LIE TO ME

Also by David Martin

Tethered
The Crying Heart Tattoo
Final Harbor
The Beginning of Sorrows

LIE TO ME

David Martin

HEADLINE

First published in Great Britain in 1991
by HEADLINE BOOK PUBLISHING PLC

10 9 8 7 6 5 4 3 2 1

British Library Cataloguing in Publication Data

Martin, David
Lie to me.
I. Title
823'.914 [F]

Hardback ISBN 0-7472-0279-6

Royal Paperback ISBN 0 7472 7956 X

Typeset in 11/13½ pt Times
by Colset Private Limited, Singapore

Printed and bound in Great Britain by
Richard Clay Ltd, Bungay, Suffolk

HEADLINE BOOK PUBLISHING PLC
Headline House
79 Great Titchfield Street
London W1P 7FN

Arabel, always

Secrets, silent, stony sit in the dark palaces
of . . . our hearts: secrets weary of their tyranny:
tyrants willing to be dethroned.

–JAMES JOYCE, *Ulysses*

1

He sits in the woods holding her hand.

It is early evening, hot July, and occasionally he sees one of them pass in front of a lighted window. He will remain here among the trees until the lights in that house across the road go out, then he will walk over there and get what is his, that's the plan. He has driven across the country, from California to the Virginia suburbs of Washington, DC, to arrive at this house he now watches from the woods where he sits holding the hand of a fifteen-year-old hitchhiker he picked up in Maryland yesterday.

Although the waiting is difficult for him, in this heat with all these bugs, he tolerates it. Squeezing the girl's hand and speaking softly, he says, 'Worth the waiting,' and then sobs in two short, dry bursts.

Prepared to wait for several hours more, he is surprised when *she* comes out of the house, moving quickly and glimmering white in this early summer night, moving girlishly even though she is fully a woman, almost but not quite skipping in her high heels which click loudly enough that he can hear them even where he is, across the road from their estate, in the woods. She wears a short white dress made of some kind of shiny material; it reaches her knees, and her legs are very long, very brown.

Out of the white house's double front doors, between white columns, down steps, on to the flagstone walk, she moves perhaps *too* quickly for a woman wearing such high heels, and he watches waiting for her to fall. But she is graceful, in control, and moving airily in the summer night's half-light, her high heels

3

breaking the quiet of this rich neighborhood – it is for him like seeing a filmed scene, all of the elements exactly right.

She holds a white clutch purse that matches her dress; incredibly long ivory earrings bounce at her neck. Then she does this: Where the flagstone walk meets the driveway, she stops and makes a complete turn while holding her hands and purse high over her head, an action that pulls her hemline to midthigh. Across the road and in the woods, he grins. She dances another circle, fingers pointing down like a matador dancing before the kill, a performance she offers for the man who is backing a black Mercedes out of the garage attached to the side of the house.

He can't see who's driving the Mercedes because the car has those smoked windows that allow *them* to look out but not *you* to see in. The man waiting in the woods knows, however, who it is driving that car, seated there behind those tinted windows, he knows.

She waits for the car door to be pushed open from the inside. Her thick auburn hair is pulled up in the back, off her long neck, and she has something white and lacy in her hair. He is taken by this, considering it a dashing touch – to wear something white and lacy in your hair.

Her lipstick is white, too, and it makes her look as if she's been eating snow, her lips appearing cold and slightly swollen, full and frosty white, lips that in this heat the man across the way finds overwhelmingly appealing. Even from where he is, the man can see such exquisite details, and when she smiles, her teeth show as white as anything she wears.

He is nodding. *Yes.* He sweats in a field jacket and a thick variety of bugs are bothering his face, but over there where the woman in white stands, it appears not to be July at all. In fact, in the evening light and wearing all that white, she offers such a heartbreakingly *perfect* sight that he has to *squeeze* the fifteen-year-old's hand, squeezing it so tightly that her knuckles make a cracking sound, which immediately gets his attention.

When the car door is pushed open for her, the woman throws

4

herself in, bouncing on to the car seat, and then she reaches back out into the world to close that door, laughing. He can hear it, her glass laughter, hearing a few notes of it before the door closes with an expensive sound, the Mercedes rushing backward into the road, screeching to a stop and then peeling off in throaty acceleration.

He imagines that they are both laughing now, that the entire departure performance – her racing out of the house, pirouetting at the driveway, the tires squealing, the car accelerating – has caused them both to laugh with head-back abandon, the man in the woods imagining that this is what they're doing right now, already half a mile away, laughing with their heads all the way back on the headrests, driving fast and absolutely delighted with themselves.

Releasing the pressure on the girl's hand, he gets up, stretches his legs, walks out of the woods, crosses the road, and steps on to their property.

He could get caught. If a resident happens to drive by right now and the man is seen, police will be called because he is out of place here, in this neighborhood where the rich live, on a road without curbs or sidewalks, houses situated artfully on large grounds, wooded lots with covenants against new construction so that everyone already in residence here can continue enjoying the illusion – country living six miles from Washington, DC.

The very sight of him will arouse suspicion here, an unshaven man with longish hair, not stylishly long but ratty looking, wearing an old Army field jacket in July, his jeans dirty and those black motorcycle boots sporting heavy silver zippers – such a man on foot in this neighborhood, walking across someone's front yard, he is out of place here, *wrong*, and the people who own property here have much to lose; if they see him, these people will not hesitate to call the police.

He doesn't hurry, however – *strolling* to the garage and trying the door, which is locked, and then walking around to the back of the house where tall hedges and closely spaced trees along the perimeter of the property prevent anyone from detecting him as he checks various doors and windows, all locked.

He stands a moment in the last light of this day, looking at the stone walls and gardens on the acre or so of ground that stretches behind the house. She was right, he thinks. The woman who set this plan in motion was absolutely right in saying that Jonathan Gaetan had become wealthy.

He reaches down and slides from his boot a large, shiny Bowie knife that he uses to pry open a basement window.

It is only when he is in their basement, standing in the dark and listening to the silent house, that he remembers the gloves, yellow latex gloves that are sold for household work, cleaning ovens. After fishing them from a pocket, he releases the girl's hand only long enough to pull on the gloves, thinking of everything he's already touched with his bare hands, the garage door and all those windows at the back of the house. But he has no ambition for retracing his steps and wiping off fingerprints; this inconstancy to detail is why he has been such an unsuccessful criminal, spending a third of his years in various prisons.

His eyes accustomed now to the dark, he finds steps leading upstairs, climbing them and opening the door at the top.

Dogs. Standing in a kitchen, knife again in his hand, he waits for dogs, waits to hear the sounds of their nails scratching for traction on polished wood floors as they rush toward him from wherever they have been resting, racing toward the kitchen to present him with their dog fury.

He knows exactly what to do, having done this before, offering an arm to the first dog that reaches him and then lifting the animal with that arm so he can bring up his other hand and slit the dog's throat. But as he waits for what does not come, he forgets why he is crouching and, after a time, slipping the blade back into his boot, he straightens up.

He walks around the kitchen, still holding the girl's hand, never in his life having seen a kitchen like this, dozens of appliances lining all those running feet of counter space, appliances with purposes he can only guess at, a double-door refrigerator, a big butcher-block island in the middle, and still enough room for a round oak table in one corner. The places where he grew up had kitchens so narrow that you could stand in the middle and put one hand on the sink and your other hand on the stove against the opposite wall. You could do that without even stretching. This kitchen, however, is big enough, well-equipped enough, that you could prepare daily meals for twenty people. But only two people live here – Jonathan and his wife.

In the refrigerator, he finds containers that he opens, smells, eats from. He drinks milk out of a carton, milk spilling from the sides of his mouth and dripping on to the shoulders of his field jacket, the white drops quickly feathering out into dark stains. When he's had enough, he drops the carton on the floor, milk everywhere.

He goes out a swinging door that leads to a formal dining room: large table covered with linen, breakfronts and china cabinets along the walls, chairs that are upholstered on the seats and the backs. He counts them, getting twelve. He counts the chairs again and comes up with a different number. Beginning the count a third time, he loses interest in the outcome and leaves the room through another door.

Their living room is large enough to accommodate several separate arrangements of furniture. He walks to one, sitting on a couch that faces the massive white and blue-veined marble mantelpiece. It must be five or six tons.

Sitting there staring at the big brass screen that shields the fireplace, he smells dead cigarettes; sliding to one end of the couch, on an end table he sees a crystal ashtray containing four butts, all of them lipstick-stained red. She must have changed her mind, putting on that frosty white lipstick after smoking these cigarettes. He notices such things. He knew, for example, that the fifteen-year-old hitchhiker he met yesterday was a smoker. He knew it the moment he touched her tongue.

He pulls at the neck of the T-shirt he's wearing under his field jacket, blowing on his chest to cool off the scratches and gashes she put there. 'You lied to me,' he says, looking down at her hand, which he is grasping with his yellow-gloved fingers. He thinks a while and then puts her hand in one of the pockets of his field jacket.

A moment later he is walking in front of the fireplace to look at the dark wood-framed pictures that line the mantel, photographs showing Jonathan and his wife in a beautifully restored, shiny black antique convertible car; showing them on a beach; camping; on a sailboat; in costumes, Jonathan dressed as a pirate, eyepatch and all, and his wife a Southern belle with flowers in her hair. In each of these photographs, Jonathan and his wife are smiling like professional models showing off their perfect teeth.

He leaves this room through a large archway, entering a lighted hallway flanked by a dozen doors, all closed, the hallway running from the house's entrance to a stairway, dark oak and wide steps, that leads Tara-like to the second floor.

He tries one of the doors off the hall, a bathroom. Flipping on a light, he looks around until he sees his image in the mirror over the sink. For some time the image does not smile, but then he says, 'Mexico,' and the face in the mirror cracks, showing upper teeth that were broken in a prison fight months ago, those teeth having subsequently died, getting darker each day. The smile in the mirror is a brief one.

He lifts the toilet lid and, while urinating, notices a delicate ceramic bowl on the sink. It is filled with brightly colored fruit, each about the size of a golf ball, and he reaches over and picks up an orange, holding it to his nose. Soap!

Laughing loudly – that awful honking sound, drawn out and dry, coming from deep in his passages; when he laughs it sounds as if he is sobbing in distress – the intruder quickly grabs handfuls of little green apples and blue pears and red bananas, smelling them and stuffing his pockets with soap.

He pops open the medicine cabinet, finding little of interest except aspirin, four of which he swallows dry before departing the room, mirrored medicine cabinet left open, toilet lid up, bowl unflushed, soap missing.

What if they come back right now and find me?

He shivers, not scared but excited, walking around in someone's house, never knowing what you might find, what's going to happen next. His original plan, calling for him to break in after they'd gone to sleep, obviously is no longer operable, and he ponders the need for a new strategy.

Another door off the hallway opens on to what looks to be Jonathan's office. The walls are filled with framed photographs so crowded that you can see the wood paneling only in narrow strips. The pictures show buildings, construction sites, men in suits but wearing hard hats, groups of men and women in business clothes standing behind ribbons, men in suits wearing hard hats turning dirt with shovels spray-painted silver in some pictures, gold in others.

He stops at a photograph of two men standing close together, looking right into the camera and smiling broadly. One of them is Jonathan and the other man is the president of the United States. On the bottom of the photograph is a carefully lettered inscription, *To Jonathan Gaetan, friend, builder, patron, patriot,* then below that is a presidential signature. When the intruder smiles at this shot of Jonathan and the president, he sees his own brown and broken teeth reflected in the glass covering the photograph, his dark smile superimposed like the Cheshire cat's directly across the face of the chief executive of the United States.

He walks around the room seeing nothing he would like to put in his pockets, nothing as intriguing as fragrant soap in the shapes of fruit, and finally ends up sitting at Jonathan's big mahogany desk, which is bare on top except for a leather pad and one brass lamp in the upper right corner. The desk has six drawers; he checks through them, flipping out files, tossing letters and memorandums, throwing stuff on the floor, unaware of what he's searching for.

The drawer on the bottom left won't open. He rattles it violently, but it does not yield. Drawing the knife from his boot, he tries to pry open the drawer, managing only to bend the knife's foot-long blade. He curses, bending the knife's blade in the other direction to straighten it and then standing up and kicking the locked drawer, bumping the desk hard enough that the brass lamp is knocked over, revealing what was hidden under its base: a small silver key.

He sob-laughs a staccato burst.

Opening the drawer with the key, he finds four Polaroid snapshots that he immediately carries out into the hallway, to study them in the light. They are pictures of a young woman dressed up like a schoolgirl, wearing a short black jumper (it barely covers her thighs) over a plain white blouse. She has on knee socks.

Her face is turned down but her eyes are looking up at the photographer, at the viewer, staring right into the eyes of the intruder, her expression shy and innocent and in stark contrast to what the rest of the picture shows.

He flips through the four Polaroids several times while making sounds like those your older brother might have made when you both were kids and your parents were out one night and he had turned off all the lights in the house and was trying to scare you.

He rubs himself, the intruder remembering when he broke into a house years ago and went upstairs, finding a teenage girl in her bed, sleeping in a room filled with stuffed animals that sat in their own little pastel-painted chairs, posters of rock stars and kittens on the walls, and one dresser covered with tiny bottles of perfumes and colognes, a dozen tubes of lipstick in various colors, six different types of fingernail polish, and she was sleeping on top of her bed, no blanket over her, wearing a T-shirt and underpants (the T-shirt had a picture of Minnie Mouse on it; the underpants were plain white cotton), and when he leaned down to her face he smelled her sleeping breath, like milk that's been left out at room temperature.

Standing in the hallway of Jonathan's house, he moves his tongue and tastes milk.

Remembering the look in that girl's eyes when she stirred from sleep and saw him standing over her, he raises his face toward the ceiling and opens his mouth, a thread of spit falling from the left corner of his lips, dropping to the field jacket's dirty collar.

Afterward, he took some of her perfume bottles, several vials of her makeup. They never caught him for that one; it was not one of the crimes for which he went to prison. A free ride, he thinks, sobbing as he looks again at the four Polaroids, shivering the way he sometimes does when taking a pee, putting the snapshots in his left pocket where he is keeping the hand of the fifteen-year-old hitchhiker he picked up yesterday in Maryland.

The intruder thinks about checking the time as he walks in and out of the other rooms downstairs – a library, a plant room that looks out on to a patio, bedrooms, another bathroom. He doesn't wear a watch. What time it was when he entered the house, he has no idea, but the way she was dressed, they must be going to some kind of party. Parties, he speculates, last until midnight at least.

Returning to the kitchen, he sees a digital clock on the microwave oven: 9:53. He closes his eyes to calculate how much time he has before they get back from their party; when he reopens them to check the clock again, it shows 9:54. Fascinated, he closes and opens his eyes once more, but this time the clock doesn't change, still showing 9:54. He tries it again, and again, and then leaves the kitchen on his way upstairs.

Running now, taking the steps two at a time, panting, he's excited to be in this house, having anticipated this night for something like seven years now, being here at last, making it happen, soon to get what is by all rights his, opening doors, looking for . . . looking for *what*, for some teenage girl sleeping in a room full of stuffed toys sitting in their own chairs, sleeping on top of the covers and wearing nothing but a T-shirt and plain white cotton underpants, her breath milky-sweet and her eyes full of such terror it would tear your heart to see them.

He finds their master bathroom, the largest and most luxurious bathroom he's ever entered. The massive, partially sunken bathtub is under a large window that overlooks the back of the house; you could soak in a hot bath while gazing out at gardens and stone walls.

Two sinks are sunk in the marble counter under a large mirror lighted around its perimeter with a continuous fluorescent tube. If you were to put on some music, this room could easily accommodate six couples dancing.

Jonathan's towels are hung neatly on racks that can be heated, but her towels are all over the place, on the floor, on the edge of the tub, two hand towels bunched up on the marble near her sink. He knows they are her towels because when he picks them up and holds them to his face, he smells her on the terrycloth.

Over at the mirror, at *her* sink, he pulls a toothbrush from a holder, her toothbrush. He puts toothpaste on it, thinking that not too long ago this toothbrush was in her mouth, brushing *his* teeth with it now, remembering what a woman who lived in a trailer said when she caught him using her toothbrush, 'Just because I fuck you doesn't mean I want you using my toothbrush.'

He plays around with vials that he finds in the medicine cabinet, taking a few of the more interesting pills, putting the vials in his pockets, and then becomes abruptly bored with their fabulous bathroom.

Next to the bathtub he sees another door, not the one he came through but a second door, one that opens on to their bedroom.

It's big, too. All the rooms in this house are so damn big, this one containing a king-size bed flanked by floor-to-ceiling windows; there are chairs here, and tables, and along the walls stand dressers, bureaus, and her makeup table with an oval mirror. He sits at that table searching through her makeup until he finds a shade of lipstick he likes, smearing it around his mouth and sobbing at his image in her mirror. He puts bluish eye shadow around his eyes and rubs rouge across the bridge of his nose. After applying mascara to both eyes, he uses an eyelash pencil to draw a thin mustache.

12

Leaning close to the mirror for a good look at what he's done, the intruder smiles. Those damn teeth. Keeping his lips back, he picks up a tube of lipstick and paints his upper teeth red. He douses himself with several perfumes and puts a string of pearls around his neck before turning in her little padded chair to scan the room.

'Such a slob,' he says softly, seeing several of her outfits on the floor where she has dropped them after rejecting them for wear tonight. From one of the dresser drawers, a slip hangs half out. Her shoes are all over the place. Why do women have so many shoes? He can remember every pair of shoes he's owned since he was four years old, this being quite literally true: the man could sit there and describe for you each pair of shoes he wore as a child, seldom owning more than two pairs at a time, wearing them until they had such holes that he could feel the sidewalks and wet grass on his feet. It's not right for her to have so many shoes scattered around this room, and he hates that anyway, the way some women are such slobs. He kept telling the woman he knew who lived in the trailer that maybe the reason her husband treated her like shit was because she was such a slob, but she said there was only one thing she had to worry about keeping clean.

He goes to the dresser and takes the slip in his gloved hands, holding it to his face and staining the white satin with makeup.

Looking over at the bed, he sees a clock on a little table. The time is 11:42, how did it get to be so late? Still not midnight, though, and he is sure they won't be home until after midnight.

From the top of the bed he takes both huge pillows and lays them end-to-end down the middle of the bed, covering them with the satin slip. He unbuttons and unzips his jeans, letting them drop; he wears no underclothing.

Maneuvering himself on top of the slip which is on top of the pillows, he takes the Polaroids from his pocket and tries to position them upright in front of his face. They keep falling over. He's having such a difficult time staying on the pillows and holding the Polaroids that he finally removes the severed hand

13

from his pocket and uses it as a prop, forcing the fingers to curl, breaking knuckles that crack like green sticks to create a perfect easel for the snapshots.

Staring at the four naughty schoolgirl poses, he begins to rub himself against her slip, humping the pillows and imagining that she is beneath him, that she likes what he's doing to her – that she is looking at him with those shy eyes.

'You like that, don't you, baby-girl?' he asks in a whisper. It was the same question he asked that teenager who was wearing only a T-shirt and underpants.

Except this time she says *yes*, she likes it.

'You want it bad, don't you?'

She says she wants it real bad.

'You're going to get it, too, bitch – get it hard.'

She says good, give it to me hard.

So he pumps harder against the slip and pillows, his thoughts back to yesterday, the way that hitchhiker begged him just like this girl-woman in the Polaroids is begging, wanting it bad and hard, which is exactly the way he gave it to that fifteen-year-old bitch yesterday, so bad and hard that her wrist bone ripped open his chest and she put cuts all across his knuckles with her teeth.

He's almost reached a conclusion when something about the face in the Polaroids begins to bother him, something about the way that girlish woman is looking out at him. He finds it so disconcerting that he immediately gets off the bed, pulls up his jeans, buttoning them but not bothering to zip up; he puts the snapshots back in his pocket and intertwines the hitchhiker's fingers with his own yellow-gloved fingers. Holding hands with her like that, he strolls around the bedroom once more.

Returning to the makeup table and seeing again what he's done to his face, he sobs and smiles and considers it inspired, this painting of his teeth. He turns his head, trying to see himself in profile, unable to catch the full profile and settling finally for a three-quarters view, posed like that, chin up, eyes right, delighted with himself.

When he looks over at the bed he sees her lying there in that white, shimmering outfit, something white and lacy still in her hair, pulling up her dress to show him what kind of underwear she has on; the intruder reaches a gloved hand into his open zipper and grasps his sudden erection, taking the girl's hand and putting it—

Someone's downstairs!

He freezes, listening to their muted voices and glancing at the bedside clock, 12:34, *what happened to midnight, where did it go?*

He can't seem to make himself move, sitting on that little padded stool in front of her makeup table and feeling ridiculous, one hand on his cock, hearing them talking downstairs, trying to remember what the plan was. He had a plan, one he'd been working on for years, speeches he rehearsed as he drove across the country, the plan was to wait until they were asleep and then break into the house, sneak up to their bedroom . . . but then she came running out in that white outfit, their car went screeching off, and he broke in while they were gone, the new plan calling for him to . . .

He remembers the spilled milk – and how he left Jonathan's office, lamp knocked off the desk, drawers open, papers on the floor. They're going to see all that and call the cops before he gets the chance to tell Jonathan what he has driven three thousand miles and waited seven years to say.

Not that's he's afraid, just confused, confused about what to do next, because if he takes out the knife and rushes downstairs right now, can he get to Jonathan and Jonathan's wife before either of them reaches a telephone and calls—

That's what he was supposed to do! He remembers now, he was supposed to cut all the telephone lines as soon as he got into the house. He's shaking his head, laughing one small and muffled sob, mocking his exquisitely unreliable memory.

Someone's coming, on the stairway, a man's voice, Jonathan on the stairway but still talking to her, the intruder unable to

15

make out what they are saying, unsure if he hears any evidence of alarm in their voices, not knowing if they've noticed the milk yet, Jonathan's trashed office. And, he thinks, I'm still sitting here with my hand on my cock, still hard, it's so ridiculous, really. He sobs, biting his lower lip to keep the sounds in.

What's Jonathan going to think when he comes up here and finds me like this, what will he do? Pull down my pants and put me across the bed to spank my bare butt? He muffles another sob, finding this hilarious. It's like being in church with his mother, trying not to laugh but needing desperately to laugh.

Jonathan is on the steps, coming up, all the way to the second floor already, stopping at the top of the stairs to call down.

'Mary! Honey, did you leave the lights on up here?'

Although the intruder does not hear her reply, he notes that Jonathan's tone is merely curious, not alarmed. Good, he thinks, they don't know I'm here.

And yet he *still* doesn't move, sitting there astonishingly serene as Jonathan comes whistling down the hallway, approaching the bedroom, almost to the door, about to find an intruder who has broken into his house, violated his privacy, what's he going to do, how's he going to handle this?

Weird. Just sitting there, makeup on his face and pearls around his neck, cock in hand, waiting to see Jonathan's face, wondering if he'll recognize him after all these years. *Hiya, Jonathan, remember me!* Too fucking weird, man, and here he is, at the door . . .

. . . and only at the last available moment does the intruder scurry into action, rushing into a closet and barely getting in, not even having a chance to shut the closet door completely before Jonathan walks whistling into his bedroom.

In the closet, the man has to keep his mouth wide open to prevent sounds from bottling up in his chest and then burbling out, trying to keep quiet and listen for Jonathan all at the same time, wondering what he's doing out there in the bedroom, has he found the pillows and the satin slip stained with lipstick?

He's nearly dancing in the closet, hearing Jonathan take out his change and put it in some kind of dish, undoing his belt, taking off his shoes. Next, he'll be opening this closet to hang up his clothes, and then what, oh, God, look at this, still got a hard-on, too much!

He releases himself, puts the hitchhiker's hand away, and crouches slowly to draw the knife. If Jonathan opens this door, I'll . . . *but it's not supposed to happen this way!* Killing Jonathan is not part of the plan; killing Jonathan *now* would ruin everything. Still, he can't prevent it, he knows exactly what's going to happen if Jonathan opens the closet door right now, he's going to bring that big blade right up into his gut and stare him right in the eye when he does. He likes to watch their eyes, you see some of the strangest expressions.

But Jonathan doesn't come to the closet.

What's he doing out there? The intruder listens, the waiting and the anticipation making him boil. Come on, Jonathan, come on, I've got something for you here in the closet, come on old boy. Unable to wait, he eases the door an inch or two wider, seeing Jonathan near the bed, his back to the closet, Jonathan standing there holding the slip and looking down at the rearranged pillows.

The intruder wonders what the hell is going through Jonathan's mind, waiting for Jonathan to *do* something, this waiting is killing him, he's done too much waiting in his life, can't wait any longer, he can't, he's too tightly coiled now, unable to tolerate waiting in the closet a second longer, knocking open the closet door, bursting out, knife in hand, penis exposed, sobbing.

Jonathan, standing by the big bed with his back to the closet, has his shoes and pants off but is still wearing his white-on-white shirt, blue striped tie, jockey shorts, black socks that come all the way up to cover his calves.

A picture! Jonathan turning in that last instant before the intruder bulls into him and knocks him on to the bed, the man sobbing even louder to see Jonathan's face in the last instant before he is hit. Jonathan's expression classic, priceless, beautiful.

Lying on top of Jonathan's back, he can't stop sobbing. You know how funny this is, how absolutely hysterical, the idea of Jonathan standing in the privacy of his own house, the fucking *sanctuary* of his bedroom, undressing to go to bed when suddenly this madman charges out of the closet, Jonathan turning just before he gets knocked to the bed, turning just in time to see who's about to jump him, this laughing, sobbing, lip-painted, eye-shadowed, pearl-wearing, thin mustache-sporting, yellow-gloved, knife-holding *madman!* Coming out of the goddamn closet! But wait. Wait here's the best part, here's what *crazes* the intruder with laughter, the thing that Jonathan did right as he was tackled, that downward flick of Jonathan's eyes, glancing down to see the madman's exposed penis, attacked by a cock, *dicked!*

The man is sobbing uncontrollably as he holds Jonathan face-down on the bed, the intruder unable to catch his breath, gulping air and exhaling prolonged sobs, keeping a knee hard on Jonathan's back but telling him, 'I'm sorry,' gasping for breath between words, 'I'm . . . sorry . . . but . . . the . . . look . . . on . . . your . . . face . . .'

From the first floor, from the bottom of the broad staircase, Mary calls up, 'Jonathan! Are you all right?'

To keep himself quiet, the intruder has to bite his lip again, biting hard enough this time that he pierces flesh and can taste the saltiness of his own blood.

'Jonathan! What are you doing up there? Are you OK?'

He whispers into Jonathan's ear, instructing him to tell his wife that everything is fine. Then he releases enough pressure on Jonathan's back that he is able to work his face free and shout down to his wife, 'I'm fine! It's OK!'

They both wait for some response but none comes.

Jonathan remains immobile under the intruder's weight, still dazed and confused from the shock of seeing an aroused monster springing from his closet.

He whispers into Jonathan's ear again, 'Don't move a muscle,' saying this as a friendly warning, as if warning Jonathan against some other danger, not himself but some third force in that room with them. 'If you move, I'll slide this big knife right up your anus.' Then he laughs a line of strangling sobs, his word choice – right up your *anus* – delighting him to no end. 'Once I stuck an icepick up a guy's ass and he was constipated for a year after that, just couldn't face the agony of taking a shit.' He relates this matter-of-factly, not threatening Jonathan as much as passing on to him some important information.

Jonathan lies there, facedown on the bed, trying to figure this out. He has obviously encountered a burglar who was hiding in the closet, a particularly violent and deranged burglar, one who has stolen some of Mary's jewelry, who has already put a string of her pearls around his neck, a burglar and a pervert who was fooling around in Mary's lingerie drawer, who has put her makeup on his face, and now, Jonathan thinks, now I have to do whatever this nut says, give him whatever he wants, wait until he leaves and *then* call the police.

Jonathan is hoping that Mary won't come upstairs, hoping that with all the noise this nut is making, maybe Mary will realize that an intruder is up here and then she'll call the police from downstairs or have sense enough to run out of the house and go to a neighbor's. Once she's safe, Jonathan doesn't mind what happens, what this guy steals. And then, he vows, the security system that he and Mary have been discussing – he curses himself for not going ahead and having it installed weeks ago – will be put in tomorrow morning. He doesn't care how much it costs or how troublesome the false alarms are, he will *never* allow something like this to happen again . . . Suddenly, the knee that has been grinding into the middle of his back is lifted.

'I want you to lay real still now while I tie you up. If you try to get funny, then you know what, don't you?'

19

Jonathan remains quiet.

'Bowie knife up the bunghole, that's what. Big blade slicing up the old chocolate highway, gouging out the windward passage.' The man stands, leaving Jonathan prone on the bed. It suddenly occurs to the intruder that he's forgotten the rope, left it in the car, but then he feels around to a back pocket of his jeans and finds it there. 'I thought I forgot,' he says to Jonathan as he uncoils a length of nylon rope, 'but now I remember I didn't forget after all.' He cuts the rope and ties Jonathan's hands behind his back.

Jonathan is hauled into a chair, its straight back shoved between his arms and shoulder blades. 'While I had you there on the bed,' the man says, 'I was going to pull down your underpants and spank your bare butt. You'd like that, wouldn't you, Jonathan? I know about you and spankings.'

'Have we met?' Jonathan asks.

The intruder laughs. After tying Jonathan's arms to the chair, he comes around and looks directly into Jonathan's face. 'Well?' he asks. '*Do* you know me?'

Jonathan stares at that bizarre face and tries to place it. I'll have to remember his description for the police, Jonathan thinks. Early thirties, average build, just under six feet, pleasant enough face under that makeup. His hair is greasy and his eyes look drug-crazed. Actually, it's hard to tell, with all that makeup smeared on his face, it's hard to tell what he might look like normally. Jonathan isn't sure if he's ever seen the man before or not.

'I have about seventy dollars in my wallet there on the bureau,' Jonathan finally says.

'Seventy dollars?' the intruder replies absently as he kneels to tie Jonathan's ankles to the chair.

'About that, I'm not sure of the exact amount, you'd have to look. I don't keep much cash on me. The usual credit cards, of course.'

'The usual credit cards?'

'Tell me what you're after. I don't keep money in the house.' Shit, Jonathan thinks – my coins. Somehow this guy has heard about my coin collection and *that's* what he wants. I'm *not* going to tell him where those coins are. 'I could write you a check, made out to cash. You could take it to a bank first thing in the morning. I won't stop payment on it.'

No reply.

'I won't, really. And the keys to my car, *a Mercedes*, they're on the bureau, too.'

But the man remains silent, still working on the ropes, tying Jonathan so tightly to the chair that he's already losing circulation in his hands.

'Tell me what you want and I'll cooperate any way I can. No reason for anyone to get hurt.' Hell, Jonathan thinks, if he knows about the coins, I'll tell him where they are. Coins aren't worth getting my throat cut. 'If necessary, I'll agree not to contact the police until you have ample opportunity to escape.'

'Ample opportunity?' He chuckles.

'I won't contact the police at all then. Whatever it takes.'

He is unusually strong, able to pick up Jonathan and the chair and turn them around in midair to face the bed, putting Jonathan and the chair close to the bed where he now sits. 'A check made out to cash?' he asks in a flat and patronizing tone. 'Really, now, Jonathan, what kind of fool do you take me for?'

Jonathan figures this guy has read about him in the newspapers, one of those nuts who believe that someone like Jonathan, a man who gives away so much money to charity, someone like that must have more money than he needs. Jonathan's lawyer had warned him about these nuts, except the lawyer said they would be writing Jonathan letters, calling his offices, trying to speak to him on the streets; the lawyer didn't say anything about one of them breaking into the house, putting on lipstick and pearls, springing from the closet with his cock hanging out.

'Jonathan?'

'Yes?'

'You didn't answer me.'

'Answer you?'

'What kind of fool am I?' He sings it, *'What kind of fool am I?'* Then he sobs.

Jonathan understands now that the sobbing is laughter.

'You still haven't answered me.'

'What kind of fool are you?'

'Precisely.'

'I don't know.'

'Precisely! But you will, Jonathan, oh, you will. First things first, however – and you know what that means don't you?'

Jonathan shakes his head.

The intruder lies back on the bed, appearing to be so unhurried that Jonathan wonders if he's waiting for someone. Does he have a partner who's already downstairs with Mary?

'Where were we?' the man asks, still lying on the bed.

Jonathan doesn't know what to say.

He sits up. 'Yes. First things first. And first thing is, we have to get your wife up here to join the party, that's the first thing we have to do.'

Jonathan tries desperately to think of a way to save her. 'She's with someone. We gave a couple a ride home and they stopped in for a drink. The man who's down there, he's a police captain and—'

'And he's got a big gun and two police dogs with him and, gee, the best thing for me to do, gosh, I'd better just climb out one of these windows and hightail it as fast as I can – something like that, Jonathan?'

'Don't hurt her, please.'

'Ten minutes into our conversation, Jonathan, and you've lied to me already. She's alone downstairs, isn't she?'

'Yes.'

'Lying to me will get you killed.'

'Listen, I have a coin collection. Mexican gold pieces, they're worth, I don't know exactly, a lot of money, any coin dealer in the country would give you—'

He slaps Jonathan on the side of the head and then leans right into his face. 'Ring your bells, honey?'

The slap was hard enough to put tears in Jonathan's eyes. His voice, however, remains strong. 'If you'd just tell me what you want.'

His face is so close to Jonathan's that, when the man speaks, Jonathan can smell foul breath. 'Do you think I'm pretty?'

Jonathan doesn't know how to answer.

He stands and pats Jonathan softly on the shoulder. 'Don't worry *your* pretty little head, Jonathan, because I *am* going to tell you what I want, precisely what I want. I've waited a long time to tell you what I want. That's the whole idea tonight, for you to be told exactly what I want. But first things first – your wife has to come up here and join the party. I have some tape . . . yes, see, some tape for your mouth, just so you won't be tempted to make any noise while I'm gone. She's really beautiful, Jonathan. You did all right for yourself. I guess any old fart with enough money can pretty well pick and choose his women, huh?'

Jonathan says nothing.

'Huh?' He slaps him across the face. 'Jonathan, if you're not going to answer my questions, this will be a very long night, believe me.' He waits a moment. 'Well?'

'Yes, she's very beautiful.'

'That's not what I asked.'

'I'm sorry, what did you ask?'

The man mutters as he unrolls a six-inch length of white tape and puts it over Jonathan's mouth. He steps back. 'If you lie to me again, I'll bust your ass wide open.' After checking the ropes one last time, he informs Jonathan, 'This is a night for telling the truth, lover boy.'

He leaves the bedroom and carefully walks the upstairs hallway, stopping at the top of the steps to listen for the woman, hearing nothing. What *is* she doing down there?

He takes the steps one at a time, stopping halfway down when

23

he smells her cigarette. Of course. That's what she's doing down there, having a smoke before coming to bed. Jonathan probably doesn't allow her to smoke in the bedroom, the intruder thinks, recalling that he saw no ashtrays in the bedroom. Good for Jonathan. I'm going to make her brush her teeth, he thinks, and then he remembers using her toothbrush – and *then* he remembers the speech he was going to give Jonathan, the speech he practiced driving out here, had it memorized and everything. I'm going to need a Bible.

He's on the first floor now, in that long center hall, creeping to the archway that opens on to the large living room. He hears ice clinking in a glass. Yes, she's having a drink and a cigarette before coming to bed.

Grinning, he draws the knife and taps its handle softly against the polished wood of the arch.

'Jonathan?' she asks.

No, he thinks, something more terrible than Jonathan, honey-pie.

Tap, tap.

'Here we are, Jonathan!' he announces happily as they enter the bedroom. He escorts Mary across the room and to the bed, having her sit there and face her husband. 'Were you worried about us?' he asks Jonathan. Then, in an aside to Mary, he says, 'Jonathan can't answer because he's kind of tied up right now.' When he honks out his sobbing laughter, Mary looks up at him with this awful expression on her face.

'First things first,' he says as he approaches Jonathan. 'We have to get this tape off Jonathan's mouth because he might have something intelligent to contribute.' With some difficulty, his gloved fingers working clumsily, he manages to loosen an edge of the tape. 'Now if I do this right, if I'm very, very gentle, taking this tape off won't hurt Jonathan at all.'

But Jonathan anticipates exactly what the intruder does – rips off the tape with a violent jerk. It makes Mary wince.

24

'Did that hurt, honey?' the man asks, rubbing Jonathan's cheeks, which have already reddened.

The first words Jonathan speaks are to his wife, asking Mary is she's OK.

'I'm fine,' she says, 'I'm OK. You?'

He nods.

'I love you,' she says.

Jonathan nods again. 'I love you, too, babe.'

'Oh, fuck me with a cathedral,' the man says theatrically. 'You know, Jonathan, I hate to be the bearer of bad tidings, but while we were downstairs, Mary offered to run away to Mexico with me, said she wanted to be *my* girlfriend and suck *my* dick three times a day, morning-noon-night, and all I had to do was come up here and kill you so she could be a rich widow and then she and I could live like royalty on all your money. What do you think of them apples?'

'Just tell us what you want,' Jonathan pleads. 'Tell us what you want and then leave, please.' This would be frustrating for any man, tied up and at the mercy of some nut case, your wife right there in the room with you but you're unable to protect her, made to listen to this idiot's foolishness and impotent to do anything except plead. It is especially frustrating for Jonathan Gaetan, however, because in the business world he wields great power and is accustomed to respect, a wealthy man who is shown deference by employees, politicians, headwaiters, and a variety of other supplicants.

The three of them wait in silence until the man finally says, 'We have to do this right.' He presses the butt of the knife handle hard against his own forehead. 'I've given this a great deal of thought, believe me, and I don't want to forget anything. Really, this might be the happiest day of my life. You'll forgive me if I get too *emotional*.' He puts his head back and hugs himself with both arms.

They can't tell if he's joking or what.

'I have to remember exactly what . . .' He has the knife butt against his forehead again, tapping harder and harder. 'Remember, remember . . . remember the fifth of September . . . or is it the sixth of September?' He tries to sing, *'Remember, remember,'* but then loses his composure completely, turning around to kick a bureau with such force that the figurines on top of it are knocked over, some of them falling to the floor where he crushes them with his heavy boots, stomping on the china and glass pieces, grinding them to dust.

Then he stops. And when he revolves slowly to face them, he is grinning and the tone of his voice is mocking. 'Now, now, just calm down, there's no need for violence.' He sobs and sobs.

After catching his breath, he walks over to the bed and sits next to Mary, draping one arm casually around her shoulders. 'That was a direct quote,' he tells Jonathan. 'What I just said about calming down, no need for violence, it's exactly what Mary told me when we were downstairs together.' He gives her a brief hug. 'She also showed me where you keep your Bible and I brought it up here because we're going to need it in a minute.' He pats the pocket holding the Bible. 'And she gave me your coin collection, too. I put the coins on the steps to remind me to take them along when I go. Terribly generous of you, Jonathan. I guess that only leaves one thing. A poem.' He clears his throat. 'Mary, Mary, quite contrary . . . suck my dick!' With that he grabs the hair at the back of her head and shoves her face into his lap.

'No!' Jonathan shouts.

Moving quickly, he releases Mary and hits Jonathan open-handed on the side of the head. 'Well, *honey*,' he tells Jonathan, using exaggerated emphasis on certain words, 'if *Mary* doesn't suck my dick, then *you're* going to have to, because *someone* has to suck my dick and I can't.' He pauses. 'I know – I've tried!' He finds this very funny, laughing in sobs and throwing himself back on the bed.

Jonathan and Mary look at each other.

'Wait a minute!' he hollers, abruptly sitting up. 'Wait just a cotton-pickin' minute. Have we cut all the phone lines yet?'

Mary nods. 'You did that before we came up here.'

'You sure we got every phone in the house?'

'Yes – except the one in this room.'

'Thank you, Mary.' Then to Jonathan, 'See what a help she's being to me, hm?' He gets up and cuts the line leading to the telephone on the bedside table. 'Now what?'

'You're crazy,' Mary tells him.

'God's not done with me yet,' he answers quickly.

Jonathan looks at him blankly and then turns his head to Mary as if to ask, Is this guy making any sense to *you?* She responds by putting out both hands, touching Jonathan's cheeks. Tears are in her eyes, too.

'You wouldn't be so lovey-dovey toward him,' the intruder says, 'if you knew he was a fornicator and pornographer, hm?'

She offers bitter laughter.

'Oh yeah? Look at these.' He takes the four Polaroids from his pocket and shows them to Mary in a peculiarly comical manner, holding them like poker cards in his right hand while keeping his left hand spread behind the photographs, ensuring that Jonathan cannot see what's being shown to his wife. The intruder does this the way a child might, allowing one friend but not the other to peek at some secret treasure.

'I found them in your desk drawer,' the man tells Jonathan. 'The desk drawer you keep locked with the key you hide under your lamp.'

Jonathan glances at his wife while Mary says to the intruder, 'I'd like you to leave those behind when you go.'

He mocks her earnest voice, 'I'd like you to leave those behind when you go,' and then makes a face at her.

Although she remains placid, making no crying sounds, Mary sits there on the bed with tears tracking her cheeks.

'You're not having any fun, are you?' the man asks Jonathan. 'I've been looking forward to this for such a long time, but you

27

haven't cracked a smile since I got here. Come on, lover boy, give us a smile.'

Trying to hold his emotions in check, Jonathan keeps his face expressionless.

The intruder asks him again to smile, and now Jonathan notices that the man has taken out the Bible and is holding it in one hand, his knife in the other. *'Jonathan,'* he says warningly, hefting the knife and moving closer to Mary.

Jonathan tries, forcing himself to pull back his lips, more of a grimace than a smile.

He slaps Jonathan across the face with the Bible, hard enough that Jonathan and the chair are knocked over, Mary crying out, and the intruder shrieking, 'No laughing in church! You will burn in hell for that, young man!'

Mary is on the floor, struggling to put Jonathan and the chair upright, and her husband uses this opportunity to whisper to her, 'Ask him to loosen the ropes, *please.*'

Once she has Jonathan righted, Mary demands that her husband be untied – immediately.

'Of course,' the intruder agrees, 'of course. Besides, the story I'm about to tell will keep Jonathan riveted to his chair anyway.' He cuts some of the ropes but not all of them, leaving Jonathan's ankles bound.

'Here's the way it works. I'll begin reading a verse from the Bible and you, Jonathan, will finish it for me. Mary, you get to be the audience. Go on, sit on the bed there facing the old pornographer, that's a good girl. One thing though, Jonathan. If you make a mistake, I'm going to cut off Mary's ear.'

Jonathan's voice is trembling now. 'I'm afraid I don't know the Bible very well.'

'Too bad you didn't have my upbringing.'

'Don't worry,' Mary tells Jonathan, 'he won't hurt me.'

'I won't, huh? Hm.' He takes the severed hand from his pocket and tosses it right on to Mary's lap. When she sees what it is, Mary screams.

* * *

'If thine eye offend thee.' He pauses, looking at Jonathan. 'If thine eye offend thee, Jonathan, dot, dot, dot.'

Jonathan is still in the chair facing the bed, but now it is the intruder who's sitting there on the edge of the bed, knee-to-knee with Jonathan. Mary is standing against a wall, both hands covering her face.

When the man raises his eyebrows, Jonathan answers, 'Pluck it out.'

'Ah.' He reaches over and pats Jonathan's shoulder. 'And if thy hand offend thee . . .'

'Cut it off.'

'Yes!'

Mary cries into her hands.

'And if thy foot offend thee?'

'Cut it off.' Jonathan's voice has become so weary that it is barely audible.

'Louder, please.'

'Cut it off!'

'Louder!' The man's face is bright red. 'Scream it out, Jonathan, for all the word to hear!'

'CUT IT OFF!'

'Hallelujah!' He raises the big knife and brings it down hard, embedding it in the edge of Jonathan's chair, leaving the knife standing like that, erect between Jonathan's legs. 'God loves you *this* much,' he says, leaning over and kissing him fully on the mouth, a hard kiss that Jonathan struggles against, using both hands in his attempt to push away that garishly painted face, to stop this obscenity.

When the intruder ends the kiss, he makes a loud smacking sound with his lips – and then he moves swiftly, all business now, as he reties Jonathan's hands and fetches Mary from her position along the wall, placing her in a chair next to her husband; he finally sits on the edge of the bed facing both of them, announcing, 'Story time, children.'

* * *

It is just past dawn when he leaves the house, walking out their front door, between white columns, down steps, on to a flagstone walk, to the driveway, and then he's trudging down the road, feeling hollowed out inside.

He walks to the small shopping center where he left his car, getting in and driving off, wandering streets and nearly falling asleep at the wheel. People are on their way to work and school, and it seems strange to him, all these men and women and schoolchildren going about their lives, acting normal, unaware of last night's profound, life-altering events. He should tell them somehow, make everyone aware that he is like a dog that's been tightly tethered all its life but now is loose among them, out and about, slipping his chain. He drives to a motel, registers, goes to his room.

Opening the sliding glass doors, he steps on to a tiny balcony overlooking a swimming pool and the parking lot. On an identical balcony across the way, a boy and girl wait excitedly for the swimming pool to open. They must be brother and sister. Must be.

The boy is wearing red trunks, holding a face mask equipped with a black snorkel that he will not be allowed to wear in the motel pool; a sign near the pool forbids their use. He is nine. His sister, two years younger, stands next to him; she is proud of her brandnew two-piece swimming suit, blue with white piping, bought especially for this trip. The girl holds a small rubber inflated ring imprinted with broadly smiling sea horses. She is talking to her brother, who points out for the girl certain accoutrements of the swimming pool, the diving board from which he will perform cannonballs, the rope and floats that mark off the deep end where she will not be allowed to go. The little girl asks her older brother a stream of questions, what time is it now, when does the pool open, how much longer are we going to have to wait, and do you think it'll be OK to go in and wake up mom and dad *now?*

He stands there watching them until the children finally see him, and then he waves. Having been warned about strangers in the city, they retreat into their room like infant animals scurrying back to the nest.

At last he gives up, stepping back into his room and collapsing on the bed, Jonathan's gold coins clinking in his various pockets.

Wednesday. He had not planned on having to wait. Wednesday, Jonathan said, and Wednesday is two days off. What he's going to do between now and then, he has no idea; his original plan did not cover having to wait until Wednesday.

A new plan. No. Not yet. He hasn't come up with a new plan yet, but he *does* have an image in his mind, an image that could develop into a plan, this image which he holds in his mind as he falls to sleep – of bright gold coins spread along a pathway that leads from where children play to a spot where he waits for Wednesday, where he waits for Wednesday and for the arrival of children.

2

When word got around Tuesday afternoon that Captain Land was going to call me in on the Gaetan case, some of the younger detectives stopped by my cubicle to give me thumbs-up. You know, the old war-horse being trotted out for one last campaign. Mainly, they thought it was a big joke, and I accepted without protest or complaint all the good-natured shit they threw my way. *In my day*, I could have told them – but no one wants to hear about the old days, not even me. Then, at four that afternoon, I got the nod, Land wanting to see me in his office *pronto*.

He was sitting behind his oversized desk, motioning for me to take a chair. It was typical of Land not to look up when you came into his office, ignoring you as if you were an interruption he couldn't quite afford. Typical, too, for him to start reading something aloud without telling you his point. He was holding a personnel jacket. 'Detective Sergeant Theodore Camel,' Land began – and I quickly got the point. 'At age thirty-five, you racked up the third-highest number of citations in departmental history. Made lieutenant that year.' He paused, glancing up at me and then back at the jacket. 'Busted back to sergeant the same year. No citations awarded for something like eight years now.' He closed the folder and put it on his desk. 'You went from being one of the department's youngest lieutenants to our oldest living detective sergeant. Fifty-three years old and just putting in time.' He looked at me expectantly.

I didn't say anything, hard times and narrow escapes having

33

taught me that, when being addressed by an asshole, you don't give an answer unless you're asked a direct question.

'In the three years I've been here,' Land said, 'you haven't done anything except fuck the taxpayer.'

Harvey Land owned all the bad adjectives: sarcastic, overbearing, superior.

'When people ask you what you do for a living, I wonder what in God's name you tell them.'

Having still not been asked a question, I volunteered no answers.

'You *used* to be a cop,' Land said, 'but I don't know what the hell you are now.'

I wasn't sure myself. I remember reading in some magazine how this writer was complaining about all the books and movies coming out these days about cops, and he said if Arthur Miller wrote about Willy Loman today, he'd have to change Willy's profession and call the play *Death of a Cop*. But I no longer trade in the fascination people have for police work. I tell them I'm a clerk, work for the county. It keeps me out of conversations.

Then Land said I was burned out.

Yes. I distinctly remember taking the occasion of my fiftieth birthday to look both directions in my life, seeing the same thing coming that had already passed. Unable to figure out the point of it all, I adopted *fuck it* as my guiding philosophy.

'I inherited you, Camel. I've asked the review board to put you on involuntary early retirement, but they piss and moan about your record and tell me to give you another six months to see if you don't come around. But you're not going to come around. You're just putting in time until you hit fifty-five and can retire on full benefits.'

Right again. You can retire on full benefits when your age and the number of years you have in the department add up to eighty, which they will for me, exactly, on my fifty-fifth birthday. Twenty-five years seniority, fifty-five years old, eighty points on the nose – and I'm out of here on full benefits. I've already bought a piece of property on the Northern Neck. Plan to work as a part-time cop for one of the local municipalities up there. Sit and fish and think. Ever since I turned fifty, I've been looking at fifty-five the way a capsized sailor looks at a spit of land on the horizon: I can make it now, because all I have to do is hold on until I reach *there*.

'But if I ever give you a legitimate order and you refuse to carry it out,' Land was saying, 'then I go to the board and *demand* they retire you early, on half-benefits. I hold my breath and stamp my feet and eventually the board goes along with my recommendation – and you're gone by the end of the year. Short of eighty points, Sergeant.'

I just kept giving him the old dead-eyes stare.

In return, he offered me his reptilian grin. 'Right?'

'Right as rain, Captain.'

Captain Asshole. He'd been a security expert in the Navy and, like a lot of twenty-year men, had chosen the Washington, DC, area for his reentry into civilian life, hoping to sop up some of the money that oozes out from the federal government like so much golden pus from so many puncture wounds. His résumé landed him a captain's job with our quiet little suburban police department, but for Harvey Land this was just a launching pad. He was already designing security systems for corporations that do business with the government, corporations whose CEOs live in our white-wine suburb. He was a forty-six-year-old go-getter who'd be rich before *he* hit fifty.

Played tennis three mornings a week. Wore green golfing slacks and a pink Banlon shirt while strolling the links with his rich friends who found it amusing, and potentially useful, to count a police captain among their acquaintances. Captain Slick.

'Even your old partner, that pirate Bodine, is coming around. He's working computers now, did you know that? He and his new partner brought in twenty-three cases of residents using out-of-state tags to avoid paying county taxes.'

'No shit.'

35

Land started to say something but then caught himself, leaning back in his big chair and grinning lizardlike. 'You don't do anything around here but shag a few loose balls for the *working* detectives, type reports, and then you're out of the building everyday at five on the nose. How come, Teddy?'

'Same reason a dog licks his balls.'

'Huh?'

'Because I can.'

'Cute.'

I didn't say anything. It was easy to rag on Land, he being such an asshole, but I knew Harvey wasn't the enemy. He was just another hotshot, the way I was once a hotshot, and the main reason I found him repellent was that he owned everything I had lost. He was cocky, confident, and getting exactly what he wanted out of life. I used to travel that track myself.

'Teddy?'

'Yeah, Harv?'

He chuckled. 'If you ever got your mind right, the way Bodine is getting *his* mind right, you and I could do each other some good.'

I kept quiet.

'When I asked Bodine why everyone calls him Lord Alfred, you know what he told me?'

'Some story about dorking the homecoming queen in high school?'

'No. He said he's called Lord Alfred because he speaks Elizabethan English.'

We both laughed and I got this sudden, sickening image of Land and me becoming friends. I stopped laughing and checked my watch.

'You in a hurry, Teddy?'

These past three years I have indeed become a clock, always out of the office by five, always in my apartment by five-twenty, always drinking that first vodka by half past five on the nose. It was four-fifteen and I could feel myself ticking. 'Time's money,' I told Land.

He tapped a pencil against his expensive teeth. 'When you and Bodine broke up, he became a real Viking.'

My former partner, Alfred Bodine, carried two hundred and forty pounds, most of it upper body weight and belly, on a six-foot frame. His face, torn up in a car accident ten years ago, looked as if it had been put back together at a drunken quilters' party. He had widely spaced little eyes, the left one drooping almost closed because of nerve damage he suffered in the crash. His sparse black hair stood straight up, each hair at rigid attention, all over his melon head. Pirate or Viking, either one was a good description. He was forty-two going on a real delinquent nineteen, and it made me wistful to think that he was getting his mind right.

'I assume you heard what happened to Jonathan Gaetan.'

Bingo.

'Well?'

'Well what?'

Land grinned. 'Too bad you didn't serve under me in the Navy.'

'Yeah, I've often regretted that myself.'

The lizard grin pulled into a tight grimace, but I just kept looking at him because that's about all I have left that still works, a pair of old eyes that don't blink.

Land picked up my personnel jacket, read a while to himself, and then put it down again. 'Do they still call you the Old Detector?'

'Some do.'

'Word was, you couldn't be lied to. Always knew if a suspect or witness was telling the truth. Never wrong. Myself, I've found that in ninety percent of the cases you already know who the bad guy is, know it from the start, but then you have to prove it. And your intuition, about who's telling the truth and who's lying, it can't be introduced in a court of law anyway. Still, it occasionally comes in handy – knowing who's lying. Word was, you really put on a performance when you interrogated.'

Yeah, I was a piece of work. But it's a hard talent to own, unable to be lied to, and it cost me a marriage, a daughter, a grandchild, one good lover, and, at age fifty, my equilibrium.

'I need you to bring that Old Detector act out of mothballs, Teddy. Will you do that for me?'

'Do what?'

He grinned again. I wondered who it was who told Land, back in his formative years, that he had a fetching smile. I wish she had kept her mouth shut. 'Talk to Mary Gaetan, Teddy, and tell me if she's lying or not. She's coming in at five. You work with me on this and we'll get you through to fifty-five standing up, OK?'

I shook my head like I was sorry as hell. 'I'm off at five, Harv.'

'You know, Teddy, sometimes when my friends talk to me about police work, they ask if I have a detective in the department who's like those detectives in the movies, you know, the guy who is always bending the rules, wrecking cars, pursuing cases on his own, upsetting city hall – a hotdog. So I tell my friends about you. How my biggest problem with you is keeping you awake at your desk. I always get a laugh with that.'

I smiled at him. 'It's true, Captain, I do have a talent for napping.'

His eyes were watering. Land had never become comfortable with his contact lenses, and when he got upset he wore the expression of a man trying his damndest not to squint. 'Talk to Mary Gaetan when she comes in at five, that's an order, Sergeant.'

'OK.'

He caught on quickly and suddenly we were pals again. 'You know what I'm saying, Teddy. Not just talk to her, but crank up the Old Detector and find out if she's lying.'

'I don't know if the old act works anymore.'

He came around from his desk and handed me a file folder. Opening it, I was confronted by a five-by-seven glossy of a naked man in a bathtub of blood. I snapped the folder shut and threw it on Land's desk.

'No, no,' he said, retrieving the folder. 'You have to study that file so you can figure out your questions.'

'Gimme a break, huh?'

'A break? You've been on a constant break for the past three years.' He tossed the file on my lap.

'I can't handle that kind of shit anymore,' I said, looking down at the file like it was something that might bite.

'Why not?'

'You know, everybody knows.'

'Tell me.'

I shrugged.

'No more cute comments, Teddy?'

'What do you want from me?'

'The truth.'

'The truth is, when I turned fifty, I turned pussy – is that what you want to hear? I used to be given all the nasty shit, but my quota's been filled, Captain. I can't handle it anymore. Gives me an acid stomach. You make me look at that file and I'll throw up all over your carpet.'

He laughed. 'Make you a deal, Teddy. You put on the Old Detector act for Mary Gaetan, and I won't make you look at those nasty pictures. OK?' When I nodded, the lizard grinned. 'I knew we could come to an understanding.' He glanced at his watch. 'I'll give you a quick rundown on what we got. Jonathan Gaetan. Biggest builder in the District, our richest resident. More money than God. Fifty-three years old, same age as you, Teddy. Married to a woman twenty-five years his junior. A real doll. I know because I've been to their house for dinner.' At this point, he actually smoothed back his hair with both hands, leaving me to wonder who cast this asshole for a part in my life.

'How does that make you feel, Teddy? Same age as you but he's a multimillionaire, *gives* away more money in one year than you'll ever make in your lifetime, married to an authentic beauty – kind of makes you feel like you were born without a dick, doesn't it?'

'Where is he right now?'

'In the morgue.'

I nodded.

Land took the folder from my lap and began flipping through it. 'There was even talk of his being appointed an ambassador to someplace. Who knows why a guy like that, on top of the world, why he kills himself, huh? I mean, if I walked in here one morning and they told me that Detective Sergeant Teddy Camel slit his throat the previous night, *that* I could believe. But not Jonathan Gaetan.'

'So you're thinking it wasn't a suicide.'

'Interesting question.'

'You think his wife killed him?'

'Another interesting question.'

I'd already passed the point in the afternoon when my relationship toward the first drink of the day changes, from wanting it to needing it, and I was in no mood for Land's forensic games. 'Why don't you just tell me what you want me to find out from Mrs Gaetan, huh?'

'The only statement she's given is the one she gave to the officers on the scene, right after Jonathan was found. She was obviously rattled, so maybe things didn't come out clearly. Maybe she was confused.'

'About what?'

'It was early Monday morning, about seven. According to her statement, Jonathan was in the head, she couldn't get any response from him, the doors were locked, and when she went to call someone for help, she found that all the telephone lines had been cut.'

'Cut?'

'Yeah.'

'Any signs of a break-in?'

'None. The house was checked over, nothing out of order. Which points to a suicide, right? Except Mary did something unusual when she found the phone lines cut. Instead of walking over to a neighbor's house to call, she drives to her lawyer's place, twenty minutes away, and he follows her back in his car, but he can't rouse Jonathan or get the door to the head open either, so he goes out to his car and places a call to the department from his car phone. Two uniforms arrive, take one of the doors off its hinges, and find Jonathan dead. Very dead.'

'In the bathtub.'

'Right. I mean, the man was earnestly deceased. Wrists slit, throat slit, and his cock hanging on by a thread.'

'His . . .'

'Apparently he was trying to amputate that most tender member when he passed out and bled to death before he could finish the surgery.'

'Ouch.'

'The preliminary pathology report says that the wounds on his wrists and throat and penis are consistent with those that could have been self-inflicted. But we got certain *discrepancies*. He had rope burns on his wrists and ankles, contusions on his face and head. All those preceded his death by several hours and they were *not* self-inflicted. Another thing – the knife he used was a cheap, chrome-plated replica of a Bowie knife, something you might pick up at a pawnshop for ten bucks. Definitely not the kind of knife Jonathan Gaetan would own. I've been skeet-shooting with him for chrissakes and I've seen his shotgun, a beautiful job from Purdey's. If he was so desperate to kill himself, why didn't he use *that*, huh?'

I shrugged. 'Momentary lapse of good taste.'

'Yeah, well, I'm left with a momentary lapse of good ideas. While pathology is willing to conclude that the actual cause of death was self-inflicted knife wounds, they don't know what to say about the rope burns and bruises. And while I'm more than willing to let this go as a suicide, what happens if it turns out that Mary *was* somehow responsible for Jonathan's death? It'll look like I let one of my social acquaintances off the hook. On the other hand, the Gaetans have a lot of influential friends, and the publicity about the suicide has been bad enough. If I start making noises about this being more than a suicide – and if I'm wrong – then I create for myself a whole raft of very powerful enemies. See my dilemma?'

I said I did.

'So I need to know if she's telling the truth.'

'Put her on the machine.'

'Are you crazy? Her lawyer's not going to allow that. We haven't charged her with anything. Believe me, this is not a woman you want to offend.'

'If I question her like I used to question people, she's going to be offended, I guarantee you.'

'Yeah, well . . .'

Exactly. Land had a future to protect, I didn't.

He looked at his watch again. 'She'll be here at five. What else do you need to know?'

'It's never very complicated, is it, Captain? If it's a homicide, the reason is money, sex, or family.'

'Well, it's not money. Jonathan carried a couple of big insurance policies but nothing out of line, considering his holdings. Mary is already co-owner of the Gaetan Development Company, she didn't need to kill him to get his money.'

'Sex then. Maybe the beautiful young wife had a beautiful young boyfriend.'

'No. Married seven years, they still acted like newlyweds. Remember, I know them socially. She was devoted to Jonathan.'

'Maybe he had a girlfriend then, and the wife found out—'

'No, no you're way off base. Jonathan wasn't a skirt chaser, believe me. Word was, he didn't even date before he married Mary. In fact, there were rumors around that he might be queer. You know, a good-looking guy like that, in his forties and never married. Then he meets Mary and—'

'There you go. A former boyfriend of *his* shows up and threatens to blackmail Jonathan. Distraught, Jonathan kills himself and even tries to cut off the offending member.'

Land seemed briefly interested in the theory. 'And the rope burns and bruises? The boyfriend did those when he was trying to put some teeth in his blackmail proposal?'

'Could be.'

He was shaking his head. 'If Jonathan killed himself, if it was a bona fide suicide, I'm thrilled. I'm over there comforting the widow and you can go back to napping at your desk.'

'What about the blackmailer?'

'Leave the speculations to me, Teddy. You don't have to sniff any deeper in this case than finding out one thing: Was Mary Gaetan involved? Does she know how Jonathan got those rope burns and bruises, that's your assignment. You do this for me, Teddy, and I'll let you go back to fucking the taxpayers for the next two years so you can retire on full benefits – OK?'

I nodded. My plan exactly.

Mary Gaetan didn't show for her five o'clock appointment. Her lawyer called and assured Captain Land that they would be in by six, but it was nearly seven before Land summoned me to his office, and for once I hurried there like a good little soldier, desperate for that overdue drink. If I stay sober too long I begin wondering how it is you go from being golden, which I was once, to being whatever it was I had become.

This time, Land stood when I came in. 'Hi, Teddy. Mary, this is Detective Sergeant Teddy Camel. Teddy, Mary Gaetan.'

We shook hands, checking each other out. Her auburn hair was arranged in no particular style, looking as if she had simply run her hands through it, pushing it back from her face. She wore a blue cotton V-neck sweater with nothing underneath, and at the sides of the V you could see the swelling edges of her high breasts. She looked as if she'd been crying hard for a long time. Gray eyes.

She wore jeans and when she crossed her legs, one white shoe dangled loosely from a set of brown toes. She was smoking.

'Teddy, you know Mrs Gaetan's attorney, George Trenter.'

43

'It's been a long time, Teddy,' the lawyer said, holding out a hand that I didn't notice for several embarrassing moments.

She was the first woman I'd ever met who had eyes that particular shade of gray, slate gray and looking right at me and no one but me ever since I walked into the office.

'I've assured George and Mrs Gaetan that this will be very brief,' Land was saying. 'I've explained how much we appreciate their coming in on the heels of such a tragic . . .'

But I wasn't listening. She must be accustomed to this, I thought – men staring at her. She wasn't a knockout beauty, but Mary Gaetan owned gray eyes and a great mouth. Women have gotten by on less. And there was something alluring about the way she kept looking at me, like she was trying to get a message across. She wore no makeup, and her mouth reminded me of someone famous.

'So if we can all just sit down and relax as best we can under the circumstances. I'll be recording this, of course, and . . .'

I still wasn't listening. Rich women – rich, elegant women, women with a touch of class, women like Mary Gaetan – are able to reach right down inside of me and twist something. My wife was in that category.

'Anytime you're ready, Sergeant.'

Land was behind his desk operating the tape recorder; Mary, her lawyer and I were sitting in chairs facing the desk. Everyone was waiting for me to begin, but I was thinking about Jonathan Gaetan. My age, wealthy, and on top of the world, that's what Land had said. Then why did he butcher himself, especially if he had a package like Mary to wake up next to every morning? Whatever demon pursued him, it must have been worse than any I could imagine.

'Sergeant Camel?'

Unless, of course, Mary was his demon.

'Teddy?'

I could tell from Land's increasingly anxious tone that he was getting worried I might embarrass him in front of these people, so I tried to build up the steam I would need to put on the act. Right at that moment, however, the message she'd been trying to send my way finally got through, arriving on one of her I'm-trying-to-be-brave smiles, Mary asking me to be careful with her. Please don't hurt me. And then I had to make a serious mental adjustment, realizing that Mary was six years younger than my daughter.

'*The tape recorder is on.*'

'Yes.' Yes, everyone looking at me, waiting for me, let's go, Teddy – showtime. If I didn't come through for Land, he might not be able to force me into early retirement but he certainly could make my life miserable on a daily basis for the next two years. Until Lord Alfred got *his* mind right, Land had him guarding six-packs at the local 7-Elevens.

I ordered a rearrangement of the chairs, moving lawyer George behind Land's desk and pulling my chair over in front of Mary, close enough that our knees almost touched. I was surprised to feel myself pumping so hard. I used to love doing this, back before I turned soft, really used to get off on ferreting out the truth. I was good at it.

You start out slowly, keeping your voice soft and reassuring. 'I know you've already explained to the other officers what happened yesterday morning,' I told Mary, 'but I'm going to ask you to tell it all over again. Only one difference this time.'

She nodded, her face like that of a schoolgirl who's been sent to the principal's office.

'Don't lie to me.'

Her lawyer launched a protest. 'I hardly think that's necessary—'

But Mary called him off. 'It's all right, George. I have no intention of lying to anyone.'

'If there's something you don't want to tell me,' I said, 'that's fine, just shake your head or remain silent, I don't care. In fact, I don't care how much or how little you say during this interview. I only care about one thing – that you not lie to me.'

Her gray eyes widened and her lawyer whined another protest, but I went on talking, a certain quiet menace growing in my voice, keeping my eyes locked on hers, telling Mary that I was a sweet old softy except for one thing – I hated lies. They are an affront to me. I smell them coming before they are even spoken. Lies make me violent. 'So don't do it. Don't lie to me.'

'I think we get the idea,' George Trenter said. He knew my reputation.

Placing my hands on my knees and leaning close to her, I asked, 'What happened yesterday morning, Mrs Gaetan?'

'My husband killed himself.'

'Why?'

'I don't know.'

Lie. The second question and she lied to me. The Old Detector act called for me to acknowledge this lie, to stand up and kick a chair over and start hollering at her, letting her know that I could see through her goddamn lies. I looked at her for a long time and then decided to take another tack. 'What did you and your husband do Sunday night?'

'We went to a fund-raiser for FONZ.'

'Fonz?'

'Friends of the National Zoo.'

I smiled. 'And when you got home?'

'Jonathan went up to get ready for bed, and I stayed downstairs to have a drink. An old habit of mine, a cigarette and a drink before going to bed.'

No cigarettes and lots of drinks before going to bed is a *current* habit of mine, I thought, and one I'm sorely missing right now. Let's get this over with. 'Did Mr Gaetan come back downstairs?'

'No. After I finished the drink, I went up to our bedroom.'

'And where was he then? In bed?'

'Yes.'

'Asleep?'

'No. Jonathan always waited up for me.'

'And then what did you do?'

'Do?'

'Did you and your husband talk, read in bed, listen to the radio, watch TV, go right to sleep – what?' I let the impatience show, picking up the tempo of the questioning, my voice becoming sharper.

'We had sex.'

I nodded, silently scoring a point for the very composed Mrs Gaetan. 'And what did you do afterward?' I asked softly.

'We went to sleep.'

'Anything unusual happen during the night? Did your husband get up, make any phone calls, speak to you?'

She shook her head.

'And then in the morning?'

I saw the tears coming. 'Something woke me up early. Jonathan wasn't in bed. I saw the bathroom light on, saw it under the door because it was still kind of dark out, and I just assumed Jonathan was planning to leave for work early that morning. I listened but didn't hear anything. I might have slipped back to sleep, I don't remember, but eventually I became worried enough about not hearing any sounds from the bathroom that I went to the door and called his name. He didn't answer and the door was locked. So was the other door, the one between the bathroom and the hallway. When I went to call the rescue squad, I found that Jonathan had cut all the telephone lines in the house.'

'Jonathan cut them?'

'I assume he cut them. *I* certainly didn't.'

'And no one else was in the house that morning or the previous night?'

She shook her head.

I stared hard at her. 'Why would he cut the telephone lines?'

'I don't know.'

'What did you do after you found the phone lines cut?'

'Drove to George's house.' She was crying now, not making

47

any weeping sounds but letting the tears run down her face.

'Why'd you go to your lawyer's house instead of a neighbor's? If you thought your husband was in that bathroom dying of a heart attack or stroke or something, why in the hell did you waste time getting your lawyer?'

'Jonathan told me to!'

'I thought you couldn't get an answer from the bathroom.'

'I couldn't! But he told me a long time ago that if anything ever happened to him, the first person I should contact is George.'

'Why?'

George supplied the answer. 'The Gaetan Development Company in involved in some sensitive projects, projects with a great deal of money at stake, much of it invested because of Jonathan's personal—'

I cut him off by asking Mary what happened after she and George returned to the house. She responded with what Land had already told me: George calling the department from his car phone, two uniforms arriving, taking a bathroom door off its hinges, finding Jonathan in a bathtub of blood.

As she was offering this weeping, halting account, I interrupted with a rude question. 'How in the hell did he get those rope burns?'

'What?'

'Did you think we were going to miss that little detail, Mrs Gaetan? Your husband had been tied up several hours before he died and now you're telling me you didn't know anything about that? He had bruises on his head, too, and they *weren't* self-inflicted. What happened, did that FONZ party you went to get violent? If you don't have an explanation, then you'd better go out in the hall and talk with your lawyer because—'

'I tied him up.'

'*You* did?'

She wiped at the tears and reached for her purse, looking for cigarettes.

I put my hand on her wrist. 'Come on, Mrs Gaetan, you don't need a cigarette to tell the truth.'

'Take your hand off her, Camel,' the lawyer said. Then he told Land that as far as he was concerned, this interview had just concluded.

But Mary said no, it was all right. She fished out a cigarette, quickly lighting it and elevating her chin as she exhaled. She looked at me very somberly. 'Are you married, Detective Camel?'

'Used to be.'

'Did you and your wife ever play games?'

'Games?'

'Bedroom games.'

Surprisingly enough, I found myself embarrassed.

'Well, if you *did* play bedroom games with your wife,' she said, 'I'm sure you wouldn't want to describe them for that tape recorder. And neither do I.'

'What are you saying?'

She just sat there, staring at me and smoking.

'Are you saying that when you and Jonathan had sex Sunday night, it involved the use of a rope?'

Mary nodded.

'Can you produce that rope?'

'I threw it out.'

'Why?'

'*Why?* Because I obviously no longer have a use for it. Did you want to borrow it?'

But I could tell that her sudden toughness was a façade, and it wasn't going to hold much longer. 'How'd your husband get those bruises on his head?'

'I loved Jonathan. I would've done anything for him. Sometimes . . . he liked to be treated roughly. George, do I have to answer these questions?'

'You certainly do not.' He came from around Land's desk.

Had to work quickly now. 'So Sunday night you and Jonathan

49

come home from a fund-raising party for the zoo and, aroused by the thought of all those caged beasts, Jonathan has you tie him up and slap him around, is that what it took for Jonathan to get his mojo working?'

'That's quite enough,' George said, taking Mary's arm and trying to get her to stand.

'Then the next morning,' I said, raising my voice, 'after a night of bondage and S & M, this pillar of the community gets up early, cuts all the phone lines, locks himself in the bathroom, fills the tub, and commences butchering himself – all without a word of explanation to you, no suicide note, nothing, is that what you call the truth, Mrs Gaetan?'

'This interview is concluded,' George announced, still trying to get Mary on her feet.

'Come on, Mary, tell me what *really* happened! Where'd Jonathan get that cheap knife he used on himself? Or did somebody else use it on him?'

She was sobbing.

'Did you kill him?'

She called me a bastard.

'Did you?' I was shouting at her.

'No!' she screamed back.

'Captain,' the lawyer said, 'you better call off your detective or I'll file a harassment suit against both of you.'

'Camel—'

'He killed himself!' Mary shrieked.

'Why?'

'I don't know!' She allowed George to escort her to the door.

'Don't lie to me!'

'Alive or dead, Jonathan was more of a man than you'll ever be!'

'I'm sure he was, Mary.' My voice, coming so softly after all that screaming, seemed to surprise everyone in the room. Mary's entire demeanor changed, her outrage collapsing into something vulnerable, begging me again with her eyes the way a woman does when that's all she has left, the power to plead. I remember seeing it in my daughter's eyes.

Land had rushed after them and didn't return to his office for nearly fifteen minutes. I was sitting exactly where he'd left me. 'Got kind of rough there, didn't it, Teddy?'

I didn't say anything.

'George was making all kinds of noise about a harassment suit, but Mary told him to let it drop. I explained that you were over-zealous but basically a good detective.'

'Thanks, Harv.'

'Hey, no need getting a complaint lodged when a few soothing words—'

'Of course.'

'That was quite a performance. What's the verdict?'

'The verdict?'

'Was she telling the truth? I couldn't read her. I mean, sometimes I thought she was being straight with you and then, the business about tying Jonathan up and knocking him around, well, if you knew Jonathan, it just doesn't wash.' He paused, staring at me. When I still didn't say anything, Land asked, 'So?'

'Dead on, Harv. She was telling the truth.'

'About everything?'

'Everything.'

'Kinky sex, not knowing where he got the knife, no suicide note, not having a clue about why he did it – *everything* she said was the truth?'

'Yes.'

'You sure?'

'Never been wrong yet.'

'Jonathan Gaetan's death was a suicide.'

'Yes.'

'And this isn't going to bounce back on me?'

'Guarantee it.'

He exhaled as if he'd been holding his breath for a long time. 'Great. Beautiful! Now I'm going to hold hands with the

51

coroner, the D.A., and anyone else who'll hold hands with me, and we're all going to come out singing *suicide, suicide.*'

'I'm happy for you, Harv.'

'Hey, Teddy, there are a lot of things you and I could work together on, you know that? Let's go talk about it over a drink.' The man was absolutely beaming.

And I remember thinking, here's your chance, Teddy. You got two more years working with this hotshot asshole, so why not make it easy on yourself? A few drinks, let Land pick up the tab, come in late tomorrow . . . 'I think I'll pass, Captain.'

'How come?' He was still grinning.

'I take drinking seriously, and I don't drink with people I don't like.' Totally unnecessary.

Land stopped smiling. 'Play it your way.'

I started to leave his office but he called to me before I got out the door.

'I'm going to need that report on my desk first thing in the morning.'

I asked him what report he was talking about.

'*Your* report, of course. One of the reasons I feel so confident about allowing Jonathan's death to be ruled a suicide is that one of my veteran detectives reviewed the case folder and he, like me, concluded that there was no foul play. So I'll need your written conclusions on my desk by nine tomorrow morning.' He hit the eject button on the tape recorder. 'You'll need this tape to do your report.'

I just stood there.

'I guess you'd better get back to your desk and start working.' He was putting on an expensive suit coat. 'You got some overtime coming your way.'

It was almost ten by the time I finished hunting and pecking the last word of my superfluous report, cursing Land and my own attitude problem with every typo I made. As I stood at the Xerox machine, two huge arms encircled me. 'Lord Alfred,' I said without looking around, 'you fucking pirate, you.'

'What're you doing here this time of night, Teddy Bear?'

'Reproducing.'

'Yeah, I heard Land was giving you the Gaetan case.'

'Land gave me shit.'

Alfred took one of the copies of the report and began flipping through it. 'Is it true Gaetan cut his dick off?'

'Tried to.'

'Why?'

'Nobody knows.'

'Bruises and rope burns, too,' Lord Alfred said, looking from the pages to me. 'And we're letting this ride as a suicide?'

'His wife tied him up the night before he killed himself. Bedroom games, she called them.'

'Really?' His good eye flashed several times. 'Can you introduce me?'

'She's out of your league, buddy.'

'You should know.'

'Meaning?'

He didn't reply. And even though I knew exactly what he meant – it was a league I had played in and lost – I pushed for an answer. 'What do you mean, I should know?'

Alfred pretended he was reading my report. 'You believe everything this Gaetan woman told you?' he finally asked.

'It's all there, *Lord* Alfred.'

'I can read the goddamn report, I'm asking if you think she was telling the truth.'

We didn't speak for a while after that, Alfred returning the pages to me and then waiting while I collated everything. The breakup of our partnership had been messy, each of us still resentful about certain details of who did exactly what to whom.

When I left the Xerox room, Alfred followed along. I put one copy of the report under Land's locked door; another copy went on the pile of stuff heading for Central Filing. Then I went back to my cubicle, Alfred still trailing me in silence.

I sat in my chair, exhausted and sober. 'You told Land that people call you Lord Alfred because you speak Elizabethan English?'

His scarred face rearranged itself into something that could pass for a smile. 'Actually, I got my nickname at our high school homecoming.'

'Yeah, I know. I've heard that story.'

'Loribeth and I left the dance and snuck out to the bleachers and—'

'And when you dropped your pants, Loribeth hollered out, "*Lord, Alfred*, you ain't sticking that ugly ole thing in me." I *know*, I've heard the story.'

'You are such a shit, Teddy.'

'Yeah. Listen, I gotta go, Alfred. Way overdue for my drinks date. You working the second shift?'

'Yeah, I'm meeting my partner here for some training.'

'Of course. Land told me you got your mind right. Becoming computer literate, huh?'

Alfred started getting angry all over again. 'You bet your ass I got my mind right. Land says jump, I ask how far. Land says shit, I ask how brown. And once I qualify on the computers, then I'm in line for a promotion. So if you think that's—'

'Hey, I think it's wonderful.'

He eyed me for sarcasm. 'Have you met my new partner?'

'I've seen him around. A nice-looking kid.'

'Nice-looking? Hell, he's prettier than two of my ex-wives. In fact, I figured on using him to troll for pussy, you know, sitting at some bar with him and just waiting for women to come around, then after he takes his pick I get first choice of the leftovers. But Melvin Kelvin is a real Boy Scout. No bar crawling, no skirt chasing. He intends to stay true to his wife.'

I laughed. 'What's happened to *values*?'

'Exactly! Come on, I'll walk you down to your car.'

54

On the way to the elevator, I asked Lord Alfred how he was occupying his spare time now that he had a partner who didn't engage in bar crawling or pussy chasing. He said he had devoted himself to literature.

'Literature?'

'Yeah,' he replied. 'In fact, I just began a new book last night – *Horny Housewives and the Plumber Who Loved Them.* I'm finding the extended plumbing metaphors a bit intrusive, however.'

'Everyone's fucking critic.'

He wanted to know if I cared to hear the book's opening line, and I said I did not. But when we stepped into the elevator, Alfred grabbed my sleeve. 'It starts with a quote from our hero, DeWitt. "Welcome to my humble abode, faggot," DeWitt growled menacingly as his pet pit bull, Penelope, urinated in nervous anticipation of a row.'

When I asked him what that had to do with plumbers and horny housewives, Lord Alfred said it was a long book.

The elevator opened on the ground floor. 'Give my best to Melvin Kelvin,' I told Alfred.

'It's not his fault he's got a funny name.'

I waved and walked away.

'Hey, Teddy Bear.'

'Yeah?'

'Since you're no longer interested in active police work, if you turned up anything on a hot case, like this Gaetan death, you'd give it to me, wouldn't you, buddy?'

'Land's going to let it close as a suicide.'

'My file could use a little good news.'

'I just write reports.'

He stepped back into the elevator, punching a button and letting the doors close between us.

By the time I reached my apartment, I was making a conscious effort not to hurry. It would be unseemly, I thought, to rush in there and grab the bottle from under the sink, pouring and

55

probably spilling the vodka in my effort to set up that long-delayed first drink of the day. I was convinced I could handle the entire procedure in a somewhat stately manner.

So I turned on the lights and glanced through the mail, thinking I might fix a fried-egg sandwich . . . but then I decided, *fuck it*. I took out the bottle and poured a glass half full, sitting there at the kitchen table with the tumbler right in front of me, feeling better already. A few of these, I told myself, and Mary Gaetan's gray eyes would be long forgotten.

3

He watches the little girl bouncing.

Having awakened to a darkened room, he stands now at the sliding glass doors and watches the scene in that other room, brightly lighted and curtains open, the room across the parking lot where mother is working at an ironing board, father and son sit in plastic chairs in front of the TV set, and daughter bounces endlessly on a bed. He is surprised that no one hollers at her to stop that bouncing and wonders how it would be to have a little girl bouncing on *his* bed, becoming intrigued with the idea of taking her to Mexico with him. Yes, he can imagine it easily, awakening every morning to the little girl bouncing on his bed in a stone house by the sea, walking along the warm ocean waters, painting sunbursts around her eyes, making her into his little doll-girl.

I could do it, he thinks – just walk over there and knock on their door, grab the man when he answers, cut his throat, tie up the woman and boy and leave them in the bathroom, take the girl and bring her back here . . .

But when he reaches down for his knife and discovers it missing, he realizes once more that he's going to have to wait until Wednesday to take the girl.

He has trouble waiting, hates waiting. Jonathan told him he'd have to wait three days to get his money, that it would take three days to get that much cash together, and the man has already waited two of those three days, the waiting making him boil in his motel room just the way he boiled in Jonathan's closet.

57

Two fucking days waiting here, ordering in pizza, staring at TV, napping during the day so he could stay up nights, spending most of his waking hours watching that happy family from across the way, the little girl and her brother playing in the swimming pool, the father and mother always smiling at their kids, all four of them hugging and kissing, and now – if he had his knife with him right now – he'd love to go over to that happy little room of theirs and share with them some portion of his terror.

He walks around the room, a petulant and deadly child, unable to delay gratification but having no choice: forced to wait. Becoming angrier, cursing and kicking walls, wondering if it really takes three days to get his money together or has Jonathan used that delay to contact the police who will be waiting there when he arrives on Wednesday to pick up what Jonathan owes him? He can't figure it out, telling himself that it is *his* money and, even if the cops are there waiting for him, they can't do anything to him, he can't get in trouble for coming by to pick up his own money. Wide awake, he lies on the bed, the scabs across his chest pulling loose and stinging. The bitch, cutting him up the way she did. Then he recalls that there *is* something he can get in trouble for, of course, something the police would love to talk to him about, that fucking hitchhiker.

He has to come up with a new plan, a way to get his money and escape before they connect him to that hitchhiker.

Tomorrow is Wednesday, he is sure of it. Wednesday is when Jonathan said he'd have the money ready. He needs a way to grab that little girl and . . . The coins! He remembers the image. He'll do it tomorrow before he goes to Jonathan's house, lay a path of shiny coins from the swimming pool, down the hill, away from the parking lot, down to where those three trash dumpsters sit on a concrete pad, to a spot hidden from view, and when the kids come down there following the coins, he'll break the boy's neck and take the girl, cool and wet in her little blue swimsuit.

It's a good plan, a plan that doesn't require him to have a

knife. And tomorrow's Wednesday, the day he's heading for Mexico, so it's perfect. He'll grab the girl down by the dumpsters and then drive directly to Jonathan's house, getting his money and leaving immediately for Mexico. By the time they find the boy and miss the girl, he'll be half the way home. With all that money, he'll be able to treat her like a princess. He'll keep her all to himself. Then see if mommy and daddy go around smiling all the time the way they have these past two days, once they find their little boy with his neck broken and their little girl gone, see if that doesn't wipe the smiles off their happy goddamn faces.

The room's noisy air-conditioner is not keeping him cool; he sweats and his head hurts and the heat makes waiting all the harder. Tomorrow. All those years of waiting in prison have not made waiting any easier for him.

He walks to the room's half-size refrigerator, opens the little door, and bends over to peer in, seeing her blackening hand grasping a can of Pepsi. At first startled, he quickly sobs his laughter. He remembers now, wrapping her hand around the can like that, pleasing himself with his peculiar sense of humor.

He wishes now he'd never ever stopped to give the bitch a ride, because if he hadn't met her, then he'd have no reason to be afraid of the cops waiting for him at Jonathan's house. Parole violation maybe, he could do that time standing on his head, the money waiting for him when he got out. But if they connect him to the hitchhiker . . .

When he straightens up from the refrigerator, he again feels that pulling pain across his chest. Opening his field jacket, he discovers that the wounds have become foul, crusting and oozing. Why haven't they healed like the scratches on his face? When he rolls the cold soda can across his chest, the sensation causes him to inhale sharply.

She lied to him and laughed at him – the bitch deserved whatever she got, exactly what she got. He walks over to a chair and sits, putting his head back and trying to sleep, but he can't sleep, having slept too much during the day. Noticing that he has brought the hand with him, he looks at it for a moment and then throws it over against the little refrigerator where it bounces like something made of rubber. He drinks some of the soda. This is unbelievable, this waiting. He thought he'd be in Mexico by now, living like a king.

He reaches into his pants and fondles himself. I should've fucked Jonathan's wife when I had the chance, he thinks, still not sure why he passed up the opportunity. He takes out the Polaroids and studies them for a long time, still playing with himself. Then he puts the pictures away and thinks back several days, to when he somehow got himself lost in Maryland, driving along a little two-lane highway and seeing her standing there with her thumb out, telling himself he'd stop and ask her directions and then give her a ride to the next turnoff, that's all. He wasn't going to do anything foolish, nothing that might jeopardize the big plan he'd been waiting seven years to execute.

She was a tough-talking skinny teenager with rat-teased red hair and a bad complexion that she tried to cover with too much makeup. Once he got directions from her on how to reach Washington, he offered to drop her off at the next road, but she said she'd go to Washington with him.

'Well, it's not exactly Washington I'm heading for,' he told her.

She said that was all right, she'd ride along with him anyway.

'I don't have time to screw around,' he insisted.

She said she knew a place they could go, not too far from where they were at that moment, down a blacktop road and then a place back in the woods where she'd fuck him for forty dollars. He thought about it a moment and then agreed, giving her two twenty-dollar bills and following her directions to this place in the woods.

After they finished, she sat against a tree and took out a cigarette. She was wearing only a T-shirt; her jeans, with his two twenty-dollar bills in them, were rumpled up next to her.

'I thought you didn't smoke,' he said to her. 'That's the first thing I asked you when I picked you up, and you said you didn't smoke.'

She smirked as she lit the cigarette. 'I told you that you were the best lay I'd ever had. You believe that, too?'

'Well, it wasn't worth forty dollars,' he said quietly.

She laughed.

He asked her what was so funny.

'You weren't even hard. I had to *work* for that forty bucks.'

'You said it was good.'

She laughed again. 'I've had better.'

He stepped over to where she sat. 'Tell me about them.'

She inhaled and then blew smoke in his direction, smiling. 'You like hearing about it, huh? That's cool. Tell you what, for another twenty dollars I'll describe the five best fucks I've ever had.' It was a serious offer, but she was taunting him, too.

When he leaned down and tried to touch her hair, she brushed his hand away. 'How old are you?' he asked.

'Old enough.'

He withdrew the big knife from his boot. 'Give me your hand.'

'Hey, come on, I wasn't laughing at you.'

'Sure you were. Said I wasn't even hard, said I was a lousy fuck.'

'I didn't say that. Come on, put the knife away and we'll go back to your car. I won't smoke all the way to Washington, promise.'

'Promise?'

'Yes.'

'I can't begin to tell you how many promises have been made to me. How old did you say you were?'

'Fifteen,' she replied immediately.

'Now give me your hand.'

She offered her left.

'No, I want the hand that's holding the cigarette.'

She crushed the cigarette out in the dirt. 'Listen, if you want to

61

screw again, we could. Really, on the house this time. I could get you off, I know ways.'

'Tell me.'

'Put the knife away first. I'll tell you while we're driving.' Her smile was crooked, unsure.

'Nancy,' he said, coming at her with the knife.

She stood, her back against the tree trunk. 'Stay away from me! Please!'

'*Please!*' he mocked her, grabbing her right hand.

'Stop fooling around, huh?'

'I'm not fooling around.'

Neither one of them was sure he was going to do it, was actually going to cut her with that knife, but when the girl brought her left hand up and scratched his face, struggling to pull away, he tightened his grip on her right hand, raising the blade high and bringing it down as hard as he could on her wrist.

She screamed.

The knife had cut halfway through, her bone showing white in all the sudden blood. 'See!' he shouted. 'I knew if you didn't hold still I was going to have trouble getting it off.'

'Oh God, please!'

Again the heavy blade came down on her wrist, hitting in another place, more blood, the girl struggling and screaming and scratching his face with her free hand, the man hacking at her wrist, blood all over both of them, the girl jerking to get away from him as he kept chopping at her wrist – until finally she pulled free, leaving her right hand in his grasp, the girl struggling backward and looking at her mangled wrist, one jagged bone sticking up where her hand had been.

'Oh, God,' she said again, looking from her wrist to the man who held her hand, trembling and wondering if she should still try to escape.

He stood there staring at the severed hand, amazed at what he'd accomplished.

She had bumped against the tree again, holding her bloody

forearm, still naked from the waist down, sliding to the ground, unable to take her eyes off the spot where her right hand used to be, unable to breathe.

He didn't know what to do next.

She finally looked up at him. 'Hospital. You got to . . . get me to a hospital. Please, I don't want to die out here, you got to get me . . .' She became hysterical.

'You want it back?' he asked, holding out her hand.

Confused, slipping into shock, she actually reached for it. But he quickly put it behind his back. 'Say please.'

She began heaving.

He knelt beside her, using her own severed hand to smooth her ratty hair, blood dripping on to her face, the man whispering, 'Make love to me.'

'Hospital,' she said dreamily, looking at the bloody stump, moving her lips but saying nothing more.

He was suddenly close, feeling between her legs.

As if awakening abruptly from a nightmare, she jerked her head around to stare into his face, screaming, 'NO!' flailing at him with both arms, her left hand scratching and slapping his face as the jagged bone sticking out of her right wrist made deep cuts across his chest. She fought, spitting like a cat, rolling from side to side, fighting to avoid this final humiliation.

But he managed to stay between her legs, shoving his fist into her mouth as he entered her, bashing her mouth with that fist as he screamed, 'This is how you like it, ain't it, whore?' Ramming her as hard as he could. 'Ain't it, Nancy?' Pumping against her, screaming, crazed as he kept hitting her face and stabbing between the legs.

When he finished, he pulled out quickly and rolled away, sitting up to look at what he'd done to the girl. She lay there as if dead but still breathing, the blood dribbling now from her jagged wrist.

He stood over her, knife in hand, telling her, 'Now we're going to take a look at what you've done to your lungs.'

She opened her eyes. 'My name's not Nancy.'

Holding the Bowie knife in both hands high over his head the way you might hold an axe, he screamed obscenities at her and began chopping.

In his hotel room, the oppressive heat has lifted and he suddenly feels cold, so cold that he shivers. He holds up his sweaty hand, making it into a fist.

Then what *was* her name?

When he stands, the fever returns to his face, but he's still shivering. I got an infection, he thinks – that bitch gave me an infection.

He walks into the bathroom and, remembering the soap he took from Jonathan's house, he searches pockets until he finds a small red bunch of grapes, rubbing it under the water and trying to make it lather. Have to clean these cuts on my chest, he thinks, but the water remains cold and the grapes refuse to lather.

Finally, he turns off the water and drops the soap into the sink, returning to the sliding glass doors, looking out, seeing that the happy little family have turned off their lights. They're sleeping but he can't do anything, not yet, not until Wednesday when he will pick up his money and leave for Mexico with the girl.

He goes to the bed and sits, unable to sleep and not wanting to sleep. It's better just to catch naps during the day, because when he goes to sleep at night, in the dark, that's when the nightmares begin. He reaches over and switches on the motel's battered box of a radio, someone's cheery voice just then announcing midnight.

4

I was surprised to hear the guy on the radio say it was midnight. I'd missed my usual bedtime by more than an hour and was still sitting there at the kitchen table, the glass of vodka still in front of me, untouched. You have to sit a long time, stone sober, to figure out how it happened that everything could have gone so wrong.

'Marry a woman who loves her daddy,' an uncle advised me back when I was a teenager, 'because those kind of women make the best wives.' And my wife did indeed adore her daddy but, unfortunately, the son of a bitch hated me on sight.

Linda and I met in college. I fell in lust with her before I found out about the family, filthy with money that went back several generations on both sides. Her old man owned an architectural firm in Florida.

'In many ways, Linda is still an adolescent,' he told me on my maiden visit to their 'compound.' I got the idea this wasn't the first little chat he'd had with one of Linda's beaux. 'At least she's still having adolescent flings. Last year it was a Bohemian writer who'd dropped out of college to "gather experiences." ' The old man, white-haired and patrician, smirked. 'Then she took up with a roustabout she met in Louisiana during summer vacation. Do you understand what I'm telling you?'

'Not exactly.' I was only nineteen.

He closed his eyes and opened them slowly. 'Your father's a policeman, right?'

I nodded, telling him that I was in prelaw and intended to

become a criminal defense lawyer. He just laughed and walked away, ending my audience without saying another word.

You superior son of a bitch.

A few months later, Linda was pregnant, we were married, and on my second visit to the Florida compound, Daddy wasn't nearly as jolly about my plans for the future. He wanted me to transfer to Harvard or at the very least to the University of Virginia; he had connections both places. He'd take care of all the expenses. 'Do well in school and treat my daughter right,' the old man said, 'and I think maybe we can make this thing work.'

That's when I let it drop that I'd already quit school and joined the Army, an announcement that caused the old man to jut out his lower jaw and walk away from me without speaking, just the way he had at the end of our first visit together. Except this time he didn't exit laughing.

Yeah, I thought, looking at the glass on the kitchen table, I showed him. Turned my back on an all-expenses-paid trip through law school and then an easy life in Florida just for the pleasure of wiping that smile off the old bastard's face.

Linda's sense of humor about my rebellious nature had dimmed after two tours in the Army, so instead of signing up for a third hitch I went back to school on the GI bill. Then my father died when I was thirty and, before finishing college, I joined the suburban police department where I still work.

Linda and I had a major, three-day argument about asking her father for the money we would need to buy a big brick house she'd fallen in love with, Linda finally contacting him behind my back. He called me one evening saying he'd give us the money if I returned to school. I told him I was happy being a cop. 'When I was ten years old,' he said, 'I wanted to be a fireman, but like most boys, I eventually outgrew that ambition. You know what a policeman is, don't you, Teddy? A public *servant*.'

I told him what he could do with his money, he said he'd never give us a dime, and Linda and I had to settle for a dinky little ranch house we could afford. My father-in-law's high-handed treatment pissed me off, but it also made me determined. Detective grade when I was thirty-three, detective lieutenant at thirty-five, I was working sixty hours a week, using up my overtime quota and then working without being paid – I didn't care because I was a hotshot back then. And it didn't matter that the cases were seldom more glamorous than burglaries and car thefts, I was going to be the best damn detective in suburbia.

I put my finger and thumb on the glass of vodka and told myself to go ahead and drink the goddamn stuff because this was too stupid, sitting there going over an old story that had been gone over too many times.

Linda took care of the house, handled the finances, and reared our daughter, Margaret; I was too busy for any of that. Linda and Margaret became like sisters, spending all major holidays and three months every summer with my wife's family in Florida. I didn't care; I was aiming to make captain before I hit forty.

I raised the glass halfway to my lips and then put it back down again. I hated this part of the story.

Even though I was not really a member of the family, showing up at our house only to eat and sleep, I still had good instincts for plots, for whispers and for those secret looks that conspirators pass between them.

'OK, what's going on?' I asked Linda one Sunday afternoon when I happened to be home.

'Going on?'

'Yeah, going on. Every time I see Margaret she's crying. When the two of you are talking and I come into the room, conversation stops. You want to tell me about it?'

Linda closed the magazine she'd been reading and folded her hands on top of it. 'Margaret's pregnant.'

'Pregnant? She's barely sixteen!'

Linda laughed. When I married her I thought she had a wonderfully aristocratic face, but over the years it had grown horsey.

'Who did it?' I asked.

She laughed again. '*Who did it?* A normal person might ask, Who's the father? But you want to know who did it. Like a crime has been committed, right?'

'OK then, who's the father?'

'We've decided not to tell you.'

That did it. I walked over to her and knocked the magazine out of her lap, putting my face close to hers. 'Decided not to tell me? How many of her friends do you think I'll have to roust before one of them gives me a name, huh?'

Margaret, who'd been listening from the hallway, came running in to beg me not to talk to any of her friends. 'You'll just embarrass me, daddy.'

'Then you tell me, honey. Who did – who's the father?'

'It's too late for you to start getting interested in my life.' She was crying. 'Mom and I can handle this on our own.'

'Hey, baby, you can't keep any secrets from your father, you should know that.'

Linda was on the couch, laughing again. I asked her what was so fucking funny. 'Just the idea that no one can keep a secret from you,' she said. 'We didn't want to go into all of this yet, but I might as well tell you. Margaret and I are moving to Florida.'

'The hell you are.'

Margaret was holding my arm. 'I don't want my friends to know about this,' she said. 'Mom and I have talked it all through, please don't mess things up, Daddy.'

I finally got Margaret to her room and then came back to Linda, asking her when all these decisions had been made.

'They've been in the making for a long time, Teddy, you were just too wrapped up in being supercop to see it.'

I was trying to get everything straight in my mind. 'She's going to have the baby down in Florida and then you're coming back here and—'

'We're not coming back. I'm divorcing you.'

'What?'

'Let's face it, Teddy – you don't know shit about secrets. I've been seeing someone, a man I knew a long time ago. This past summer, he and I—'

'What the hell, wait a minute, what are you saying? Summer vacation? Is that when Margaret got pregnant.'

My wife nodded.

'What, the two of you cruised the beach together? She gets anyone under twenty and you take on the thirty-plus crowd? What kind of shit is this? Hey, nobody's going to Florida, I'll let you in on that little secret right now.'

'Oh yes we are, Teddy – everything's been arranged.'

'Bullshit. Who is it, Linda, somebody I know?'

'Which one?' she asked coolly. 'My lover or Margaret's?'

I walked over to the couch and slapped her across the face.

Linda stood, holding a hand to her cheek. 'No one can keep a secret from the great detective Teddy Camel, right? Then you tell me how much money my family has given us since we've been married.'

'Money? Not a goddamn dime as far as I know.'

'Yeah, as far as you know. You ever wonder why we aren't in debt like everyone else you work with? Do you really think I can live on your salary? Did you really think I was going to be happy in this ranch house the rest of my life?'

'Who're you fucking down there in Florida? Have I met him?'

'It's too late for you to start asking questions, Teddy.'

'You've been lying to me from the start, haven't you?'

'Easy to lie to a man who isn't paying attention.'

'I want to know—'

'Want to know what? *Everything?* It's too late, Teddy. You didn't know Margaret was pregnant, you didn't know I was having an affair, you didn't know my family has been giving us money, you don't even know I was fucking someone when you were in the Army, pathetic, really—'

The second time I hit her, I knocked her down.

*　　*　　*

I got up from the kitchen table and went into the bathroom, careful to avoid the mirror.

Lawyers handled all the details. I was quickly paid off: given the car, the house, and what money we had in our bank accounts. In return, Linda dropped the assault and battery charge against me. Visitation rights were a moot point because Margaret informed me that she never wanted to see me again, ever, and that she was going to make sure I never saw her child, either.

A year after they left me, the final humiliation arrived anonymously by mail: a newspaper clipping describing the double marriage ceremony, mother and daughter, both of their new husbands employed in my ex-father-in-law's firm. I'm convinced he was the bastard who sent the clipping. A separate photograph showed my daughter holding her son; the caption said his name was David. That's the only picture I've ever seen of him.

I sold the house and moved into an apartment, and it was then that I developed my specialty, my talent – unable to be lied to. I became so profoundly, so genuinely affronted by lies that I could read them in the faces of men we arrested for burglary, teenagers who'd taken cars for joy rides, women who were brought in for shoplifting. Especially the women. As soon as they started lying to me ('I put it in my purse because I didn't have a shopping cart with me but I intended to pay for it, I just forgot'), I became so screaming mad that Alfred would have to hold me back. This was no good cop-bad cop routine; I really was bad.

Bad enough to get demoted to detective sergeant, and I probably would've been fired if word hadn't gotten around about my reputation, the Old Detector; neighboring jurisdictions began calling me in when they needed to know if certain witnesses or suspects were lying. I managed to remain employed.

A woman lived with me in the apartment for about a year, the best lover I ever had, but I couldn't leave her alone either. Expert at reading the lies in the faces of people accused of crimes, it became casually easy for me to know when a lover was lying. *Who'd you have lunch with today, what'd you talk about, and*

*that guy who came over for dinner last night, an old friend from
school you said, did you ever sleep with him? Come on, don't lie
to me.*

So she walked out, too, and at age fifty I finally decided –
fuck it. But now, three years after that decision, here I was back
at the kitchen table, well past midnight, going over the story one
more time.

Mary Gaetan lied to me. She might have been telling the truth
about Jonathan's death being a suicide, but she lied when she
said she didn't know why he killed himself, and she lied about
those rope burns and bruises, too. Then I turned around and
convinced Land she was telling the truth about everything.

Have I become so pathetic that I give a free ride to a woman
younger than my daughter simply because she dangles a white
shoe from brown toes and asks me with gray eyes not to hurt her?
Pathetic is right.

And stupid. Stupid to be sitting here past midnight wondering
again how my grandson turned out, if he's tall, if he plays ball,
and what in God's name have they told him about me?

Stupid, yes, but mostly what I felt when I finally hauled myself
to bed that night was sober – terribly, vulnerably sober.

5

At ten o'clock on Wednesday morning I was taking a nap at my desk in the usual manner, head on my hands, elbows on some opened report, my back to the bullpen. Sleeping sober hadn't been good for me last night but, as I told Land, I have a breathtaking capacity for the nap.

'Detective Camel?'

The woman's voice put me on instant alert. Keeping my back to her, I quickly held up one finger. 'Just a second, I have to finish this.' I grabbed a pencil and made a couple of marks on the report I was supposedly reading and then turned, pleased with my performance.

She stepped smartly into my little cubicle and sat very straight-backed on the straight-backed chair next to my desk.

'Pathetic.'

Yeah, I'd heard the word applied to me before.

'This morning, on the way here, I saw a bum sleeping on a park bench, but at least he wasn't collecting a paycheck.'

I couldn't stop blinking. Who was this woman? And why hadn't I been told she was coming to see me? A glance out at the bullpen answered the second question, three detectives standing there grinning, the bastards having sent the woman to my cubicle without announcing her because they knew I was napping. *Ha, ha*, assholes.

'What can I do for you?' I finally asked, still blinking.

'I have some information,' she announced. A lot of what she said came in the form of announcements.

I nodded and waited for the information. She was in her late thirties, dark brown hair in a shoulder-length flip that was at least a decade too young-looking for her, heart-shaped face with pointy chin and a really ugly nose sporting a fat little bulb right on the end of it. Except for the nose, she wasn't an eyesore. Brown eyes and large breasts. She wore a dark blue skirt with matching jacket, which she carried over her arm; her plain white blouse, straining to contain its cargo, was buttoned up all the way to her neck. Very large breasts.

'My name is Jo-Jo Creek. I am, was, Jonathan Gaetan's personal secretary. I understand you're in charge of the case.'

Oh, Jonathan, you cad: Mary Gaetan to keep you blissful at home and this mammary centurion to guard you during the business hours, why did you ever butcher yourself the way you did?

I cleared my throat. 'A terrible tragedy, Miss Creek.'

She eyed me. 'I can do without your officious expressions of sympathy. Jonathan Gaetan did not kill himself.'

'He didn't?'

She snorted. Although fifteen years my junior, the woman was making me nervous the way nuns once did. I sat up straight, putting both hands on my desk, hoping she wasn't going to start hollering at me as I asked, all wide-eyed, 'You don't think it was a suicide?'

'He was murdered, you twit.'

It suddenly occurred to me to wonder why I was sitting there listening to her abuse. Jonathan Gaetan's death was not my case; it was Land's and he had already let it close as a suicide. 'Do you have any evidence to support your conclusion?' I asked her carefully.

'If I had the evidence, Detective, I would be sitting in the D.A.'s office, not your little cubbyhole. I believe that's included in your job description – assembling evidence, making arrests, et cetera, et cetera.'

'Of course.' I had to bite back a grin. For some strange reason, I was beginning to like this little Hun. 'Do you have any clues, as we call them in the trade, any theories, suppositions, suspects, et cetera, et cetera?'

She snorted and said, '*Cherchez la femme.*'

I guess I looked at her blankly.

'Not even high-school French, Detective Camel?'

'I was absent that day.'

She took a breath, inflating her breasts dangerously against the blouse buttons, and began what was obviously a rehearsed speech. 'I started working for Jonathan Gaetan when I was twenty-two. Fifteen years ago. I was his secretary and book-keeper when his business was nothing more than a construction trailer, rented equipment, and day laborers. I went through *everything* with him, the struggles and finally the successes, even the times when I had to take money out of my own savings account to help the company make its payroll. I own stock in the Gaetan Development Company, but I kept on working as Jonathan's secretary because I admired the man.'

And you were in love with him, I thought.

'The company really took off about twelve years ago. We moved into our new offices in Washington. I was Jonathan's personal secretary when *she* came to work in those offices eight years ago.'

'Mrs Gaetan.'

From Jo-Jo Creek's expression you'd think she'd just belched something from a cheap breakfast. 'Her pursuit of Jonathan was relentless. And quite effective, too. A year after she began with us, the two of them eloped to Las Vegas even though she was only twenty-one. Were you aware of that?'

'No, but—'

'I didn't think the marriage would last beyond however long it took for her to lay claim to some portion of Jonathan's money but, give the devil her due, she stayed married to him these past seven years.'

I leaned back in my chair and tapped a pencil on my teeth until I remembered seeing Captain Land doing the same thing.

Tossing the pencil away and sitting up, I asked her, 'What role, exactly, do you think Mrs Gaetan played in her husband's death?'

She snorted again, as if she found my stupidity tiresome.

'Miss Creek?'

'Yes?'

'Be very careful before you make any accusations.'

'I haven't made any accusations, *yet*.'

'Then what's your information?' I needed to know because I was the one who had lied to Captain Land about Mary Gaetan telling the truth. 'Miss Creek?'

Her voice was not so strong as it had been before. 'I don't want you to make the mistake some people do, Detective Camel, thinking I'm one of those prim and proper executive secretaries who has always been secretly in love with her boss, who secretly hates the boss's wife, one of those secretaries who believes her boss is a hero while his wife is a shrew. I know the syndrome and I wouldn't want you to think I'm an example of it.' Then she locked eyes with me. 'I thought about this a great deal before coming to you, because I realize that certain matters are going to be exposed. I was reared in Oklahoma, I have four older brothers, I *know* how the world works. It's not that I'm overly embarrassed by what's going to come out in this investigation, but Jonathan did prize my discretion.'

I didn't say anything, deciding to let her tell it her way.

'I admired Jonathan a great deal, but I have no illusions about him. He was heir to the weaknesses all you men have for women like Mary, bubbly little fluffballs like her, always smiling and always happy, a talent for making men laugh and forget themselves. But there's something behind that famous smile of hers, Detective Camel – something bad.'

'I don't understand what you're trying to say.'

Jo-Jo gave me a look that seemed to say she'd get to the point in just a minute. 'Mary made Jonathan happy, I know that, I have to live with that, how much happier he was with her than he ever was with . . . than he was before she came along. But I knew him longer than she did, better than anyone did. Psychologically, he was even-keeled, a very disciplined man. He did not kill himself.'

I offered my line about a man and his demons.

'Yes,' she agreed, 'but if Jonathan did have demons I didn't know about them and if they *had* driven him to suicide, he certainly wouldn't have killed himself in the way they say he did, in a rage like that, butchering himself. That was the work of someone else.'

'Who?'

'I think Mary wanted out of the marriage. Maybe she was bored being married to a businessman – and that's what Jonathan was, heart and soul. A businessman. Maybe she found someone more exciting, I don't know, but I think she asked for a cash settlement in exchange for a quickie divorce. Then something went wrong and she killed him or had him killed, staging his death to make it look like a suicide.'

I was shaking my head. 'I tried to warn you, Miss Creek. Accusing someone of homicide, I don't think you realize how much trouble you can get yourself in. Listen, I've been sitting on some information I probably should have given you right in the beginning. The final report from the coroner has come in, and the pathology clearly shows, shows conclusively, that the wounds causing Jonathan Gaetan's death were self-inflicted. There's no way around it, I'm sorry, but he did kill himself. Whatever drove him to it, whatever or whoever caused him to act out of character and go into that self-destructive rage, I don't know, but Jonathan Gaetan killed himself. OK?'

She was unfazed by my announcement. 'I've been sitting on some information, too, Detective. Jonathan called me Monday morning, right before his death.'

I adjusted myself a little straighter in the chair. 'He did?'

'If you had been investigating his death as a potential murder instead of trying to close the case as quickly as possible to avoid

inconveniencing his widow, then you would've examined his telephone records and you would have discovered that call to my
apartment. I've been waiting for you to contact me.'

'How could he have called you if all the phone lines in his
house were cut?'

'From his car phone.'

'Oh.' Then why didn't Mary use that car phone instead of
driving over to fetch her lawyer? 'He must have called you
around daybreak.'

'Yes. Jonathan sounded terrible.'

'What'd he want?'

'Money.'

'Money?'

'He said that as soon as I got to work that morning, I was to
transfer money from his various business accounts into his personal checking account. Then I was supposed to withdraw the
money from the checking account, withdraw it *in cash*, and
have one of our security men deliver it to Jonathan's house in a
suitcase.'

'In a suitcase?'

'Yes, I know. Very unusual. Jonathan had never made that
kind of request before. I could've had the money for him that
very day, but Jonathan didn't want anyone to ask questions, so I
was supposed to cash a few bonds and sell some securities, transfer the money in bits and pieces into his household checking
account. Doing it that way, it would take a couple of days at
least, but Jonathan was very insistent about this being handled as
quietly as possible. The cash was scheduled to be delivered to his
house Wednesday morning, *today*.'

'How much money are we talking about?'

She paused for effect and then said, 'One hundred forty-five
thousand, six hundred dollars.'

OK, I was impressed. 'Exactly that amount? A hundred and
forty-five thousand, six hundred dollars.'

'In twenties and fifties and hundreds, he wanted it all in

78

twenties and fifties and hundreds, in a suitcase.'

'Jesus.'

'Exactly. Now I know you're going to get sidetracked into thinking that Jonathan was involved in something illegal, a business payoff or a drug deal, something like that, but I worked for the man for fifteen years and I know everything about him, his personal life and his business dealings. Jonathan was a straight arrow. He'd never been involved in anything shady, at least not something requiring a suitcase full of cash.'

'Then what?'

'To pay off Mary. Maybe *she* was involved in something illegal and he was bailing her out, I don't know, but I think you'll agree that it deserves to be investigated.'

'Where's the money now?'

'As far as I know, it's still sitting in their joint checking account. After what happened to Jonathan, I certainly wasn't going to send the money to his house. I should've come to you earlier but, as I said, I was torn between my loyalty to Jonathan and my obligation not to allow his death to be labeled a suicide – which it wasn't. He told me, when he called that morning, he instructed me not to tell anyone about the money. I've been waiting for you to contact me.'

'Does Mrs Gaetan know about the money?'

'That would be an interesting question to ask her, wouldn't it?'

I started to protest, but she interrupted me: 'That woman is a seducer, and I'm not talking about sex, either – at least not sex exclusively. She has a talent for making herself into whatever another person wants her to be. I've seen Mary in action, believe me.'

So had I. I assured Miss Creek that the money angle would be investigated fully and that if Mary Gaetan was involved in any illegal—

She interrupted me again, this time by snorting. 'I'm sorry. But you men *always* think you're invulnerable to a woman like her, you think you can play with her the way she's playing with you and you'll never get caught. Jonathan thought that. And then you men always turn out being wrong.'

I nodded. 'I'm going to have to ask you some questions.'

'I expected that.'

'Apparently there were rumors about Jonathan, before he got married . . . apparently he didn't date much and there were these rumors about the possibility that he was homosexual.'

'Untrue.'

'That could be the angle for the money, you know. A former boyfriend of Jonathan's shows up, threatens to embarrass him unless he gets a payoff.'

She took a breath and blew it out, pausing a moment before saying, 'Until Jonathan got married, he and I worked ten hours a day, six and sometimes seven days a week. That's what it takes to go from a construction trailer to a multimillion-dollar operation. He didn't have time to date.'

'Maybe he didn't have the inclination, either.'

'You'd love to find out he was gay, wouldn't you?'

'I'm just looking for a possible—'

'Even if he'd had the time for other women, Detective Camel, he didn't *need* them. He had me and I was convenient.' She raised her head the way women sometimes do to prevent tears from forming. 'And I was going through a lot of trouble in my life back then, too, so I guess you could say our affair was *convenient* all around.'

'Listen, Miss Creek, I'm not saying I believe those stereotypes about a man in his forties who doesn't date, has never been married, but—'

'Haven't you heard anything I've told you? He didn't date because he was screwing me – in the trailer, in his office, on the floor, propped up on his desk, believe me, I know whereof I speak. There is no homosexual connection.'

I got the message: the man was a hog for pussy. 'Were you in love with him?'

'After he married *her*, I loved *and* hated Jonathan. I'm not blind to the effect she had on him, making him a man who was happier with life . . . I don't know what my mistake was. Being too convenient, I guess. When the two of them eloped, I could have killed him myself, but I kept on working there because, in a way, being with him during the office hours was better than not being with him at all. He was a bastard, the way all men can be bastards, dropping me for her without an explanation but, yes, I loved him. Yes.'

'Did your affair continue after they were married?'

'No. I made suggestions a few times but Jonathan was too "in love" with her.'

'Why do you think he asked for that money to be delivered to his house today, that specific amount?'

'I have no idea.'

'Did he ever mention having troubles with his wife, that maybe he was suspicious about her and another man?'

'No. He never talked to me about their marriage, at least he had the decency not to do that. I, of course, was the one who was suspicious of Mary, of her motives, and I did a little poking around on my own, trying to find out if she had anyone else on the line.'

'And?'

'As far as I could tell, she was faithful to him.'

'During your affair with Jonathan, did he ever like to try different things?'

'Different things?'

'Bedroom games,' I said, using Mary's term. 'Did he like to be tied up, knocked around, did that sort of thing arouse him?'

'What an extraordinary question.'

'It's important.'

'He liked his sex straight and often. The idea of Jonathan being involved with ropes and whips is ludicrous. My God, he was a businessman!'

I laughed.

'What?' she asked.

'Nothing, I'm sorry.' Maybe Mary was the one who had introduced him to some of the more exotic practices, and maybe that was her hold on him.

When I glanced at Jo-Jo's face, I noticed she was blushing. 'What is it?' I asked.

'He liked to do it between my breasts sometimes,' she said quietly. 'Does that count?'

I glanced at her chest and shook my head.

She asked me what else I needed to know.

'Nothing else at the moment. But I'd appreciate it if you didn't discuss any of this with anyone until I have a chance to check out a few things.'

'Of course. I told you, discretion is one of my virtues.'

'Yes, well, I appreciate your coming in, Miss Creek. You did the right thing.'

'In view of the conversation we've just had, I think you should call me Jo-Jo.'

'And my name's Teddy.'

'I'll wait to hear from you then.'

'This is a police matter now, you understand that, don't you?'

'Of course. Just be careful with her. There's an element of evil in that woman, and I know what that sounds like, coming from me, but you're going to have to take my word for it. If you let her, she'll seduce you, too. You'll end up talking yourself into it, without even knowing you've been seduced. I've seen the way she operates.'

When I said I'd be careful, Jo-Jo offered a barely audible snort and then stood, shaking hands and leaving me there to wonder what the hell I should do *now*?

The smart thing, of course, would be to march right into Land's office and tell him everything, tell him that in view of Jonathan Gaetan's last telephone call being a request for a hundred and forty-five thousand, six hundred dollars to be delivered in cash to his house, the case should be reopened, and then I'd admit maybe I was wrong about Mary telling the truth when I questioned her in his office. Afterward, I could come back here and resume my nap. That would be the smart thing to do.

Instead, I called Lord Alfred at home.

The phone rang eight times before he picked it up. 'This better be good,' he said, sniffing loudly and then hacking to clear his throat.

'It's Teddy. How's about coming down this afternoon?'

'I worked last night.'

'I might have something for you on that Gaetan case after all.'

'What?'

'I'll tell you when you get here.'

'I don't have to be in until noon—'

'Hey, forget it then. You're the one who asked me to—'

'OK, OK. I'll catch a shower and be there in half an hour. Is Land letting you handle this on your own?'

'I haven't talked to him.'

'Why are you being so mysterious?'

'Listen, Alfred, I think maybe this case should be reopened. Even if Gaetan did kill himself, something else is involved. I should just walk in and give it to Land, but maybe if you take it to him, he'll give you the case.'

'Take what to him?'

'What I'm going to tell you when you come in.'

'OK.'

'In other words, I'm doing you a favor.'

'OK.'

After hanging up, I sat at my desk trying to figure out why I was getting so excited. I wasn't supposed to care about this kind of shit anymore. Mary Gaetan had lied to me and I covered for her, but now the whole matter was going to be reopened and whether Land handled it himself or gave Lord Alfred a piece of the action, I wasn't going to be involved. Someone else would have to *cherchez la femme*, not me. Not this time.

6

The boy floats facedown in the swimming pool.

Any moment now his parents will see him, will start screaming his name, and then he'll pop his head up, all smiles, laughing because he's just doing the dead man's float, which he learned in the Scouts. If he can only hold his breath a little longer.

His mother, in fact, looks concerned and is beginning to rise from her plastic-webbed pool chair near the diving board when her husband puts his big hand on her forearm and shakes his head. He is smiling. He is one of those wonderfully unflappable men whose serenity arises from a combination of inward calm and blunted imagination. The world is a good place in his view. They are from Iowa, this family, and the father knows his son is plotting a trick, knows that the boy can't possibly hold his breath much longer.

Then the boy hears his name being called, even with his ears partially submerged he hears his name clearly, so he raises his head, gasping for breath and grinning, looking toward the diving board and seeing his parents still in their chairs, still placidly reading the books they purchased specifically for this vacation. His mother glances up at him, smiles, and waves with one hand before returning to her book. Then who was calling his name?

'Billy!'

He turns toward the shallow end of the pool. *His sister. She's* the one who ruined the trick. Disgusted, he dog-paddles away from her.

'*Billy!*' she insists. 'Come here and look at this, Billy.'

He wishes she had been born a boy.

'Billy!'

It's a good thing there aren't other people here at the pool because then her constant calling of his name would really embarrass him. 'What?' he finally answers, making a show of his irritation.

'Come here. Billy! Look what's over here.'

Reluctantly, he climbs out of the pool and walks to the chain-link fence where she stands. Probably sees a butterfly, he thinks. Girls get excited about the stupidest things. 'What?' he asks again in his best bored-brother voice.

'*There,*' she whispers excitedly, pointing to the grass on the other side of the fence. 'See it? And another one, there. Do you think they're real?'

He glances back toward the deep end of the pool. His father's book has already collapsed on his white chest, the man sleeping while Billy's mother, able to relax now that both kids are out of the water, has lowered her chair so she can lie flat and get some sun. 'You stay here,' he instructs his sister, 'and I'll go around the fence and get them.'

But the little girl is having none of that. Mother instructed them not to leave the pool area, she reminds her brother, and besides *she* was the one who saw them first so if anyone's going to go over there and get them it's got to be her, not him.

Billy sighs. At nine, he considers himself worldly and mature compared to his seven-year-old sister. He argues that what their mother really meant was that they weren't supposed to go out and play in the parking lot. He's sure it would be perfectly permissible for him to walk around to the other side of this fence and pick up a couple of coins.

'Why don't you go ask Dad if it's OK then?'

Because I want to surprise them, Billy thinks. Just like the trick he was trying to pull doing the dead man's float – *surprise!* 'The gate's right there,' he tells his sister. 'You stand here so if they wake up they can see you, and I'll go out through the gate and get the coins.'

She shakes her head repeatedly, resolutely. 'No,' she says in case he still hasn't received the message. '*I* saw them first.'

He kicks lightly at the fence with his bare toes. 'OK, we'll go together.'

She looks over toward their parents.

'Come on,' he insists. 'We'll be back before they even know we left.'

Penny follows Billy because this is a dream come true, to go on an adventure with her beloved older brother.

In the grass, they pick up the two coins Penny spotted from the fence and then see three others. These, however, are farther down the hillside, which slopes precipitously, or so it seems to a nine-year-old boy and a seven-year-old girl, the hillside falling away from the pool and the parking lot, sloping steeply down toward a dirty-looking place where three trash dumpsters sit on a concrete pad. Billy wants those extra coins down there, but if they leave the crest of the hill they will be out of sight of their parents. He tells Penny to stay right where she is while he goes down the hill for the coins.

She shakes her head. No way. If he's going, she's going, too.

'I could've had them by now,' he says.

'Well, let's go then,' she says quietly, urging him on with a waving motion of her tiny hands, the way you might shoo chickens in front of you. As long as she's with her big brother, Penny is unafraid.

They walk down and pick up the three additional coins, standing on the side of the hill to examine their treasure.

'How much is it?' she asks in an awed whisper.

'I don't know, but I think they're really valuable.' The five coins in Billy's hand seem unusually heavy. 'They're foreign,' he announces as he looks at the strange lettering on the faces of the coins. 'Gold.'

Penny covers her mouth with her hands. *Gold!*

Her brother continues turning the coins over and over, humming and grunting like a numismatist. 'They might be worth millions,' he suggests, warming to the possibility. 'Maybe some drug dealer from South America dropped them while the cops were chasing him.' Billy watches television.

They both hear something down by the trash dumpsters, something like a man crying, and when they look there, Billy thinks he sees a shadow move by the end of the far dumpster. Maybe a rat. His father told them stories about big rats in Washington, and maybe rats are out here, too.

Then Penny grabs his arm. 'There!' she shouts, pointing at that far dumpster. 'Billy, it *is* a treasure!'

He sees it, too. An entire pile of gold coins by the corner of that third dumpster, coins stacked there like poker chips, must be a dozen of them.

When his sister shouts his name again, Billy puts his hand over her mouth. 'You go back and tell Mom and Dad. I'll stay right here and keep watch, in case someone comes along and tries to take them.'

She removes his hand from her mouth. 'I'm not leaving you here, no I'm not!'

'Why? We'll split 'em fifty-fifty.'

'But I want to go down there and get them with you.'

Before he has a chance to argue his case, Penny is off running down the hillside, the incline drawing her down more quickly than she wants to go, running faster and faster to keep herself from falling, heading for the treasure pile shining in the morning sun, right there by the corner of that far dumpster.

He has to go after her, of course, not only to protect his little sister from rats or whatever other danger waits there on the refuse pad, but because this is also his dream coming true: finding a treasure of golden coins!

She has managed to slow herself to a walk now, stepping gingerly on to the concrete pad. When she bends to pick up the coins, a hand with scabbed-over wounds all across its knuckles snakes out from the corner of the dumpster to encircle Penny's ankle.

She screams – and at that exact moment her father comes to the crest of the hill and calls her name. 'Penny!'

The boy stops, looking down at his sister and then up at his father. What's going on?

She kicks her leg the way an animal does when suddenly snared. Then, when her father calls her name a second time, the leg comes free and Penny, golden coins all forgotten, runs as fast as she can up the hill, past her brother, into her father's arms.

When Billy arrives at the top of the hill, he and his sister both talk in such a jumble of words that their father has to put his hands on their shoulders and keep saying, 'Shh. Shh. One at a time now. Shh.'

Penny insists that someone grabbed her foot when she was down there.

Billy tells of seeing what he thought was a rat.

'Dear God,' the man says, bending to inspect his daughter's feet and ankles and legs, finding no bites, no injuries, checking all over her body, asking repeatedly if she hurts anyplace, if she felt herself getting bitten, and Penny keeps telling him no.

From behind the fence, the mother has one hand over her eyes, shading them from the sun as she asks what's wrong, but now the kids are showing their father the coins they found, five golden coins and, look, Dad, there's a whole stack of them down there by that trash bin.

He instructs them very sternly to stay exactly where they are, the big man then walking down the hill, picking up the coins there, walking carefully all around the three dumpsters, and then coming back up the hill to herd his children to their mother at the pool.

The children's excited stories are repeated to the woman, who looks from them to her husband. He opens his hands to show her the coins. 'Good Lord,' she says.

Back in their room, the woman is convinced that her children have had too much sun; she makes them lie on the beds with wet washcloths across their foreheads. Their father spreads the coins across the top of the TV set, examining each of them before declaring that they are valuable, real gold coins he thinks, lost by a coin dealer maybe.

'Or stolen by drug dealers!' Billy sits up to suggest, his mother tsking as she eases him down on the bed again, repositioning the washcloth on his forehead, telling him he has to rest.

'We'll take them to the police,' the man announces. He is from Iowa. Then, while his children rest under wet cloths and his wife sits on a pink plastic chair fanning herself and keeping watch over Billy and Penny, the father delivers a soft-spoken, heartfelt sermon on the subjects of obedience to your parents ('You both were told not to leave the pool area'), the dangers of vermin ('Rats can be vicious'), and an older brother's responsibility for the safety of his younger sister ('You shouldn't have let her go down there, Billy, she's just a baby').

'I'm *not* a baby,' Penny protests weakly as she drifts toward sleep.

In his room, he pounds an opened can of soda on the table until it foams over, making a brown sticky mess that spreads everywhere. He had her! Actually had his hand around that sweet little ankle. And then the big hero arrives. *Daddy.* Fuck Daddy. If I'd had my knife with me, he thinks, then we would've seen what kind of hero Daddy was – just wait until I get another knife, just you wait, hero!

It enrages him, the way they were all hugging each other when they got back to the pool, showing off *his* coins, goddamn them anyway, they think they're so much better than everyone because they're so fucking happy, wait till I get another blade and then we'll see.

He's burning up with the heat, pulling at an undershirt to get it over his head, scabs coming loose from his chest, feeling like he's been doused with lighter fluid and then set afire. Goddamn it, he thinks, I'll slit all three of their throats and then take her to

Mexico with me and then we'll see how hugging and happy they are then!

Noticing the blackening hand on the floor, he gets up to kick it across the room, its putrefying stench jolting the air, making him curse.

She was a whore and a slut and a liar, he thinks – just like Nancy. It was *her* idea to go to that place in the woods and get fucked for forty dollars. He turns around and screams an obscenity, just then remembering that he left the two twenty-dollar bills he'd paid her. Left them in her jeans! *Damn!* Why doesn't anything ever go right for him? If she hadn't laughed at him, *asking* to get it, then he wouldn't have had to kill her and the cops wouldn't have anything on him, he could walk right into Jonathan's house today and pick up his money and nobody could've said anything.

But she had to laugh at him, didn't she? Laughing at him because he didn't get hard enough, because he was never very good at it like that, plain sex, sex unadorned by terror, managing only half an erection, fumbling between her legs and ejaculating before he was even fully inside her, and then she lit that cigarette and started . . .

Nancy smoked constantly, coming into his room and smoking one cigarette after another, telling him *lies* about how she was going to get the both of them out of that apartment, whatever crummy apartment they were living in at the time, get them away from the crazy woman, take him with her to live someplace nice, and he treasured those lies until she got old enough to start fucking boys, fucking her way out, coming back on increasingly rare occasions, returning to smoke cigarettes in his room and repeat her wonderful lies, and then she never came again though he still waited for her, waited for her every night.

He goes to the bathroom and splashes water on his chest. Today is Wednesday, he's sure of it. And he has a new plan, too – go to Jonathan's house, get his money, come back here and grab the girl, then hightail it as fast as he can to Mexico. Yes, Mexico. He couldn't believe it, the day that the crazy woman showed up and told him how he could live like a king in Mexico on a hundred dollars a week.

It stinks in here, he thinks as he returns to the bed, sitting there and wondering if he should get rid of it. Does he have anything else of hers, anything else that could tie him to that hitchhiker? Her makeup? He looks over at his field jacket but remembers then that he left her lipstick on the ground next to her head. He remembers. After he finished chopping open her chest, he found her purse and took out the lipstick and drew lines all around her eyes, putting lipstick on her battered mouth, too. Just the way Nancy used to do to him.

He leaves the room and gets into his car, heading for Jonathan's house to pick up his money. On an impulse, however, he pulls off the road and into a gas station, thinking he'd better call Jonathan first and make sure the money's there. He walks over to the outside telephone, finds the piece of paper in his field jacket pocket, punches the number. No answer. 'Come on, you bastard, answer the goddamn telephone!' The phone rings and rings, no answer. He hangs up and tries again, punching the number and listening to the unanswered ringing, cursing, hitting the side of the telephone box with his flattened hand, sweating in this unbearable heat, wanting to be in Mexico where there's always a breeze off the ocean, wishing he hadn't killed that girl, wishing Nancy had come back for him like she said, wishing . . . exploding inside with all of his hot hatred for the way things turned out, his fucking head hurting so bad he could cry, goddamn them all . . .

'Hello?'

7

He tries to remember.

'Hello?'

Rubbing his hurting head, he demands that she put Jonathan on the telephone.

Her reply is a short burst of laughter, breathy and rueful and not caused by anything funny.

'What?' he asks.

'You know.'

'I don't!' he insists.

She makes that bitter laughing sound again.

He asks her what the hell is going on.

'Don't you remember?'

'Put Jonathan on the goddamn phone. I want my money. It's Wednesday!'

'He's dead.'

His mind twists around and around with the possibilities, tricks being played on him.

'Hello?'

'What're you trying to pull, huh?'

'It was on the front page of the *Post* yesterday.'

'What was?'

She doesn't say anything.

'What are you talking about?' Sweat is running down his face.

'Jonathan is dead.'

'I don't believe you.'

'Believe what you want, it doesn't change the fact that Jonathan is dead.'

He tries to remember. 'I didn't kill him.'

She laughs that breathy, humorless laugh once again.

'I didn't!' he insists.

She says nothing.

'Goddamn you, I didn't kill him and you know I didn't, you were there and you know—' Then an insight, an inspiration. '*You* did, you killed him.'

No reply.

'You did, didn't you?'

Still no reply.

He rubs his temples. 'It doesn't change anything, you know the deal, Jonathan still owes me that money. It's up to you to get it for me.'

'I will.'

'If you don't, I'll fucking kill you, I'm fed up with this shit.'

'I said I will. But you're going to have to wait until Friday, it's going to take me at least that long to—'

'Friday!' he screams, collecting stares from people who are filling their cars with gasoline. 'Fuck you Friday!' He has traveled right to the edge of madness waiting for Wednesday, waiting for *today*, no way is he going to be able to hold out for two more days, until Friday, no fucking way! Panic mixes in with his rage, the man sensing his world coming apart again, Jonathan dead and the payment in jeopardy, everything unraveling at the edges.

'Listen to me,' she says.

'I can't wait until Friday!'

'Calm down and listen to me.'

'I don't want to listen to you! I don't want to calm down! *I want my money!*' He wants his money. 'I'll come over there and slit your fucking belly open!' He will, too. 'I was supposed to get my money today!' *Today*.

She is silent.

'I didn't kill him,' he says in a quieter voice.

'Don't you remember?'

'I didn't kill him!' he screams.

'That doesn't matter now, what matters is getting you your money. And I will. I'll have it for you on Friday.'

'I'm coming over there now!' he screams. 'I'm coming over to get my money right now!' Enraged he is, holding the receiver slightly away from his face, the better to shriek at it.

She is telling him that she doesn't have the money, that his coming over to her house is not going to help him get the money because she simply doesn't have it. 'If Jonathan hadn't died—'

'I didn't kill him, goddamn it, I didn't!'

'If he was still alive, he would've been able to get your money by today, like he promised, but his death has tied up the assets in his business accounts. All I have access to is our joint checking account, and there's only a few thousand in that. Do you understand what I'm telling you?'

He stands there breathing heavily into the receiver.

'I'm working on it,' she tells him earnestly. 'I know what the arrangement was, and I'm not going to deny you your money, believe me. But I need some time. Jonathan's being buried tomorrow, and then I should be able to . . . listen, I could give you a few thousand right now, if you wanted to leave for Mexico today. Then I could wire you the rest.'

'Wait a minute!' Instead of just rubbing his temple, now he's hitting it violently with his free hand. 'Wait a fucking minute, will you!' His circuits are overloading. Wait till Friday, get a few thousand today, wire the rest to Mexico . . . 'How'd you know about Mexico?'

'You really have fried your brains, haven't you?' she asks, her voice sounding genuinely concerned.

'How'd you know I was going to Mexico!'

'You told him, don't you remember?'

He pauses a moment. 'Yes,' he lies. But he doesn't remember telling Jonathan, and if he's forgotten about that, maybe he's forgotten about killing him, too. That hitchhiker and now

Jonathan, *shit*, he's not going to escape this mess, not if he has to hang around for two more days, the cops are going to . . . 'I can't wait until Friday,' he finally admits to her, his voice soft and weary.

'Then leave right now.'

'Not without my money.'

'Then wait until Friday.'

'Fuck you,' he mutters.

'Wherever you're staying, keep in your room and wait. Don't do anything stupid. Don't do anything that'll get you involved with the police. Watch television for two days. Then come over here to the house on Friday, about midday, I'll be waiting for you with the money – promise.'

'Promise?' he asks incredulously.

'And bring those photographs with you, the ones you took from Jonathan's desk. I want them back.'

He is suddenly very tired. 'I don't care about your pictures, I just want my money.'

'Of course you do.'

'I can't wait until Friday,' he says in a seething voice, frustrated and betrayed, everyone always jerking his leash, goddamn them, goddamn them all.

'You *can* wait until Friday and you *will* wait,' she tells him sternly. 'And those coins you took, don't try to sell them around here. You don't want them to be traced back to Jonathan. Wait until you get out of this area before you try to sell them – OK?'

'I already gave 'em away.'

'*Gave* them away?'

'To my girlfriend.'

'You have someone with you?' she asks, her voice rising.

'She's going to Mexico with me.'

'Does she know about you and Jonathan, did you tell her?'

'Not yet.' He sobs, enjoying this, putting Mary on the defensive.

'You're going to ruin everything. If you'd just calm down, stay

96

out of trouble, don't tell anyone about Jonathan – two more days and then you can leave for Mexico. If you haven't already told the woman about Jonathan, for God's sake don't—'

'Not a woman,' he says. 'A girl. A *girl*friend.'

'Don't do anything stupid, *please*.'

'I had another girlfriend, too,' he says, 'but she couldn't go to Mexico with me because she had a chest operation!' Sobbing. 'And she got her hand cut off in a smoking accident!'

'Oh, God,' Mary says, more to herself than to him.

He tells her he's horny.

'What about your girlfriend?'

'She's cherry. I'm saving her for Mexico. But I could come over and fuck you.'

'Oh, Philip.'

Hearing his name spoken like that causes him to jerk the receiver away from his ear, as if a spark has arched out, burning him. He quickly hangs up, keeping one hand over that ear, staring at the telephone.

Obsessed with the idea of fucking someone, he drives toward the District and gets caught in rush hour, wandering aimlessly with the flow of cars until he goes around a traffic circle and sees several black prostitutes. He drives the circle three times before pulling to a curb; they've been watching him and one comes immediately to his car.

She leans into the passenger window and asks if he's looking for a party.

'Looking for a piece of ass,' he replies sullenly.

She keeps smiling that false smile. 'I got a little room two blocks down. Sixty bucks'll make you a new man.'

He looks her over, a black woman in her thirties, twenty pounds overweight, large breasts bulging out of a bright orange Spandex top. She is sweating, her hair is greasy, and over that fake smile her eyes are somewhere else faraway.

He doesn't remember how much he has left from his original

stake, having made no effort to watch his money because he assumed he'd be rich by today. Recalling again that forty dollars he left in the hitchhiker's jeans, he curses.

'You a cop, honey?' she asks.

'Forty fucking dollars,' he mutters, still thinking of his lost money.

'Yeah, well, forty dollars'll get you what you need,' she says, opening the passenger door.

He watches her get in. 'I'll give you twenty to blow me right here.'

She laughs. 'I got a room.'

'How much is that going to cost me?'

'Twenty.'

'Back up to sixty, huh? How about I just give you forty and we go down that alley there for a stand-up?'

She laughs again, reaching over to grope him without finesse or feeling. 'Once you go black, you never go back.' She says this by rote, too, not caring. 'Come on, twenty for me and twenty for the room, let's go, peckerwood.'

He follows her directions to a dilapidated three-story former townhouse that now displays a cardboard sign in its first-floor window: ROOMS.

After he parks, she tells him he has to use a rubber, which she'll supply. 'For your own protection,' she adds, laughing.

He laughs, too – thinking that as soon as he gets her in that room, *he'll* be the one giving orders, making her do what he says, or else. When she gets out, he looks at her broad ass straining at a pair of white shorts that are stained in the crack, the sight of it putting the taste of pennies in his mouth.

He gets out and stands there on the sidewalk with her. 'I want a blowjob.'

'Still got to wear protection.'

'For a blowjob?'

'I like the taste of rubber.'

He laughs.

'You got to give me the twenty for the room now 'cause I have to pay the man inside.'

'Fuck that.' What does she take him for?

'Then you go home and suck your own dick, honey.' She is tired of the game. 'You fresh off the farm or what?'

'Fresh out of the joint.'

'Mm.' And for the first time she really looks at him, her eyes focusing on his face. She decides to pass.

But he's bringing out a wad of bills, putting together two fives and a ten, which he hands to her, shoving the rest of the money, mostly ones, back into his pocket.

She climbs the four concrete steps but by the time *he* reaches the door it has closed, giving him that sinking feeling of being taken again. He bangs on the door with the flat of his hand.

A very large black man who is not sweating at all opens the door. 'Yeah?' he asks in the most casual of voices.

'I'm with that woman.'

'What woman?'

'Don't hand me that shit! You opened the door for her. I already gave her twenty bucks.'

'You did?' The black man is bemused, eyebrows arching. 'And why did you give her twenty dollars, sir?' The way he says *sir* is especially intimidating.

'For a fucking blowjob, what do you think, baldy?'

The man rolls his dark eyes upward and then runs a hand over his hairless head. He is smiling more broadly now. 'Paying a woman for sexual congress is illegal in the District of Columbia.'

Philip bends down, going for his knife, coming up empty-handed, of course. Then *he* smiles. 'Tell that whore to give me back my money. I've changed my mind.'

'I'm sure I don't know what you're talking about, sir.'

'That whore's got twenty dollars of mine and I ain't leaving here without it.'

'If you have a complaint to lodge, may I suggest that you contact the District police? If you consider it an emergency, you may dial nine-one-one.' Then, still smiling, he closes the door.

Philip tries the handle and then kicks the door several times with his heavy motorcycle boots.

When the large black man reappears, he is not smiling. 'You touch that door again, I'll break your fucking leg.'

'I'm not afraid of you.' If you're afraid in the joint, they pass you around like a piece of meat. His hands gripped tightly into fists, Philip steps back to give himself enough room to swing, unfortunately stepping back too far, falling backward down the concrete steps.

The black man rubs his bald head and laughs loudly, genuinely amused. Then he closes the door.

While Philip is regaining his feet, three people stop on the side-walk to watch him. 'What're you looking at, assholes!' They move on.

He stands there staring up at the closed door, screaming, 'I'll fucking firebomb this place!' He keeps muttering about it as he gets back in the car, hitting the steering wheel with both hands, hollering curses out the window before he drives off in a hurry, a man on a mission.

But the gas station he stops at won't sell him gasoline in anything but an approved two-gallon can, which he can buy from them for $7.95. He insists they put gas in the empty whiskey bottle he has found, no fucking way is he going to spend eight bucks for a can he'll be using only once, everybody in this town ripping him off. He is shouting, an argument ensues, and Philip is chased off the property by two mechanics wielding large crescent wrenches.

He drives around, not caring about what Mary said – stay out of trouble until Friday – singular in his intent, worse than a predator, searching for whores and hitchhikers, slipping his chain, something terrible out and about, loose on our streets.

She is young and has a sweet little face, although the big blond wig she wears makes her look ridiculous. She can't weigh much over a

hundred pounds, a too-small T-shirt pulling tightly over her padded bra. She offers the usual patter.

He looks at her leaning in the passenger window. 'You listen to
me, 'cause I'm only saying this once. I'll give you a hundred
dollars to go over there in that alley and fuck me standing up.
Now don't give me any shit about more money for a room or
anything like that. Just yes or no. 'Cause if you don't want the
hundred, there's a lot who do.'

She considers it. If she got a hundred dollars from this guy, she
could go home afterward, watch a little television, put her baby
to bed herself and save some money on the sitter, too. She could
really use that, getting home early for once. The only thing that
makes her hesitate is how pissed this guy seems to be. 'A hundred, right?'

He jerks out the wad of bills but then stuffs it quickly back into
his pocket before she can read the denominations. 'Yes or no!'

'Still awful light out for a stand-up, honey.'

'Yes or no!' He races the engine.

'You got to wear a rubber.'

'Yeah.'

She smiles. 'Then you go ahead and park this car, honey – we
got ourselves a date.'

He smiles, too, and sobs his laughter.

8

By the time Lord Alfred arrived at the department that Wednesday afternoon, I had changed my mind about giving the case away. I wanted to know *for myself* why Jonathan Gaetan arranged to have one hundred and forty-five thousand, six hundred dollars delivered to his house in cash, and I wanted to question Mary Gaetan again. OK, maybe I wanted one last chance at a headline, too.

I know, I know – I was supposed to be immune to those old fevers, but losing your immunity is what happens when you stay up past midnight stone sober, going over all the old mistakes one more time: you start thinking about redeeming yourself, being a hero, going down to Florida to meet that grandson you've never met, showing up with your name in the papers. Fifty-three years old and still looking for happy endings.

I needed to convince Alfred we could work this case ourselves, no need to get Land involved yet, so I took my ex-partner into an empty office and told him about Jo-Jo Creek's visit that morning, her suspicions regarding Mary, and Jonathan Gaetan's last request, that a suitcase full of twenties, fifties, and hundreds be delivered to his house on Wednesday, *today*.

Alfred thought the money might be for a drug deal or a business payoff, or that Jonathan was cooking his books and needed the cash to keep some deal liquid. I explained what Jo-Jo had said about Jonathan being a straight arrow and also what Land's perfunctory investigation had turned up, that Jonathan's business was rock solid.

'What does that leave us with then?' Alfred asked.

I didn't know.

'What about the Old Detector? You interviewed Mary. Was she lying to you or not?'

I shrugged.

Alfred ran a hand over his scarred face and then just sat there looking at me.

'What?' I asked.

'You ain't sure, are you?'

'Well, I don't have any solid theories if that's—'

'No, I mean you ain't sure now if she lied to you or not – are you?'

I shrugged again. 'I think it's blackmail. I think someone had something on Jonathan, and Jonathan agreed to the payoff but then killed himself. Mary's keeping quiet either because she doesn't want Jonathan's secret to come out or because she's afraid of the blackmailer.'

'If he's such a straight arrow, why's he being blackmailed?'

'I keep going back to the possibility that maybe earlier in his life Jonathan was actively queer, that one of his former boyfriends came across some article about the respectable and fabulously wealthy Jonathan Gaetan, being considered for an ambassadorship and all that – so the boyfriend shows up to collect some retroactive palimony. It fits, doesn't it? Jonathan agrees to pay the guy off but then he's so ashamed that Mary has found out about his past that he butchers himself in the bathtub. Your usual suicide just wants to get the job done but Jonathan was heavily into punishing himself, even trying to cut his dick off. Maybe the boyfriend has AIDS and Jonathan went crazy that night, thinking that he had it, too, and might have passed it on to Mary. Land's the one who got me thinking in this direction, saying that there had been rumors around before Jonathan married Mary, rumors that Jonathan was quietly queer.'

'And Mary's role in all this?'

I shrugged. 'I think if the money had showed up at her house today the way it was supposed to, the way Jonathan arranged it in that last telephone call he made, then Mary would have just let the payment go through. The suicide itself is getting enough bad publicity, especially with all the details coming out now. Why make matters worse by revealing that Jonathan was also paying off an old boyfriend?'

'I don't know, Teddy. It's not such a big deal anymore, somebody being found out as a queer. And you'd think that if an old boyfriend had put Jonathan in such a state that he killed himself, then Mary would be so pissed that she'd let us know right away that the guy was trying to shake Jonathan down, get his ass arrested and to hell with the publicity. Besides, from what Jo-Jo Creek told you, it sounds like Jonathan was a pussyhound from the word Go.'

'I still think Jonathan had *something* nasty in his past, something that came back to haunt him Sunday night.'

'Why did he ask Jo-Jo to deliver that specific amount, a hundred and forty-five thousand, six hundred dollars?'

'How about this – in his earlier days Jonathan was heavily into rough sex, let's say Mary was telling the truth about that, and one night it got a little too rough and he ended up killing someone. So he agrees to pay a third party a certain amount to cover up the mess or take the rap for him or something along those lines – except Jonathan never came through with the payment. The third party finally catches up with Jonathan and wants his money plus interest.'

Alfred laughed and then asked me when I was going to lay all these speculations on Captain Land.

'He's out for the rest of the day. I thought I'd go over and talk to Mary, see if I can get some straight answers out of her, and then I'll tell Land about it tomorrow.'

Alfred stood and reached down the front of his trousers to adjust his scrotum, a habit of his that a lot of people did not find endearing. 'Then what am I doing here?'

'I thought you and I could work together on this sort of

105

unofficially. At least until we find out who's doing what to whom.'

He was shaking his head. 'Unofficially, my ass. You got to report to Land what this Jo-Jo Creek told you about the money.'

'I will.'

'When?'

'Tomorrow, I told you.'

'This isn't even your case. The only reason Jo-Jo Creek went to you with the information is that a couple of the guys sent her to your cubicle because you were sleeping. You go nosing around in this, messing with Land's social acquaintances, and he'll have your balls.'

'I forgot.'

'Forgot what?'

'Forgot that you got your mind right. You play it by the book now, don't you? That's fine, Alfred, really. Just pretend this conversation never took place. I haven't said anything to you about anything. I'll handle everything myself. Then if I get in trouble with Land, your efforts to become computer literate aren't jeopardized.'

He told me that I should fuck myself. 'I'll play a couple rounds with you, Teddy, just to see where this whole thing is heading. But tomorrow morning we're turning everything over to Land. If we've developed some leads and he lets us pursue them, fine. But if he decides he's going to reopen the case and handle it himself, that's jake with me, too. OK?'

'Yeah.'

'You're saying "yeah," but you're meaning, "we'll see." '

'Yeah.'

Alfred laughed and then asked me what *we* were going to talk to Mary about.

'I thought we would kind of split up assignments. You check out the file on Jonathan's suicide and see if anything strikes you as wrong. You know, see if Jo-Jo Creek's theory about Jonathan's death being a *faked* suicide holds any water.

Meanwhile, I'll go over and talk to Mary, then we could meet back here and—'

He interrupted me by laughing again. 'You got a hard-on for her, don't you?'

'Shit, Alfred, I haven't had a hard-on since last January when the furnace went out and I woke up in the middle of the night to a freezing apartment and a full bladder.'

'Come on now, numbnuts, this is Lord Alfred you're talking to. I was your partner long enough to know where your kinks are. You get all dreamy-eyed over them high-toned rich bitches, don't you?'

'Mary's not like that.'

He made a disbelieving sound.

We sat there trading accusations, lies, and epithets until the telephone rang. Jo-Jo Creek for me.

'Mary came into the office this afternoon,' Jo-Jo said. 'She's still here as a matter of fact, asking about Jonathan's various accounts, wanting to know if she can draw money out of any of them.'

'Which means she doesn't know about Jonathan's call to you Monday morning, doesn't know the money is already sitting in her joint checking account.'

'Apparently.'

'Did you tell her?'

'I most certainly did not.'

'Do you have a contact at the bank? Can you let me know when the money *is* withdrawn from that checking account?' She said she could. 'Great. One more thing, let me know when Mary leaves the office, OK?' Jo-Jo said she would.

I filled Lord Alfred in on the other half of the conversation he'd been listening to and then, to deflect further suspicion that I was interested in this case only because I lusted for Mary Gaetan, I said *both* of us would go visit her after she left Jonathan's office and returned to her house. 'Meanwhile, you check that file and—'

'And see if there's any possibility that someone else could have butchered Jonathan and made it look like a suicide.'

'Right. I'll call around to some of the other jurisdictions and find out if they've had any recent homicides or assaults involving a big knife. Land seems to think that Jonathan Gaetan would never have owned a cheap Bowie knife like the one we recovered at the scene.'

Alfred said he'd like to take a look at the knife, and I told him it was still down in evidence as far as I knew. Then we split up, me returning to my cubicle to make the calls.

The information I got wasn't encouraging. In the Washington, DC, metropolitan area during the past week, there'd been so many assaults, rapes, robberies involving knives (and all the victims reported that the knives were *big* ones) that it would take Alfred and me a month to check them all out, to see if any of them might be connected to what happened in the Gaetan house Sunday night or Monday morning.

On my eighth call, a guy I know who works at the Maryland State Police headquarters asked me if I was following a lead on the Lipstick Murder.

'The what?'

'Christ, Teddy, even if you don't read those alerts we send you, you must've seen it in the papers. Once some reporter gives a case like this a name, it really turns up the burners. We're working on nothing else, except we got nothing to go on.'

'I must've missed it, Mack. I've developed this allergy to bad news, so mostly I stick to the comics and the sports page.'

'I ought to make you go find the alert we sent out.'

'Come on, Mack, I'm an old man.'

He made an unkind remark about that and then told me what one of their troopers had found just this past Sunday morning. 'She was only fifteen, Teddy. They put the time of death Saturday afternoon. She'd run away from home so many times that her mother didn't even report this last episode. Won't run away anymore.'

'Killed with a knife?'

'Raped, beat up, her entire chest chopped open, and—'

'Jesus.'

'He chopped her hand off and took it with him.'

'*Jesus.*'

'The papers are calling it the Lipstick Murder because of the way he painted her face, real gruesome shit, Teddy. Used her own lipstick to draw lines around her eyes. I saw the photographs.' He paused, waiting for a comment. 'Teddy?'

'Did you recover the weapon?'

'No. I told you, we got nothing solid.'

'Anybody speculating on what kind of knife it was?'

'Something big enough, heavy enough to chop through her rib cage.'

'Bowie knife?'

'You *do* have a lead on this, don't you, Teddy?'

'No.'

'How come you said Bowie knife?'

'Seems obvious, doesn't—'

'If you have something on this case, Teddy, you better let me know right now. You wouldn't believe how hot this is.'

'I'm just doing a statistical report for Land, comparing the severity of crimes committed with firearms to those committed with knives.'

'Twenty years a cop and he's got you doing term papers?'

'Yeah.'

'Listen, you might come across something I could use, anything at all involving a cutter, someone who likes butchering, especially if he smears lipstick on the victim, anything at all like that, you call me, huh, Teddy?'

'Hey, Mack, you know me. Two more years and I'm retiring to a fishing cabin. I—'

'It's in our jurisdiction.'

'I know that.'

When I hung up, I noticed my palm had left wet marks on the receiver.

Twenty minutes later, back in the empty office, I told Alfred about the call to Maryland. He, of course, *had* read the alert from the Maryland State Police and had read about the Lipstick Murder in the newspapers, too. 'But Jonathan's death is still suicide,' he said.

'Maybe the guy put the knife in Jonathan's hand and—'

'It's a suicide!' Alfred insisted. 'If you'd read the file, really read it, you'd know that yourself.'

'It wouldn't be the first time someone faked a—'

Alfred slapped one big hand on the table. 'Listen to me. When Jonathan Gaetan began carving on himself in the bathtub, he sprayed blood and water everywhere, all over the floor. The officer who found the body had the presence of mind to keep everyone out of the bathroom until the lab team got there. The only footprints on the floor, the only marks made on all that blood and water, were those made by the officer. In other words, shit-for-brains, the only way someone could have killed Jonathan and then got out of that bathroom without leaving any footprints in the blood and water would be if that person could fly.'

We sat in silence until Alfred said that maybe *Jonathan* killed the girl Saturday afternoon and then, distraught at what he'd done, he used the same knife on himself. But when we checked the file, we found that Jonathan had played golf on Saturday, from noon to four. His partners included a federal judge and a loan officer from Riggs Bank.

Alfred laughed. 'Maybe there's a gang of perverted rich guys who provide each other with alibis so they can go out and chop up young girls.'

'Yeah, or maybe aliens from the planet Xerox did it. In any case, we got to get the Bowie knife over to Maryland.'

Alfred stood to rearrange his balls. 'No can do.'

'What do you mean?'

'Mary Gaetan's lawyer picked it up this morning.'

'He got it out of evidence?'

'No reason for us to keep it. Jonathan's death was already ruled a suicide. The knife was the widow's property.'

'But why in hell would she want it?'

'We'll make sure to ask her that. Is she home yet?'

I said I hadn't heard from Jo-Jo. 'You know, if the money was scheduled to be delivered to Jonathan's house today, then maybe the blackmailer—'

'If there is a blackmailer.'

'Maybe he's still going to show up at Gaetan's house today – and that's why Mary has been at the office trying to raise the cash. She doesn't know that Jonathan called Jo-Jo before he died, doesn't know that the money is already sitting in her joint checking account. Some guy's going to be wanting his suitcase full of cash, and Mary will be sitting there empty-handed.'

Alfred suggested that we go over there right now.

'Let me call Jo-Jo first.' I put the call through and found out that Mary was still at the office; Jo-Jo repeated her promise to let me know the minute Mary left.

While we were waiting – my five-thirty drinks date having passed unconsummated for the second day in a row – Alfred's current partner showed up.

'You guys have already met, haven't you?' Alfred asked, making the introductions anyway. 'Teddy, this is the amazing Melvin Kelvin. Melvin Kelvin, this is the unremarkable Teddy Camel.'

He was thirty, the same age I was when I started in the department, although I was convinced I never looked as innocent as this kid did. His hair was combed with amazing precision.

'Melvin Kelvin's teaching me computers,' Alfred said like a father bragging up his boy.

'Yeah, except we missed this afternoon's session. Where were you?'

'I might have to miss tonight's shift, too,' Alfred replied.

The kid looked at me. 'You guys working on something?'

I shook my head.

111

'Melvin Kelvin attended Princeton University, didn't you Melvin Kelvin,' Alfred said.

'He never calls me by my first name,' the kid said. 'It's always both names together like that. Part of his ongoing effort to keep me humble.' He was smiling.

'Ah, Melvin Kelvin, you knows I love you,' Alfred replied. He was grinning, too, and I felt like someone's ugly cousin visiting from New Jersey.

'None of the other new guys wanted to work with him,' the kid said, still talking to me. 'I volunteered because I think, even with all the recent innovations in police work, a person could still learn a thing or two from veterans like you and Alfred.'

The little shit.

Alfred apologized to him for having missed their training session that afternoon.

'It's OK. I picked up something new anyway. Somebody turned in some coins, and I've been identifying them.'

'You a numismatist?' I asked.

'Hey,' Lord Alfred bellowed, '*nobody* calls my partner a chicken fucker!'

Melvin Kelvin laughed and told me, 'He's a fascinatingly complex personality, your ex-partner. Having grown up in circumstances that didn't prize a man for being overly intelligent or sensitive, he plays the dumb country boy and goes to extraordinary lengths to mask his sensitivity. The kind of man who yearns for fidelity and companionship but seeks out a constant series of one-night stands. The kind of man who wants to write poetry but, instead, reads pornography. Fascinating.'

Lord Alfred was rocking on his heels, beaming. 'Cute little fucker, ain't he?'

I had to agree.

Ten minutes after Melvin Kelvin left to run a computer check on his lost coins, Jo-Jo Creek called to tell me that Mary had just left the Gaetan offices. I asked her if Mary had found out about the money in her checking account, and Jo-Jo said no. 'Are you sure?'

'I called the bank at the close of business, and the money still hadn't been withdrawn.'

On the way to Alfred's car, I told him that something about this case was making me nervous. I admitted that I knew Mary had lied to me in Land's office yesterday, but I could no longer be sure of that line separating her lies from the truth. 'Or maybe my problem is being sober for two days running now. What do you think?'

'Hmm,' he replied, shoving a hand down his pants and thoughtfully hustling his balls.

9

She's sorry now.

A big mistake, coming into this alley with a man who's acting so strange, so hyped. What's he on, anyway? I fell for the oldest trick in the book, the young prostitute thinks, the *promise* of big money, and now look where it's got me, back here in a dark alley against a dirty brick wall.

'Come on, baby,' she urges, fighting to keep her voice smooth and coaxing, fighting against her growing fear. She has performed these stand-ups before, but usually the men are so excited that they finish quickly.

Not this guy. He's fumbling around, half hard, becoming angrier and angrier as if it's her fault he's only half hard. Incredibly stupid, she thinks, coming here with him before I had the hundred dollars in my hand, thinking I would get home early and see my baby, and now he's getting my clothes dirty, hurting me.

Her friend Annie always told her never let them touch you until you got the money in your hand, but the young woman accepted forty dollars instead of a hundred because she had no choice at that point, the man thrusting forty dollars at her and then shoving her to the brick wall, and now he's humping against her while she tries to do her job, raising her skirt with one hand and exposing his half-erect penis with the other, attempting to get the rubber on while urging him toward a more workable firmness. The toughest forty dollars I ever earned, she thinks.

'Come on, baby, going to be so good when you push it in me

standing up like this and maybe somebody comes along and sees us but we don't care, do we baby, we don't care who sees us fucking, huh, come on now, you don't have to be bumping against me so hard like that, wait till I get this on you and then we're going to take care of you, baby, yes we are.'

His face is buried in her neck where the synthetic strands of her white-blond wig make his nose itch. He reaches up to squeeze her small breasts, but it's not going to work for him unless . . .

He stands away from her, both of them looking down at the flaccid member resting sluglike in her hand.

'You give me the rest of my money, baby,' she suggests, 'and I'll go down on you, guaranteed.' When he sobs his laughter, she despairs of ever seeing that sixty dollars. 'What is it?' she finally asks him.

He whispers something.

'What?' she asks.

His voice is surprisingly shy. 'Act like you're scared of me.'

'Scared of you?' That wouldn't take much acting, she thinks.

'Like I pushed you up against this wall to rape you.'

She laughs a little through her nose. 'Pay me the rest of the money and I'll scream like a white girl.'

But he's given her the last of his money. He calls her names, no shyness in his voice now, shoving her to the dirty brickwork and bumping against her with his hips, pumping her with his rage.

'You're hurting me,' she says, telling the truth. His face again buried in her neck, she looks over his shoulder at the dark alley, garbage-strewn and stinking in this DC summer, all the lights long ago broken.

But when she complains again that he is hurting her, she feels his cock respond, growing firm in her hand. All right then if that's what it takes, she decides, let's get it over with even if she has to settle for the forty dollars already in the small red purse which she has dropped at her feet. 'Oh, God, you're *hurting* me!' She speaks right into his ear. It's all acting, her friend Annie told her. You lie to your boyfriend about what a good fuck he is, so you may as well lie to some white dude and get paid for it. She and Annie had laughed at that, women and their secrets. 'Please don't hurt me!' There. Good. He is hard and the rubber is on. It won't take long.

Now he's holding one of her wrists back against the wall and banging against her, his face still in her neck. 'I fucked a nigger boy in jail.'

She freezes, stepping out of the role because her brother, eighteen, two years younger than she, is in jail right now.

'Knelt him down on the floor and bent him over his own cot, holding his arms behind him, my knees on his legs so he couldn't move. Late at night, you know, and I had to use half a bottle of hair oil before I was greased up enough to do the job but then I busted that little black puppy real good.'

She closes her eyes against what he is telling her.

'And all the time he's begging and crying and asking me please don't put it up his ass.' He sobs. 'But I told him if anyone hears him squealing, that'll just make him a more valuable piece of ass 'cause ain't nothing makes a piece of ass more valuable than when it squeals.'

She hates the son of a bitch who is now having sexual intercourse with her, but the young woman knows that the only way this scene will end is for him to get his rocks off, so she steps back into character, squealing into his ear that he's hurting her – and then to seal that false bargain, she darts her tongue into that ear.

Her tongue is the spark that ignites him, Philip jumping back from her as he puts one hand to the ear she has violated, rubbing it violently as if some small and vicious biting insect has lodged itself there, and with his other hand he slaps her hard across the face.

No theatrical slap, the blow hits her with full force, knocking the slight woman to her knees, causing her head to ring and her eyes to water, her jaw hurting something awful. While down there amid the garbage, on her knees, she retains enough presence of mind to grab her little red purse.

'I'll fucking kill you!' he is screaming down at her as he continues to ream his wet ear with his index finger.

He remembers Nancy coming into his room after one of her 'dates,' how she would come creeping into his room to fill it with her smells, perfume and liquor and cigarettes, and she would kneel by his bed to watch him sleep and then, to awaken him, she would stick her tongue into his ear and he would bolt upright, rubbing at the ear as he watched her laughing. She looked so beautiful when she laughed, and he would start laughing at the joke, too, telling her never to do that again, and she promised she wouldn't although both of them knew she would. He adored her back then.

When she starts to get up, he slaps the young woman on the back of the head, dislodging but not quite removing her blond wig. While still on her knees, she extracts from her purse the utility knife she always carries with her, better than a straight razor because the utility knife has a shaped handle upon which she can get a good grip, the triangular razor at the end of the handle very sharp and held securely in place with a screw. When he steps close to hit her again, she reaches up and stabs his right thigh.

He stumbles backward, bending down to cover the wound with his hand, shocked by the pain. Although the blade is barely over an inch long, it went full-length into his flesh, and when he speaks, his voice is full of betrayal. 'You *whore!*'

She quickly regains her feet, holding the utility knife in his direction. 'You come near me and I'll cut your throat,' she warns, sidestepping around him.

He straightens up. His grin, which even in this dim light shows broken and discolored teeth, unsettles her. He says something about liking knives as he moves sideways to block her escape out of the alley.

She wonders what to do. If she can get a head start, his wounded thigh will prevent him from catching her, they both know this, but if she turns to run too soon, while he is within lunging distance, he'll still be able to grab her. So what she has to do is *ease* away from him a few more feet, get the head start while keeping the utility knife high and in his face, looking the Devil in the eye.

She commits the prey's mistake, however, bolting too soon – and even with a bad leg he is able to lunge and grab her before she can start running, bringing her down as she turns back toward him and with an upward stroke of the blade lays him open from his right hipbone, across his belly, all the way through his left nipple. The gash is not deep, barely below skin level, but it is long and it has cut through the festering wounds already on his chest, and the pain it causes him is large and immediate.

He has her on the ground, one knee on her chest, bending her wrist until he forces her to release the knife, which he then takes in his own hand.

She looks past the triangular blade that he's holding above her face, looks right into the man's ruined eyes. She says, 'Please, friend, I have a little boy waiting for me at home.'

Philip pauses. Her reference to the child has no effect on him, but he is puzzled by her calling him *friend*, a usage that seems too quaint and gentle for the circumstances.

'His daddy's in St Louis and I'm the only one in the world that little boy has to keep care of him.'

He waits to hear what else she's going to say.

'Why don't I just give you your money back and then we can both—'

She is interrupted by the sudden squeezing of her throat, both of her hands going immediately around his wrist as she tries desperately to ease the pressure, her head jerking back and forth in small, manic movements. '*Please*,' she manages to say.

He tells her to stick out her tongue.

She's in a panic now, trying to scream but unable to make a sound, and the choking does indeed cause her tongue to appear between her heavily painted lips – but he can't get a hold on it.

'Stick it out, goddamn you!' he shrieks.

119

She's still jerking her head back and forth, still trying with both hands to ease his grip on her throat.

He begins slashing her face with the knife, ripping right through her cheeks until the sight of it causes *even him* to pause, seeing her entire face open up when she tries to scream, that hideous mouth opening he has created exposing all of her teeth, even those gold-capped molars in the back. Blood is everywhere, soaking and warming his hand, which is still on her throat.

To stop her from making those awful sounds, he puts his entire weight behind his bloody hand, crushing her windpipe and causing her eyes to bulge until you'd think their sockets would soon lose them.

Then he steels himself and actually reaches into that lurid mouth opening, grabbing her tongue between his thumb and bent forefinger, pulling . . .

Someone behind him!

Philip turns to see two black kids coming up the alley. They haven't spotted him yet, but he hisses at them anyway, spitting out his words like a night beast caught in this act of defilement. 'Get the *fuck* out of here!'

Seeing the man on top of the woman and thinking they have come upon a couple screwing in the alley, the two teenagers laugh.

'Get . . . out . . . of . . . here,' he growls.

They laugh again and saunter away, leaving the night beast to complete his surgery.

But, ten minutes later, the two boys are waiting for him at the mouth of the alley. One of them is holding a short length of pipe, the other a split two-by-four – items they picked out of the trash because this is nothing they had planned on doing, catching this white guy in the alley, just an opportunity come their way. They're both tall and thin, both sixteen.

While he's still in the dark of the alley, he speaks to them softly. 'Come on, children. Let's see what you got.' He steps into the light from the street, holding the utility knife casually in his right hand, beckoning them with a chilling whisper, 'Come on, children.'

It is not the little triangular blade that scares them, not his calm challenge, his obvious willingness to fight; they run because of the very sight of him, all that blood on his jacket and over his entire face, like a vampire who hasn't bothered to wipe his mouth yet, like something stepping from a charnel house, a butcher in the alley.

He calls them 'Punks!', an epithet that carries a more unflattering connotation in prison than it does out here on the streets. Then he makes it back to his car, limping and sated.

He uses a rag from the floor, an old T-shirt, to bandage his thigh, but the diagonal slash across his chest is hurting worse, and all he is able to do for that is hold a forearm tightly against the pain and then drive one-handed.

When he finally finds his way back to the motel, this nighttime trip having taken twice as long as it should have because of all those wrong turns, he sits a while in his car, the wounds becoming even more painful as they stiffen up. Although it hurts too much to move, he knows he has to reach his room before someone sees him and all this blood.

For once in his life he gets lucky, encountering no one on his way to the room. He sits on the bed, holding a pillow to his chest and taking pills that he finds in his pocket, pills from Jonathan's house. He tries to think.

If Jonathan really is dead, if she was telling the truth about that, then that's the last of them: Nancy, the crazy woman, and now Jonathan. All gone, leaving him alone. He sits there knowing he will not sleep tonight, will not sleep until he gets what is his.

Maybe the little girl is bouncing on her bed in that room across the way. He would feel better if he could watch her bouncing, he really would, and he tries to get up, but it hurts too much to stand.

10

About halfway to Mary's house I began planning to say something that I knew would come out wrong, would be misunderstood, would hurt Alfred's feelings. Sitting there in the passenger seat of his car, I was planning to say something that, once said, I would immediately have to begin retracting, insisting that what I had just said wasn't what I really meant. And, in spite of knowing exactly how it would all turn out, I went ahead and said it anyway.

'You're going to have to watch yourself with Mrs Gaetan, Alfred.'

'How so?' he asked in a cheerful voice.

'Hillbilly charm isn't going to melt her, believe me. She's the kind of woman who has to be handled very carefully.'

He pursed his little mouth, but that didn't stop me. 'She's going to require a certain . . . a certain *sophistication*. From both of us. I'm not just talking about you, of course.'

He turned that melon head slowly in my direction, sent one grim look, and then returned his attention to the road.

'All I'm saying—'

'Yeah, I know what you're saying.'

'I didn't mean—'

'I'll try not to fart in her presence.'

'Hey, come on.'

'Let the elegant and *sophisticated* Teddy Camel handle all the talking.'

'I knew you were going to take this wrong. My only point is

that, both of us, sometimes we come on a little strong, a little crude.' I was hoping Alfred would appreciate the understatement.

But now he was acting wounded. 'Don't worry, *partner*, I won't embarrass you.'

'I'm not worrying about that, I'm just trying to suggest the best—'

'Sure you are. What you really want is to meet with her alone so the two of you can sit there sipping brandy and exchanging meaningful looks, 'cause you got this complex about your social betters – you always have had – and you're afraid I'm going to spoil the mood by telling jokes about midgets with hard-ons.'

'How does that one go, the one about the midget with a hard-on?'

'Fuck you, Teddy.'

'No, fuck *you*, Alfred.'

We drove the rest of the way to Mary's house in silence.

It was a big place, white pillars across the front but otherwise displaying Jonathan's wealth quietly, in a setting – well back from the road with woods generously distributed – that looked more upscale rural than suburban. A gentleman's country home.

Alfred pulled into the driveway, I got out, he stayed behind the wheel.

'What?' I asked.

'I'll wait in the car.'

My laughing didn't help matters but, after all, the man was forty-two years old, sitting in the car pouting the way my daughter did when she was twelve and just learning to cultivate moods.

'Come on,' I told Alfred.

'No, you go ahead. I'll be fine here, really.'

I told him this was like being married again; he didn't laugh. 'If you don't come with me,' I said in a wheedling voice, 'I'm going to tell Mary that my partner feels kind of shy about meeting her and then I'm going to ask if she'll come out here and try to talk you out of your shyness. How would you like that, huh? And you know I'll do it. Alfred, you know I will.'

'Asshole,' he muttered, getting out of the car and following me to her front door.

She opened the door only a crack, peering out with orphan eyes.

'I'm sorry for showing up here without calling,' I said.

She opened the door reluctantly, Mary wearing a simple white cotton dress with a red sash around her waist, very much the señorita look. Her eyes and nose were red from crying (in fact, she had a small handkerchief wadded in one hand) and she wore no makeup. When she sucked in her lower lip and began chewing on it, I thought then that I should have planned more carefully what I was going to say to her.

After I introduced Alfred, he hung a lopsided grin on that disfigured pirate face of his, stepped forward, and put out a big paw. 'Nice to meetcha, Mrs Gaetan.'

We stood there like that, in her doorway, until I asked if we could come in and 'chat' for a moment, very unofficial, off the record, and so forth.

She took a moment to consider the request and then nodded, turning to walk down the long central hallway while Alfred and I followed her. I smelled something sweetly familiar in her wake as she led us to a large living room where the three of us stood again in uncomfortable silence, just as we had at her front door.

I decided to redress whatever grievances Alfred still held against me by giving him a straight line. 'You know, Mrs Gaetan, down at the department, this gentleman is known as *Lord* Alfred.'

She dabbed at her nose with the handkerchief, widening her eyes and asking Alfred, 'Why's that?'

He shook his head.

I attempted to deliver the gift a second time. 'Quite a story on how he got his name.'

'Really?' she asked.

'Oh, Theodore,' Alfred responded in a prissy voice, 'I don't

125

think Mrs Gaetan would be interested in *that* sort of story.'

I muttered something.

She was facing him. 'I think you're going to have to tell me the story, Lord Alfred.' Saying it more out of politeness than genuine interest.

'I doubt you'll find it amusing, ma'am.'

Mary said she could use something amusing in her life right now.

My stomach turned a little acidy when Lord Alfred put back his head and grinned, patting his beer gut with both hands and letting his voice slip back to its origins: 'Growing up in Possum Holler back there in southern West Virginia, well, ma'am, I was always vexing my mama . . .'

Vexing my mama!

'. . . vexing her something awful, and when I performed some especially mischievous deed, she would step to the door of the old home place . . .'

Old home place? He really was shameless.

'. . . and she'd holler out from the porch, "Lord, Alfred, you're going to be the death of me yet!" Like when she caught me stringing her geese.'

'Doing what to her geese?' Mary asked.

'Stringing 'em, ma'am. See, one of the jobs I had as a strapling boy was to keep moving mama's geese from one weed patch to the next, 'cause although they're god-awful ornery creatures, they do a good job of keeping the thistle down. I was having the usual trouble herding them when I came up with this idea. I don't know if you've had much goose experience, ma'am—'

'Call me, Mary, please. My experiences with geese have been limited.'

Alfred laughed at that like it was funnier than anything *he'd* ever said, his laughter causing Mary to smile, making me wonder what I'd unleashed here.

'Well,' he continued, 'if you feed a goose a piece of pork fat, it'll pass right through him. You've heard that expression, like fat through a goose, haven't you, Mary? It's true! You can feed 'em that pork fat and just stand there and wait for it to exit.'

'Extraordinary,' she said.

'So I tied me a goodly length of string to this hunk of fatback and fed it to the first old gander and, sure enough, he passed it in a few minutes, and I picked it up and pulled the string right through his innards until just a foot or so was hanging out his mouth, the rest leading out from his rear portal, if you catch my drift.'

'I'm afraid I do.'

'I fed the fat to the next goose in line, and the same thing happened. I kept feeding that fat and pulling the string and feeding and pulling until I had the whole entire flock of geese strung on a single line like some kind of living pull-toy. Tying a stick to the back end of the string, behind that last goose, so it wouldn't pull through, I go around to the first goose and pick up the end of the string hanging out of his mouth, and I'll be darned if I couldn't lead them geese wherever I wanted. 'Course, when my mama saw what I'd done, she hollers out the front door of the old home place, "Oh, Lord, Alfred, my poor geese, my poor geese!" Things like that happened with such regularity that folks just naturally took to addressing me as *Lord Alfred*.'

Mary and I were both smiling, except mine was a ruthless little smile. 'Lord, Alfred, I do believe you lifted that story from a book I lent you about Errol Flynn.'

He offered me a fuck-you smirk.

'I don't care where he got it,' Mary said, 'it was exactly the kind of thing I needed to hear.'

He closed his little eyes and raised his chin and I'll be damned if the oversized turd didn't snake down one hand for a quick and furtive adjustment of his groin.

Mary suggested we all have a drink.

'We really don't want to take up your time,' I mealymouthed. 'And I apologize again for coming over here without calling first, but I did want to tell you I'm sorry for being so aggressive during that interview yesterday.'

She heard me out and then turned to Alfred. 'Nothing for you, either?'

'Well, hell's bells, ma'am,' he said, on a roll, 'might as well have a little something 'cause it's too wet to plow and too windy to haul pea gravel.'

She shook her head and walked over to a bar in the corner of the room, asking Alfred if he'd like a rum and tonic.

'Sounds dee-licious!'

'Got to get some ice,' she said from the corner of the room, picking up a silver bucket and leaving through a side door.

I sat on the couch facing the fireplace, drumming my fingers on the armrest; Alfred sat way over at the other end of the couch, whistling tunelessly. I didn't want to say anything but couldn't help myself. 'Too wet to plow and too windy to haul pea gravel?'

He looked over at me with a grin that fell somewhere between shit-eating and canary-swallowing.

Just before Mary returned, Alfred told me that her mouth reminded him a lot of Elvis Presley's.

As Alfred and Mary sipped their drinks and made small talk, I caught another whiff of her sweet, clean smell and remembered when my daughter began using perfume. I went into Margaret's room one day and saw her little dressing table lined with those unbelievably tiny bottles, a few of the names sticking in my mind, Tatiana, Stephanotis, Florissa, and I wondered if she was more taken with the names and the little vials than she was with the scents. When did she get old enough to start using perfume? How could I have missed such a progression, smelling baby powder one day and Paris Twilight the next. 'How do you like it, Daddy? It's called Paris Twilight.' I told her she smelled like she took a bath in it and the whole idea was for a scent to be subtle – when I should have said, 'Ooo-la-la,' and hugged her as tightly as I could, even if I had to gag on the odor of Paris Twilight. The mistakes you make when you're not paying attention.

Mary seemed nervous, trying to keep up her end of the conversation with Alfred even if her heart wasn't in it. She was complaining about the rudeness of reporters who had been trying to interview her and about the crassness of some of the men who had called her since Jonathan's death, supposed friends of the family who wanted to know if there was anything around the house that needed a man's attention. 'Like I'm a poor widow who can't afford a plumber,' she said quietly, stealing glances at me, wondering why I wasn't talking. Alfred told her he'd recently read a fascinating book about a plumber, but I wasn't listening to them anymore.

I was becoming lost, thinking that if I *had* found out who'd made my daughter pregnant when she was sixteen, if I'd found out who my wife was screwing, if I'd gone down to Florida and killed those bastards in a rage – I probably would've been out of jail by now. Crimes within the family, however, are not so quickly punished. For almost eighteen years, my daughter has kept me locked out of her life and her son's life. I can no longer picture the faces of my wife and daughter and I have no idea what my grandson looks like, all grown up. I should've gone down to Florida years ago, told him who I was.

I used to write letters asking for a picture of the kid, but my daughter wouldn't even send a snapshot. I got interested in my family too late, and my daughter turned out to be too much like me, like the way I used to be – a hard case. I have talked to my ex-wife a few times on the telephone, and she tells me everyone there is happy. *Happy*, she says, enunciating the word carefully, as if it still might not be in my vocabulary. I've never asked what they've told the kid about me. Does he know I'm up here working as a detective, still doing time?

'Teddy!'

I turned toward Alfred.

'I was just telling Mary,' he said, 'that she doesn't have to worry about *you* hitting on her because, like you were saying just today, the last time you had an erection was back in January when your furnace went out and you woke up to a cold apartment and a full bladder.'

129

I thanked him for passing along that bit of information and then I looked at Mary. 'I think of you more as a daughter.'

She stirred, leaning toward me, touching my knee. 'That's a very sweet thing to say.'

I glanced over at Alfred who had a peculiar look on his face. Then I turned back to Mary. 'Alfred and I, if you're in some kind of jam, I mean we don't necessarily have to play this exactly by the book. I could, we could provide you with some discreet protection.'

'What an extraordinary thing for a policeman to say.'

I could see from Lord Alfred's face that he was thinking the same thing. 'I guess I haven't expressed myself very well,' I said.

Mary asked me if I was sure I didn't want a drink.

I shook my head. 'Actually, I think I need to use the bathroom.' She started to give me directions, but I said I could find it myself, thank you.

I knew there had to be a couple of bathrooms on the ground floor, but I went up the big staircase, checking doors on both sides of the second floor hallway until I found it: the master bathroom, where Jonathan died. Why was I here? I wasn't going to find anything that had been overlooked by the lab team. There wasn't going to be a message on the wall, Jonathan leaving a note for *me*, explaining *to me* what his demons were.

The room was spotless. Had our men left it this way or did Mary pay her housecleaner a bonus to make sure all the blood was cleaned off the tile floor, off the porcelain of the big tub?

Why did you do it, Jonathan? Who was blackmailing you? What secret could you possibly have terrible enough to put you in such a black rage that you had to butcher yourself? Did you scream while you were cutting yourself up, did Mary hear you scream? Or did someone else take that big knife to you?

I stepped to the tub. Over it was a window approximately three feet high and six feet long with three sliding glass panels. I suddenly saw how it could have been done: dragging Jonathan into the tub, slitting his wrists and throat while standing behind him, so it would seem the wounds were self-inflicted, slashing his penis, forcing his hand around the knife to get a good set of prints – and then while he's thrashing in the water, spreading blood and water all over the floor, the killer could have climbed out the window. He could've used a rope to get down to the ground, putting rags around the rope so it wouldn't leave marks on the window frames, lowering himself and then pulling the rope free with a slipknot. When Jonathan was found, was the window open? Did anyone check for footprints on the ground below this window? Could someone have done this, killed Jonathan in the bathtub and then escaped out the window without Mary hearing anything?

No, homicides are never that complicated. As I told Land, the motivation is money, sex, or family – and in this case, Jo-Jo Creek had already uncovered the money angle for us. There's no such thing as a locked-room murder, and when the reason for Jonathan's death finally comes out, it'll be something obvious and crude. I went back downstairs without peeing.

As soon as I walked into the living room, Mary stood. 'Find any clues?'

I raised my eyebrows as if I didn't understand the question.

She was shaking her head, using the handkerchief on her eyes. 'You said you wanted to apologize for the way you questioned me yesterday. You even made that extraordinary speech about wanting to help me, protect me. Then you sneak off upstairs to get a look at the crime scene.'

I started to give her my cover story, that I'd gone upstairs looking for a bathroom, any bathroom, not the one that . . . but then I got tired of lying. 'Sorry.'

'Please leave.' She was crying.

'What I said before, Mary, about helping you—'

'*Please leave.*'

Alfred came over to me and signaled with his eyes that leaving was a good idea.

'I'm sorry,' I told her again. I should have it engraved on my effing tombstone. *I'm sorry, I'm sorry.*

131

Mary was already heading down the hallway, showing us the way out. I stopped a few feet away from her. 'Why didn't you call the police from the car phone? When you found all the phone lines in the house had been cut, why didn't you—'

'Get out!' She opened one of the double doors. 'My car doesn't have a phone in it. Jonathan's does but I forgot about it. I was in a panic. All I could think of was what Jonathan had told me a long time ago, if anything ever happened to him I should—'

'How come your lawyer came to get the knife? We were holding it in our evidence lockup and he—'

'Get out of my house, *please*.' She looked at Alfred who was staring at his feet. 'The knife was part of Jonathan's collection.'

'Collection?' I asked. 'In Land's office, you said you didn't know *where* Jonathan got that knife.'

'I don't. But he collects, Jonathan used to collect different things, and I assume the knife came from his collection.'

'I know you're angry with me. I know I have no right to come into your house and start with these questions again, but it's very important to me . . . Mary, please listen to what I'm saying. It's important that I get that knife back from you.'

'What in God's name for?'

'I—'

'I threw it out. All of them, all the knives in his collection, it made me sick, the idea of those knives still in the house, so I threw everything away. I wanted them gone from here, destroyed, that's why I asked George to get that knife back from the police. Is that so hard to believe?'

I took out a card and tried to hand it to her. 'It has my home and office numbers. If you are in any kind of trouble, if you think you're in danger, call me anytime, night or day. Alfred will give you—'

'I already did,' he said quietly.

She refused to take my card, so I put it on a hallway table. 'Mrs Gaetan, I know someone else was here with you and Jonathan that night.'

Her gray eyes widened in astonishment.

'If you're scared of this other person—'

'He killed himself!' she shouted. 'Why can't you just let it go at that? Why do you keep bothering me? Don't you realize what I've been through these past few days? Can't you leave it alone?'

My daughter had asked me those kinds of questions eighteen years ago.

'Who was it, Mrs Gaetan?'

Alfred pulled tentatively on my arm, but I couldn't stop, had to know. 'Who was it? Someone Jonathan had business with – or an old friend of yours?'

She gave me one last astonished, frightened look and then walked away, running up the stairway, Alfred taking me by the arm and closing the door behind him.

Back in his car, Alfred said, 'You certainly handled that with a large dose of finesse.'

'Hell of a lot of support I got from you.'

'Hey, didn't sound like you needed my help. Doing fine all on your own. Coming in and telling her how sorry you were for those rude questions you asked yesterday in Land's office, saying you thought of her as a daughter – a nice touch, that. Then you sneak upstairs to check out where Jonathan died, come downstairs and start blasting her about the knife and who was with them that night. Jesus, I mean I know the idea is to keep the witness, or maybe I should say the suspect, off balance but, damn Teddy, three days ago her husband was found in a tub full of blood and you go after her like she was a child-killer.'

'Fuck you.'

'Was she lying?'

'Goddamn right she was lying! Someone else *was* with her and Jonathan. Lying about that knife, too!'

'OK, OK. Now what?'

'I'm going to stake out her house tonight, in case the other party shows up for his money.'

'I'll call in sick.'

'No,' I told Alfred. 'You work your shift tonight and then come back and relieve me at seven in the morning. We have to keep this house under constant surveillance because we have no idea when the guy's going to show up.'

'*If* he's going to show up. If there even *is* someone else involved.'

'Fine, then don't relieve me in the morning—'

'All I'm saying is that we don't know *why* Jonathan arranged for that money to be delivered to his house. He was obviously out of his mind and . . . OK, I'll drive you around and drop you off at the other side of those woods. I'll be back at seven in the morning to take your place.'

I nodded, saying nothing.

'Then what're you going to do?' Alfred asked. 'After I relieve you. You going to go to Land and tell him everything?'

'Yes.'

'*Teddy.*'

'I will!'

He drove me to a spot where I could enter the woods across from Mary's house without being seen. I asked him to bring me some coffee and sandwiches.

'What're you going to do, out here all by yourself, if some blackmailer *does* show up?'

'You can bring me back a radio, too. If it looks like I need some help, I'll call in.'

'We shouldn't be doing this on our own.'

I shrugged.

'Hey, in spite of your little talk on the way over, how I should watch my p's and q's, I think I really charmed her.'

'Yeah, you were Fred-fucking-Astaire.'

11

Back when Alfred and I were making our reputations, certain people assumed we were like George and Lenny in *Of Mice and Men*, with me as the smaller, smarter one and Alfred the big, dumb, and potentially violent half of the team. That assumption was correct only in terms of our respective sizes, however. I was always more volatile than Alfred, always the more dangerous one. He worked as a detective the way he played college ball for West Virginia University, wanting his side to win, of course, but carrying no personal hatred for the opponents. Defeat them, yes, but once the game was over, Alfred was always ready to shake hands. He didn't turn roguish until *after* we divorced as partners, feeling betrayed by me, bored with his new assignments and new partners, suffering through the collapses of his second and third marriages. But now he's finally got his mind right.

Sitting in the woods across from Mary Gaetan's house, I opened one of the sandwiches he had brought for me. I couldn't tell what the meat was, something that should have been micro-waved but wasn't. The coffee was lukewarm and tasted thin. Mary still had her lights on.

The hardest kind of case to figure is when a person is killed by someone who claims the death was an accident. 'I didn't mean to shoot her. I was cleaning the gun and it just went off.'

Sometimes you can uncover a sound motive for homicide and sometimes the physical evidence will help make your case, but often only the person who did the killing knows whether it was

135

accidental or not. It's a secret they hold to tightly. And if that person won't take a lie-detector test or if the results are inconclusive, what do you do? I remember when Alfred and I were called in because this kid in the District, sixteen years old, ran over his father in their driveway, said it was an accident, his foot slipped off the brake and hit the accelerator, he was as sorry as hell but that's the way it happened.

I kept hammering at him, *goddamn it, son, don't you dare lie to me*, just the way I went after Mary in Captain Land's office, the way I pursued the various truths being held so closely by my daughter and wife. *Don't lie to me!* It wasn't even my case, and the only points I'd made in helping 'break' it were the points that would be added to my reputation. Can't be lied to.

Finally the kid broke down and admitted that maybe it wasn't *totally* an accident, that his old man wasn't going to let him use the car that night, and he knew his father was somewhere back there, and although he didn't mean to kill him, not really, he did let his foot slide over to the gas pedal, he was just pissed because of the way his father was acting. He was only sixteen. But I nailed him. And he was convicted of manslaughter.

I remember how the other detectives slapped me on the back when I stepped out of the room where I'd been interrogating the kid. What kind of man takes glory in doing what I'd done, getting a sixteen-year-old boy to admit that he killed his old man? If I hadn't shown up, that child could have, given enough time, convinced *himself* it was an accident. He could've learned to live with it. But I took what was in his mind during those two or three seconds when his foot slipped off the brake and hit the accelerator, and I made that brief, murderous secret public. Sent him to jail because of it. Another citation in the jacket.

I drank some more of the bad coffee, tensing up when a car slowed down past Mary's house. It didn't stop, and I wasn't interested in the second sandwich.

I remember when the detectives from Fairfax County called me in to talk with a young woman, twenty-six years old, three

kids in three years and the third one born after she and her
husband were divorced. The baby drowned in the bathtub, she
said. She just went to answer the phone, I wasn't gone but a
second, she said, but I guess the baby slipped or something
because when I . . .

You look back at all the people whose lives you've affected,
and it has a way of making your soul cringe. Mary Gaetan turned
her lights off, and I spent a long night in the woods across from
her house.

12

He's gone mad.

Truly. He has on occasion suffered *episodes* of insanity, when he chopped up that hitchhiker, what do you call that except insanity, totally crazy because he was so hopped-up about the prospect of seeing Jonathan after so many years and because she laughed at him and because she was the first woman he'd been with in eight years and . . . But he returned from that particular trip into insanity and was able to perform – brilliantly, he thought – at Jonathan's house the next night. This time, however, he can't find his way back. Lost, mad.

His pain is a living thing that his own body has given birth to, the puncture wound in his thigh, the slash across his already festering chest, and especially the awful way in which that living thing screams, SCREAMS, inside his head.

He has taken all the pills in his possession, able finally to stand and lurch to the sliding doors and look across the way, toward the dark room where that happy family is staying, all of them so peacefully asleep, smiles probably tugging at their mouths as they sleep, the little girl cuddled up in the same bed with her brother. He wonders if it is possible that, in her sleep, the little girl awaits his arrival.

Philip stands there on the balcony and *wills* her to come to him, to arise from her bed in a trance and leave her family and come to him, into this room, into his arms, joining him in the madness he has become. He has tried this before, it never works.

He finally returns to the bed, sitting on it and knowing he will not sleep, not tonight. He may never sleep again. He looks around the room, which is stained in various places with his blood, and wonders how he's going to get his money. Friday is out of the question, that much – and perhaps only that much – is clear in his mind. No way can he make it until Friday. The police are going to connect what he did tonight to that whore and what he did to that hitchhiker, and now time has become another enemy, something else that's against him, one more thing he has to fight.

Tomorrow. He has to get his money tomorrow. Then he'll leave for Mexico. He can still pull it off, still get away – just as long as she has his money for him when he shows up tomorrow. And if she doesn't, if she doesn't have his money like Jonathan promised, then . . .

His eyes close and slowly he slumps. NO! Can't sleep. No. Never wake up if you go to sleep now.

He's dry and his tongue works the inside of his mouth like something over which he has no control, unable to make his tongue stop rolling around in his mouth. Crazy.

She was crazy. He knows that now. He didn't realize it when he was a kid, but he knows it now, crazier than a bedbug. When they came to inform him that she'd died, he felt nothing. *Nothing*. Not even gratitude for her telling him Jonathan's address, for suggesting how much of Jonathan's money he should demand, for explaining that he could live like a king in Mexico on a hundred dollars a week.

He is slumped on his bed; his eyes bug out and then begin blinking. Must have some of those pills left, he thinks, searching in his pockets, finding the Polaroids, two pieces of soap, a picture he took from the whore's purse. He finds his forty dollars, too.

When he was still in the alley, before he went out to meet the two black kids, he remembered his money. He wasn't going to leave it this time, not the way he forgot that forty dollars in the hitchhiker's jeans. So he took his wad of money out of the whore's little red purse and then dumped the rest of the contents on the ground. She had three ones and two fives of her own, neatly folded and clipped with a large pink plastic paperclip; he took that money, too. He also found a photograph of a two-year-old child wearing a cowboy outfit, chaps and fringed vest and two silver six-shooters in their holsters, big western hat and all. The photograph was heat-sealed in plastic.

On the bed in his motel room, he stares at the picture thinking even a whore's kid has it better than he did. Not fair. *Not fair.* But he evened a few scores tonight, yes. Philip tries to sob but can't summon the energy for it.

He couldn't paint her lips because he had ruined her mouth, so he picked the lipstick tube off the ground and drew lines around her eyes, lines radiating like spokes on to her forehead and temples and down to where the mouth wound touched cheekbones.

On the floor of his motel room, near the severed hand, lies the young prostitute's brassy blond wig. He doesn't even remember bringing it with him. What *does* he remember? Giving her sunburst eyes, he remembers that. 'Now you got sunburst eyes,' Nancy would say after she had painted his face and held up a little round mirror so he could see.

And he remembers getting the biting urge, too – his teeth on the flesh of her neck, and the harder he bites down, the more compelling the urge becomes.

Something else in his pocket, too. Sobbing to see it in his hand now. Did he really do it? Of course. He holds the evidence right in front of his face. I warned her about my biting urge.

No longer pink and wiggling the way it looked when he went in her mouth after it, going in after it the way a disturbed child pulls some terrified animal out of its den, it has turned gray. He brings it toward his lips, weeping as his discolored teeth pierce her flesh again, the living pain behind his eyes having grown too large for his skull to contain, screaming into the back of his eyeballs. It is fibrous, tasting of death.

And he is like water poured out on the ground, a lost soul taking final communion, fat tears running down his cheeks, sobbing now for real as in madness he searches for solace, the terror terrorized. Gone, mad.

13

Lord Alfred arrived in the woods across from Mary's house at exactly seven Thursday morning, bringing me hot coffee and fresh rolls. I told him nothing had happened during the night, and as we stood there talking, Mary pulled out of the garage in her little gray BMW. 'Maybe the payoff has been set for some-place else,' Alfred said, but I reminded him that Mary can't make the payoff because she never withdrew the money from her checking account.

Then I complained about being too old and too soft for this shit, spending a night in the woods, Alfred countering with his own list of complaints – putting in extra, unpaid time on this unofficial investigation, possible retaliation from Land when he discovered we were staking out Mary's house without his authority, and the plain *wrongness* of not letting the Maryland State Police know that we have a hunch on the Lip-stick Murder, regardless of how wild and unsure that hunch might be.

I assured Alfred that I'd tell Land everything as soon as I got to the department.

'You'd better.'

'I said I would.'

'Yeah, well, you'd better.'

'Why do you keep saying that?'

'Because you're blowing hot and cold on this case, Teddy – that's why. Half the time you want to protect Mary from what-ever trouble she's in and the other half of the time you want to nail her for lying to you.' He paused. 'I don't feel right, working with someone who's as out of whack as you are.'

'Give me the keys to your car.'

'You radio me as soon as Land's been told.'

I nodded, holding my hand out for the keys.

''Cause if you haven't told him by noon, I'll call in and tell him myself.'

I kept standing there with my hand out.

He gave me the keys and I left without saying anything more. As soon as I got to my apartment, I took a shower. When I turned off the water, the telephone was ringing, and I hurried to answer it without bothering to dry myself or even grab a towel.

It was Jo-Jo Creek. 'I must have called you a dozen times last night.' I hadn't said hello yet. 'Don't you own an answering machine?'

'Yeah, but I keep it off.'

'That's smart.'

'Something depressing about being out all night and knowing, because there are no messages on the machine, *knowing* you didn't get any calls. It's better to imagine that—'

'I've got some news for you.'

I was getting chilled, looking around for something within reach that I could use to wipe the water off my chest and belly.

'Teddy?'

'Yeah.'

'Jonathan is being buried today.'

'I know.'

'That's not the news. The news is that Mary was just over here at my apartment. I've never seen her so upset. I mean, that woman is a model of self-control, believe me, but she was very upset this morning, and I think something more than the funeral is bothering her. She wants me to go back to her house with her after the burial. Just me. She said she needs to talk to me, privately, something very important.'

'Are you going to do it?'

'Of course.'

'What do you think it's about?'

'The money.'

'How so?'

Jo-Jo snorted. 'I told you I called the bank at the close of business yesterday and the money I had deposited in that joint checking account still hadn't been withdrawn.'

'Right.'

'My contact at the bank called me back around five – and this is why I was trying to get hold of you all night – and she said that although the money hadn't been withdrawn, Mary *did* call the bank to check on the status of her account, and she was informed that nearly one hundred and fifty thousand dollars had been deposited to the account over the last two days. She was obviously surprised to hear this, and when she asked who made the deposits, the bank told her that I had.'

'So now Mary wants to find out how much you know.'

'Yes.'

'But she didn't ask you about it this morning?'

'No. She's going to play it cagey, waiting until Jonathan is buried.'

I stood there trying to think what this all meant, distracted because I felt foolish being buck naked and shivering in the air conditioning.

'And here comes the bomb, Teddy.'

'There's more?'

'Yes! When Mary found out the money was sitting in her account, well, the bank was already closed and you can hardly take a hundred and fifty thousand dollars out of the teller machine, so she got the bank president on the phone and arranged to have exactly one hundred forty-five thousand, six hundred dollars in twenties, fifties, and hundreds to be delivered to her house. Sound familiar?'

'So there *is* going to be a payoff.'

'My contact at the bank, who's not supposed to be telling me any of this, of course, but she and I have known each other for years and she has the same opinion of Mary that I do, *she* said that the bank president was anxious as hell about being responsible for the delivery of so much money in cash, but the bank does a lot of business with the Gaetan Company so he finally agreed to send the money over with a couple of security guards. It's going to be delivered to Mary's house Friday morning at ten.'

I told Jo-Jo we'd be there to intercept the payoff.

'Don't you think I'd make a great detective?'

I agreed she would. 'But you'd better come up with some excuse why you can't go to Mary's house after the burial today.'

'Why?'

'We can't tip our hand that we know about the payoff and—'

'You think I'm so stupid I'm going to tell her I've been to the police?'

'No, but—'

'If I *don't* meet with Mary today, then she's going to be suspicious about what I know and don't know. In fact, she might become so suspicious that she'll cancel the payoff.'

It made sense. 'What're you going to tell her about—'

'I'll just tell her that Jonathan called me Monday morning and asked me to have that money deposited in his account, which I did, and he instructed me not to mention it to anyone. I'll say I have no idea why he wanted me to make those deposits, that it was none of my business and that I haven't told anyone about it. After all, I didn't even tell *her*. She knows how much Jonathan prized my discretion. Once she's assured that I'm ignorant of whatever she's up to, that I'm simply the dutiful little secretary doing what her boss instructed, then Mary will go ahead with the payoff tomorrow and you can be on hand to find out who she's paying off and why. And how it all led to Jonathan getting killed, too.'

'I don't know, Jo-Jo. This thing could—'

'I'm not in any danger, if *that's* what you're worried about. Whoever is getting that money isn't showing up until tomorrow at ten. Mary's already made the arrangements. No one's going to be at her house except the two of us. I can handle her, believe me. I'm familiar with Mary's technique, pretending she's sweet and innocent and needs a big strong man to help her. Exactly what she pulled on Jonathan. And she's probably tried it on you, too. But it doesn't cut any ice with me.'

'Someone will be watching the house when you're with her this afternoon. I think we'll put a wire on you so if things do get hairy, we can come in and—'

'And save me?'

'Something like that, yeah.'

'Have you done a background check on her yet?'

'Not yet.'

Jo-Jo snorted. I started to say something but she interrupted me again. 'I guarantee you, Teddy, that a *thorough* background check on little miss Mary will turn up something interesting. I checked her credentials myself when she applied for that job with us eight years ago. After high school she went to a junior college and then six months with a secretarial school. She arrived here when she was twenty, married Jonathan at twenty-one. A little too pat for me.'

'A lot of young women get out of college and then work as secretaries.'

'Jonathan was *forty-six* when he married her.'

'That's not a crime, either, Jo-Jo.'

'If it had been up to me she would never have been hired in the first place.'

'Well, that was a long time ago—'

'You check her out, Teddy.'

'I'm running a check on her as soon as I get to the department. In fact, I have to get going right now. You caught me in the shower. Didn't even have a chance to dry off or grab a towel.'

'You mean you're *naked?*'

I laughed.

'Well, you'd better get dressed and get on the job, Detective Camel.'

147

I started to say something, but she snorted and hung up before I had the chance.

I immediately called the department and got Melvin Kelvin's home number. 'I know you pulled the second shift last night,' I told him, 'and I'm sorry to be calling you this early, but I could really use some of your computer expertise.'

'No problem, Teddy.'

'I want you to run a complete background check on Mary Gaetan.'

'I *knew* you and Alfred were up to something.'

'What'd he tell you?'

'Alfred didn't tell me anything.'

'Yeah, well, I need this kept on the q.t. You have any problems with that?'

'I guess not.'

'Can you run the check this morning?'

'We were just leaving for the zoo. I promised my wife and little girl that we'd spend the morning at the zoo.'

I thought of all the outings with *my* wife and daughter that I had canceled over the years, canceled because I had more important things to do. I told Melvin Kelvin that he should definitely go to the zoo with his family. 'But if you could come in early this afternoon, I'd appreciate it.'

'Sure, Teddy. I was planning to work on the computer this afternoon anyway. We still haven't found out who those coins belong to. It's getting a pretty big play, twenty gold coins, some of them really valuable, and yet there's absolutely no report of coins like that being stolen or lost. Strange. Did you see the segment they did about it on TV last night, the honest family from Iowa turning in a small fortune in gold coins and all that?'

'No. Listen, I need everything you can get on Mary Gaetan. Where she's lived, the jobs she's worked, where she went to school, any previous marriages, criminal record, anything and everything. You'll find her maiden name and Social Security number and all that in the Gaetan file.'

'You reopening that?'

'You do this for me and I'll owe you one, OK, Melvin Kelvin?'

'If you can get Alfred to stop calling me Melvin Kelvin, I'll consider us square.'

'You got it, Mel.'

I hung up and got dressed, intending to go to the department right then, but I checked the time and saw that it was only quarter past eight. Land wouldn't be in his office for nearly an hour – and after being up all night I could use an hour's nap. I had just gone into the bedroom, in fact, when it occurred to me that I'd better call Jo-Jo back and make specific arrangements for her to come by the department before going to Mary's house after the funeral. Then again, wire or no wire, Land might nix the idea of Jo-Jo meeting Mary, but by that time it would be his case, his decision – not mine.

I called her apartment but Jo-Jo didn't answer, probably in the shower herself. I left a message on her machine: 'Jo-Jo, this is Teddy Camel. I'm no longer naked but I bet you are. Listen, call me right away, OK? If you miss me here, I'll be at the department. It's important. 'Bye.'

I got the alarm clock from my bedroom and set it for nine, then stretched out on the couch. I kicked off one shoe before falling backward into a deep, black, and dreamless sleep.

I didn't come around until past two that afternoon. Impossible, I thought, looking at the clock. Used to be, I could lie down for a nap and awaken in exactly thirty minutes, totally refreshed. But now I had slept for almost six hours, slept right through an alarm clock and probably Jo-Jo's call, too – feeling as if I had awakened from a drunk.

Shit. When I didn't check in with Alfred by noon, he probably called Land just as he said he would. And Jonathan Gaetan is already in the ground, Jo-Jo with Mary right now. I sat there holding my head for a moment more. You think of detectives blowing cases because they're pursuing the wrong leads,

149

overlooking evidence, violating someone's rights. Not me, though – I blow it by oversleeping. Pathetic is the word that comes to mind.

Everything unraveling. I rushed out of the apartment without bothering to put on a tie or brush my teeth.

As soon as I walked into the bullpen, I knew something was wrong. Detectives were looking at me with the queerest expressions on their faces, and when I nodded at them, they responded with thin smiles before finding somewhere else to put their eyes.

Two of the detectives who were often assigned to internal affairs investigations were in my cubicle, going through my desk drawers.

'What's the problem, Officers?' I asked, smiling. You know, a joke – the line you get from every citizen who's stopped for a traffic violation. These two guys didn't laugh, however. One of them pointed with his chin toward Captain Land's office.

Shit. Alfred has told Land about our stakeout of Mary's house, about Jo-Jo Creek's information on the money, and now I'm about to get reamed. *I was going to tell you all about it this morning, Captain, but I overslept.*

I knocked on his door and then opened it without waiting for an answer. 'Harv?'

He motioned me in and, after I was seated, went to the doorway and called in a court reporter. I watched as she set up her apparatus, a tape recorder and a microphone that covered her mouth like an oxygen mask, into which she would repeat everything we said, for later transcription. After Land closed the door, I asked him, 'What's the problem, Officer?' He didn't laugh, either.

'You know your rights, Sergeant Camel, so I'm not going—'

'Rights? Hey, Harv, I realize you're upset but don't you think you're overreacting just a bit?'

He sent one grim look my way and then noted, for the reporter, the time and date, my full name, rank, and badge number. 'This is an initial inquiry into charges—'

'Charges? You were out yesterday afternoon, but I was going to tell you all about it this morning. I just . . . just got a little behind schedule.'

'Sleeping off a drunk?'

'What?'

'I indicate for the record that Sergeant Camel's appearance indicates he is not fit for duty. He appears either to be intoxicated or having recently awakened from a binge. His clothes are in disarray, wearing no tie, his eyes bloodshot, and—'

'Oh for chrissakes, Harv.' I knew he was going to be pissed, but this was ridiculous. 'Give me five minutes to explain and—'

'I want your sidearm and your badge on my desk.'

I laughed.

'On my desk *now*, Camel!'

I complied, asking Land if he was worried I might shoot him and take the reporter hostage. He didn't crack a grin and when I looked over at her, all I saw were dead eyes and those jaws working silently into that black mask.

'Yesterday morning, Wednesday morning, Jonathan Gaetan's secretary, Miss Jo-Jo Creek, came in and talked to you, is that correct.'

I nodded. 'Yes.'

'But you never reported her visit to me, even though I was in charge of the investigation into Jonathan Gaetan's suicide, is that correct?'

'Yes, but . . . Come on, Harv, the suspense is killing me. What are you charging me with?'

'While Jo-Jo Creek was at your desk, you made certain sex-ually suggestive remarks to her, is *that* correct?'

I laughed again. 'No, that is *not* correct. Where'd you get this nonsense?'

'Do you deny—'

'You bet I deny. I don't know where you got this crap, Cap-tain, but you sure as hell didn't get it from Jo-Jo Creek.'

Then the lizard grinned. 'Right here,' he said, holding up a

151

piece of paper. 'A handwritten complaint from Jo-Jo Creek, brought in by her personally.'

'I don't believe it.'

'I'll give you copies.'

'This is crazy.'

'I've never seen a woman so distraught.'

'Jo-Jo?'

'Yes. You really did a number on her, Camel.'

'Did she tell you why she came to see me yesterday?'

'Yes. She said she was making some routine inquiries about Jonathan's death, wanting to know if it had been ruled a suicide yet.'

'Harv, if you can take a break from being sanctimonious for the record, I'd like to point out that if you had simply asked me about this matter, instead of launching a goddamn official inquiry, I could have cleared up the whole mess for you in five fucking minutes.'

'You watch your language in this office, mister.'

Unbelievable.

'Your record and your seniority aren't going to pull you out of this little mess, Camel.'

'I didn't make any sexually suggestive remarks to her – and you know I didn't.'

'Maybe you don't remember. Maybe you were under the influence that morning. Maybe you are right now.'

'Why don't you bring in the fucking Breathalyzer, Harv, huh?'

'According to Miss Creek, she was not planning to take any action regarding the pass you made at her when she was at your desk Wednesday morning. But since that time, according to these complaints, you have called her residence repeatedly, demanding that she have sex with you. She warned you that she was going to approach your superiors, but you continued making the calls.' He paused for a significant moment. 'Do you deny these charges?'

'Yes,' I said without enthusiasm.

'You called her at an early hour just this morning and told Miss

Creek that you were naked and masturbating while you were talking to her.'

I laughed, my face feeling suddenly hot. 'You have no idea what an ass you're making of yourself, Harv.'

'Me? That's an interesting interpretation. Do you also deny that you called and left a message on her answering machine, making a point of telling her that you were *not* naked during that particular telephone call? Before you deny that, Sergeant, I should tell you that Miss Creek also dropped off the cassette from her answering machine.' He held it up. 'Shall I play it for you?'

I shook my head. What was Jo-Jo trying to pull? Of course, all I had to do was tell Land about the money and point out that Jo-Jo's failure to mention the money to him obviously proved that her complaints were a charade. But I wasn't sure I wanted to play that particular ace, not yet.

He was pontificating about my betrayal of the public trust, how reprehensible I was for sexually harassing the poor woman on the very day that her boss was being buried, and so on and so on. When he paused for breath, I asked him if he was finished and he said he was waiting to hear what I had to say.

'I say you're a prick.' I watched the reporter's eyes widen above her mask. 'Did you get that, ma'am. *Prick*.'

'I think you've pretty well proven my point about your irresponsibility,' Land said quietly. 'You're suspended from active duty pending a full hearing on these charges.' He dismissed the court reporter, walking her to the door and then returning to his desk. 'Teddy, Teddy, Teddy,' he said when we were alone. 'We have some excellent programs for the alcoholic who is serious about recovery.'

'Fuck you.'

'You're going to be lucky to get out of this with nothing worse than forced retirement on half benefits.'

'Fuck you.' I remember thinking that I was probably losing this debate on points.

'You go on home now. And listen to me. You are not to have
any contact with Jo-Jo Creek, in person or by telephone. That's
an order. She's waiting at her apartment for me to call and
confirm that I've talked to you and that you're not going to
bother her anymore. I'm going to give her my promise that you
won't contact her again. I hope you understand what I'm saying,
Teddy.'

I sat there staring at him.

'Maybe I can convince her to soft-pedal these charges against
you.'

'What about desecrating the public trust?'

He laughed. 'I just want to get you out of this department,
Teddy, I don't want to ruin whatever is left of your life. You
work with me on this, pal, and we'll get you quietly retired
without a scandal. Now, you're going to have to excuse me
because in fifteen minutes I'm leaving to give a speech to the
Lions Club.'

I stood. 'You are such a screaming asshole.'

He just laughed at me. 'Monday morning at ten, that's when
we're holding the hearing. You be here on time and sober, huh?'
He gave me a quick flash of his white teeth and then busied
himself with some other paperwork that was on his desk.

In the parking lot, I met Lord Alfred and immediately began
screaming at him. 'What the hell are you doing here! You're
supposed to be watching Mary's house.'

He screamed right back. 'You were supposed to call me by
noon!'

'Sorry, *pal*, but—'

'But shit! Half an hour ago Melvin Kelvin calls me on the radio
and says you had him doing a background check on Mary Gaetan
but now he doesn't know if he should continue with it or not,
because the word is that Jo-Jo Creek is filing sexual harassment
charges against you. He wants to know what's going on.'

'So do I. I'm heading for her apartment right now to find out.'

154

'Alfred stood there taking deep breaths. 'Did you hear there's been a second Lipstick Murder? This one in the District. They found her body this morning, a hooker with lipstick around her eyes just like that runaway in Maryland. The thing is, the killer didn't use a big knife this time. Used some kind of razor instead. You see what I'm saying, Teddy? It makes the connection between the Lipstick Murders and Jonathan all the stronger, because the Bowie knife was left at Jonathan's house – so the killer *had* to use something else on that hooker.'

I couldn't make my mind focus on what Alfred was saying. Jonathan was killed by the same person who committed these other two murders? Why? How was Mary tied in? And if Jo-Jo was so hot to nail Mary, why had she filed those phony charges against me?

'Teddy? Teddy! Listen to me. We got to tell the Maryland people and the District people everything. The money angle and everything. That hooker last night, the killer ripped her tongue out and took it with him. She had bite marks all over her neck, too.'

'Jesus Christ, Alfred.'

'Yeah, exactly. I'm going to go in and arrange for someone else to watch Mary's house and then I'll tell Land what we know and he can decide how he wants to proceed notifying—'

I didn't hesitate lying to Alfred. 'I already filled Land in.'

'You did?'

'Told him everything. The money, the stakeout, our suspicions about a possible connection to that killing in Maryland – everything. He wants Melvin Kelvin to continue working on that background check of Mary. We don't need a stakeout on her house because the payoff has been rescheduled until tomorrow morning at ten.'

'How do you—'

'I'll explain everything to you later. Go in and help Melvin Kelvin with the computer work. Whatever you get, take it back to your apartment and I'll meet you there when I finish talking with Jo-Jo.'

He eyed me suspiciously. 'You sure you told Land everything?'

'He's already left to meet with the District homicide people. All you have to worry about is getting that computer information.'

'I don't know, Teddy. You're acting so fucking strange, man.'

'Ten minutes with Jo-Jo Creek and I'll have all the answers we need.'

He nodded but I could tell from Alfred's little brown eyes that he still wasn't sure about me.

14

He's in hell.

He is! It's where he lives now, a wish fulfilled, traveling among the levels of hell and suffering diverse curses, physical pain, and a tormented mind – failure! ridicule! – and that special hell of sleeplessness, awake all last night and awake all day today, daring not to sleep because when he's like this the madwoman comes to him in his sleep, pulling back the covers to see if he is hard, and if he is – just a boy, ten years old, tumescent from bladder pressure, what did he know from being hard, what it meant, how could he possibly explain it to her or defend himself when she stood over his bed, screaming and demanding to know what he was dreaming about, with whom did he fornicate in his sleep, in his dreams – *your sister!* – I'm going to cut it off, she would scream, her eyes reddened from all the crying she did, threatening to cut it off and free him from the lust that he's inherited from his fornicating father, how could he know at his age that it was all theater, she was only trying to make a point, to frighten him, shouting, *O, Sweet Suffering Jesus, give me the strength to do it;* of course he believed her, he was only a little boy begging, *please don't cut me, please, I won't do it anymore,* confused about what it was he'd been doing that was wrong but promising on his life not to do it anymore, *promise.*

Then, *sometimes,* Nancy would come in to save him, throwing herself on top of him, shielding him with her own body, he still remembers that richly potent mixture of feelings, Nancy covering him with her body, the boy grateful for her protection but

157

confused why it should make him hard again because being hard was what brought the woman and her craziness. As he got older, Nancy was home less frequently, and the woman would pull him out of bed and make him get down on his knees to pray with her, *rid this boy, O Lord, of his lust, wipe away his father's stain*, shrieking at him, *pray with me you little fornicator or I swear to God I'll wait until you go back to sleep and then I'll come in here, I swear I will, and cut it off, pray louder!* and he would, screaming right along with her, praying all night long, released only when it was time to go to school.

For weeks after one of these late-night horror sessions, he would of course be afraid to sleep, would make silent pledges never to sleep again, staying awake forever if that's what it takes, napping by his favorite tree on the way home from school, the better to stay up all night, but eventually he would have to sleep and, eventually, she would come to him in his sleep and throw off his covers, awakening him with shouts and prayers, the boy living this terror until he was old enough – big enough, strong enough – to fight her off, push her away and curse her God right to her face, telling her that he hated God, saying it just to watch how it made her all the crazier, but he was too big for her to do anything except weep and warn him he was going to hell with his father and his sister, the three of them would dwell in hell while she looked down from heaven still praying for them. He laughed at her, saying that if she was waiting for him in heaven, then, yes, he *wanted* to go to hell.

A wish fulfilled in a motel room six miles outside of Washington, DC.

In hell, he waits. He can move around now, his mind becoming numb to the pain in his thigh, across his chest, and he has decided to wait until dark and then he will go get his money and leave for Mexico. That's it, that's his final plan – leave tonight for Mexico.

He remembers, sitting there on the bed and waiting for night, he remembers how bad it got after Nancy left and there was no one to protect him from the crazy woman, Nancy promising to come back but never coming back.

He remembers his magic tree, developing an obsession about it, because if he touched this tree in a certain way, one hand on one limb, the other hand . . . he believed with all his heart that if he followed a certain routine with this tree on his way home from school, then he would be protected from her during the night. If it worked, he was proven right. If it didn't work, he hadn't followed the routine correctly and would have to try harder the next day.

One afternoon he discovered a kid who was a year or two younger that he was, this kid carving on *his* tree with a penknife, *ruining* the magic, so he attacked the boy, grabbing away the pocketknife, knocking the kid to the ground and telling him he was going to cut off his dick, the fear in that boy's eyes electrifying Philip for a lifetime.

This was to become his solace from terror, the ability to instill in others a fear strong enough to overpower his own.

On the ground behind the tree, he made the boy unzip his pants, Philip playing the pocketknife's blade on the boy's tiny penis, telling the kid he was thinking about doing it, really doing it, really doing it, as punishment for messing with his tree, the younger boy begging the way Philip begged at night, *Please, please don't!* Laughing at the kid and keeping the penknife for himself, his first knife.

The motel maid comes in at noon, using her passkey after receiving no response to her insistent knocking. She takes two steps into the room and then sees it on the bed, excusing herself and backing out immediately, hurrying to the manager to tell him about the big blond woman in room 337, sitting on the bed sobbing, her hair matted and the whole room filthy, smelling something terrible, like hamburger meat gone bad, the maid said. No, she didn't see the blond woman's face, saw only her back, big shoulders in a dirty green field jacket, it was awful, those sounds she was making. The manager checks some records and says that room 337 is rented to a man, a single, there isn't supposed to be a woman staying there but, then, well you know. 'Just skip that room today', he tells the maid, who goes away muttering about the room needing a fumigator because she sure as hell wasn't being paid enough to go in there and clean up that kind of mess, you wouldn't believe the smell, really.

So here he sits in that stinking hellhole of a room, waiting for darkness and wearing the whore's blond wig, her severed tongue still squeezed in his left hand, what's left of her tongue.

Infection from his various wounds has spread throughout his body, veins tracing red along his chest and into his armpits, burning up with the poison in his blood, the fever robbing him of whatever ability he once had to string thoughts, able to remember only hazily what Jonathan's wife told him on the telephone about money and Friday, no hope of placing what day it is today, knowing only that when it is dark enough he will go to Jonathan's house and collect what is his, one way or the other. He needs to go to the bathroom but cannot summon sufficient motivation to rise from the bed, sitting there and fouling himself sobbing.

Hours later, he manages to stand, to stumble to the balcony doors where he sees that it is not yet night, barely dusk, still too much light for him to move safely out there in the world, looking from hell to see the swimming pool, the parking lot, those three green dumpsters on their concrete pad at the bottom of the hill.

It is hot. The Washington summer presses upon him from the outside like a goddamn pressure cooker, its heavy, humid fever matching his own internal temperature, too hot, too goddamn hot, he thinks as he sees them walk out from behind the dumpsters.

While their parents pack the car for a dawn departure (Dad likes to get on the road early, six hours of driving in by lunchtime, that's his goal), Billy and Penny search for more coins, seeking to relive the glory of finding treasure in gold coins, interviewed by a policeman who wore a suit instead of a uniform, who told them that when the coins' owner was located they might get a reward, and if the owner is never found, then the treasure is theirs to keep! Interviewed on TV! Just wait until the kids back home hear about this.

The only problem is, their father told them *specifically* not to go by those dumpsters because the policemen had already made a search for more coins – there were none – and trash attracts rats and one of them might have brushed against Penny's ankle that day, don't take any chances, stay where we can see you, keep away from the pool and the dumpsters.

They disobeyed him by degrees, sitting on the crest of the hill, looking back and forth from their car to those dumpsters, walking down a few steps to check the hillside for coins that might have been missed, neither of them *saying* anything, grazing the hillside, getting closer to the dumpsters, wanting one more look, that's all, one more quick search for treasure.

Penny finally decides they should go back right now but no sooner does she make this suggestion than Billy finds a quarter a few feet from the middle dumpster. See! It's just an ordinary quarter, he admits, but if the policemen didn't find *it*, maybe they missed some more of the coins, too. Penny, remembering the rat (and it *didn't* just brush her ankle, she doesn't care what anyone says, it *grabbed* her), becomes increasingly afraid. It's getting dark, we should go back. She stays away from the dumpsters, standing by the building, keeping her back against the double doors that lead into the motel's ground floor, arguing all the time with her brother who says don't worry, it'll take Mom and Dad forever to pack the car, we'll be on top of the hill before they miss us, here, you hold the quarter.

Leaving his room with his left arm cocked and pressed against his chest to keep pressure on the pain there, Philip walks the halls with the whore's little knife in his right hand. Following stairs and hallways all the way around the building, he passes one couple who flatten themselves against a wall to give him

161

plenty of room to pass, avoiding at all costs being *touched* by him.

Rushing now, he is around to the other side of the complex of buildings, shuffling down a ramp leading to a set of double doors. When he pauses to rest, noticing hair in his face, he looks up and sees the wig, sobbing because now he knows why that couple gave way to him. Removing the wig from his head and stuffing it into a pocket, he sobs once more before moving to open the doors.

A dime! 'Hey, Penny, look . . .' But Penny is gone. Where is she? She was standing by those doors just a second ago, where is she now? Billy glances up the hill. She couldn't have gone back to the car without his seeing her. 'Penny?' No answer.

He's going to get it now. If she tells dad where they've been, where Billy is right now, then he's in big trouble, and finding a quarter and a dime isn't going to save him. *'Penny?'* No answer.

In this dying light, dusk lingering the way it does in summer, Billy becomes suddenly afraid. She wouldn't have left without saying something to him. Maybe he hasn't been calling her name loudly enough. *'Penny!'* No answer.

Then he looks at the double doors where she was standing, noticing for the first time that the one on the right stands slightly ajar. She's gone in that way. Girls are so stupid, she'll get lost in the corridors, she'll never find the room by herself. Billy transfers the newly found dime from the right hand to his left, reaching out with the right to open one of the double doors. It's dark in there, the boy whispering into that darkness, 'Penny?' A man answers.

162

15

I arrived at Jo-Jo Creek's door in a righteous mood, eager to confront her, pumping anger the way I always did before interrogating a suspect. Being genuinely pissed, that was the key, showing them you're *not* just doing your job, you're taking this personally, getting angrier and angrier at them for lying to you, becoming so goddamn screaming mad that your partner has to hold you back. I used to be good at it, really good.

And I figured Jo-Jo would be scared seeing me there on her doorstep, especially after Captain Land had guaranteed her that I wouldn't bother her anymore – yet there I would stand, a betrayed man about to launch his rage at her. Yeah, I figured I knew exactly how this little scene was going to play.

But I figured wrong. When Jo-Jo opened the door, she looked at me with nothing more than disappointment in her eyes – as if she was expecting someone else.

It was funny. There I stood pumped up and ready to launch, while Jo-Jo just shrugged – as if I were an old boyfriend who kept showing up at all the wrong times, some guy named Ralph who spent too much time talking about his mother. She simply walked away, leaving the door open for me to follow her in.

As I trailed her through the big apartment, I was surprised to see that Jo-Jo owned such a classy place, that it was furnished so expensively, tall cylindrical silver vases sporting tasteful arrangements of cut flowers, Georgia O'Keeffe prints in chrome frames on the walls. I don't know, I was expecting maybe she would live in a cramped and fussy apartment with a lot of cats and books. I'd pegged her wrong several different ways.

When we finally got to the bedroom (Jo-Jo leading, me following), she immediately began working on the several suitcases that were open on her bed, clothes all over the place. Since I'd lost my anger, I decided to see if I could at least make her snort. 'Going somewhere?'

Nothing. Jo-Jo was acting like someone who'd just returned from the doctor's office with all the bad news on her charts. I sat in a chair and watched her throwing clothes into one suitcase and taking them out of another. 'Why'd you do it?' I finally asked.

She stopped fooling with the suitcases long enough to glance at me – as if *I* were the one who had disappointed *her*. Then she went over to find a Kleenex and blow her nose.

When I repeated my question, Jo-Jo sat on the bed and worked on her reddened nose with a wad of blue tissue. 'You're mad at me,' she said. It was a statement.

'I got suspended because of you.'

She was quiet for a long time and then said, 'Mary is planning to talk to your Captain Land on Monday, smooth everything over, get you off the hook.'

'What does Mary have to do with this?'

'Are you going to rough me up?'

I laughed. What made the whole thing even crazier was the hopeful look in her eye.

'Mary wanted you out of the way,' Jo-Jo said.

'Why?'

'Did you tell Captain Land about the money?'

'No.'

Jo-Jo was blowing her nose again, nodding her head. 'Mary knew you wouldn't. I kept saying that when you told Captain Land about the money, then Land would be after me, wanting to know why I didn't mention it when I filed those complaints against you. But Mary, she's an expert – she knew you wouldn't tell him about the money.'

'Yeah, well, you warned me about her. But *you*. I thought you and I were working the same side of the street, Jo-Jo. I knew all along that Mary was lying to me about something, but what the hell are *you* up to?'

'I know. I'm the one who convinced you to pursue this case, and now I've arranged to have you taken off it – you have every right in the world to be angry with me.'

I asked what the hell had happened to her today.

'Things. Lapses in judgment, being too emotional after too many years of holding everything in. Wanting too much and then hurting too much when I didn't get it. I don't think I can explain—'

I stood and kicked over a small table. 'I'm in no mood for rambling conversations, goddamn it! I'm looking at mandatory retirement on half-benefits because of you, so don't give me any shit about how hard it is for you to explain. I want answers. I want to know who's coming by tomorrow to collect that money from Mary. What does it have to do with Jonathan's death? And how in the hell did she get to you?' I went over to the bed and took her by the arm. 'Come on now, don't fuck with me.'

I guess she knew it was a performance, kicking over that table and then grabbing her, because Jo-Jo looked up at me as if she felt sorry for the both of us. Her unforgivably plain face and that big nose appeared all the worse for the crying she'd been doing.

'Someone from Jonathan's past wants that money and Mary is going to pay him off to avoid publicity, avoid ruining Jonathan's name. She wants you out of the way because she's afraid you'll mess up the payoff tomorrow, she said you weren't as "pliable" as your partner. This person from Jonathan's past, he's going to leave the country as soon as he gets the money, so by Monday it'll all be over. I agreed to help.'

'By filing those charges against me.'

'Yes.'

'Smear me to keep Jonathan's name clean, huh?'

'Yes.' Then she caught herself. 'Well, that was part of it. I saw

165

no reason to push Jonathan's reputation any deeper in the mud but mainly, I guess, the primary reason I filed those charges against you was to help Mary.'

'I thought you hated her.'

'I did.'

I returned to the chair and sat there rubbing my face. 'How long are we going to keep dancing like this? Come on, Jo-Jo, tell me something I can understand. I thought you were so no-nonsense, so businesslike – tell me what's going on, please.'

'Did you know that I was present when Jonathan fell in love with her, that I actually saw it happen?'

Groaning, I covered my face with both hands, too tired for this shit.

'Mary had been working in our office for a few months when somehow she organized a birthday dinner for Jonathan. Normally he didn't go for that sort of thing, parties and office celebration, anything that distracted people from their work. You think *I'm* businesslike? You should've known Jonathan.'

'I'm beginning to feel like we were fishing buddies.'

'But somehow she got him to agree to this dinner at a restaurant after work, seven of us, Jonathan and me, two of the vice presidents who had their wives come in from the suburbs, and Mary there by herself, unescorted – a clever bit of business, that. It was all very irregular, a *secretary* arranging a party for the company's owner and then inviting herself, but that was Mary, always getting her way.

'The rest of us, the three couples – if you include Jonathan and me, if you could have called us a couple – we ordered our meals very carefully. The two vice presidents were Jonathan's age or older, their wives a couple of those anorexic, birdy women with leathery skin from too much tennis, too many vacations in Bermuda, devoting their lives to staying thin and spending money. They ordered salads with no dressing, no butter on their vegetables, Perrier to drink, nothing for dessert, and then afterward they wouldn't even have coffee or tea, just hot water in a cup, good for their digestion they said, sitting there with these strained smiles on their faces, sipping hot water.'

'This is all very fascinating, the eating habits of corporate wives, but—'

'Oh, the men ate the same way, poached fish with no sauce, ordering these tiny portions, worrying about their hearts and their cholesterol, their salt intake, drinking a little white wine with the meal but no hard liquor, decaffeinated coffee afterward.

'The six of us, we were *careful* people, picking at the food as if it were slightly poisonous, as if we were too delicate for real food, invalids afraid of living too hard because, well, for the men at least, they were at that age when some of their friends had already had heart attacks, and they were becoming afraid that something inside of them might break, treading lightly – afraid of dying, you know?'

'Yeah.'

'But Mary!' Jo-Jo smiled. 'My God, she ordered half the menu, crab meat in a thick cream sauce, a big steak, rare, of course, baked potato with butter *and* sour cream, the rest of us flabbergasted by all the food she ordered, rich and spicy food – drinking martinis before the entrees arrived, silver bullets she called them, and you could see the men practically drooling, because of course they *used* to drink martinis. She drank beer with her steak, right out of the bottle, greasy fingers and all.

'She ate like it was a privilege to be hungry, and Jonathan watched her the way some man watches a waif he's taken off the streets and treated to a meal. You know, the satisfaction that comes from seeing a person really enjoy something, not just the food but the way Mary was enjoying *life*.

'It was a spectacular performance on her part, I can appreciate that now, Mary laughing and eating and smoking, not bothering to ask anyone's permission, did the rest of us mind her smoking, she just went ahead and . . . Like Mary was the only person at that table who was truly, fully alive, do you see what I'm saying?

167

The rest of us were traveling carefully through life, traveling at a safe speed, but Mary was galloping, laughing, damn-the-torpedoes. She wore this low-cut black dress that I guess she brought with her from home, changing at the office before we went to the restaurant. It was *sexy*, no denying that.

'I wear things . . . because my breasts are large, I wear things that downplay their size, and I envied Mary that night, envied not her body as much as how proud she was of it, that she could get away with showing it off like that, dressing sexy but acting so innocent, screeching and covering her mouth when one of the men said something slightly off color, which absolutely delighted the men, of course. And really frosted the women. All three of us, not just the two wives, but me, too. We thought she was common and silly. But when I watched the men's faces watching Mary . . .

'Not that they were lusting for her, although I'm sure a kind of secret lust was part of it, but mainly they looked *wistful*. They were intrigued by the way she ate and talked, her laughter and how she made her eyes go so big in surprise, how she could develop this type of rapt interest, like putting a wonderful mask on her face when one of the men was talking. Maybe they were remembering when they could eat the way Mary did, remembering when their wives looked at them with that kind of interest on *their* faces – back when their wives laughed at their jokes. Mary represented the time . . . for the men, she *was* that time in their own lives when they were tough, more than tough – back when they were invincible, when they could drink martinis and eat steaks and never think about dying.

'The way Jonathan made love to me that night, I knew Mary was on his mind. Of course it hurt, knowing right then that it was Mary he wanted, needing that life force of hers, wanting it injected into his own life like some kind of serum, I could have told you right then, that night, the way he made love to me, trying to prove something – not to me but to himself. I knew what was going to happen.'

She put a hand across her forehead – the way you check a child for fever. 'And I was right, of course. He didn't "come to his senses" the way I hoped he would. They eloped and Mary made him happy.'

Made him happy until this past Monday morning, I thought.

'After the funeral today, we went back to her house from the cemetery, just the two of us. It was flattering, in a way.

'She said she knew about the affair Jonathan and I had before he married her. I told her it ended when they got married and she said she knew that, too. Mary was very complimentary to me, saying some very sweet things, how she envied the way Jonathan admired me, admired my tact, or at least my discretion. She said no one in the world would miss him as much as she and I would, and that was the truth of course. The two of us on her couch, both of us crying, holding each other. She . . . Mary kissed me.'

When I caught her eye, Jo-Jo nodded. 'On the neck. She began kissing me on the neck. I was so startled, I didn't know what to do, and then I had my hand on the back of her head, touching her hair. Mary's a beautiful woman.

'Mary said she read in a magazine once that some women become sexually aroused after a funeral because sex is a way of affirming life and that's what they need to do after burying someone, affirm life. I told her it was odd, both of us Jonathan's lovers, both of us sitting there knowing what Jonathan did in bed, the things he enjoyed doing and enjoyed having done to him. He was dead but *we* were together, and although he would never touch either one of us again, we *both* knew what his touch felt like, Mary asking me if I remembered, if I remembered how it felt making love to Jonathan.'

Her eyes lost their focus.

'Of course I remembered, remembered everything, the way he would suck my nipples, slipping his fingers into his mouth while he was sucking, and then I could feel his tongue and his teeth and his fingers all at the same time, everything working on my nipples like that. I used to close my eyes and imagine . . .'

169

She started to raise a hand to her breast but then stopped halfway there and allowed the hand to fall back to her lap. Jo-Jo looked at me.

'I can't believe I'm telling you this. I have no discretion left, none. Mary told me I had wonderful breasts but she's the one with . . . She told me . . .

'Mary began unbuttoning her dress and I put my hand . . . It was very arousing, and at the time . . . She asked me to do it the way Jonathan did.

'I guess because of all the emotion of Jonathan's funeral, everything that's happened this week, I'd barely stopped crying when all this began to happen, and my entire face was still wet, makeup a mess, and when she put her breasts against my face, or I put my face against her breasts, I'm not sure now how it happened, but I was suddenly down there, in her open dress, Mary holding the back of my head, my tears making her nipples wet before I even touched them with my mouth, Mary asking me to suck her the way Jonathan used to do it, and it sounds so weird to be saying it now, telling you, but at the time it didn't seem like we were doing anything perverted, Mary was pulling the top of her dress down and I was unbuttoning my own blouse – and then suddenly it didn't have anything to do with Jonathan, just Mary and me. I think she's wanted me all along.'

When I came over to sit by her on the bed, Jo-Jo quickly got up and moved away. She kept her back to me. 'You think it's impossible for so much to happen in the space of one afternoon. For me to go from hating Mary and wanting to prove she was somehow responsible for Jonathan's death and then end up betraying you to help her out, but you'd understand if . . .' Jo-Jo turned around. 'Teddy, if Mary ever concentrated her attention on you the way she did on me this afternoon, you'd understand. She makes you feel like you're special, she says things, you forget about everything else because she touches you like you were made out of gold, like she can't believe *her* good fortune, that

170

she's the lucky one to be with you. If that ever happens to you, then you'll know what I'm talking about.'

I told her it would never happen because Mary was too frightened of me.

'Frightened?'

'She knows I can't be lied to, that's my talent, Jo-Jo, and Mary realizes it makes me dangerous to her, which is why she used you to get me out of the way.'

'Used me,' she said, pondering its truth.

'Well—'

'Yes, used me. But not you, huh?'

I was becoming weary all over again, wanting my answers without listening to any more monologues. 'Who's Mary paying off tomorrow?'

'Maybe you're right, maybe she is scared of you. After she told me the whole story, she said you were the only one who could mess things up, and she was thinking of filing a complaint against you herself, for coming to her house and questioning her again, but she was afraid of alerting Captain Land, making him curious about what you were investigating. So I volunteered . . . there's the thing, Teddy. I *volunteered* to betray you, saying I could file a sexual harassment complaint and use that message you left on my answering machine as evidence.'

'I know all that, Jo-Jo. What I'm trying to find out now is who the guy is – who's Mary paying off?'

'After I'd written my statement to Captain Land and was getting ready to leave Mary's house so I could come back and get the tape from my machine, I told Mary that I'd like to have dinner with her, that after dropping everything off with Captain Land, I could return to her house and we could spend the afternoon together, make dinner together. Maybe I'd put a few things in a bag and spend the weekend with her, just so she wouldn't have to go through with the payoff alone.'

'And?'

'She said she needed to be alone and maybe we could have lunch next week. Lunch! What does that sound like to you?'

171

I told her I didn't know.

'Sounds like a man, what a man says after he's taken you to bed but doesn't want to see you again. We'll have lunch. Because lunch is safe. I saw it in her eyes – a brush-off.'

Jo-Jo returned to the bed, bending over near where I was sitting. She took some clothes out of a suitcase, speaking to me in a soft voice, as if whispering a secret she didn't want anyone else to hear. 'Jonathan was married before.'

'He was?'

'Yes, and he had two kids.'

'You should've told me yesterday.'

'I didn't know! In fact, I'm not supposed to be telling you now. Mary made me promise not to say anything about it, but I'm no longer discreet, am I? I'm like the good little girl who suddenly decides to go down for anybody and everybody. Who's next? I don't care anymore.' Jo-Jo left the bed to get another tissue.

'What does Jonathan's first marriage have to do with the money?'

'All those years with him and I never knew he was married, which just goes to show you exactly how stupid I really have been.'

'*Jo-Jo.*'

'He got married when he was nineteen and then six years later his wife took off with the kids and just disappeared. Funny, huh?'

'Funny?'

'Jonathan being such a womanizer when he was young. That's why his wife left him. It's funny because when I met him, when I began working for him, he didn't date or go out with women at all – which is why there were those rumors about Jonathan being queer. What I didn't know was that he was trying to swear off women, like an alcoholic taking the pledge, Jonathan needing to keep away from women so he wouldn't mess up his life again. And I helped him stay on the wagon, isn't that funny?'

'You didn't know about Jonathan's first marriage, but Mary did?'

'Yes. Jonathan used to live in California. His daughter was five when the wife left Jonathan; his son was a year younger. After a while, Jonathan finally gave up looking for them and came east, starting his construction business. I assume he eventually got a divorce from his first wife, I don't know how that all worked, but it was his son who showed up last Sunday night. Philip.'

'*His son?*'

'Yes.'

'And it's the son who's getting the payoff?'

'Yes. Mary says he's crazy. He's been in prison.'

'In California?'

'I guess.'

'Why was he asking for such an odd amount of money?'

'He told Jonathan that he wanted a hundred dollars a week for every week of every year that Jonathan was "missing" from his family in California – twenty-eight years of abandonment, from when the boy was four until now, age thirty-two. At a hundred dollars a week, that comes to one hundred forty-five thousand, six hundred dollars.'

'I'll be damned.'

'He told Jonathan and Mary that he's going to take the money and go to Mexico – which is exactly what Mary wants him to do. Leave the country, avoid more scandal. I agree with that part of it. I don't see why any of this has to be publicized.'

'And this long-lost son, Philip, he's the one who tied up Jonathan and put those bruises on him?'

'Yes. Mary said he's a real nut case. He accused Jonathan of being responsible for everything bad that happened to him and his sister and mother, telling Jonathan that the sister, Jonathan's daughter, died of a drug overdose when she was still a teenager – and I guess that's what broke Jonathan's heart. For the first time since it happened, I understand, now I understand why Jonathan killed himself – having his past thrown in his face like that.'

But it still didn't make sense to me. 'Why was he blaming himself? It was the wife who took off with the kids.'

'Because it was Jonathan's screwing around that forced the

wife to leave. Then, a lifetime later, Sunday night, Jonathan finds out that his son is a crazy ex-convict and his daughter died a junkie.'

We sat a while in silence, me on the bed and Jo-Jo in a chair, holding a tissue to her face. Then she said it was all up to me now, how this thing was going to end. 'You can be at Mary's house tomorrow when Philip comes for his money and you can arrest him for whatever it is he's done wrong, assaulting Jonathan that night, I suppose. But you can't get him for extortion, because Jonathan willingly arranged for that money to be given to his son, figured he deserved it.'

But I still wasn't buying it. Even if she was desperate to save Jonathan's reputation, Mary wouldn't have lied to us *and* seduced Jo-Jo to bring her in on the conspiracy *and* endangered herself by agreeing to face Jonathan's crazy son alone tomorrow. Those are the kinds of things you might do to save your husband's life but not his reputation. Those are the kinds of things you do to save your own ass.

'Jo-Jo. Twenty-eight years of abandonment you said and the boy was four back then, the daughter five – right?'

She nodded.

'And Mary is how old?'

'She was twenty when she joined the firm, she married Jonathan a year later and they were married seven years.'

'Twenty-eight. OK, that makes her four years younger than the son and five years younger than the daughter.'

'So?'

'So she could've known one of them in California. Maybe she had something on Jonathan all along, which means that if the son goes public, not only does Jonathan's reputation get smeared, but Mary finds *herself* in trouble, too.'

'Mary didn't say anything about knowing the son.'

'And you believe her?'

'Yes. But of course I don't have your talent for not being lied to, do I?'

174

I didn't say anything.

'So why don't you arrest Mary, too? And then, of course, you can arrest me for filing false complaints against you. Hell, Teddy, you can put us all in jail – but that doesn't change anything. Jonathan *did* commit suicide and the money is a legitimate gift or payment, whatever you call it. A lot of wrong things have been done and maybe some laws broken, too, but no one's been murdered.'

But of course I knew different. I asked Jo-Jo if Mary had told her anything about the knife.

'The knife Jonathan used on himself?'

'Yeah.'

'No – why?'

'Did the son bring the knife with him?'

'Mary didn't say.'

'Could it have been Jonathan's knife?'

'I have no idea.'

'Mary told us that Jonathan collected knives, that the Bowie knife he used to commit suicide could have been from his collection.'

'I have no idea.'

'You don't know anything about a knife collection?'

'Before today, I considered myself an expert on Jonathan Gaetan, and I could have told you with absolute authority that he never collected anything except gold coins – but now I'm not sure of myself. I didn't know he was married before, so, sure, maybe he collected knives and maybe he was bald and wore a toupee, I'm no longer an expert on that man.'

'Coins?'

'Yes, Mexican gold pieces.'

'He kept them at his house?'

'Yes. Jonathan was like a little boy with those coins, always telling me about the latest one he'd acquired, how much he paid for it, how much it would be worth in ten years. He said he was a fool for not keeping them in a safety deposit box, but he couldn't

175

deny himself the pleasure of taking them out whenever he wanted to, looking at them and—'

'Did he give them to his son?'

'I can't imagine Jonathan giving those coins to anyone, but maybe he did. Mary didn't mention anything about that, why?'

I shook my head. 'Did Mary say she knew where Philip was staying?'

'No.'

'Are you sure? This is important.'

'Positive. He called her once. He didn't even know that Jonathan had killed himself, and Mary had to tell him that it would take an extra couple of days for her to get the money together. She said he went crazy when he heard he'd have to wait until Friday for his money.'

I got off the bed and went over to stand near her. 'Jo-Jo, did it ever occur to you that one of the reasons Mary is so eager to pay off this son is so he won't get a lawyer and make a claim on Jonathan's estate?'

'No.' She shrugged. 'You're probably right, though. Mary has undoubtedly thought of that angle.'

I walked back to the bed, fingering one of Jo-Jo's suitcases, 'Where're you going?'

She said she didn't know. 'I think I'll just go out to Dulles and get on the next plane that's going somewhere very far away. That's daring of me, isn't it?'

I smiled, trying to keep my voice soft and reassuring. 'You're going to have to stick around, you realize that, don't you, Jo-Jo? You'll have to withdraw your complaint against me, and we're going to need your statement about the rest of this mess, Jonathan's son and all.'

'As soon as you walk out of here, I'm going to Dulles – I give my word on that.'

'I could take you in right now.'

'What you mean is, you could call a policeman who isn't suspended, one who has *not* been given orders by his captain not to contact me, and then *he* could take me in.'

176

She had a point.

'You want my advice, Teddy – do what I'm doing, just walk away from this whole thing. Go back to napping at your desk and let Mary take care of business. She's tough and she's going to get her way in the end, believe me. The best thing you could do is just stay out of her way.'

'I can't do that.'

'I mailed a letter before you got here,' Jo-Jo said. 'To your Captain Land, telling him that my complaints against you were all a big mistake, that I was confused in my grief over Jonathan and that you never made any untoward remarks to me, that your actions were always totally professional, that you should be given an award for dealing so patiently with a hysterical woman like me. Mary promised me, if you were still on the hook come Monday, she promised she would do everything she could to get you off.'

'Promised, huh?'

'You still don't get it, do you, Teddy?'

'A lot of people have been asking me that lately.'

'People like Jonathan and Mary, people who are tough inside and have all that money, they do things like this all the time, paying to keep their old mistakes secret. Come on, you know how that works.'

'Maybe not this time.'

She snorted. 'Well, the fact of the matter is I don't care. I don't care what happens to Mary or to Jonathan's son or to you. I'm going to get on that airplane and make fucking arrangements with the first person who gives me the eye.'

'I'm sorry you feel—'

'I'm sorry, too!' She began crying again. 'And you're going to end up just like me if you don't stay away from that woman.'

'I have to find out what's going on.'

She was standing over a suitcase, taking clothes out and then putting other clothes in. 'The only thing I have to find out is who's next in line to fuck me. Beyond that, I *just don't care.*'

'Yeah,' I said, leaving Jo-Jo as I'd found her, packing and unpacking, 'I know the syndrome.'

177

16

Lord Alfred opened the door to his apartment and stood there glaring down at me, his drooping left eye nothing more that a slit. 'You didn't tell Land *nothing!*' he shouted as I tried to get in, Alfred determined not to let me pass. 'Land didn't go to the District to see the homicide people, you lied to me, man – he was off giving a speech to the Elks.'

'Lions,' I corrected him.

'Man, you are messing with homicide investigations in two different jurisdictions, lucky if you don't get charged with obstruction yourself.'

'I need a gun,' I said, squeezing past Alfred. 'You still keeping your arsenal in that chest of drawers?'

Lord Alfred rushed after me, grabbing a shoulder. 'You're crazy! The last thing in the world I'm going to do is arm you. I'm glad Land suspended you. Did you hear me, asshole – I'm glad you don't have a badge or a gun! You're dangerous, man.'

I kept my voice calm. 'I also need to know where those coins were found, the ones Melvin Kelvin was working on.' When I looked down at Alfred's hand and then up at his eyes, he released me. 'Please hurry,' I told him. 'A gun and the name of the place where those coins were found.' He stood there dumbfounded. 'I'm waiting, Alfred.'

'And I'm waiting for you to get down on all fours and start barking like a dog.'

I walked toward the chest of drawers where he keeps his hardware, Alfred trailing behind me and asking, 'Don't you want to

179

hear what Melvin Kelvin and I found out from the computer check?'

'If you hurry. I don't have much time.'

'Jonathan Gaetan was married before and he had two kids.'

'Yeah, I know. A boy and a girl.'

'You knew?'

'Of course. I'm a detective.'

'What's going on, Teddy?'

But I'd already reached the chest, pulling out the bottom drawer and asking Alfred if all the pistols were in working order.

He took me by the arm. 'Jonathan's son has done time. Lots of time. In fact, he just got out a week ago from an eight-year stretch for assault with a deadly weapon.'

I didn't know that, of course, but I couldn't pass up the opportunity to astound Alfred one more time. 'Yeah, he was in prison in California. What else did Melvin Kelvin's magic computers came up with?'

'You're the man with all the answers.'

I shrugged, bending down to select a weapon.

'OK,' Alfred said, 'stop me if you've heard this before. The son – he goes by Philip Jameson – has been in and out of prisons most of his life. This last stretch was for assaulting a woman in her house trailer, threatening to slice her tits off with a butcher knife. That alone makes him a good bet for the Lipstick Murders.'

I stood. 'Now here's what I found out. The young Jonathan Gaetan, when he was married and living in California, was screwing everything that wasn't tied down at both ends, which is why his first wife took off with the two kids, Jonathan never seeing either of them again until Sunday night when the son, Philip, shows up asking daddy for a hundred dollars a week for every week that daddy had been missing from Philip's life, twenty-eight years worth.'

'I suppose that adds up to the hundred and forty-five—'

'Yeah. Mary's going through with the payoff tomorrow

180

morning at ten. Jo-Jo agrees with Mary's thinking. Jo-Jo filed that sex complaint to keep me out of the way, so I wouldn't interfere with the payoff. Apparently neither one of them has connected Jonathan's crazy son with the Lipstick Murders, they're just trying to keep the Jonathan Gaetan shrine as untarnished as they can. Now do you know where those lost coins were found or not?'

'Hold on a second.'

'I don't have a second!'

'Then fuck you, I ain't telling you nothing about the coins.'

I bent to the lower drawer again and picked out something big, an Army Colt in a shoulder holster – something that would stop a man with one shot. Then I decided I'd better have a back-up, too, choosing for that purpose a little silver .38 in an ankle holster.

While I was strapping everything on, Alfred asked, 'How did Mary plan to get *me* out of the way? Didn't she know I was working with you, wasn't she afraid *I'd* mess up the payoff?'

'I think the operable word was *pliable*,' I said. 'If you showed up, Mary figured she could sweet talk you into staying out of the way.'

He responded to this insult with what he was hoping would be a little bomb of his own. 'Melvin Kelvin's over at Captain Land's house right now, showing him the computer readouts and convincing him we got a line on the Lipstick Murders.'

I shrugged. 'I'm asking you one last time. Do you know where those gold coins were found?'

'Hey, numbnuts, we worked on that computer for *hours*, because *you* asked us to, remember? You have any idea the trouble it is, checking records that go back twenty or thirty years? From Jonathan's Social Security number we found out that he was married before and from those records we found his first wife's Social Security number, then—'

I stared at him as blankly as I could.

'OK, you're not interested, fine. But you ain't going no place, especially with my pistols, unless you tell me what you're up to. The way we figure it, Philip somehow learned that Jonathan was his father. Maybe his mother told him. Melvin Kelvin found only one record of Philip's mother visiting her son in prison, on Philip's twenty-fifth birthday, but regardless of how he found out, as soon as he is released from prison, he hightails it here, somehow gets distracted by that runaway and kills her, shows up at Jonathan's house and kills him, and then while he's waiting for his money, bored I guess, he kills that hooker in the District. Is that the way you're figuring it?'

'Close. I still think Jonathan committed suicide. He *voluntarily* arranged for that money to be handed over to Philip and then killed himself because Philip told him that the daughter had died of a drug overdose while she was still a teenager, which really put Jonathan over the edge.'

'Makes sense. The daughter, Nancy, had a juvenile record, but Melvin Kelvin couldn't get access to it. He did find out, though, that the state paid her hospital bills for a live birth. No father listed. She gave the kid up for adoption. After that, the daughter, Nancy, just dropped out of sight, nothing more on the computer.'

'I have to go *right now*, I'm stopping by the department to look at that lost-and-found file myself, since you won't tell me who turned in those coins.'

'What is it with the coins?'

'Jo-Jo said that, to her knowledge, Jonathan didn't collect knives, but he did collect gold coins.'

Lord Alfred's good eye suddenly opened wide. 'And Philip took the coins and then somehow lost them!'

I was nodding.

'Why didn't you tell me that in the first place? Two kids found the coins. Tourists. The family is staying at the Common-Wealth motel off Sixty-Six.'

'Which is where the coins were found?'

'You think Philip's staying there, too?'

182

'A good place to start looking.'

'I'm going with you.'

'You armed?'

'Does a fat baby fart?'

On the way to Alfred's car, I asked why he and Melvin Kelvin ran a computer search on Jonathan when it was Mary whose background I wanted checked out.

' 'Cause we couldn't find anything interesting on her, that's why. She graduated high school in a little place outside San Francisco, went to junior college for a couple of years, secretarial school for six months, and then came out here and got a job with Jonathan's company. No priors, no previous marriages, no nothing.'

'What was her maiden name again?'

'Wilson. Her records are clean, man, it's Jonathan with all the secrets.'

'Hmm.'

'Hmm *what?*'

'The daughter's dead but maybe Mary doesn't want to share Jonathan's estate with a son or with a previous wife who never got a settlement, so she lies to us and plans to go through with the payoff because it's a hell of a lot cheaper than some big legal battle over what Jonathan might owe to his other family.'

'None of which makes much difference now, does it?'

I had to agree.

As soon as we got into Alfred's car, he called the department and asked for backup to meet us at the motel. He also requested that a message be put through to Captain Land's house, telling Land and Melvin Kelvin that we were heading for the Common-Wealth motel off Highway Sixty-Six and had reason to believe that Philip Jameson might be staying there. Then Alfred pointed out to me that we were only five minutes from the motel and would arrive well before anyone else.

'So?'

'So are you sure you're up to this?'

'I'm fine, I'm fine, let's go.'

Although the engine caught on the first hit, Alfred turned the ignition a second time, grinding the starter and cursing. When I asked him how *he* was, he replied, 'I'm fine, I'm fine.'

Sixty seconds later, racing through residential streets, I admitted I was scared, not so much about confronting this Philip as about the consequences of having totally fucked up the entire investigation. Maybe if I'd gone to Land with Jo-Jo Creek's information as soon as she told me, someone could've made the connection to Philip *before* he killed that prostitute. 'Scares me shitless to mess up as bad as I have.'

Alfred didn't argue the point.

17

Billy is *trying* to be brave.

He remembers last summer when he was very brave, his moment of glory, actually, and how proud his father was of him then; right now, Billy is trying hard to keep this former triumph in mind, because he needs to be brave, sitting as he is, naked on a crazy man's bed.

Last summer, Billy and his friend Jimmy were riding double on Jimmy's two-wheeler, going too fast downhill when they crashed into a doghouse with a tin roof of all things, both boys hitting hard and getting bad cuts, Billy a gash on his knee and Jimmy's forearm laid open. It was a Saturday, both of their fathers home, so the two men carried their sons into Billy's father's car and drove off in a hurry to the emergency room.

When they got there, Jimmy's father warned him not to make a big fuss in front of everyone, but Jimmy began crying when he saw the needles and then became so hysterical, squirming away from the doctor, that three men had to hold him down before his arm could be sewed up. Jimmy's father hollered at him the whole time, 'Come on don't be such a goddamn little sissy!' But that just made things worse.

Billy was next. All his father said to him, in a quiet voice, was, 'Try to be brave, son.' And he tried – and he was. Very brave. It hurt something terrible, that first needle going in to deaden the nerves around the cut so that Billy wouldn't feel the other needle, the one that would stitch his knee closed. But he *did* feel that second needle, and it hurt, too, Billy *willing* himself to sit there

185

on the table and not cry, and the more it hurt, the harder he squeezed his father's hand. Some tears ran down his cheek but he didn't cry out loud, not once.

While they were all in the emergency room, Billy's father didn't comment on his son's bravery, because he didn't want to make Jimmy or his dad feel bad, but when they got home, Billy's father crowed to his wife and daughter how Billy had sat there so bravely, not crying, taking all twelve stitches without a whimper, he couldn't stop talking about how brave Billy had been, not a sound. When Billy's father picked him up and said, 'I'm proud of you, son,' he had tears in his eyes. It was the first time Billy had ever seen that.

Now, naked and sitting on a filthy bed, his sister next to him, naked too, an absolutely crazy man stumbling back and forth in front of them, rambling on about things neither of the children understands, *now*, even though this is a thousand times worse than getting your knee stitched up, now Billy is *trying* to be brave because he wants his father to find him being brave – and Billy is sure that, any moment now, his dad is going to be kicking down that door, rushing in here to save them from this horrible man. His dad can do anything. His dad is brave; he knows everything.

Except he was wrong about the monsters. It happened a few months ago: Billy had these awful nightmares about monsters coming into his room, manlike monsters with canine teeth sticking out of their mouths, terrible dreams that made Billy scream in his sleep, his dad rushing into his room to hold him and tell Billy that there are no monsters. 'The things that hurt you in life,' his father explained, 'are accidents – like when you hurt your knee – and sickness and sometimes even the people you love can hurt you, when your friends at school say mean things or when people who are close to you die, like when Grandma died at Christmas, remember? So I'm not saying you're not going to get hurt in life, but I guarantee you one thing, son – there are no monsters.'

But there are! Billy and Penny are in a room with one, a

monster who is wearing a blond wig, who is filthy, and he's got blood all over him. He's holding this little knife with a triangular blade that he keeps waving in Billy's face, threatening to cut him up in a dozen different pieces. He smells awful, especially when he gets close, and the entire room stinks of something more terrible than sweat. But worst of all, this monster has made Billy and Penny take off their clothes. Billy has heard about this sort of thing – that Den Leader in their hometown who got arrested because he was giving Cub Scouts dollar bills to pull down their pants so he could take pictures. Billy and his sister have been carefully instructed not to let anyone, except for the doctor, touch or look at their private parts – but what do you do when a monster grabs you and pulls you by the arm to his room and threatens to cut you open unless you take off your clothes and sit there naked on his filthy bed so he can look at you? Billy knows it is wrong, but he had no choice. Penny is crying and holding tightly to her brother's arm. 'Billy,' she keeps saying in a soft and frightened voice.

The monster's eyes are red, his mouth and tongue are performing strange antics, the mouth occasionally opening and stretching as if he's doing some kind of bizarre exercise, his tongue rolling around the insides of his lips, making them bulge out. He's talking, but the only word Billy recognizes is *Mexico*. Sometimes, when the monster grins, not a smile but more like a grimace, Billy can see that his front teeth are cracked off and brown.

The most terrible thing he does, however, is sob, an awful honking sound that makes Billy shiver.

He worries about where all the blood came from, blood on this guy's pants and jacket, Billy worrying that this monster has had other kids up in his room, cutting them into parts just like he said, getting *their* blood on his clothing and then burying their bodies before going out to search for new kids to butcher. Billy and Penny are next! *Where's Dad?* If it weren't for his trying so hard to be brave, Billy would screaming for his father right now.

The monster stops pacing in front of them. His lower jaw moves rapidly back and forth, tongue darting in and out, and he is not looking *at* Penny and Billy as much as he's looking *through* them. 'You kids like shiny coins, huh?' Then he sobs and sobs, as if suddenly overwhelmed by despair.

Billy and Penny glance at each other with eyes nearly as large as the coins they found – because now they get it. For the first time since this man grabbed them, *now* Billy and Penny understand why. He's mad at them for taking his coins. He lost them and he thinks Billy and Penny stole them. Billy allows himself a measure of hope, now that something makes sense, and he ventures to speak.

'We gave all the coins to the police,' he says, his mouth very dry and his voice coming out in breathy trembles.

The monster kneels in front of Billy, who keeps both hands cupped over his genitals.

'Swear to God, mister, we didn't steal any of your money.'

'Don't swear to God in front of me, you little fuck.'

Billy swallows hard. 'All you got to do is go to the police and ask for them back.'

'The police!' He sobs.

'Really,' Billy insists, working this angle as earnestly as he possibly can. 'The policeman told us that when the owner shows up, he gets all the coins returned to him. We didn't steal them, we just *found* them.'

Penny whispers something to Billy about giving up their 'award.' She holds her brother's arm with one hand, keeping her other hand firmly between her legs.

'The policeman said we might get a *reward* from the owner,' Billy explains, 'but we don't want anything, really, you can just have all your coins and let us go, OK?'

Philip looks through them for a long time, his eyes dimly lit, his mouth hanging open. Then his attention abruptly returns and he tells the children that he *wanted* them to find the coins. 'I knew you were a couple of greedy little fucks, but I don't care because I got what I want.' He leans close to Penny, touching her knee with one finger.

'*Billy,*' she begs, as if he can do something about that finger on her knee.

When Philip tries to stand upright, his right leg gives way and he crashes backward, sprawling on the floor, cursing, his knife slashing the air. Billy glances toward the door. Did the monster lock it when they came in? Billy doesn't remember. Can they make it? If he grabs Penny's hand and rushes toward the door, can they reach it before he reaches them, can they get the door open and run down the hall before he . . .

But Philip has already turned over, on his hands and knees and then grabbing on to a chair to pull himself up, standing, wheeling around to see their reaction to his fall, staring, sweating, his face red with rage. Being naked in front of this man is worse than having ten thousand stitches in your knee.

He comes to the bed and sits next to Penny – Penny between the monster and her brother – and when the man touches her bare shoulder, Penny again speaks her brother's name in that pleading voice, '*Billy.*'

The man takes something from his pocket as he strokes the girl's hair. 'Bringing you to Mexico with me,' he mutters, more to himself than to Penny. 'My little virgin bride, living with me in Mexico.' He plays with her hair, stringing it among his fingers. 'You'd like that, wouldn't you, being my little princess in Mexico, hun?'

That's what her father sometimes calls Penny, 'my little princess.' She turns her back on the monster and desperately asks Billy, 'Where's Dad?'

'You think your daddy's going to save you?' That crazy tongue darts in and out to wet cracked lips. 'I hope he does. I hope to fuck he tries it, 'cause I'll gut him as soon as he walks in and then we'll see what kind of hero Daddy is, when he's stumbling around the room tripping over his guts.'

Sobbing, the monster grabs Penny's hair and pulls her head

189

back, exposing her terrified face, and with the lipstick he's taken from his pocket, he smears her mouth a garish red. Penny is crying, hysterical.

Then the monster pushes Penny back on the bed; she manages to keep one hand on her brother, one hand still between her legs. Billy watches open-mouthed as the monster draws lipstick lines radiating from Penny's horrified eyes, putting circles of red on her cheeks, and now Billy realizes that the man's sobbing is actually some kind of terrible laughter.

Penny struggles upright, holding on to her brother with both hands now.

'My little doll-girl,' Philip says dreamily, petting her. 'My little Mexican doll-girl.'

With some effort, he gets off the bed. 'Not much time,' he says as he stands in front of them. 'Dark out now.' His mouth opens and closes, opens and closes. 'Go get the money and then you and me leave for Mexico.' He touches Penny's thigh and asks her, 'Want to see how pretty you are?'

She shakes her head and tucks herself even closer to Billy, some of the lipstick from her face rubbing off on her brother's arm.

The man stands with his hands to his temples, muttering about how much it hurts, and although Billy distinctly hears the word, 'hurts', he can't figure out whose pain the man is referring to.

Philip pulls off the wig and throws it across the room, scratching his head with both hands. He lurches to the little refrigerator, opens it, looks inside for a long time, and then slams the door so hard that it bounces back without latching; he leaves it open. 'Nothing cold to drink,' he says in a sad voice. 'In this fucking heat and not a goddamn . . . Mexico, in Mexico there's always a breeze off the ocean.' He hurries, stumbling over to Penny. 'You do want to go to Mexico with me, don't you, little doll-girl?' And he really is pleading with her.

But Penny shakes her head against Billy's arm.

'How about if I paint your face some more, huh?' he asks,

waving the lipstick by her eyes as if it were a weapon, weaving as if he were drunk, sobbing softly to himself as he begins to draw lines on her cheeks.

She is still shaking her head against Billy's arm, whispering, 'No, no.'

Philip pulls her away from her brother and shoves her back on the bed, both of Penny's hands now instinctively between her legs, the monster grabbing one knee and then pulling on her hands, trying to take them away from that place, kneeling on the floor in front of the bed, moving his head toward her – until Billy screams as loudly as he can: *'Don't!'* And then the nine-year-old boy hits the monster with a clenched fist, the blow bouncing off the side of Philip's head.

He moves back from the bed, looking at Billy as if the boy were a piece of furniture that had suddenly become animate, lashing out at him. But the astonishment passes quickly, Philip grinning his broken teeth. 'You little fuck,' he says, almost happily. 'Wait right there, I got something to show you.' He begins looking around the room, kicking trash out of the way, searching under pizza boxes, sobbing and muttering and cursing.

When Penny says her brother's name now, 'Billy!' she is pleading more for him than for herself, because something terrible must be in store for a boy brave enough to hit a monster.

Unable to find whatever it is he's looking for, Philip stalks back to Billy and slaps the boy's hand, the one that he has over his genitals.

'I got an idea,' Philip says, his face so close to Billy's that the boy feels like gagging, sour stuff rising in his throat. 'How'd you like to grow up dickless, huh?' Then the monster sobs.

Billy is not actually crying – crying is when you make crying *sounds* – but tears are on his face and he is lost in a vast hopelessness. No way is his father going to make it here in time to save him, Billy is convinced of that now.

'You're coming with me.' Philip tells him, pulling on Billy's arm. 'In the bathroom, sucker. I'm going to fix you real good.'

191

Penny holds on to her brother with both hands; she is crying hysterically.

'Hey, little doll-girl, don't cry. I'm taking *you* to Mexico.' Then from his pocket he comes up with a tiny red apple, handing it to her. 'Soap. *Really*. Go on and smell it. Soap,' he says again, as if he is offering her something magic.

When Penny refuses his gift, the monster moves away from the bed grabbing a broken valise and walking around the room stuffing clothes in it, muttering about his money and Mexico, leaving a belt on the floor, picking up a length of rope. He stops to search in the pockets of his field jacket once more, finding some photographs that he studies with a puzzled expression before returning them to the pocket. He looks over at Billy. 'You know what you should be worrying about, kid? Once I get you in that bathroom, you'd better worry about what happens if I get the biting urge.' Again that wretched sobbing laughter.

Philip continues moving around the room, putting things in the battered valise. When he bends over near the TV set, he suddenly shouts. 'Here it is.'

Delighted with himself, he carries it in both hands, this *thing*, which he shoves into Billy's face, the odor worse than the monster's breath – this blackened, rotting, severed hand.

'I cut her hand off,' he whispered to Billy. 'You should've heard her begging me, just like you're going to be begging me when I get you in that bathroom, except begging didn't do her any good – just like it ain't going to do you any good, you little fuck. *I'm going to make you a doll-boy.*'

'Billy! Penny!'

Hope! It is carried into this room – muffled but unmistakable – on the sweet familiarity of a mother's voice.

'Billy! Penny!' Although the room's windows are closed, curtains drawn, there is no denying the names the woman is calling out from the parking lot below.

'Billy! Penny!'

Her voice isn't registering panic, not yet.

The monster hurries to the curtains, peeking out – then turning to grin at the naked children. 'Oh, I've been watching you all right, your happy horseshit family, all that hugging and playing together, I've been watching you all right, but you ain't home yet, kid. Me and you got an appointment in that bathroom there.' The triangular-bladed knife is in his hand again, and he is pointing it toward the green door of the bathroom. 'Come on, *doll-boy*.'

Billy looks toward the bathroom, wondering what's in there – the bodies of the children this monster has already killed? That's where he does it, Billy thinks. He takes them into the bathroom and cuts them up in the tub.

Philip comes to Billy and whispers right into his ear. 'I am the terror.'

He knocks the boy off the bed, flat on the floor, Penny yelling: 'Billy!'

With his heavy motorcycle boot, he shoves Billy toward the green door. 'Get in there, hurry up.' Kicking him hard enough to make Billy stand. 'That's it, dolly-boy, go on in.'

But Billy stops at the door, both hands against the doorjamb, his feet firmly set, turning his terrified face toward his sister. 'Penny! Get dressed, Penny!' he yells, finally really crying because he can't help it, too scared, sorry, Dad, I just couldn't help it.

Penny slips off the bed and quickly begins putting on her clothes, the terror making no effort to stop her. In fact, he tells her, 'That's right, you go on and get dressed for the trip, doll-girl.' Then to Billy: 'Get your ass in there!' He shoves the boy, but Billy holds on.

'Billy! Penny!'

Now the woman's voice sounds frightened.

And Billy sees a chance for his sister, because if he goes into the bathroom with this monster and if whatever torture awaiting him in there takes enough time, then maybe his mom and dad will have become so worried that they'll call the police – and when this man who is the terror hears sirens, he'll run away.

'Penny! Billy!'

Dad! Now *he's* hollering for them, too. It won't be long now.

'Hey, *Billy*,' Philip says, mocking the boy's name, 'I ain't got the time to fuck with you, huh? You either get in that bathroom or I'm slitting your throat and your sister's throat and letting both of you bleed to death on the fucking floor, what do you think of Mommy and Daddy finding you like that, huh?'

Billy knows he has to do it – it's his sister's only chance – and Billy is trying to be brave, but Sweet Suffering Jesus, this boy does *not* want to go into that bathroom with a monster.

The terror pushes the cold, dead flesh of the rotting hand on to the nine-year-old's bare back, making Billy's skin turn instantly into goose-flesh. He is openly crying, he can't help it.

'Billy! Penny! Penny! Billy!'

The boy releases his grip on the doorjamb and takes the first tender step into the unlit bathroom, still *trying* to be brave.

18

Alfred went tearing into the motel's parking lot and nearly ran into the ten people who were milling around one of our department's patrol cars. The two uniformed officers glanced up from their clipboards to give us dirty looks.

'I thought we were going to get here first.'

'I don't see how anyone could've beat us,' Alfred replied.

'Who're the uniforms?'

'A couple of new people. I know their names but I can't—'

'Let's find out what we got.' But I couldn't get the car door open. 'I keep thinking, if he's killed someone else, it's my responsibility.'

Alfred still didn't try to talk me out of it, grabbing my sleeve and saying, 'You just sit there and get a hold on yourself, I'll go see what the skinny is and come right back.'

I nodded and Alfred lumbered over to the group, talking to the two uniformed officers and then returning to me with the most unreassuring expression on his face.

'*What?*' I asked.

'Strange. They don't know anything about Philip Jameson. They were called here ten minutes ago to check out a report of two kids being missing.'

'Kids missing! The same kids who found the coins?'

Alfred immediately returned to the group, talked briefly with the patrolmen again, and then rushed back to me. 'Yeah. It's the same two kids, the ones who found the coins. A Hammermill family from Iowa, that's the parents there giving statements.

195

They were packing their car and the kids were supposed to stay in sight, but when the car was packed, the parents couldn't find either kid. A boy, nine, and a girl, seven. We got their description, what they were wearing and everything. Been missing for about half an hour I guess. Billy and Penny Hammermill.'

My pulse fluttering, I found it difficult to draw a good breath. 'Teddy?'

'OK . . . Uh, let's get everyone off this parking lot. Right now! Back in their rooms. You fill in . . . what are their names?'

'The uniforms? Terry and—'

'Fill them in on what we're up against here, and I'll go around to the office and see if anyone matching Philip's description has checked in during the last week. You kept a copy of the readout?'

Alfred pulled the computer paper from his coat pocket and handed it to me. I hurried around to the motel's office, finding a skinny twenty-year-old with Coke-bottle glasses and bad skin; he was standing by the window watching the action in the parking lot. 'What's going on out there?'

'You the desk clerk?'

'Yeah. Who're you?'

I reached into my coat but then remembered I didn't have a badge to show him. 'I'm looking for someone who might have registered here sometime within the past six days.' I glanced down at the computer readout. 'Male Caucasian. Age thirty-two. Five feet, eleven inches. One hundred and eighty pounds. Brown hair. Gray eyes. Uh, let's see. His front teeth were cracked off.' I looked back at the kid. 'Anyone like that staying here?'

He was unsure he should answer. 'Are you a detective?'

I nodded. 'The guy we're looking for might have had California tags.'

'Could I see a badge?' he asked timidly.

I pulled back my jacket and showed him the big forty-five. 'If you remember anyone matching the description I just read, you better tell me right now, son 'cause I don't have time to dance with you.' A Hollywood stunt, but it got the kid talking.

196

'Room three-three-seven.'

I had to keep my mouth open to get enough air.

He spoke by rote, like a tour guide at the end of a busy week. 'You go around the office here, into the door, turn right, up two flights, halfway down the corridor, the room will be on your right.'

'Only that one door to the room?'

'Yes. It has a balcony that overlooks the parking lot and pool, but you can't get out that way without making a very long jump.'

'A back way?'

'Out of the room?'

'No! You just said there was only one door to the room. Come on, asshole. Is there a back way to the hall that—'

'Yes!' he replied, his voice breaking. 'Follow the sidewalk along the parking lot, past the pool, and then in the double doors at the end of the building. Up two floors, halfway down the corridor, the room will be on your left coming that way.'

'Do you know if he's in, if he's in his room right now?'

The kid shook his head. 'What'd he do?'

'Give me your passkey.'

He handed it over. 'Does this have anything to do with those coins the kids found?'

I left without answering him. Lord Alfred and the two uni-formed patrolmen met me with their pistols already drawn. 'You two get around the back way. Alfred and I will go in the front.' I gave them the layout. 'But if you reach three-three-seven before we do, wait there for us in the hallway. We're going to need that backup.'

Alfred said he'd already called it in again. 'Melvin Kelvin and Land are on their way, too.'

'Let's do it then.'

Alfred and I had just stepped into the front door of the motel building when someone came up behind us, startling me enough that I drew the .45 and stuck it in the guy's face.

Alfred put a hand on my chest. 'It's the kids' father, Mr Hammermill.'

197

He was big, almost Alfred's size. In his late thirties, polyester slacks, Hawaiian shirt, worried eyes. 'What's wrong? I mean, you've all got your guns out. Do you know where my children are?'

I told him he was supposed to wait in his room. 'But don't go back across the parking lot now. Just stay right here.'

'You know something, don't you? Please . . . Don't start shooting if my kids—'

I eased him back against the wall under the stairwell. 'Just stay here and keep your mouth shut. Understand?'

He nodded, the panicked expression on his face firing my own panic.

We rushed up the stairs, my heart squeezing so hard that I felt pain radiating throughout my chest, thinking this would be a hell of a time for a heart attack. On the third floor, I signaled to the two uniforms who were waiting there for us, halfway down the corridor. I had to take a moment to catch my breath.

'Jesus, Teddy, you look like you're going to pass out.'

'I'm OK.'

We walked the corridor and met the other two at the door to room three-three-seven. All of us had our weapons out now.

'I'll kick it.' Alfred said. 'Everyone ready?'

I held up the passkey in my left hand. The other three stood there waiting for me to open the door, but I couldn't make myself move, couldn't figure out the simple logistics of how to use the passkey while holding that .45 . . . Do I put the gun away and unlock the door with my right hand, or will I be able to use the passkey with my left hand? Paralyzed.

'Let's do it, partner,' Alfred said, his voice tender. *'Teddy.'*

'Yeah,' I replied quickly. 'Yeah.' I sensed the three of them getting increasingly nervous, embarrassed for me. I had been holding the passkey by the doorlock for only a few seconds but the delay seemed to stretch out in both directions forever.

'Camel!'

I looked down the corridor to see Captain Harvey Land

striding toward us with great authority, Melvin Kelvin puppy-dogging right behind him.

'Wait right there, Camel.'

With my left hand, I slipped the key into the lock and pushed open the door, rushing in with Alfred and the other two following close on my tail.

The room stank. Looking around at the mess, paper trash on the floor and chairs knocked over, my eyes were searching less for Philip Jameson than for either of those two kids, Billy and Penny.

All six of us were in the room now, Land telling me I'm on suspension until *he* takes me off, and furthermore I'm not authorized to be carrying a—

But I was already opening the door to the bathroom, someone telling me to be careful. I had it half open, standing there in the doorway with the others behind me trying to see what I was seeing.

Someone else asked me what's wrong and Alfred spoke my name. Land told me to get the hell out of the way.

I stepped into the bathroom and shut the door behind me, locking it and going instantly to my knees, putting the .45 on the floor because a gun wasn't going to do me any good against what was wrong in that tiny room.

19

Penny finally makes up her mind; she's not going to think about it.

She is wearing jeans, white tennis shoes without socks, a pink T-shirt with a picture of a unicorn on the front, two blue ribbons that Penny's mother put in her hair, and lipstick that he smeared all over her face. She is in a car with him, this crazy man who is muttering things Penny can't understand as he speeds up and then abruptly touches the brakes to slow the car within the speed limit.

Penny wants to see her mother and father. She wonders what happened to Billy. But this wanting and wondering is too large for her seven-year-old-brain to hold – being kidnapped by a crazy man who put lipstick all over her, watching Billy being led into that bathroom and then the crazy man coming out alone, worrying about what the man is going to do to her, wondering if they're really going all the way to Mexico. That's too far away, her parents will never find her in Mexico. All of this wondering and worrying is too much for Penny, so she sits rigidly quiet in the seat and decides not to think about anything. She doesn't pray or cry or watch out the window, because every last bit of her will is required for this one saving effort: not thinking about it.

Philip is thinking, however. About Mexico. About getting caught. About how nothing ever works out right for him.

It was a simple plan: drive across the country and go directly to Jonathan's house, announce that he was Jonathan's son, tell Jonathan the whole sordid story, especially the part about his daughter, Nancy, being dead, demand the money, go to Mexico, live like a king. A simple plan. Except that hitchhiker in Maryland laughed at him, Jonathan got killed, the money wasn't ready in time . . . he curses and jams his foot on the accelerator until he remembers that he doesn't want to be picked up for speeding, so he presses the brake and slows the car to fifty, thinking about how everything has gone wrong for him once again.

Still, he could've gotten away with it. That hitchhiker and then that whore in Washington, neither of those killings put him in any immediate danger of getting caught, Philip is convinced of it. No witnesses. Those two black kids in the alley, they didn't see him get into his car. No way to trace him. The cops didn't know where he was staying. Mary had no reason to turn him in because he didn't kill Jonathan, he's almost sure of it.

No, even with everything that'd gone wrong with his original plan, he might still have ended up living like a king in Mexico – until what happened tonight.

Those damn kids and their happy little family, they're the ones to blame. The cops will be called in to look for the little bastards and eventually his room at the motel will be searched and they'll find the boy – and then they'll know. Put out a bulletin for this car Philip is driving. Pull him over and even if he uses the girl as a hostage, how far can he get? Not to Mexico, Philip's distorted brain is working well enough for that conclusion to be obvious – he ain't getting all the way to Mexico now.

How long will it take them to find the boy in his room? Let's say the cops are arriving at the motel right now. A room-by-room search will take how long? An hour? If they start on the ground floor and work their way . . .

Goddamn, it's hot! He's sweating, too hot to think straight – too enraged, too full of pain, too sleepy. How long has it been since he's had any sleep? Too long. How did things get to be this bad? He can't figure it out, can't reconstruct the details.

I don't even know where I'm going, he mutters – just driving.

He should come up with a new plan. Should turn around right now and go to Jonathan's house and collect my money from that bitch who kept laughing at me on the phone. Mess her bad and *then* head for Mexico, at least I'd have the money. Why didn't he go there when he left the motel? Philip remembers now, because she said he killed Jonathan and if that's true then the cops would be at the house waiting for him – except he's almost sure it *isn't* true. He didn't kill Jonathan.

Speed up, slow down.

Let's see . . . what – what was he trying to figure out? The cops at the motel, yes, how long will it take them to put out a bulletin on his car? An hour, it has to take them that long to check every room in the motel. Unless they start at the top floor and work their way down. Unless someone saw him leave with the girl. He looks over at her.

Penny is scrunched up in the corner of the seat, her head turned toward the door beneath the window, silent and not thinking.

It's all over unless he can come up with a new plan. Get rid of this car, that's what he should've done right off. If he gets rid of this car, ditches it someplace and steals another car, then the cops won't have any way to find him. Steal two or three cars in quick succession and then, maybe by the time they figure out what car he's driving, he'll be far enough away. How far is far enough away, Philip doesn't know, but at least now he has a new plan and it provides him with some small measure of comfort; get off this highway and find a different car.

He passes a sign announcing the next exit, two miles. Great! He drives, speeding up and slowing down, but when he reaches the sign that says the exit is one mile ahead, his rearview mirror catches flashing lights close behind him.

He glances at the speedometer, sixty. Surely he's not being pulled over for doing sixty. But then why?

Philip and the girl left the motel five minutes ago, not more than ten minutes tops, so the cops couldn't have found his room yet. Now what? Go for it? No, no, keep calm, he tells himself, this is just a traffic violation, keep calm. But it entails a tremendous effort on Philip's part, keeping calm, and he is rigid with this effort as he slows the car and guides it to the shoulder, thinking no way is he going to jail again, not when he has all those years of living like a king in Mexico *this close* within his grasp – no fucking way.

He has stopped, the cop car parking behind him, the state trooper calling in his tags to see if the computer has anything on Philip's car. This is the critical moment, Philip knows it, because if the cop sitting in the car behind him right now picks up a bulletin about the kidnapping, then all hell is going to break loose. More cop cars will be called, or maybe this trooper will cowboy it on his own, coming on strong with his gun drawn, shouting for Philip to get out with his hands over his head.

But if he's being stopped for a traffic violation, then the cop will just walk to the window and ask to see Philip's license.

Which is it going to be, just wait and see, Philip tells himself, wait and see, except he hates to wait, waiting tears him apart. He sits there and presses one temple as hard as he can.

There, in the rearview Philip sees it, the state trooper getting out and walking toward him, and although the cop's hand is resting on his gun butt, the gun isn't drawn and *the cop is coming to the window*, shining his flashlight on the back of Philip's head, keeping close to the car – a regulation approach for a traffic violation.

Philip knows the cop is right there by him, standing right next to the car and slightly behind the window, but Philip doesn't want to turn around and let the cop see his face, because one look at his face and the cop will draw his gun, Philip knows this, so he muffles a sob and waits.

Penny turns in her seat and looks. It's a policeman! If you get lost in the crowds, her father told her and Billy when they started out on this vacation, just find a policeman who's wearing a uniform and ask him for help. *This* policeman is wearing a uniform.

'May I see your driver's license and registration, sir?'

204

A little closer, Philip thinks, just a little closer. He grips the utility knife in his right hand – but the state cop knows better than getting too close to the window; he stands right next to the car, behind the window, out of range.

'Policeman!' Penny screams. 'Policeman!'

Philip looks at her, his rage so abrupt that he almost takes the triangular blade to her throat, shut the bitch up for good.

Unsure what's going on, wary now, the state trooper draws his revolver and bends down to look into the car, to see what's wrong with the girl in the passenger seat. Why is she screaming like that? He shines his light on her face. Something's wrong, all that red.

'Hospital,' Philip says, looking forward, not daring to face the cop, not yet. 'I'm trying to get my little girl to the hospital, she's had an accident!'

The trooper moves to the driver's window, bending down, looking in.

'Billy's in the bathroom!' Penny screams. 'Billy's still in the bathroom!'

The trooper can't figure it out.

'Come on, goddamn it!' Philip shouts at him, though still not looking at his face. 'Can't you see she's bleeding, huh? Can't you see she's hurt!'

It does look like blood, the trooper thinks as he bends closer to the window, leaning toward it just enough to make a mistake.

Philip's left hand bolts up, grabbing the trooper by the shirt collar, his thumb hooking inside the collar, grasping enough material of that taut-fitting shirt that he's able to pull the trooper's head into the car, the Smokey Bear hat getting knocked off, Philip incredibly strong the way he's holding on to the trooper who tries to bring his revolver up but finds that his shoulders are blocking the window, giving him no room to maneuver.

'Help me!' Penny screams right into the policeman's face, which has been pulled all the way to the steering wheel now, Philip's right hand already on its way, delivering the little blade to the cop's throat in one slashing movement, the blood instantly vomiting out on to Philip's lap.

'Oh, shit, oh, shit,' Philip says, sobbing with a kind of mad, exquisite delight, acting as if he had just opened a bottle of champagne that is now gushing all over him, Philip still pulling hard on the trooper's shirt, keeping him jammed in the window.

Outside the car, the trooper's legs perform a crazy shuffle. He drops the revolver and puts both hands against the car, trying to push himself free.

Inside the car, his eyes have rolled so far back in his head that nothing but white shows. His mouth is open, his tongue sticking straight out.

'Oh, shit, oh, shit,' Philip keeps saying as the hot blood soaks his lap and fills the car with its smell.

Penny closes her eyes and turns her head away, putting both hands over her ears so she doesn't have to listen to the policeman gagging like that. She gets off her knees and bunches up in the corner of the seat, pressing herself against the passenger door. Once again, she makes up her mind not to think about it, and, that decision made, Penny becomes deathly silent.

Philip, however, is still sobbing. He keeps shaking the cop by the shirt, looking down at all the blood pooling in the seat between his legs, sobbing in great heaves at what's he's done.

20

When I was a young man, a new father, I would on occasion awaken at three in the morning with an iron weight on my heart, imagining an unspecified, unresolved danger that faced my infant daughter. What it was, I don't know, I never found out. Maybe fathers always dream dangers for their children. The worst part of entering the motel room's small, dirty toilet was that I saw the nightmare for real, the danger specified, the terror resolved.

He was stripped naked, red marks all over his body and face, tied up and sitting on the oval toilet seat, eyes wide open, too stricken to speak, something obscene jammed between his legs.

Lengths of rope had been tied around his thighs, his knees, his ankles; his hands were bound behind his back. Mouth open, silent, he looked at me the way a rabbit looks at a dog when escape is no longer even a possibility. I couldn't help staring at it, what was between his legs, that blackened hand with its rotting fingers curled around the boy's genitals, cupping them as if the hand had come up from the sewers to grab him like that.

I kept shaking my head, not wanting to deal with this kind of shit anymore. I was too old for it, had grown too soft. I wanted to go home and sleep and let someone else handle these nightmares that really do happen, this filth.

I was almost sure the boy wasn't seriously injured. That is to say, the red marks on him were lipstick, not blood, but when I asked him – stupidly – if he was OK, he didn't reply, sitting there and looking at me as if I were the next guy in line to do something bad to him.

When I took out my pocket knife and unfolded the big blade, he began shaking his head. It was heartbreaking, and I couldn't remember his name. Someone on the other side of the bathroom door knocked lightly, and it struck me at the time how genteel it sounded, like there was a person out there needing to use the facilities and he was politely, almost shyly, urging me please to hurry up. Then I remembered the boy's name.

'Billy? I'm a policeman, a detective, OK? And I'm going to cut these ropes off you, OK?'

No response, just those terrible eyes watching me.

I started with the rope around his ankles, then the one around his knees, and then carefully sawing through the rope that tied his thighs together. When that final rope was cut, he immediately spread his legs, letting the severed hand drop into the toilet, both of us looking between his legs to see it in the water – and then we looked at each other.

I lifted him to a standing position and closed the toilet lid before turning him around and cutting the rope that bound his hands behind his back. I noticed the knife shaking in my hand and decided I'd better sit on the edge of the tub before I fainted, Billy remaining where I'd stood him, fingers casually locked together in front of his crotch, not looking at me, trying hard not to cry.

'Camel! Goddamn you!' The knocking at the bathroom door had ceased being polite, had become more like the pounding you do with the butt of your fist. 'If you're fucking with evidence in there,' Captain Land said through the door, 'I'll have your ass.'

I told Billy that the guy doing all the screaming was my boss. He turned toward his clothes, which were in a pile under the sink. 'Let's get that lipstick off you before you get dressed, OK?' He still wasn't answering me. I went over to the sink and ran the water until it was warm; finding a halfway clean towel, I held it under the water.

I knelt on the floor and motioned for him, Billy coming to me only reluctantly, not liking the idea of being touched. What Land had just said about destroying evidence bothered me enough that I took a moment, there on my knees, to think things through.

Philip Gaetan had committed those Lipstick Murders and had drawn on this boy the same kind of lines he put on the two women he killed. Depending on how the case broke, Billy's painted face might be the key evidence that ties Philip to the Lipstick Murders – in which case I shouldn't touch the boy until we get some photographs of him.

But it wouldn't be right, opening that bathroom door and letting the other cops see him, making his parents see him like this, keeping him naked and painted like a sacrifice until we could get a police photographer down here.

'Camel!' Land was kicking the door.

Besides, there was the hand in the toilet – evidence enough for any jury. I found a little piece of soap in the shape of an apple and began rubbing it on the towel, telling Land through the door: 'I'm questioning the boy. Be done in a second.'

Then Alfred's voice: 'Is he all right?'

'I think so.'

Land again: 'Camel, you're treading shit in there. If you ruin our chances of getting a conviction, I'll have your balls bronzed, I swear to God I will!'

'Nice guy, huh?' I asked Billy as I used the towel on his face.

'Camel!' Land was practically whining, but then his voice changed and he announced he was going to kick the door open so I better make sure the children were out of the way.

Children? I shouted to Alfred: 'Don't let him come in yet! *Alfred*, not yet, OK?'

They began arguing on the other side of the door; I was able to make out only the part where Land told Alfred that now *he* was suspended.

When I finished with his face, I handed the towel to Billy. 'You go ahead and wash the rest of it off.'

He made a half turn away from me and began scrubbing hard at the lipstick on his torso, at the long lines down his legs. He

209

started crying, and the harder he rubbed, the more he cried; the more he cried, the harder he rubbed.

'*That bastard*,' I whispered.

Alfred rapped on the door several times. 'Teddy, how's the girl?'

Billy stopped washing his legs and looked at me, speaking for the first time. 'Didn't you find Penny?

'Your sister?'

'I thought you already caught him and found Penny.' His voice was full of panic.

Jesus, I'd forgotten about the girl.

'He's taking her to Mexico! That's what he said, taking her in his car so they could drive to Mexico!'

I went to the door. 'Alfred! He took the girl in his car. Get someone down there to the registration desk so you can get a bulletin out.'

'Melvin Kelvin already went to take care of that, Teddy,' Alfred replied. 'Hey, buddy, things are kind of sticky out here. The boy's parents are waiting in the hall. Can't you bring him out now?'

When I looked at Billy, he asked if he could get dressed first. 'Absolutely,' I told him – and then informed Alfred we'd be out in five minutes. I went back to sit on the edge of the tub.

'I've become stupid,' I said to Billy as he put on his underpants and jeans. 'Lazy and stupid. I should've put out a bulletin on that guy's car before I even came up here, should've asked you about your sister right away.' He pulled his T-shirt over his head and then sat next to me on the tub to put on his socks and shoes. I nudged his leg. 'What that jerk did to you, don't let it mess up your mind. Jerks like that, I don't know. I don't know what makes them the way they are, what makes them do the things they do, but you got to try as hard as you can not to let it get to you, huh?'

He shrugged, tying his shoelaces.

Then there was the question I didn't want to ask. 'Did he do anything else to you?' No reply. 'You understand what I'm asking, Billy?' Asking him because his parents will be asking me. 'Did he touch you down there, did he—'

'No!' He said it angrily, as if I had no right to ask.

I apologized. 'We got to know, son. If he did anything to you, your folks will want you to get checked by a doctor.'

'He didn't touch me like that, like what you're saying. Just touched me to put on the lipstick.'

I still knew when someone was speaking the truth and, for once, this was a truth I was glad to hear. He was dressed now, but we kept sitting on the tub. Billy waiting for me to tell him when it was time to leave the room. I didn't know what *I* was waiting for.

Then came his quiet voice. 'He threw my clothes in here and said I could get dressed when I got the ropes off. But they were too tight. He said he didn't have time to do what he wanted to do. He said he was going to cut it off – but he didn't have time.'

'The guy's a monster. Sick in the head. We're going to nail him so you don't *ever* have to worry about him again, not ever.' We sat some more. I kept expecting someone to knock on the door and say the five minutes were up. 'I saw the scar on your knee. Stitches, huh?'

He nodded.

'You get hurt playing ball? Falling out of a tree?' Then I knew what I was waiting around for, why I was delaying our departure – to see how it was spending time with a boy, talking to a boy the way I never talked to my grandson.

Billy told me he fell off a bike.

'Two-wheeler?'

'My friend's. Jimmy's. We were riding double down this hill and he couldn't reach the brakes.'

I wanted to ask him what kind of day it was when he went riding double down that hill on his friend Jimmy's bike, was the bike red with an aluminum basket in front, was the sun shining, who took him to the hospital, how many stitches, did he—?

'Are you going to catch him before he takes Penny to Mexico?'

'You betcha. Then he goes to jail for the rest of his life, so neither you or your sister ever has to worry about him again.'

He began rubbing his eyes. 'It was my fault, my idea to go down there one more time and look for coins. Dad said we were supposed to stay where he could see us, but I thought maybe there might be a couple more coins down there. That's why he kidnapped us, you know – they were his coins and he thought we stole them. Dad's going to be mad at me.' He was crying.

'No, your Dad won't be mad at you. It wasn't your fault, no one's fault except that jerk with the lipstick. They weren't even his coins, he'd stolen them from someone else.'

'Who?' Billy asked, still crying.

His father? No, I wasn't going to get into that. 'Some rich guy.'

'I hope you kill him!'

'Yeah, well it might come to that.'

Then the knocking I'd been expecting finally came. 'You ready to face everyone now?'

'I guess so.' He'd almost stopped crying.

We stood and I smoothed his hair with both hands, taken with a sudden need to reach down and kiss his head, hug him, but I knew it would only confuse the boy, frighten him. 'Do you have a grandfather?'

He nodded. 'Two.'

'What do you call them?'

'Huh?'

'Grandpa, grand-dad . . . pa-pa . . .'

'I just call them grandpa. Grandpa Morris and Grandpa Hammermill.'

'When I was growing up, I only had one grandpa. He lived on a farm. He'd dead now, dead a long time. I used to call him Poppo. I guess you think that's a pretty silly name for a grand-father, huh – Poppo.'

He shrugged.

Where was I coming up with this stuff? I'm glad no one else

but the boy was there to hear me. I told him I had a grandson. 'He's lot older than you. Seventeen. He lives in Florida.' Jesus. 'I guess we'd better leave now, huh?'

He nodded. 'Does he call you Poppo?'

I shook my head. Someone was knocking on the door again. 'You ready, son?' I asked.

'Yes, sir.'

When I opened the door, Land took a step toward me and started to say something belligerent, then he spotted the boy standing behind me. 'You OK, Billy?' Land asked. 'Your parents are waiting for you in the hallway.' He motioned to one of the officers, who brought in the Hammermills.

The mother was crying, saying her son's name over and over, going down on her knees in front of him, hugging him then drawing back to look at his face. The man stooped over them, his arms around wife and son, his face in my direction – asking me the question with his eyes.

'He's all right,' I said. 'The guy put some lipstick on him, took his clothes off and tied him up, threatened him – but he didn't harm him physically.'

The man nodded. His wife got to her feet and rushed over to me, asking about her daughter.

Land started to say something but I interrupted him. 'There's a bulletin out on the man who took your daughter, and I'm pretty sure we'll be picking him up in the next few minutes. I don't think he's hurt her, either.'

'How do you know?' she demanded, her face as ruined as Jo-Jo's was earlier in the evening.

'Well, for one thing, he just hasn't had time. The first two officers arrived here right after he left and he's probably been driving ever since, trying to put as much distance behind him as he can. We'll pick him up on one of the highways leading out of here, somewhere on the Beltway probably.'

'Where's he taking her?' she asked.

'Mexico!' Billy exclaimed. Everyone in the room looked at

him. 'That's what he said,' Billy added in a quieter voice. 'Said he was taking her to Mexico.'

With both parents suddenly asking questions, I had to speak quickly. 'Every police officer in every jurisdiction around here, every state trooper, they've all been alerted. We know what kind of car he's driving. He won't get away.'

Captain Land, having had enough of my role as officer in charge, began issuing his own orders, telling an officer to take Billy and his parents to their room. 'Get a complete statement from the boy, I'll be there in a few minutes.' When they'd all left, he turned to Alfred and me.

'I don't even know where to start,' he began. 'Camel, before you began reassuring those people about the multiple-state dragnet you somehow organized from inside the bathroom there, you mentioned the boy had been painted up with lipstick. That connects our man to the Lipstick Murders. But the boy's face was clean when you brought him out of the bathroom, wasn't it? You wanted to make him presentable before his parents saw him, very admirable. Also very stupid. If you've fucked up our chance to link this guy with the Lipstick Murders—'

'Go look in the commode, Captain.'

'The commode?'

'Yeah, it's got a severed hand in it. From the runaway who was killed in Maryland. We're not going to have any problem, nailing him for those homicides.'

Land made a funny face and it took a moment for him to regain his outrage. 'Your entire conduct in this case goes well beyond being unprofessional, Camel. It's criminal. And you bet your ass I'm bringing you up on charges.'

I shrugged.

Then it was Alfred's turn. 'And you, Detective Bodine, I thought you and I had reached an agreement. You sat there in my office and swore to me you were through with being a cowboy, that you were going to work with Detective Kelvin, mend your ways, make me proud of you. So I gave you another chance, and you show your gratitude by defying me in front of other officers, preventing me from kicking that door open so I could stop Camel from destroying evidence. Well, mister, you're going up on criminal charges right along with your old drinking buddy here. If there's one good thing that comes out of this mess, it's that you two fuck-ups won't be impersonating police officers any longer.' He let all that sink in and then asked: 'Either one of you got something cute to say?'

Alfred and I looked at each other. We didn't .

'I've already put in a call to our crime scene people,' Land was saying, 'but the chances of them getting anything useful out of this room now are—'

Melvin Kelvin opened the door and looked at us with crazy eyes. 'Captain! A state trooper's been killed out on Sixty-Six less than five miles from here. Had his throat slit by someone he stopped. They got the description of the car, tags and every-thing – it's a match! It's our man, the guy who was staying in this room!'

I asked Melvin Kelvin if there was any report of a little girl being with him.

'I don't know. Jesus Mary, I was just calling in our bulletin when they told me that every cop in Maryland, Virginia, and the District is already looking for the guy. They're asking us to put out all available manpower, every car we have, they want every-thing on the Sixty-Six corridor.'

'When did it happen?' Land asked.

'I don't know, couldn't have been long ago. A few minutes. The Virginia State Police are going crazy. I told them we have reason to believe that the guy driving that car was also respon-sible for the Lipstick Murders, so now, Jesus Mary, Captain, they want you to call the watch commander so you can coordi-nate your people. Each department is being given a specific sec-tor to patrol. I never heard anything like this before, on the radio, geez, it sounds like there's a war going on out there.'

Land looked scared. 'You two are temporarily off suspension.

215

You buddy up in Bodine's car. Get on Sixty-Six right now. As soon as I find out the sector we're supposed to patrol, I'll have it called in to you. Kelvin, give them a description of the car. You'll be riding with me. Come on, we'll radio the department from my car.'

The four of us went down the stairway together, Land and Melvin Kelvin splitting off as soon as we got outside. I walked with Alfred to his car but didn't get in.

'Let's go,' he urged.

I shook my head.

'What now?'

'There's an army of cops out there looking for this guy. If he's on the road somewhere, you'll find him. One more old detective isn't going to make any difference.'

'Teddy!'

'You go for it, buddy.'

He started the engine and raced it. 'Get in, Teddy.'

'Car chases give me motion sickness.'

His face was livid. 'Blocking that bathroom door for you, that's the last time, Teddy. The absolute last time. You and me, we're finished. Hear me? Finished! Now get in this goddamn car!

I shook my head again and stepped away from the door, Lord Alfred calling me a bad name and then racing away.

I stood in the parking lot until Billy's father walked over and asked me what was going on. 'Those two officers were questioning my son,' he said, 'when all of a sudden that young detective came in looking for Captain Land and then he told something to the two officers and everyone went running off.'

'They'll be back.'

'It's about the man who has our daughter, isn't it? They've found him.'

'We got a good lead on him but, no, he hasn't been picked up yet.' A cab was letting out a couple by the front of the motel. 'Listen, I have to catch that cab. You just stay in your room, someone'll be back to talk to you.'

216

'My wife and I, we want to thank you. Billy told us about how you cleaned him up.'

The cab was starting to pull away, so I signaled the driver. 'I got to go.'

When the cab came over, I got in quickly but then just sat there, saying nothing, unsure of my next move. 'Where to?' the driver finally asked.

I wondered what truths would come out when they finally caught up with Jonathan's son and got him talking. The driver turned around in his seat and looked at me. 'Hey, where to, huh?'

I gave him Mary's address.

21

Philip needs her.

He took the girl because he *wanted* her, had become obsessed by her and her family, but everything has changed now. Adrenaline is clearing his mind, lifting the fog of sleeplessness, blunting his pain, and now Philip has become singular, knowing *exactly* what he has to do: Escape. And to do that, he *needs* Penny. Predator is prey, he's being chased, a contest now, Philip against the cops again, a game he's played before except this time they're not going to win, not this time. And Penny has become useful to him. That state cop would've never leaned close to the car window if Penny hadn't been there. She's going to come in handy.

Philip is driving residential streets, looking for a car to steal, not much time before they find that dead cop back on the highway – and then they'll be searching for Philip with a terrible vengeance, Philip knows how they are when one of their own has been killed, tribal, so he has to locate another car quickly, has to come up with a way of hiding his own car.

Maybe go to a shopping center and tuck his car among all the others in the parking lot, use Penny to attract some shopper's attention, steal his car. But what time is it? Too late for shopping centers to be open? And if he steals a car from someone who reports the theft right away, the cops will know that he's driving a stolen car, will still be on his tail. No, he has to come up with another plan. He pauses at a stop sign to think.

Think! Inside the car, the blood's salty protein odor is

overwhelming. Philip leans his head out the window to breathe night air. Quiet. Penny, bunched up in her seat, hasn't said a word since she called out for help from that *policeman!*

His gun is in Philip's waistband. He held the trooper in that window, bleeding, until there was a break in traffic, then he pulled the body around to the other side of the patrol car and left him lying, wide-eyed and still bleeding. Maybe it'll take a while for some motorist to stop and find out why the patrol car is sitting there, lights flashing, no one inside. Maybe it'll take a while for other patrol cars to be sent out to learn why the trooper Philip killed isn't answering his radio. Maybe it'll take a while for that killing to be linked to the boy they've surely found by now in the motel room.

These hopeful speculations are broken by a siren that sounds nearby, then two more in the distance, another one close by, just a few streets over, more sirens sounding from other directions, a dozen of them in different places in the night, like dogs howling, each howl calling forth others, the night full of these dogs, searching for him.

Philip sits there gripping the steering wheel as a cop car goes screaming by *right in front of him*, on the street he's facing, past the stop sign at which he waits. In his rearview mirror he sees flashing lights race past on another intersecting street. All heading for the highway. They've found the cop – and soon they'll return to these residential streets, moving slowly then, looking for him, knowing exactly what kind of car he's driving. They'll also know I have his gun, he thinks, which means they won't be taking any chances, not with an armed cop-killer. They'll shoot as soon as they see me and claim later they were firing in self-defense.

He looks over at the silent Penny. Except they won't shoot if they know I have the girl.

Philip pulls away from the stop sign, slowly cruising another street, no time to find a parking lot, he's going to have to steal some car along here and then just hope the owners won't notice it missing for a few hours, hope the cops won't find his own car parked on this street, not for a few hours at least because he needs at least a few hours to get away from the sirens, needs time to do one more thing before he makes good his escape, but the sirens are so common now that it sounds as if the city is under some kind of attack, sirens warning about an enemy out and about, warning of danger, stay indoors, sirens carrying away those already dead; it's a war, and at a few houses Philip passes, people have come to their front porches to look out into the darkness, to see if they can discover what it is about this night that has caused a hundred sirens to sound.

He crosses an intersection, looking to his left and seeing a patrol car cruising the street with menacing slowness, the car's spotlight illuminating vehicles parked on the driver's side, another cop in the passenger seat, checking cars on that side with a flashlight. Philip drives to the next intersection and takes a right, goes a block, makes a left. Two streets ahead, another patrol car passes slowly into and out of view, spotlight and flashlight working both sides of that street, too.

He takes his breaths in shallow droughts, driving on, turning – not much time now, not much time at all. His mind works on what he's going to do when they spot him, put their lights on his car, and tell him to get out. Show them the girl, yes, but even if they allow him to drive off, they'll just follow and wait for their chance. Even if they don't shoot, they'll surround him and wait. Time and numbers are on their side. He's sweating but too nervous to be sleepy, too excited to register his pain.

There! He has passed a house where the garage door has just opened. Philip stops, checks the street behind him, and then reverses to the driveway. He pauses a moment in the street. An old guy is standing in the lighted garage, the house dark, this old man having just lifted the garage door, and now he's at his car, standing by the driver's door, keys in his hand.

He doesn't notice Philip's car until it's in his driveway, hurrying into the two-car garage, parking right next to the old man's brand-new Buick. The guy has a funny little smile on his face, thinking this must be someone he knows, someone who saw him in the garage and decided to pull in for a chat. He walks around the back of the Buick, trying to see who it is, still smiling.

Philip leans to Penny. 'Start crying, like you're hurting.' Penny *is* hurting but she just sits there, refusing to acknowledge his existence, so he pinches her *hard* on the belly, Penny squealing and then, yes, crying, although she sounds more terrified than injured.

When Philip gets out of his car, the old man's smile twists into a grimace, his face horrified to see all that blood. Philip glances down at the stains and when he looks up again he sees that the old man is getting ready to run out into the street. Just before the guy bolts, Philip talks to him.

'You got to help us, mister, my little girl's been injured and I'm out of gas.'

Not at all sure about what he's hearing, the man pauses by the back bumper of his Buick, still ready to run for it, except there *is* a little girl in that car and she *is* crying – and there's something all over her face. Blood? 'Dear God, what happened?'

'She cut herself with a kitchen knife,' Philip says, again looking down at his stained clothing. 'Can't you see all this blood I got on me, her blood? I was heading for the hospital but I knew I wouldn't make it, not enough gas. Saw your garage door open. Can you drive us?'

He's sixty-eight years old, a dapper little guy in mustard yellow slacks, white linen shirt, a snap-brim straw hat. Two Christmases ago, he was mugged in the parking lot of a shopping mall. Some young punk, a white kid, tripped him and took his wallet right out of his back pocket; stole both bags of Christmas presents, too. They never caught him, they never do. His back has been bothering him ever since. He has become a wary man.

'She's bleeding to death!' Philip shouts, glancing out into the street, knowing he has to get that garage door closed before one of those cop cars comes by.

The old man cranes his neck, trying again to get a good look at Penny, who has stopped crying, who has retreated to a corner of the seat. Something's funny, the old man thinks. You can't be too careful these days. This guy with the blood on him, he looks awfully rough. Wild-eyed, hair a mess. Maybe this is some kind of scam, the old man has heard about these scams, a thief using a child to talk his way into your house and then he knocks you over the head and robs you.

On the other hand, how's he going to feel if the girl really is injured, and then she dies in that car and her father tells everyone that she might have lived if she'd been taken to the hospital in time except he ran out of gas and the one man he asked to help, he wouldn't help, he was too suspicious, how's he going to feel when his friends hear about that?

Philip considers rushing over and grabbing the old fart, pulling him deeper into the garage and shutting the door – but the man seems so frightened, so ready to run, still leaning toward the street. In his mind, Philip can see everything going wrong again, chasing him into the street, a struggle, shouts, lights coming on in other houses, cop cars pulling up from both directions. No, he tells himself, don't scare him off, lure him in, use Penny.

'Oh, my God!' Philip exclaims as he leans into his car. 'She's dying! Hold on, Penny, we'll get you there, we'll get you to the hospital, hold on, darling!'

Scrunched up in her seat, she looks at him blankly.

Philip straightens up, looks at the old man. 'She's unconscious! Can't you at least call an ambulance?'

The old man knows what he has to do, you have to do what's right even if there *is* something terribly odd about this character, the way he keeps looking out to the street, not acting frantic the way you think a man would act if his daughter is dying in the car, the old man remembering when his own daughter got hit and broke a leg right there on the street in front of the house, back when she was twelve, a couple of kids riding double on one of those damn motor scooters, riding right on the sidewalk . . .

223

'Hey!'

Of course he's going to do the right thing. 'Put her in my car,' the old man says. 'My name's Charlie Warren. I'll drive you to the emergency room myself.'

Perfect. Philip goes around to the passenger door of his car, opening it and bending close to Penny, telling her to keep quiet. Then he calls to the man. 'She's dead!'

'God, no,' Charlie Warren says, hurrying over, his face worried and scared, sorry he'd been so suspicious, regret-filled for not agreeing to help as soon as the man drove into the garage – but when he reaches the open door where the young man is standing, Charlie can see clearly that the little girl in there is perfectly alive. She has what looks to be lipstick on her face and her eyes are closed, her hands over her ears – the way Charlie's own daughter used to act on the Fourth of July whenever anyone lighted a firecracker – but the little girl obviously isn't dead.

'Asshole,' Philip mutters, sobbing as he grabs the man's shirt and pushes him with an easy effort to the concrete floor. He pulls the state cop's revolver from his waistband and points it at Charlie's head. 'You stay down there or I'll blow your fucking brains out.' Then he hurries over to the garage entrance, takes one last look up and down the street, and closes the door. He can relax now.

I knew it, Charlie thinks as he sits there on the concrete floor.

'Give me the keys to your car,' Philip orders when he returns from the door.

Staying on the floor, the old man reaches up one hand, offering the keys and thinking, Good, he's just going to steal the car, that's all. It's insured.

'You weren't going to help us, were you?' Philip asks, kicking him lightly in the ribs. From the floor, the man does not reply. 'Stand up, you old fart.'

It takes him a while to get on his feet. He brushes off his yellow pants, refusing to look at Philip.

'We're going to take your car, but I don't want you reporting it missing until tomorrow at noon. We'll need that much of a head start at least – OK?'

Charlie is nodding. He has tears in his eyes. If this punk had tried to pull something like this on me twenty years ago . . .

'You give me your word you won't call the cops until noon tomorrow?'

'Yes, yes,' he says, his voice breaking. Even now, if that punk didn't have a gun, I'd . . .

Philip leans against his car, scratching his face with the gun barrel. 'Look at me. How do I *know* you won't call the cops until noon, huh?'

What frightens Charlie the most is the way he is being played with, that taunting voice, the young man no longer in a hurry. 'I *won't*, I promise.'

'Oh, you *promise*, huh? I've had promises made to me before. Yeah,' he says, seething, 'I know what promises are worth. Where were you going?'

'Going?' Charlie asks back, looking around, confused.

'Yeah, Pops, you were about to leave in your car. Where were you heading off to, huh? Someone expecting you at their house?'

'Get something to eat. My wife's away.' Had he already mentioned that? 'I don't like cooking for myself, it doesn't taste the same when you cook it yourself.'

'Awful late for an old guy like you to be going out to dinner. Sneaking off to meet some bimbo while the wife's away, huh? You paying some young cooze to see if she can still get the meat hard, huh?' Philip sobs that laughter of his.

'No, of course not,' Charlie snaps. If one of his sons ever talked to him like that, he'd get backhanded. 'I was going to Denny's. Open twenty-four hours. Sometimes I can't sleep. Please, go ahead and take my car, just leave me alone.'

But Philip is enjoying this. 'So no one's expecting you to be anywhere tonight. If your old lady calls and you don't answer, she figures you're asleep.'

'She already called tonight. Our daughter's having her first baby. She hasn't had it yet, though. My two sons have two children each, this'll be our fifth grandchild. My wife's helping out, she's done that with every grandchild we've had, doesn't matter where she has to travel or what time of year it is, she—'

'Yeah, right. Listen to me. I'm taking your car but I'm going to need a week's head start, so you wait seven days before reporting the car stolen. OK?'

Charlie is already nodding. 'Yes, yes, of course.'

Philip steps toward him, pushing Charlie hard in the chest, the man tottering backward several steps and then falling rather gently on his ass. 'Liar!' Philip screams. 'Everyone *lying* to me, all my fucking life. I didn't even believe you when you said you wouldn't report your car stolen until noon tomorrow, but we *both* know you're not going to wait a whole week before you call the cops. Soon as I leave, you'll run in your house, make sure all the doors are locked, and then you'll be on the phone to the cops, crying about how this awful man took your nice new car. *Lying* to me. You won't wait an hour. Lies, lies, lies.'

Sitting on the garage floor, Charlie waits. Philip comes over there and kicks him in the back.

Charlie begins to weep. 'What do you *want* me to say. I don't understand what you want!' The old man is sobbing now.

This is what Philip wants, to see that terror come oozing out, creating in others the terror that has filled his own life. 'I *know* how to make sure you don't report your car stolen,' Philip says he puts the gun in his waistband. From a pocket of his field jacket he pulls out the knife with the small triangular blade. 'Oh, I *know* how to make you keep your word, all right.'

Charlie gropes around trying to get his hands under him so he can struggle to his knees. 'Please.'

'*Please*,' Philip mocks him.

'Don't hurt me in front of your little girl, don't make her watch you do something like that.'

'Oh, she's seen worse.'

But Penny is seeing nothing. Although the passenger door is

open, she still has her eyes tightly shut, hands over her ears.

'Who are you?' Charlie asks.

Philip goes behind the kneeling man, flips off his hat, grabs him by one ear.

'Hail Mary,' Charlie begins, 'full of grace, the Lord is with thee.'

'Yeah, yeah,' Philip says, bringing the blade quickly across the old man's crepey neck.

Inside the car, Penny presses her hands more tightly over her ears but, still, sounds reach her, almost precisely the same sounds that policeman made, gagging and choking – Penny trying as hard as she can not to think about it.

Philip stands there and watches, fascinated by Charlie crabbing around on the floor, one hand holding his neck, a futile effort to stop the blood, eyes wild, mouth working up and down producing only blood, no words, blood all over that white linen shirt, Philip finally tiring of the display, kicking Charlie in the head, knocking him supine and then getting down on the floor to push Charlie under the car, still alive under there, still gagging on his own blood.

Now Philip moves quickly, pulling Penny from his car and putting her in Charlie's Buick. He finds a quart of oil and pours it over the bloodstains on the floor, dropping the container there to make it look like oil's been spilled, nothing more. He takes a tarp from one of the shelves and uses it to cover his car, standing still for a moment to determine if Charlie is still making noises. He isn't.

Philip looks around the garage. *Perfect*. No one's going to be searching for me in that Buick. I have time now. One more thing to do. No one will miss the old man until tomorrow and that'll give me plenty of time to do what I have to do.

He walks over and gets into the Buick. Except what about Penny? The cops won't be looking for him in a brand-new Buick, but they *are* searching for a man who has kidnapped a little girl, and if they see Penny, especially with that lipstick on her face . . .

The truth is, he doesn't *need* her anymore.

227

22

'I don't think I can let you in,' Mary said as if the decision wasn't hers, unsure of her *authority* to admit me.

'Let me make it easy for you.' I pushed the door with my shoulder, knocking it away from Mary and giving myself room enough to enter.

'I'm calling Captain Land,' she said.

'You want the number?'

She stepped to the telephone on the hallway table, made the call, talked to someone for a few moments, and then said to me, 'He can't be reached, but I left a message. If you leave before he calls back, I won't mention this to him.'

I didn't say anything.

'My husband was buried today and I've been hounded by reporters all week, I think common decency—'

'What're you drinking?'

We both looked down at the glass in her hand, then Mary raised her eye to mine. 'Scotch.'

'Perfect.'

She sighed, her shoulders slumping. 'Come on, then.'

We went into the living room, Mary sitting on the couch that faced the mantel and indicating to me where the liquor was, at the bar in the corner of the room. I walked over there and found a heavy cut-glass decanter that was half full of something golden brown. I poured three fingers over two cubes in a squat crystal cocktail glass and then went to stand at the mantel facing Mary.

'Cheers,' I said without enthusiasm, taking a sip while keeping my eyes on her face. It was the good stuff.

Mary had on a red robe that she kept wrapped tightly around her, but it didn't take much imagination to tell that she wasn't wearing anything underneath.

'Guess what,' I said. 'Philip ain't showing up for his money tomorrow.'

She started to say something but then changed her mind, reaching for a cigarette instead. After she got it lighted, Mary asked if I was there at her house in an official capacity.

'I'm off suspension, if that's what you're getting at.'

'Suspension?' she asked, all innocence.

I nodded. 'We can dance as long as you want, Mary, doesn't matter to me. It's all going to come out before the night's over.'

'You don't like me, do you?'

'Hold that thought,' I said, putting my glass on the mantel and walking out into the hallway to call the department. They hadn't found Philip or the little girl yet but there were reports placing his car in a residential area just off Sixty-Six, west of where the trooper had been killed – Philip still heading away from here. When I returned to the living room I told Mary everyone was looking for her friend.

'My friend?'

I didn't say anything.

Mary inhaled deeply from her cigarette and then stubbed it out. 'Actually, Teddy, I'm glad you're here.'

'Really?'

She was fingering the rim of her glass. 'Would you like me to freshen that drink?'

I shook my head.

Mary shrugged, getting off the couch and going to the bar to make another one for herself. 'You sure?'

'Positive.'

She brought the Scotch over anyway, leaving the decanter on

the mantel and then standing there almost touching me. 'I know all about you.'

'Really?'

'George told me all about you. My lawyer.'

'Yeah, I know George.'

She returned to the couch, tucking her legs under her. 'George said you're burned out.'

'Could be.'

'He also said that once upon a time you were a real hotshot, had a reputation for being a human lie detector.'

'A talent that hasn't entirely left me.'

'Which is why you're here,' Mary said, sipping her Scotch. 'To put the lie detector on me.'

'I've already had it on you, in Land's office and then when Alfred and I came visiting. You lied both times.'

'I know why you're obsessed with me.'

'I'm not obsessed with you, I just want to know what happened Sunday night and what your connection with Philip is.'

'When you were here yesterday with your partner, you said you wanted to help me, to protect me. Said you thought of me as a daughter, remember?'

'I remember.'

'So you were lying to me then?'

'You want some truth, I'll tell you some truth. Jonathan's son was here Sunday night but you didn't mention that, you lied to us, and that means you're responsible for Philip killing a woman in the District and, just tonight, a Virginia state trooper. He also assaulted a little boy and kidnapped the boy's sister. And that's not counting the fifteen-year-old runaway he killed before he showed up at your house Sunday. Your lies – and the fact that I covered for you – that's why people are getting killed, Mary.'

She had a frightened look on her face. 'Have they caught him yet?'

'Not yet. I left your number with the dispatcher, he'll call me as soon as they have word.'

231

Mary began crying. 'I can't be blamed for what Jonathan's son did.'

'The hell you can't. Accessory to murder.'

It required several sips of Scotch and another cigarette for Mary to digest what I'd just said. She had stopped crying but when she spoke, her voice was unsure. 'I'll have to call George.'

'Go ahead. But I'm not here to arrest you, if that's what you're worried about. I'm leaving that to Captain Land and all the other cops who'll be over here as soon as they catch Philip and he starts talking. You think the press has been tormenting you these past few days, wait till they find out the whole story. Make you a media star, Mary. And when all that comes down, yeah, you'll definitely need George by your side, but you don't need a lawyer for what you and I are going to do, Mary. I just want to hear the truth from you, that's all I want.'

She was dabbing at her eyes. 'Whatever I tell you now is off the record?'

I stood there looking at her.

'How wonderful it must be,' Mary said, suddenly dry-eyed. 'Caught me in all my lies and now . . . I know how you got your information, too – Jo-Jo crying on your shoulder about the evil Mary Gaetan.'

'Yeah, I talked with Jo-Jo tonight.'

'I bet you did.'

'You fucked her up real good, Mary.'

She made a sound in her throat and then got up from the couch to take our glasses over to the bar for more ice. When she returned to the mantel, she poured Scotch into both glasses and then stood there close to me again. 'She tell you she wanted to be my girlfriend?'

'She said you seduced her.'

'And you believed her?'

I nodded.

'Then your lie-detecting abilities are for shit. I guess she told you it was my idea to file that complaint against you, too, huh?'

I started to reply, stumbling on my words.

'The fact is, I tried to talk Jo-Jo out of filing that complaint because I thought it would just complicate matters, but she was very determined to get on my good side, to save me. Jo-Jo's a dyke.'

'Bullshit.'

'Bullshit? Really? Have you checked her out? Did you talk to any of the people who worked with her and Jonathan in the beginning? Back then, Jo-Jo was openly lesbian and didn't care who knew about it, either. Jonathan was screwing her because he had messed up his life too many times over women and he figured she was a safe lay, figured he definitely wouldn't fall in love with her and make a fool of himself over it.'

'The way he did with you.'

'What Jonathan and I had was good.'

'If Jo-Jo's a dyke, what was she doing screwing Jonathan?'

'Well, gosh, Teddy, I don't know,' Mary said, grinding the sarcasm. 'I guess little old Jo-Jo just swung both ways. And besides, Jonathan was letting her buy into the company and I suppose Jo-Jo saw the two of them as this neat little business team, hoping maybe Jonathan would marry her so she could put her dyke days behind her.

'Don't make me out to be some kind of spider lady, seducing the virtuous and formerly queer Miss Creek and commanding her to do my bidding, because that's just not the way it happened.'

'OK, then how *did* it happen?'

Mary stared hard at me but then abruptly lost her grip on my eyes. Looking away, she said, 'It was all very confused. We were sitting on the couch talking about Jonathan, hugging each other, crying. I noticed that her hand had slipped down from my shoulder. Jo-Jo was touching my breast. I was so torn up about Jonathan, about everything that happened this week, I didn't realize . . . didn't tell Jo-Jo to stop. Then she was suddenly kissing me, opening my dress. I guess the fact that I didn't stop her immediately, I guess Jo-Jo took that as encouragement. When I finally got my wits about me, Jo-Jo was already saying she was going to pack a bag and spend the weekend with me. She said it would be easy to file a complaint against you and get you out of the way until after the payoff tomorrow.

'The answer is, Teddy, I *don't know* why I let her grope me, but it was all Jo-Jo's doing, not mine. *Her* idea to file that complaint, not mine. So am I telling you the truth or not – what's your lie detector reading?'

I wasn't sure, the *certainty* of it eluding me. I had believed Jo-Jo's version but now I was believing Mary's too. Losing my talent. 'What's your connection with Philip?'

'He's my stepson.'

'Come on, don't fuck with me.'

'Listen, Teddy. I'll tell you the truth – OK?' She went over and sat on the couch, lighting another cigarette and then leaning forward enough that I could see down her robe, see her breasts bare and white on her tanned chest. 'That night, Sunday night, was the worst night of my life. No one will ever know how bad it was. You know how you remember a certain moment, remember every detail of that moment for the rest of your life? Like when President Kennedy was killed. I was in second grade and the principal came in to our room and she was crying when she told us, every detail of that moment is burned in my memory. That's true for everyone, right – you can remember exactly where you were and what you were doing when you heard the news. Well, Sunday night, there are a thousand of those moments for me, a thousand things that I'll remember in exact detail for the rest of my life.

'The crazy way Jonathan's son was acting, how he kept hitting Jonathan, the way Jonathan totally gave up when he heard that his daughter had died of drugs when she was still a teenager. That broke Jonathan's heart, it really did – I'll never forget the look in his eyes, *never*.

'Jonathan killed himself because of the guilt he felt about his daughter, because he fucked around so much in his early days. His wife caught him in bed with her sister, for God's sake, but when she took off with the kids and Jonathan couldn't find them, he came out here and got rich. It's a dirty little story, Teddy, and, yes, I tried to keep it quiet. That's all I'm guilty of though, trying to prevent everyone from finding out what Jonathan was so ashamed of, what he butchered himself over.'

She was telling the truth, I was almost sure of it, but I kept probing anyway. 'You knew Philip in California.' Mary shook her head and, looking at her eyes, I became suddenly unsure of the truth. 'If Jonathan had no contact with his family after he left California, then he didn't get a divorce from his wife – which means you might not get a dime of his estate. That's the way I figure it, Mary. You lied about Philip being here and you were planning to go through with the payoff because otherwise you stood to lose everything.'

'You're just fishing.'

'Yeah, and looks like I caught you.'

'Poor Teddy. Your wife leaves you for another man, your daughter refuses any contact with you since she was a teenager, you become a glorified clerk down at the department – but now you're going to be a hero by exposing me, hm?

'George's got a big mouth.'

'I told you I know all about you. Too bad you didn't do *your* homework. Jonathan divorced his wife ten years ago.'

'But—'

'Jonathan was becoming wealthy and his lawyer didn't like the idea of a wife being out there somewhere, so they hired someone to find her and she made a settlement.'

'And the two kids?'

'The daughter had already died by then and Jonathan's wife didn't know where the son was.'

'Is the wife still alive.'

'No, she died seven or eight years ago.'

'About the time you and Jonathan got married.'

'Yes. So what does all this leave you with?'

I wasn't sure.

'I'll tell you, Teddy – it leaves you with nothing. I get Jonathan's estate because I'm his legal wife. I tried to pay off his son to protect Jonathan's reputation – no one's going to put me in jail for that.'

She was probably right.

'You came after me the way you did because you hate women – because of what your wife did to you. Do I remind you of her, is that it?'

'Bullshit, you're younger than my daughter.'

'Oh, that's right. Of course – I remind you of your daughter. The one who has a son you've never seen. What, you're surprised I know that, too?'

I was.

'The only difference between your family skeletons and Jonathan's is that yours were never very secret. What's his name, your grandson.'

I told her.

'And you've never even talked to him on the telephone?'

'I tried a few times, but my daughter . . .' I told Mary I wanted to meet the boy back when he was young enough to call me Poppo, which is what I called my grandfather. I felt suddenly stupid saying these things, embarrassed.

Mary's voice came to me softly. 'Jonathan doesn't have a chance to make up with his family, but you still do.'

'My daughter won't even talk to me.'

'Then go down to Florida and find your grandson on your own, you're a detective.'

I wasn't feeling like much of one, though.

She came to me at the mantel. 'I haven't done anything bad, not really.'

I shrugged, looking away, and Mary put a hand on my waist. 'Stay here with me until they catch Jonathan's son, will you do that?'

236

I told her I would.

'You want another drink?'

I said I'd better not.

'There's a telephone in my bedroom, you could come up and wait for the call there.'

I just looked at her, not figuring it out.

'You know where the bedroom is, where I'm sleeping?'

I nodded.

'I'll wait for you upstairs – OK?'

I said OK.

23

He's back.

Sitting against a tree, Philip sees the upstairs light go on across the road and although he is suffering again from that crippling pain, Philip spirits immediately elevate: *She's home*. He sobs his laughter and squeezes the hand.

Inside the house, lying on one of the couches in the living room, Teddy Camel is thinking and drifting. He's called the station several times and been told that Philip Jameson hasn't been apprehended yet. They think he's out of the area, having slipped away before the roadblocks were in place. The search is being extended farther west.

Philip rests the back of his head against the big tree, so sleepy. But he can't let himself sleep, not yet. Think of something else – of how you outsmarted them.

Yes! He drove right past cop cars, gripping the steering wheel, breathing shallowly from fear, a strong hand squeezing his heart – and then the exhilaration, the *happiness* of having made it back here without getting caught.

Philip sobs.

Before he left the old man's garage, he washed his hands and face in a utility sink, finding a comb in the medicine cabinet above the sink and using it to bring some order to his hair, looking at himself in the mirror there and deciding that, except for the eyes, he could pass for normal. Finding aspirin, swallowing six tablets without water, putting the bottle in his jacket. He reversed out of the garage in the old man's new Buick, stopping to close and lock the door, then driving off in a direction that would carry him away from the sounds of sirens.

He saw two roadblocks but they were on other streets, Philip wasn't going that way, he was coming here instead. He stayed on the small streets, drove right at the speed limit, kept his eyes straight ahead. No one stopped him. He drove by two cop cars – but no one stopped him! Outsmarted them is right, proving that—

Jesus, it hurts. Now that the thrill of escape has passed, all the old pains are fiery again; and his eyes, deprived of sleep these past days, they itch and hurt and seem to be squeezing even more pain back into his head where there is already too much pain. He brings that screaming headful of pain forward and stares with hooded eyes at her house, waiting for the bedroom light to go off, squeezing the hand harder as he waits.

Lying on a couch in that house, drifting and once again about to display his prodigious ability for napping under even the most adverse of circumstances, Teddy Camel wonders how he could have been so wrong about so many things. A hell of a time to lose my talent, he thinks – with everyone lying to him and getting away with it.

But as Camel drifts, his mind keeps laboring. He knows he shouldn't go to sleep until Philip is caught, but Camel is seduced by a river dream: floating on a slow barge, drifting with the current, an engine room making muffled sounds somewhere far away.

Jonathan Gaetan had two kids. Philip is thirty-two and if the daughter, Nancy, had lived, she would be thirty-three – a year younger than my daughter, Camel thinks. Mary is twenty-eight. Even if she and Jonathan's kids had gone to the same high school in California they wouldn't have been in high school *together*, Mary's too young, so why am I still trying to connect Mary to

Jonathan's kids, why I am still trying to find something to *blame* her for? Maybe she's right, it's because ever since my wife and daughter left me, I've been wanting to prove what liars women are.

I don't know, Camel thinks as he allows those thoughts to drift on that slow river, I just don't know – Teddy Camel drifting away to sleep, an engine room deep in his mind still working on the possibilities.

But Philip is *fighting* his need to sleep, struggling against his pain – coming up with a brand-new plan.

As soon as her bedroom light goes off, he'll go into the house and wake her up and get his money. Then he'll wait until daylight and take Jonathan's Mercedes, leaving the Buick in the garage because even if the cops have already found the old man with his throat slit, they'll be looking for a Buick, not Jonathan's Mercedes.

He'll dress up in Jonathan's clothes, too – a nice suit, clean white shirt. The cop won't stop him then, not dressed like that and driving a black Mercedes. My daddy's boy, Philip thinks, sobbing.

Then switch cars three or four times on the way to Mexico, *buying* them because he'll have plenty of money, drive straight through and for once in his life make a success of something.

When the upstairs light across the street goes off, Philip immediately puts his right hand on the butt of the gun in his waistband, quietly sobbing his laughter.

24

He walks out of the woods holding Penny's hand.

Philip pauses at the street, still searching the night for signs of a trap, desperate not to get caught, not at this late stage, not when he's so close. He tries to cross the street in a hurry but is unable to run, that puncture wound in his right thigh hurting too much, forcing him to crab and scurry his way across, limping to the side of the garage and then making his way behind it, stopping there to rest, breathing heavily, tired all the way down to his demented soul.

He leans his head back against the garage wall, closing his eyes, and – incredibly – he falls instantly to sleep. Standing there holding Penny's hand, asleep.

When Philip awakens with a start, he lunges forward and falls to his knees, still holding her hand. *Shit*. He struggles to his feet. How could he have dropped off like that, standing up, and how long was he out, no more than a few seconds, a minute at the most, but I have to be careful, he tells himself, never make it to Mexico at this rate.

At the back of the house, Philip checks the basement window he pried open last Sunday but it has been locked and he can't possibly pop it open with the little utility knife in his pocket. He tries ground-floor windows, finding them all locked, too. Holding a flap of his field jacket against a window pane to muffle the sound, he taps the glass with the state trooper's pistol, tapping harder and harder until the glass cracks. Then he works the broken pane out and reaches in to unlock the window.

Once in the house, Philip quickly finds the center hallway, pausing at the bottom of the steps to listen for sounds.

Teddy Camel is lying within thirty feet of where Philip stands, Teddy dreaming of his daughter and of those moments Mary Gaetan was talking about, when news arrives so unexpectedly, so bad, that for the rest of your life you never forget the *details* of that moment. Like when Teddy's wife told him their daughter was pregnant and the two of them were leaving him, easy to lie to a man who doesn't pay attention, she had said – Teddy will never forget the details of that moment.

Teddy remembers and dreams of the last time he gave a bath to his daughter, still a toddler, telling his wife that he thought the girl was too old for him to be giving her a bath, his wife laughing good-naturedly at his confused embarrassment.

The exact details of a telephone call – Teddy drifting and dreaming and remembering – when his daughter called him at work and said, 'Daddy, I've got some bad news,' explaining to him that the president had been shot in Texas. Even though Teddy and the entire world had known about it for hours, his daughter announced the news carefully, as if she needed to break it to him gently.

And now she won't even take a call from him, won't send him a snapshot of her son, Teddy's grandson, a boy who's all grown up now and too old to call him Poppo even if they *were* to meet at this late stage.

Teddy rolls over in his sleep.

At the bottom of the steps leading to the second floor, Philip decides it is nothing, just his ears playing tricks on him. He had been watching the house for a long time and didn't see any cars parked nearby, didn't see any cops wandering around. They haven't made the connection between me and Jonathan, they don't know I'm here, just go on upstairs and do it, he urges himself – *do it*.

He creeps along the second-floor hallway, stopping at the bathroom door, which is open. Although the lights are off, the big window over the tub illuminates the room well enough that Philip can see it is empty, no one lurking there to catch him. The next door on the right will be hers, steady now, almost there . . .

'I have to go to the bathroom.'

Startled, Philip immediately halts and looks down at Penny as if he has forgotten he's been pulling her along with him all this time. Until now, she's been totally silent, not complaining or resisting even when he had to haul her through that window with him.

It requires a moment for Philip to recover his composure, recover from the surprise of this mute creature suddenly speaking, but soon he has his hand clamped over her mouth, bending down to tell Penny, 'Keep quiet,' and then releasing his hand to find out if she's going to comply.

'I have to *pee*,' she whispers again, standing on one leg and then the other. 'I *have* to.'

Annoyed, Philip tells her to go in her pants.

'I can't do *that*,' she insists, pointing back to the bathroom doorway. 'In there.'

'Damn,' he mutters, wishing now he had followed his instincts and left Penny in the garage with that old man. After all, he doesn't *need* her anymore.

But when Penny pulls on his hand, Philip allows himself to be tugged along to the bathroom.

Why did he take her with him, putting her on the front floor of the Buick, covering her with a blanket, warning her not to make a sound or he *would* kill her? Why go to all that trouble when he no longer needed her? It wasn't a lack of resolve, he tells himself, because he could've easily slit her little throat . . . but then why didn't he do it?

Because he still wants to take her to Mexico with him.

No, he can't. The cops'll be going out of their heads looking for a man traveling with a little girl, stupid to take Penny with him. But he doesn't want to go alone, that's the thing . . .

Take Mary along! The three of them could pass for a family, the cops won't be looking for *a family*, and being part of a regular family appeals to Philip.

Once in the bathroom with Penny, he closes the door to the hallway and keeps the lights off. 'Go on,' he whispers to her, 'you don't need the lights to pee.' Only when she begins twisting her small hand in his does he realize that the reason she can't walk over there and pee is that he's still holding on to her.

Philip releases her hand and at the same time he lets go of his stupid dreams, traveling to Mexico with Penny and Mary as if they were a regular family. Because the only chance he has of making it is to leave Penny and Mary in this house and go off on his own like always, leaving them here with their throats slit.

Penny is standing at the toilet, looking back at Philip and waiting. 'I can't,' she finally whispers. 'I can't go to the bathroom with *you* in here.'

He rubs his temples. 'Well, I ain't leaving you here on your own.' Then Philip creeps to the door adjoining the master bedroom, opening it quietly and seeing Mary sleeping alone in that big bed. He shuts the door carefully and turns toward Penny.

She's still just standing there, dancing again, whining as one hand grasps at her groin. 'I have to *go*,' Penny implores.

'Well, *go*,' he replies.

'Not with you watching.'

'I ain't watching.'

'You have to go out and wait for me,' she says, glancing at the door to the hallway.

He shakes his head.

'*Please*.' Penny has begun to cry.

Looking worriedly at the door to the bedroom, Philip warns her, 'If you wake anyone up . . .' He steps to the center of the room. 'Tell you what, I'll go in there, in the tub, and I'll pull the curtain so I won't be able to see you, but then you got to hurry up and pee. And listen to me, little girl, if you try to run away I'll really take care of you, understand?'

Penny nods.

He walks to the tub and steps in. 'I'm closing the curtain, but remember what I told you.'

She nods again.

Still worried he's making a mistake, Philip stands in the tub waiting and listening, hearing nothing. 'Hey,' he whispers.

'I'm *trying*,' she tells him.

'Are you on the pot?'

'The what?'

'Are you on the toilet?'

'Yes.'

'Well, go ahead and pee.'

'I told you, I'm *trying*.' Silence. 'You have to be quiet, I can't go if you're talking to me.'

Philip mutters something.

'*Shhh.*'

This is crazy, he thinks as he sits in the tub. Waiting and listening, Philip still can't hear her peeing. He finally lies back, whispering once more for Penny to hurry.

'Shhh,' she tells him again.

He curses halfheartedly.

The big bathtub is too much like a bed, Philip lying there waiting, listening, looking out through the window over the tub and seeing stars, his eyes too heavy to keep open, and even with all of his willpower he can no longer resist, can no longer bear the weight that presses down on him, eyes closing, not enough struggle left within him, unable to hold off what has already arrived, sleep.

25

He stops his car a block away from Mary's house and parks on the side of the road, dousing the headlights but then just sitting there, Detective Sergeant 'Lord' Alfred Bodine taking time to calculate the angles.

It doesn't make sense, Teddy's refusal to come along on the manhunt. He might have burned out years ago, but he is no coward.

Alfred sits and thinks. Until the past hour or so, he'd been too busy patrolling his sector to worry about Teddy, but as it became increasingly clear that the killer had eluded them, Alfred began wondering what angle Teddy was playing. Then it came to him: Teddy had returned to Mary's house to wait for the killer.

And now here I am, Alfred thinks, putting my ass on the line again after *swearing* that the episode in the motel room was absolutely the last time I'd risk my career to cover for him. Bodine glances at his radio. In twenty minutes he's due back in his sector for a radio check. Damn Teddy anyway.

Alfred drums his blunt fingers on the steering wheel. Got to check out the house, he thinks, find out if Teddy's here, if Mary's all right – and then get back to my sector before Land discovers I left without permission. Shouldn't be doing this without backup. Shit.

He gets out and walks down the road, standing a while outside the big house, looking for lights. Maybe he was wrong about Teddy. Maybe he just went home, Mary's in bed asleep, and Philip Jameson is holed up a hundred miles from here. Alfred decides to check the perimeter.

Flashlight in his left hand, revolver in his right, Bodine walks around to the back of the house and immediately spots the open window with the broken pane. *Shit!* All of it becoming instantly clear to him: Philip *did* return here, broke in the house, found Teddy and Mary, killed them both . . .

Procedure requires Bodine to return to his car and call this in but, instead, he climbs through the open window and flashes his light around the room, a library.

Pumping adrenaline now, more frightened about finding bodies than he is of meeting up with Philip, Alfred moves quietly, surprisingly light on his feet as he leaves the library and finds himself in the central hallway, doors closed on both sides: the bodies, or Philip, could be anywhere.

Lying on the couch that blocks his view of the hallway, Teddy Camel is suddenly awakened by a message delivered to him from that engine room deep in his mind. *He knows.*

But now that Teddy knows, what's he going to do with that knowledge? Run upstairs and awaken Mary, confronting her with the truth? And what then? What if she pulls back the covers and invites him to join her, naked, in her bed?

My God, he thinks, it can't be true – but of course it is. And for the moment, Teddy reacts to that truth by doing what he's done since he turned fifty: nothing. By doing what he's done about reconciling himself with his daughter and meeting that grandson he's never seen: nothing. The only reason Teddy finally moves at all, in fact, is because the big .45 has been digging into his ribs, Teddy rearranging the holster and finally getting an elbow under him to raise up.

Having just reached the archway to the living room, Alfred thinks he hears someone in there. He flicks off the flashlight so it won't make him a target, going into a crouch and pointing his revolver at the back of the couch that faces the big mantel, waiting for Philip to show himself.

Alfred is, in fact, about to reach around the archway for the light switch when he hears the muffled sound of a toilet flushing upstairs. At least that's what he thinks he hears.

Alfred steps backward to the middle of the hallway and listens, hearing nothing now. What do you do? Was that a phantom sound in the living room or is Philip in there – or is he upstairs taking a leak?

Alfred climbs the steps quickly, checking doors off the upstairs hallway, casting his flashlight beam around the rooms, coming finally to the master bathroom, opening that door and pointing his flashlight immediately on a small figure sitting on the toilet.

Keeping his revolver cocked and held out in front of him, Alfred flicks on the overhead light. It's the little girl, her face painted, jeans bunched around her ankles, tiny red tennis shoes dangling inches above the floor. Alfred holds one finger to his lips, the girl acknowledging his request by nodding slowly.

When Alfred reaches Penny, he kneels in front of the toilet, his back to the closed shower curtain, 'I'm a policeman,' he whispers. 'Who else is here with you? Is there another detective here? Someone wearing regular clothes, not a uniform?'

She shakes her head.

'The man who took you and your brother to his room at that motel – is he here?'

Penny slowly nods.

'OK, honey, I'm going to bring you out to my car, you ready?'

She moves her eyes from Alfred's scarred face, glancing over his left shoulder, and then quickly looking back into his eyes.

'Penny?' Alfred swivels on his bended knee, checking behind him, seeing nothing. He turns back to her. 'Do you know where the man is right now, that bad man?'

Comes the smallest of voices: 'Yes.' She points over his left shoulder just as Alfred hears the shower curtain being swept aside, Alfred turning his head to see a figure wearing a blond fright wig, leaping from the bathtub, rushing him, Alfred trying

251

simultaneously to get his gun up *and* to keep his body between the girl and this onrushing figure.

It doesn't work. Being down on one knee makes Alfred awkward, and by the time he has executed a half-turn, Philip is on him, striking Alfred with a wide-arcing and full-force blow, the state trooper's revolver connecting with a sickening crunch against Alfred's forehead, the big man falling backward from his crouch, landing on his back on the bathroom floor, Philip pouncing on his chest, hitting him again and again, pounding Alfred's head until the struggling stops, all the struggle beaten out of Alfred, who finally lays still on the floor, arms spread and head bloody.

Sobbing with excitement, Philip pulls the razor-bladed knife from his pocket – but before he can slit Alfred's throat, Penny rushes by.

Enough! She's had enough of policemen being killed in her presence, throats slit, an old man kicked under a car – *enough!*

Slipping off the toilet and pulling up her pants, holding them up with one hand, Penny's had enough of everything and now she's running away from it, passing the crazy man who's sitting on top of the big policeman, Penny rushing toward the bathroom door.

Philip makes a wild grab for her, missing. 'Shit!' he screams, getting off Alfred and starting after Penny, it'll be easy enough to catch her, to take care of her once and for all, she's been enough trouble, her usefulness at an end and now the time's come to slit that little throat.

'Philip?'

He stops at the bathroom door, turning to see a figure by the other door, the one that leads to the bedroom – Jonathan's wife, standing there wearing a red robe that is only loosely tied at the waist, exposing her soft belly and long legs and the dark place between those tanned legs.

He comes toward her, that little knife in his right hand, smiling his broken smile.

'Philip,' she says again, except this time his name is not a question.

26

Teddy Camel is at the bottom of the steps when Penny comes rushing down. He nearly shoots her, releasing the pressure on his trigger finger and raising the barrel at the last moment. This near-mistake jellies his knees, forcing Camel to reach out for the bannister.

She stops a few steps up from him. 'I want to go home.'

The girl is a bizarre sight, holding her jeans up with one hand, face painted with those garish red lines. Her name comes instantly to mind. ' Penny. Who's upstairs, honey?'

She glances back up the steps, worrying that the answer to this man's question is about to make an appearance.

Camel looks up there, too. 'Penny, I'm a policeman, please tell me. Who brought you here?'

'*He* did.'

From the expression on her lipstick-smeared face, Camel knows to whom Penny refers. 'Where is he?' Teddy asks in a whisper, trying to keep the panic out of his voice. 'You have to tell me where he is. Somewhere upstairs?'

Penny sighs. She doesn't want to tell *this* policeman where the crazy man is because if *this* policeman goes upstairs, then he'll end up like the others. She wishes he would just do what she is asking him to do: Penny wants to go home. A policeman is supposed to take you home when you ask him to, her father said so.

'Penny? *Penny.* That man, that bad man who brought you here, where is he right now?'

She slowly looks upstairs and then points there. 'But you'd better not go see,' she warns Camel. 'He did it again.'

'Did what again?'

'Will you take me home now?'

'Yes!' He tells himself not to become angry with her, remember what she's been through tonight. 'Penny, did he hurt you? Did he do anything bad to you?'

'Not to *me*.'

'Before I take you home, I have to make sure that man doesn't hurt anyone else.' Camel is thinking of Mary.

Penny scratches her hair. 'But you'd better take me home *first*.' Or else I'll never get home, Penny thinks, because *he* will do to you what he did to the others.

'Is a woman upstairs with him?'

She sighs again. 'Another policeman came in while I was on the potty. I flushed the toilet because sometimes that helps me go. This other policeman said he was going to help me, but that man was hiding in the bathtub. Then this policeman told me everything was going to be OK. But he was wrong.'

'Another policeman? Was he wearing a uniform, was he dressed like a policeman, or did he—'

Penny knows what a uniform is. 'He had on regular clothes. His face . . .' She touches Camel's face, running small fingers across his cheeks, her touch so soft that Camel feels chills along his spine.

'You mean he had lines on his face? Scars?'

She nods. 'He was big.'

Alfred. 'What happened to him?' Teddy asks anxiously.

'He's dead,' she says softly. Then her voice strengthens: 'Just like the others and that's why you got to take me home first!'

'Dead?' Lord Alfred dead? 'Are you sure he's dead, that big policeman?'

Penny nods her head very earnestly. 'And so is that policeman who *was* wearing a uniform, who came up to the car when we were on the highway, and so is that man in the garage – and so will you be dead, too, if you go upstairs!'

'OK, OK,' He pats her shoulders. 'Now you have to listen to me, Penny, listen to me very carefully.' He takes her by the hand to a table on which rests a telephone. 'First off, I'm going to call—' Camel is interrupted when Mary's voice cries out from upstairs.

'I don't know who *that* is,' Penny says, maneuvering to get behind Camel.

Mary. Camel releases the girl's hand and steps toward the stairway. 'You're going to have to make the call for me, Penny.' He looks up the stairs and then back at her, trying to explain in a hurry what she must do. 'Just pick up the phone and punch nine-one-one, tell them your name, tell them a policeman has been killed, and then just stay on the line.'

'I don't know the address.'

He has climbed five steps when he stops to talk to her again. 'You don't have to know the address. They can trace a nine-one-one call. Please, just make the call and then run outside and hide.'

'A policeman came to our school once and he told us how to use nine-one-one, and he said you're supposed to know the address so you can tell—'

'Penny!' Camel is halfway up, on the landing now, bending so he can still see her, talking to her in quiet desperation. 'Just make that call, honey. Nine-one-one, tell them what's happened, tell them a policeman is in trouble, you don't have to know the address.' When Mary cries out again, Camel turns away from the girl and takes the remaining steps two at a time.

Penny knows what's going to happen up there. She knows what's going to happen to whoever is screaming and to the policeman who's rushing to help her. Penny has seen it happening all night; she *knows.*

Instead of making the nine-one-one call, Penny decides to hide. But not outside like the policeman said, it's too scary to go outside in the night-time like this. She walks carefully along the hallway until she sees a small door to the space under the staircase. Perfect! In her grandmother's house, there's a little door like this and when she and Billy play hide-and seek, sometimes that's where Billy hides. Penny has never hidden in there because it's the kind of place where spiders probably live. She turns the latch and looks in. When the woman upstairs cries out again, Penny ducks her head and enters the dark space, braving whatever spiders might live in here, braving even mice or ghosts because none of that is as scary as what she's been with tonight. Creeping among boxes, Penny finds a hiding spot in one of the far corners of the storage space, sitting on the floor and making a resolute decision not to come out for anyone – not even a policeman, uniformed or not – Penny making a promise to God that she's not coming out for anyone except Daddy himself.

Teddy has stopped in the upstairs hallway, flattening himself against the wall next to the open doorway leading to the lighted bathroom, trying to catch his breath. He can't. He's going to have to charge in panting.

Holding the heavy .45 straight out with both hands, he swings around into the doorway, glancing at the figure on the floor and knowing without looking at the face who it is spread-eagled there. But he doesn't have time to check Alfred, to see if Penny was right about his being dead, though dead is certainly what he appears to be, so still does he lie, so much of his blood on that expensive tilework around his head. Teddy Camel's mouth tightens.

Still panting after breath that eludes him, Camel moves through the bathroom, kicking open the door that leads to the bedroom, gun pointing straight ahead, ready to shoot.

Philip and Mary are on the far side of the bed, Philip holding her by the hair with one hand, his other hand pressing a small triangular blade against that long expanse of her throat. Mary's robe has come completely undone, hanging open, her breasts exposed, nipples very red in the light coming from the room behind Teddy, all of the body tanned except for her breasts and that bikini area around her pubic hair.

256

'The bitch says she doesn't have my money,' Philip says to Teddy, as if that explains everything.

Trying to maintain the sights on Philip's face, Teddy speaks flatly: 'I'm a police officer. Release the woman.'

'Fuck you,' Philip replies, almost gaily. He remains behind Mary, keeping the blade to her throat. Now what, Camel wonders. If Penny made the call, fifty cops should be showing up here in ten minutes – except he's not sure ten minutes are available to him or to Mary.

'We've got men all around the house, Philip.'

'How do you know my name?' he demands in a rage. 'How the fuck does everyone know my name?'

'I'm one of the officers who's been tailing you. We followed you here. That officer in the bathroom, he was the first one in the house, then I came in, and there are a dozen more outside, patrol cars on their way – it's all over, Philip.'

'Bullshit!' He drags Mary to the window. 'I don't see no cops out there. You're bullshitting me!'

'I'm not,' Teddy replies, following their movements through the sights of the .45 automatic, trying not to let the terror on Mary's face distract him, knowing he's not marksman enough to guarantee hitting Philip without endangering Mary. Have to stall, Teddy thinks. They're on their way. If Penny made that call . . . 'Philip! As soon as the backup arrives, those officers downstairs are going to come charging up here. But if you toss the knife on the bed and let the woman go, you can still walk out of here alive.'

Laughing at Camel, he pulls Mary back to the far side of the bed. 'Kind of old for this Rambo shit, ain't you, Pops?'

Yeah, Camel thinks.

'You and that big cop in the bathroom, it's just the two of you, ain't it? You and your partner got sent over here to check out the house, right? And I already took care of the big guy, so now I kill you, Pops, and then, yeah, I *will* walk out of here alive.'

To Camel's horror, the .45 begins shaking in his hands. Has *he* noticed it yet? 'When those other officers arrive, they're going to be coming up here shooting. They don't care about the woman, 'cause you're a cop-killer, and they're going to nail you. But if you release her right now, then I'll go downstairs with you and make sure you don't get shot – that's the only way to play this.'

'Bullshit!' Philip screams. 'You're the one who's going to get nailed, asshole, and I'm the one going to nail you!'

Why does he keep threatening to kill me? Teddy wonders. I have a gun on *him*, how's he going to kill me? 'I'll make you a deal, Philip.'

'Fuck your deals! And stop saying my name.'

'Release the woman and then you can go. I won't try to stop you.'

'Ha! I step away from her and you'll shoot me, think I don't know that? I'm not stupid!'

'I know you're not. A stupid man would never have been able to escape the way you have, all those cops out there looking for you, but here you are, slipped right through them, didn't you?'

'Fucking A!'

'So what're you going to do with the woman, huh? She'll just slow you down. Let her go and take off, that's the way to play this.' Camel wishes he could get a message through to Mary, telling her to drop, to let her knees buckle and drop straight down so he can get a clear shot. But even if she got the message, Camel decides, she wouldn't be able to do it, not with that blade so tight to her throat.

'I'll tell you how we're going to play this, Pops. I'm slitting this bitch's throat and then I'm killing you and *then* I'm strolling out of here – how do you like that plan, huh?'

But he's obviously not made up his mind to do it, Camel thinks, or he would've done it already. He's trying to talk himself into it. 'As soon as you cut her,' Camel says, 'I'm going to blow your ass apart, you know that. At this distance, you realize the hole a .45 slug is going to make?' The big automatic trembling in his hands, Camel is beginning to doubt that Penny made the call.

And if she didn't, how is he going to prevent this guy from slitting Mary's throat?

Philip is looking around the room, confused, his eyes red. He glances at Teddy who is staring at him with those blue eyes sighted down the barrel of that gun, which Philip just then notices is shaking. He sobs. 'Fuck you, old man. Hear me, fuck you, huh? It's just you and me, ain't it, and that's why your hands are shaking, man, 'cause there ain't no one else in this house to help you, just you and me, ain't it?'

'Yes.'

'I knew it! You lied to me, fucker!'

'But I'm not lying to you about this, *Philip* – you put one scratch on that woman, I'm blowing you away. Just drop the knife!'

Teddy is amazed when Philip does exactly that, tossing the knife on the bed – but then Philip quickly slips behind Mary and draws out a revolver, pointing it at Teddy, the movement performed so deftly that Teddy is unable to capitalize on Philip's transfer of weapons.

Philip is sobbing.

I blew it, Camel thinks – now what?

Mary remains frozen, Philip's left arm around her neck, both of her hands on that arm, unable or unwilling to attempt escape. Occasionally, her mouth opens as if she wants to speak but then thinks better of it.

No one's coming to help me, Teddy decides. The little girl was too scared to make that call. I can't shoot him because Mary's in the way, and now there's nothing to prevent him from shooting me. It's over. And with that realization arrives a certain resigned calmness; the .45 stops trembling. 'What're we going to do, Philip, shoot each other?'

'I told you to stop using my name.'

'What do you want me to call you?'

'I want you to keep your mouth shut, that's what I want.'

'Let's do it, Philip. Step away from the woman so we can

259

shoot each other, that's where this is heading, isn't it?'

'I got a better idea. Toss your gun on the bed and then I'll think about if I'm going to let you live or not.'

'No can do.' Never surrender your weapon.

'Fine,' Philip says, raising the revolver until it is pointed directly at Camel's face. Then he cocks the hammer.

And Camel can see in the man's eyes that he does indeed intend to shoot, so Camel does what you're never supposed to do, what is now unavoidable: he tosses the .45 on the big bed that separates him from Philip and Mary.

'Ha!' He is sobbing again. 'Ha! Now what have we got, huh, asshole, copper-man, huh, now what have we got! I'll tell you what *you* got, you got nothing, no gun, no other cops to help you, you got nothing!' He is practically singing these words.

Teddy straightens out of his shooting crouch, lowering his arms to his sides. Amazingly he actually feels relaxed, everything out of his hands now, standing up straight and giving his arms a rest. He looks at the woman. 'Tell him, Mary,' Camel says.

'Tell me what?' Philip asks. 'About the money? You got the money after all, holding out on me, huh, is that it, bitch?' He jerks the arm that's around her neck, making Mary's head snap back and forth. Then Philip looks at Camel who's still looking at Mary. 'Great tits, huh?' He takes his arms from around her neck and moves his hands down, over her breasts. 'I got a good feel the first night I was here,' he tells Teddy. 'She wanted to fuck me that night.'

'No,' Mary says, staring at Camel's eyes.

'Oh yes she did, wanted to fuck me real bad, but I don't need no secondhand pussy from my old man, all I wanted was what was coming to me, my money.'

'I told you,' she says, choking to get the words out. 'The money's being delivered here in the morning, Friday morning, just like I said on the telephone. You came too early, it'll be here in the morning.'

'But we ain't got that much time, can't wait till morning, can we, Pops?'

'No.' Teddy Camel looks at the two people who hold his life in their hands, Philip who can shoot him at any moment he chooses and Mary who can stop him from doing it. 'Mary, tell him,' Camel requests.

Philip raises the revolver to point it at Camel's face again, demanding: 'Why do you keep saying that? What's she's supposed to tell me?'

'She has to be the one to say it, you won't believe me.'

'*Say what?*'

Mary is shaking her head.

'Screw you both,' Philip says, pushing Mary on the bed but holding tightly to her robe so that she ends up sitting on the edge of the bed naked, her hands at her sides, making no attempt to cover herself.

Philip glances rapidly between Mary and Teddy. 'You two are trying to pull some fancy shit on me, but I ain't falling for it.' Then he sobs several times, grinning. 'You, Pops, get undressed – I'm going to watch you fuck her. Go on! I'm giving you a chance to die in the saddle!' Sobbing. 'You heard me, asshole, strip!'

Teddy Camel's reply arrives calmly, nothing to lose. 'Fuck you, Philip.'

'Hey, I'm warning you.' He still has the revolver pointed at Camel's face.

'No!' Mary shouts.

'You two think you're going to end up laughing at me, screwing me out of my money, lying to me about having this place surrounded, hey, I've been dumped on enough, no more! Jonathan was out here getting rich, laughing at the way he left my old lady, but Jonathan ain't laughing now, is he? And after tonight nobody's going to be laughing at me, you hear, *nobody!*'

'No,' Camel agrees, 'no one's going to be laughing at you after tonight.'

'Fucking A. So the only thing I got to decide now is which one of you I off first.'

Mary has moved her hands to cover her face, leaving the rest of the body still exposed.

Philip hesitates. The problem is, he can't quite get the rhythm of it, killing someone with a gun, he's always done it before with a blade, knifings that they never even found out about in California, at least never traced to him, and that's what he wants to do to Mary, watch the blade draw a red line across her throat, feel the heat of her blood on his hands, get off on the terror in her eyes as she performs that final dance – but he can't slit her throat and keep the cop covered too, so he's going to have to shoot the cop first. Just pull the trigger, he tells himself. The gun's already pointed at the cop's face – just pull the goddamn trigger.

Mary suddenly reaches for him. 'Doll-boy,' she implores.

'That does it!' he shouts at her. 'You're going first, bitch!' He turns the gun away from Camel and puts the barrel on Mary's forehead, exactly between her eyes – which are looking right at him. 'Nobody calls me that,' he says by way of explanation, almost an apology for what he's about to do.

'Don't,' Camel says, amazed that Mary still won't say it, not even to save her life. 'Don't shoot her, Philip. She's your sister.'

He stands there with the gun against her forehead, his mouth trying to form a question. What the hell is he talking about, my sister? Nancy's dead. This is Jonathan's wife. It's a cop trick.

'You don't want to kill your sister, Philip.'

'What're you talking about?'

'When you turned twenty-five,' Teddy says in a rush of words, 'your mother came to visit you in prison, telling you who your father was, where he lived, telling you that he was rich and that you deserved some of his money, you remember that, don't you, Philip, what your mother told you that day in prison, how she gave you the idea to come out here and collect your money?

'Nancy's not dead. Your mother found Nancy on *her* twenty-fifth birthday, on Nancy's twenty-fifth birthday, and she told Nancy the same thing she told you, about Jonathan. Then Nancy came looking for your father, just like you did.'

Mary closes her eyes. 'No.'

Philip steps back, removing the barrel from her forehead, staring at her.

'Can't you see it?' Teddy insists. 'Can't you see who it is? Don't you remember how your big sister looked, can't you see it's Nancy?'

Philip takes another step back, lowering the revolver. 'She can't be Nancy. Nancy's dead. If she was Nancy . . . you can't marry your own father.' But he keeps staring at her, trying to see Nancy in her face.

Gingerly, slowly, Teddy lifts his right foot, bending the knee, bringing his leg up behind him, trying to get his foot close enough to reach the .38 in the ankle holster, keeping his eyes on Philip, still talking to him. 'Eight years ago she came out here to see her father, just the way you did, maybe to get some money, like you tried to do, Philip, but instead she fell in love with Jonathan.'

'No!' Mary shouts, opening her eyes and looking wildly from Philip to Teddy.

'You didn't love him?' Philip asks quietly.

'Yes! I loved him. More than I loved anyone in my entire life, I loved him.'

'Is it you?' Philip asks, extending the robe he's been holding in his left hand; she takes it and presses it against her body. 'But I don't understand . . .' Suddenly remembering the Polaroids, he uses his free hand to fish in his pockets for them, bringing them out and holding them spread in his fingers like a card hand. His lips play shyly with a half-smile. 'I kept looking at these,' he says to no one in particular. 'I *knew* something was bothering me about these pictures.'

Having completed the agonizingly slow lifting of his leg, .38 now in his hand, Teddy straightens himself, keeping his right hand at his side, the pistol out of sight. Philip hasn't even glanced at him, so intent is he upon the Polaroids.

'It is you, isn't it?' he asks again. 'Nancy?'

'I couldn't tell you,' she replies.

'You *married* him?'

'I couldn't tell anyone.'

'I thought you were dead.'

'I was. That person I used to be, when we were living with Mom, that person is dead. I'm someone different now.'

'But you are Nancy, aren't you?'

'I'm sorry, Philip.'

'You *promised!* You said you wouldn't leave me there with her, no matter what – you promised you'd come back for me. I *waited* for you. That's why I thought Mom had to be right when she told me you were dead, because if you were alive, I knew you'd come back for me. I waited . . .'

'I tried! But my life was so screwed up and by the time I got myself straightened out, you were in prison.'

'Nancy?' he asks as if still unable to believe it. Philip has lowered the revolver to his side. 'I would never have treated you like . . . if I'd known it was *you*, Nancy, I wouldn't have been so mean to you that night I came here. You should've told me.'

'I couldn't. I couldn't tell anyone.'

He's nodding.

'I'm sorry I didn't come back for you, please believe me, how sorry I am.'

'I believe you,' he says, a great earnestness in his voice. 'If you'd been able to come back for me, you would have – I know that now. I'm just glad you're not dead. I thought everybody was dead. You, Mom, Jonathan. But you're *alive*.' He's grinning.

Mary reaches out her right hand and Philip takes it with his left, the two of them holding to each other with fingers lightly intertwined, neither of them totally sure yet of the wisdom of touching.

'I didn't kill him, did I?' Philip asks her. 'I remember almost everything that happened that night, I didn't kill him.'

'No.'

'You said I did.'

'You didn't, doll-boy, you didn't.'

'You did.'

'No, those photographs did.'

'Come on, Nancy, *you* killed him didn't you?'

She stares at his face for a long time and then nods.

Camel, standing on the other side of the bed, wonders why he is listening to all this, why he doesn't bring up the .38 that's in his hand and shoot him, right now, before Philip regains his composure. But Camel is too enthralled to act, too fascinated with the truth he's hearing.

'I didn't mean to,' she tells her brother. 'I was trying to *save* him.'

'But you killed him instead.'

'Yes.' She is crying. '*Yes.*'

'Hey, Nancy, that's all right, don't cry, I killed some people, too. So, see, we're in the same boat, it's OK.' His voice has assumed childlike qualities. 'I'm going to take care of you, it doesn't matter what you've done, you're my sister.'

'I wanted to pay you that money so you could go live in Mexico, but I had trouble getting it out of the accounts. I wasn't lying about the money, doll-boy.'

'I know.'

'I wanted you to make it,' she is telling Philip, 'but you got yourself in so much trouble.'

'It's all right, Nancy. Now that I've found you, nothing can bother us. Listen, as soon as that money comes in the morning, you and I can drive to Mexico together! They'll never catch us. You should've seen all the cops out there tonight, and I drove right through them. We can get *lost* in Mexico.'

'But those people you killed.'

'Hey, don't worry!' Philip's face is bright. Standing there and holding his sister's fingers, he seems emptied now of terror, talking happily to her. 'I'm going to protect you, Nancy.'

'You have to give yourself up, that's the only way. I'll hire the best lawyers and—'

She is interrupted by a change in his face, his demeanor darkening again, looking over at Teddy but still speaking to his sister. 'You're worried about this cop, aren't you?' Philip is nodding. 'I understand, Nancy. Because he's here, that's the reason you think we have to give ourselves up. But you don't have to worry about him. I told you, Nancy, I'll take care of everything.' He glances down at the gun, confirming that the hammer is cocked, and then Philip makes eye contact with Camel again, telling him, 'Adios, motherfucker.' He raises the gun.

But Teddy Camel is faster, bringing the .38 up and firing when his arm is level, the entire action performed in one smooth motion.

Philip is knocked backward by the concussion, falling on his ass, turning to get up but then collapsing on the carpet, legs kicking and arms pumping furiously, as if he is practicing some demented swimming stroke, making sounds with his mouth but producing no words.

Mary, still sitting on the edge of the bed with the robe clutched to her breasts, is holding her hand straight out in the air, exactly where it was when her brother was touching it, before he let go.

Later, Teddy Camel will be unable to recall hearing the shot he fired, will be able to remember only the sounds that followed that shot: Philip gurgling and choking, his arms and legs scratching at the carpet, and then, *after* Philip becomes still, that is when Mary begins to scream.

27

Even though Philip had an ugly red hole in the middle on his chest, I kept the .38 on him as I kicked the revolver away from his body and then reached down to confirm the obvious: the man was dead. I retrieved the revolver and looked at Mary.

She was sitting on the edge of the bed, holding the robe to her body, the screaming replaced now by a strange kind of whining. No time to deal with her. I rushed to the bathroom and knelt beside Alfred, placing two fingers to the side of his neck, enjoying the feel of his strong, steady pulse. I made him as comfortable as I could with towels and then ran downstairs to call for an ambulance and find Penny.

Shouting her name in the hallway and receiving no answer, I stayed on the phone until I was sure that the dispatcher understood exactly what I was talking about – that I had shot and killed Philip Jameson, the Lipstick Murders suspect, and that my partner was unconscious and needed an ambulance ASAP. After hanging up, I looked at my watch: 4.35 in the morning. By quarter to five, this house would be crowded.

I went outside and called for Penny, but she was apparently too frightened to answer. We'd have to organize a search as soon as enough men arrived. I returned upstairs to check on Alfred, his pulse still strong.

In the bedroom, I found Mary on the floor with Philip. She was naked, cradling his head in her lap. 'Put something on, for chrissakes,' I told her.

Mary stood to get her robe. 'Everything turned out so bad,'

she said, crying and searching around for a cigarette. She found a pack on the bedside table but it was empty. 'Do you have a cigarette?'

I shook my head.

Mary sat on the bed and ran her hands through her hair. 'I guess when everyone gets here, you're going to tell them who I am.'

'What do you think?' I went around the bed to Philip, the hole in his chest appearing even uglier. What looked to be a cheap blond wig was sticking halfway out of the right pocket of his field jacket. I took a sheet from the bottom of the bed and covered him.

'Poor Philip,' Mary said.

'I guess you didn't count on him ever showing up, huh?'

'Teddy? No one has to know about me.'

'What do you mean?'

'I mean, well, your investigation will turn up certain facts, that Jonathan was married before, that he had two kids – and that Philip was his son, of course. But who besides you knows that I'm the daughter?'

'No one. I didn't figure it out until tonight.' I went over and sat beside her.

Mary was trying to smile. 'See? No one else has to know.' She took my hands and moved them into her lap, leaning toward me. 'What's the point in telling people who I am, what does that accomplish?'

'People were murdered because of your lies.'

'No! Philip killed those people, *I* didn't. Even if I'd told you about him from the beginning, who's to say you could've caught him and stopped him from hurting anyone? He killed that girl in Maryland before he even got here, and I didn't even know where he was staying. Why punish me for what my brother did, a brother I haven't seen for eighteen years!'

'You're incredible.'

'I could make you happy, Teddy, I really could.' She was nodding eagerly, gray eyes wet and shining.

'Like you made Jonathan happy?'

'I *did!* For all those years we were married, I made him a happy man.'

'You told Philip you killed him.'

'No! When he found out who I was, that's what killed Jonathan! The secret killed him, finding out the secret, that's what I meant.'

I pulled my hands out of her lap and stood. 'You couldn't tell the truth if your life depended on it.'

'My life depends on it right now, because if you tell people who I am, I swear to God, Teddy, I'll kill myself – I'll commit suicide just like Jonathan did.'

'Tell it to Captain Land, Mary. He's going to be here in a few minutes with a lot of people who'd love to hear—'

'You know what I'm going to say? I'm going to say that when Philip came here demanding money last Sunday night, that was the first time I ever laid eyes on him. I'm going to say I didn't know anything about any murders, I was just trying to protect Jonathan's reputation, trying to protect myself from getting hurt by Jonathan's son.'

'And simply not mention the fact that you happen to be Jonathan's daughter, huh?'

'That's right, Teddy.'

'Don't be an idiot. You got a juvenile record, one fingerprint check and it'll be a cinch to prove who you are.'

'I know that.'

'Then what's the point?'

'The point, Teddy, is that I'm leaving it up to you, I'm trusting you *not* to tell.'

I stood there shaking my head.

'What?' she asked, that smile of hers working hard.

'You are amazing.'

'I don't think you will tell, Teddy, because you're going to realize there's no point to it, ruining me. And you're the only one who can do it, too, because no one else knows, Jo-Jo doesn't, and—'

'And the people who did find out, Jonathan and then Philip, they're both dead, right?'

'Please, Teddy, *please*.' She got careless about keeping her robe together. 'I couldn't go on living if it came out. It's going to be bad enough without people knowing I was Jonathan's daughter.'

'So you want me to lie for you, then you walk away from this mess, as golden as ever, huh?'

'I'll never be able to walk away from this, I'll carry it with me for the rest of my life.'

'Bullshit! You don't feel guilty about anything, you never have.'

'That's not true!' She got off the bed and came toward me.

'At least you have a solid claim to Jonathan's money, being his daughter *and* his wife, you'll have plenty of money for lawyers.'

'What in God's name have I ever done to *you?*'

'Lied to me.' I checked my watch. 'Time's up anyway. Take your chances with Captain Land.'

'I'm not going to jail,' she insisted. 'Even if you tell who I am, I still won't go to jail. I lied to the police, yeah, but I did that because I was under threat from Philip, no one's going to prosecute me.'

'How about incest?'

'They won't put me in prison because of that.'

'I'll tell them you tried to bribe me.'

'What? Tried to bribe you? Is that what you're holding out for, Teddy? You mean when I said I could make you happy, you think that's a bribe? A free fuck and a half-million dollars, is that what it's going to cost to keep my secret?'

I considered it.

'You *are* going to keep my secret, Teddy.'

'I am?' I was smiling.

'Yes. Because you're not going to ruin my life the way you ruined your daughter's life.'

Then we both heard sirens in the distance. 'In about thirty

seconds, you'll find out what I'm capable of.'

'Please!' She began crying again, putting her arms around my neck, trying to make me look her in the face. 'I didn't mean for anyone to get hurt, I swear to God, come on, look at me, you know I'm telling the truth, things just got out of hand, Philip went crazy, all I was trying to do, God, Teddy, I just didn't want people to find out, you can understand that, can't you?'

I tried to get out of her hold.

'*Teddy*,' she pleaded.

The closer the sirens sounded, the more desperate Mary became. 'Listen, please, Teddy, if you want money, I'll give you anything you want, just name an amount.'

I grabbed her wrists. 'I have to get downstairs and meet them.'

'Oh, God, *please*, Teddy!' She had pulled away from my grip and was holding me around the neck again. 'I'll tell you everything, that's what you want, isn't it, to know all the details, exactly how it happened, why I did it, what I was thinking, I'll tell you everything and then you can decide, if what I did was so bad, if I'm such as evil person, then you go ahead and ruin me, play God, I don't care, but please, Teddy, at least give me a chance to tell you what happened, what really happened – the truth.'

But by then the sirens had wound down in front of the house. 'Too late, Mary.' To get away, I had to jerk her arms loose and shove her away from me, Mary hitting the edge of the bed and then falling on the floor next to her brother.

'*Please*,' she begged as I left the room.

28

Downstairs I opened Mary's front door expecting to look out on an army of faces but instead found myself eye to eye with the lone and boyish figure of Melvin Kelvin. In the driveway, two medics were unloading a gurney from the emergency wagon.

'Didn't Land get my message?'

Melvin Kelvin nodded and then immediately turned from me to hold the door for the medics. We all went upstairs and loaded Alfred, still unconscious, on the gurney, carrying him back down and then out to the wagon. Melvin Kelvin and I didn't speak until we were standing once again by Mary's front door. 'If Land got my message, then where the hell is everyone?'

Embarrassed for me, trying to find a way to answer that would soften the insult, Melvin Kelvin finally said, 'Captain Land didn't want to make the announcement until it had been confirmed.'

'Confirmed?' We went inside. 'What's to confirm? You going to hold a mirror to Philip's mouth?'

The kid wisely did not reply.

On the way back upstairs, I told him, 'I want to see how you confirm this.'

'The Captain thought, you know, with all the stress you've been under, after everything that's happened this week, he—'

'He's afraid I finally lost whatever remaining marbles I had in my possession, huh? Or maybe he thought I was drunk, making that call just to break the boredom, deciding to play a little joke on everyone, huh?'

Melvin Kelvin tried to respond sternly. 'More than a hundred officers are still out there looking for this guy, Teddy. If Captain Land is going to call off that kind of search and announce that one of his men has killed the suspect, of course he wants to make sure he got the message straight, that the dispatcher didn't garble it, for example.'

I laughed, 'Yeah.' Leading the boy wonder into the bedroom (Mary had found her cigarettes and was sitting in a chair by the window, smoking and not looking at us when we came in), I said, 'The dispatcher garbling my message, bullshit.'

'I'm just following orders, Teddy.'

I pulled the sheet off of Philip's body, telling Melvin Kelvin: 'Do your stuff.'

Incredibly, he took a faxed photograph of Philip out of his coat pocket and checked it against the dead man's face, actually glancing back and forth several times between face and photo before nodding like a racetrack steward confirming a photo finish, Teddy Camel winning by a nose.

'Satisfied?'

Melvin Kelvin insisted again he was only following Captain Land's orders. 'He said if you *had* shot someone, I was supposed to make a positive ID before I called it in.'

'So what do you think?'

'It's him, of course it's him. Congratulations, Teddy – how'd it happen?'

'Yes, indeed,' Mary said, still looking out the window, '*congratulations* by all means.'

'Mrs Gaetan?' Melvin Kelvin asked as if just then remembering his manners, starting in her direction. To shake hands, I guess.

I took him by the arm and escorted him into the hallway. 'The little girl—'

'Right! Wow, Land wanted me to ask you about her, too.'

I decided against saying anything flippant. 'She's hiding somewhere in the house or outside, I'm not sure. She's too scared to answer me, so I want you to go look for her, start outside, all around the house and in the woods across the road, too. Her name's Penny.'

'I know, I know,' he replied very seriously; a man with an assignment, Melvin Kelvin drew his service revolver.

I waited a moment to take it all in and then asked, 'What're you going to do, son, *shoot* her?'

He grinned, turning red, shaking his head, returning the revolver to its holster. 'Sorry, Teddy. Everyone's been so jumpy, you wouldn't believe what it's been like out there.'

'Been kind of interesting in here, too.'

'Tell me what happened.'

'You go find the girl first.'

'I'll start looking for her as soon as I call in to Captain Land.'

'No!' I said it so sharply that Melvin Kelvin jumped. 'You find the girl and *then* you call our careful Captain.'

'I can't,' he whined. 'He's waiting by the radio right now, told me to call in the minute I found out what the story was with you.'

'The story with me, Detective, is that until someone of higher rank gets here, I'm in charge, and my orders to you are, find the girl first, call Captain Land second. If you disobey those orders and something happens to that girl, it's your ass.'

'He's going to be really ticked off.'

'Yeah, well, I'm always getting my fellow detectives in trouble, didn't Alfred ever tell you that?'

'No.'

I directed Melvin Kelvin gently down the hallway. 'Find the girl – and be careful with her, huh? Remember what she's been through – then you can report in to Land, those are your orders, Mel.'

He nodded and walked away. I went back into the bedroom and took Mary by the hand. 'Let's find someplace to talk where there's not a body on the floor.'

Once we closed the door behind us in one of the other upstairs bedrooms, Mary laying out her cigarettes and ashtray on a small round table, I told her that because of a fluke, a mix-up in communications, we now found ourselves with a little time to kill, and if she wanted to tell me her story, the *truth*, I would listen. 'But the first indication you're lying to me, I'm walking out of this room.'

'The truth? You mean like there being a mix-up in communications, that kind of truth?'

I offered a stare that was relatively blank.

'I saw the way that young man checked Philip's identity,' Mary said. 'They didn't believe you really shot him, did they? They don't trust you, your own people, they thought maybe you killed the wrong man, and when you said there was a mix-up in communications, when you told me that just now, you were lying to me, weren't you?'

I shrugged.

'See, *everyone* lies.'

Mary pulled the robe more tightly around her body, as if suffering a chill, and then she asked, 'Who's that little girl you were talking about?'

'One of the kids that Philip snatched from a motel.'

'She's been here all along, in the house here?'

I nodded. 'Listen to me, Mary, we don't have all night, what's left of the night, because as soon as that detective finds Penny, he'll be calling Land.'

She took out a cigarette but didn't light it. 'How'd you know, can I ask you that?'

'I can't be lied to, remember?'

'Of course, that wonderful talent of yours.' Mary flashed a false smile and then lighted the cigarette.

'I figured it all out while I was downstairs, after you went up to bed.'

'I was wondering about that, too. How did Philip and that little girl and your partner, how'd they all get past you? The only reason I was able to sleep was because I knew you were

276

downstairs. I thought I was safe, but then you let a whole parade of people go marching—'

'Hey, that's how I get when I'm figuring a case out, total concentration, oblivious to everything else. I was on your couch, kind of mentally drifting—'

'Mentally drifting? What you mean is, you kept drinking after I went to bed and you got drunk and passed out, that's what you mean, isn't it?'

'I was *asleep*, OK? But even sleeping, I was still thinking about you, Mary. I couldn't figure it, you know – why you had taken so many risks just for Jonathan's reputation. It didn't wash. *You* had to be involved somehow. Then I remembered how awful you said Sunday night was, how it would stick in your mind the rest of your life the way the news of Kennedy's assassination did, when you were in second grade. But that meant you had to be lying about your age, because if you're really twenty-eight, you would've been only two years old when Kennedy was shot. All this became clear when I remembered how my daughter called me the day Kennedy was killed, and she was in second or third grade. Which makes you roughly her age, thirty-four.'

'Thirty-three,' Mary corrected me.

'Anyway, figuring out your real age was the key. You weren't twenty when you came out here to work at Jonathan's company, you were twenty-five. The same age Philip was when your mother visited him in prison to tell him about Jonathan. The same age Jonathan was when your mother left him. Once I got to that point, it wasn't hard to make the jump.'

'To believe the worst about me, you mean.'

'Yeah. Now let's hear it.'

Mary spoke without emotion. 'I was five when Mom took us away and went into hiding, Philip was four. When Mom found Jonathan in bed with her sister, I guess that really put her around the bend. Certifiable. And most of her craziness was focused on Philip, I guess because he was a boy, potential fornicator like his father.

277

'She used to come into Philip's room at night and threaten him, demanding to know if he was having unclean thoughts, no wonder he turned out the way he did. I tried to protect him, but basically I was out of that house by the time I hit fourteen.'

'Where'd you go?'

'With any guy who'd take me in for the night.'

'Those high school and college records, they're not yours, are they?'

She shook her head. 'I didn't even finish high school. This girl I knew back then, she wanted to disappear, went away with her boy-friend who was wanted by the police because . . . It doesn't matter. I took her Social Security number, her name, used her high school and college records when I enrolled in that secretarial school. And the only reason I went to secretarial school was so I could get a job with Jonathan's company. It all became part of the plan after my mother looked me up and told me who my father was.'

'The last official record we found of you – the real you – was when you went into the hospital to have that kid. Age sixteen. Then you show up here at age twenty-five. What were you doing for those nine years?'

She looked at me not wanting to answer but seeing no way around it. 'Living with different guys, hustling, doing coke, smoking heroin – whatever I had to do that didn't involve going home again and living with that crazy woman. I visited Philip, though.'

'And promised you'd rescue him.'

Mary nodded. 'But after having the baby, giving it up for adoption, I decided to drop out. I'd been busted so many times, had had so many overdoses, I figured that if anyone tried to look me up they'd see the records and just assume that I had died somewhere, the body never found. You know – suicide, overdose, killed by some john. The only reason Mom found me was that she didn't check any records, she came for me in person. Actually saw me on the street – every mother's nightmare, huh?

Seeing your daughter selling it on the street. Confirmed every crazy notion she had about Jonathan's evil influence.'

Mary stood very still, letting the cigarette grow a long ash. 'Back when I was still using my real name, I'd had two abortions. Then, pregnant the third time, I was more or less living with one guy – knew who the father was. But the bastard skipped on me when I was seven months pregnant, too late for an abortion, and having the baby involved me with all those state agencies. I had to give the baby up for adoption because I couldn't take care of myself, couldn't even get my shit together enough to go save my brother – how in hell was I going to raise a child? Then the very next year I had another abortion.'

'Jesus, I thought you were a pro.'

She was stubbing out her cigarette with a furious grinding motion, looking down at the ashtray and telling me, 'I rode 'em bareback, Teddy – just the way your daughter did.'

'Keep my daughter out of this, OK? You've been using her to fuck with my mind ever since we met.' I waited for a moment. 'All I'm asking, I mean, Christ, weren't you worried about having a kid with Jonathan?'

She turned toward me, her gray eyes wet and angry. 'Go to hell, Teddy. *You're* the one who's been making connections between me and your daughter, you didn't need my help with that. What's the matter, still horny for her?'

'Fuck you.'

'Well, you did say you thought of me as a daughter – so *fuck me* fits, doesn't it?'

I stepped toward her, remembering exactly how I felt when I hit my wife that Sunday afternoon, eighteen years ago. But instead of slapping Mary, I leaned close to her and went for the cheap seats: 'That kid you gave up when you were a teenager. Was it a boy? He should be of age now, so maybe you can look him up and complete the cycle. You know – marry your father and fuck your son.'

She slapped me across the face and I laughed, a hard-ass again after all these years.

We walked around the room in different directions for a few minutes, both of us finally finding places to sit.

Mary's voice came so quietly that I had to lean toward her. 'Ten years ago, Jonathan's lawyers made a strategic mistake, looking up my mother to cut a divorce deal with her. She had just assumed that the fornicator – that's how she always referred to Jonathan, never telling Philip or me his real name when we were growing up . . . Mom just assumed he had crawled off someplace and died. Never occurred to her that God would allow him to live and to get rich, too. She agreed to a divorce in exchange for a monthly payment that would be cut off if she ever publicized her marriage to Jonathan.

'She told the lawyers that she didn't know where either of us kids was, maybe they wanted to strike a deal with us, too. But Mom *was* keeping tabs on Philip and me. What better way to wreak vengeance on the fornicator than to sic his kids on him, especially seeing how we had turned out, me an addict and Philip doing time in prison.

'She waited until we were each twenty-five to contact us with her information about Daddy, figuring that by then we would've ripened into sufficient evilness, twenty-five being Jonathan's age when he did the dirty deed with his sister-in-law.

'I can just imagine Mom in those last years, still praying for bad things to happen to Jonathan, absolutely giddy with the possibilities of all the trouble Philip and I would cause him once we showed up on his doorstep. She never lived to find out what happened, to see her plan become such a rousing success, but you'll have to agree, Teddy – my mother finally won, didn't she?'

'Yeah.' I waited for Mary to start talking again and then asked, 'You came out here to get money from him?'

She was nodding. 'But I was a little more careful in my plans than Philip was. I wanted to work for Jonathan's company so I could check out the extent of his assets. I intended to ask for a lot more money than Philip did.

'It was the weirdest feeling, meeting Jonathan for the first time, knowing who he was but knowing, too, that he didn't realize who I was, having that secret on him. I was prepared to hate him, of course. After all, I'd been taught to hate him all my life, Mom telling us daily that the reason we kept moving around, the reason we were poor – all of it is "your father's" fault.

'But I played up to Jonathan, acting as if he was God's gift, a role I was accustomed to playing, an easy part, one that men always fall for. I got to know him pretty well. Once I arranged a birthday party for Jonathan and a few other people. He didn't usually go for that sort of thing, too frivolous, but I was teaching him to laugh.

'Then I made a gigantic mistake. He asked me out to dinner and I said yes, and, after dinner, we went for a walk and he held my hand, and then he took me home and, at the door to my apartment, I let him kiss me. That was the mistake. At any point until then, I could've said, "Listen, Jonathan, I have something to tell you. I'm your daughter, I'm Nancy." And then we could've sorted things out, come to some kind of financial arrangement.

'But how do you tell a man you're his daughter *after* he's kissed you, after you open your mouth and feel his tongue touching yours – *then* how do you say. "I'm your daughter!"?

'You don't. But that night I thought, OK, you blew it and now you're going to have to hire a lawyer and let him handle everything because no way was I going to be able to tell Jonathan on my own. I planned to quit work and let my settlement get thrashed out by lawyers, very bloodless, and I would never have to set eyes on Jonathan again, just leave him to his nightmares about that kiss. But I went to the office the next day.'

'Why?'

'I guess because having that secret was fascinating, compelling, and I enjoyed it too much, Jonathan flirting with me, Jo-Jo giving me the fish-eye because I was poaching on her territory – I liked that part especially. Scandalizing the overly protective Miss Jo-Jo Creek.

'I was hooked on the thrill of it. And I was falling in love with Jonathan. And . . .' Mary got out of her chair and came over to where I was sitting. 'Please try to understand this, I never thought I'd have to explain it to anyone but now it's very important to me that you understand.

'When you're fifteen years old,' she said, 'and guys are passing you around at a party, you miss out on any kind of normal life. I mean, I used to go into a bedroom with anyone who was nice to me, that's all it took, for him to tell me I was pretty, then I started having these instant fantasies, he would be my lifelong love, my knight, he'd take me away and we'd live happily ever after, never mind the fact that we hadn't even exchanged names yet, that I'd already fucked someone else at that same party, *this* time it was true love. So I'd go into the bedroom with this new guy and do whatever he asked me to do, trying with all my heart to please him, and then he'd leave, not even a kiss on the cheek, and I'd get dressed and come out and stand around until the next one showed up, telling me that he'd noticed me as soon as he came in, that I had beautiful eyes, and I started thinking, well, OK, *this one* is my soulmate, and I'd go off with him, and so on and so on.'

Mary cleared her throat, putting a hand on my shoulder. 'When you're living that kind of life at fourteen and fifteen, peddling it by the time you hit sweet sixteen, when most girls are still worrying if they should let their boyfriends touch their titties, that kind of life, the life I led, it's devoid of any tenderness, you have no thrills, at least no innocent thrills, nothing exciting about sex because, what's the big deal, I'm just getting fucked again.'

I put my hand on hers.

'Jonathan returned my innocence to me, Jonathan and the secret I had, because when he held my hand, I was thrilled by his touch, and when he kissed me – knowing who he was and knowing how wrong it was to be letting this happen – I would start trembling and sweating and I'd actually blush, *me!* He used to say I was the first woman he ever went out with who really blushed.

'Poor Jonathan thought I was the last nervous virgin in

America, all trembly and reluctant with each step we took, that's what really charmed him, you know, the fact that I wasn't faking it, I really *was* trembly and reluctant, nervous. But I let it go too far, and when we finally became lovers . . . I'll remember that night for the rest of my life, too. I was crying and Jonathan was comforting me, thinking I guess that he'd forced himself on this poor young thing who was without experience in these matters, actually apologizing, telling me everything was OK, that what we'd done was beautiful, and I'm crying my eyes out, unable to tell him why, and when we made love the second time that night, I had such orgasms, never anything like it before in my life, doing such a forbidden thing, keeping such a secret, I screamed and clawed at him, these big rolling waves of orgasms . . .'

When I began shaking my head, Mary left me and returned to her cigarettes. 'After we went to bed that first time, the big question was, would I be able to keep my secret? Was there any way Jonathan could ever find out? See, he was my father in a *technical* sense, but it wasn't like he'd raised me and we'd spent our lives together as father and daughter before we suddenly launched ourselves as lovers. I somehow separated my father, that man my mother condemned on a daily basis, I separated him from Jonathan, who was someone else, although of course, the fact that he *was* my father, that's what made him so thrilling to me – am I making any sense at all?'

'I think so.'

'We were in love. You look bewildered, but it's the truth, Jonathan and I were in love – and I was scared to death that the secret might come out and destroy the only good thing that had ever happened to me, finding Jonathan and falling in love with him. So I spent hours trying to figure if anyone could ever *ever* find out. My mother, of course – she was one obvious connection, the *only* connection as far as I could determine. She died after I'd been working in Jonathan's office for about a year.'

'That must have been right after she visited Philip in prison and told *him* who his father was.'

'I didn't know she'd told Philip, of course. At the time, all I could think of was that her death removed the last barrier between Jonathan and me. We would've been married sooner except I kept putting him off because I couldn't marry him as long as Mom was still alive. No one else could've known who I was. That girl whose name I took, she was dead. Mom was the one person who could connect Jonathan and me and I just couldn't take the risk. But with her dead . . . I finally said yes to Jonathan.'

She stood there looking at me.

'Please, Teddy, I really need for you to understand. When I first let Jonathan touch me, kiss me, those were impetuous decisions, yes, but after that, I gave this whole thing a great deal of thought, and believe me, I would *never* have married him if I thought there was any possibility in the world that he would ever find out, that anyone would ever find out. You see, as long as it was *my* secret, a secret that would go to the grave with me, then who was being hurt? No one, absolutely no one. You think what I did was wrong, but I don't know about that. Maybe the truth wasn't wrong, just when the truth came out, that's what was wrong.'

'What did you tell him about your past?'

'I said it was checkered.' She turned toward the ashtray, flicked her cigarette, looked back at me. 'Aren't you going to laugh?'

I shook my head.

'Jonathan never asked for details. I told him I'd had some hurtful affairs and had sworn off men, which is why I was so emotional about getting involved with him, and he told me about his first marriage. You can't imagine what I went through when he explained how much he loved his children and how it almost drove him crazy, having them taken away from him, never seeing them again.'

'So why didn't he try to find you and Philip?'

'He said he didn't have enough money to hire private

detectives when he was younger and by the time he could afford to search for my mother, Philip and I were already in our twenties, and Jonathan didn't see any point in interfering in our lives at that stage.'

I snorted.

'I'm sorry none of us lives up to your moral standards.'

'Yeah, well . . .'

'Anyway, Jonathan and I pretty much ignored the past and concentrated on the present, making each other happy.

'And we were great together, Jonathan and I. I made him happy, no one can ever take that away from me. Before I came along, Jonathan lived for one thing only, his business, but I showed him how to enjoy life. We traveled, we went to parties.'

Mary paused, shaking her head. 'That sounds so shallow, traveling and going to parties, that's not what I mean at all. We made each other happy because we were in love, and we would've been happy even if Jonathan was poor.'

I didn't say anything.

'All the little things we did for each other, that's what was important, the silly gifts we bought for each other, leaving love notes, taping them to the bathroom mirror, folding them under each other's coffee cups in the—' Mary caught herself, stopping these recollections either because they were too painful to remember or because she just didn't want to be telling them to *me*.

'I made Jonathan happy, that's the point. And he gave me a brand-new life, a clean slate, reasons to respect myself for the first time in my life. I took classes, you know, and I learned about things, about paintings and how to decorate a house and how to *comport* oneself at formal dinners. We even went to the White House.'

I laughed.

'Yes, I know, this is all very funny to you, but—'

'It's not funny.'

'At first Jonathan was embarrassed to be marrying someone

so young, and of course he thought I was five years younger than I really was, but we never talked about our age difference when we were alone – it was a problem other people had with the marriage, not us.

'And, yes, Jonathan did want to have children, but that last abortion, after I had the baby . . . scar tissue and . . .

'You won't believe this, Teddy, but it was the *secret* that made the marriage so good for me, that absolutely guaranteed I'd never get bored – because I had a *secret*.

'You know the power of secrets, don't you, Teddy? You of all people. That's your famous talent isn't it? – going after secrets. Secrets are magic. When you were a little kid and you saw two of your friends whispering, remember how that would drive you crazy? They had a secret but you didn't. That secret made them somehow better than you, it gave them a certain power. A kind of magic.

'I remember once reading a survey which supposedly found out that in one-forth of all marriages, at least one of the spouses has a secret that, if revealed, would destroy the marriage. I thought that was fascinating, all those people out there living with dangerous secrets – just like me.'

'And then Philip shows up and there goes your secret.'

'No!' Mary was shaking her head, frustrated that I apparently still didn't understand. 'I told you before, I wasn't afraid of Philip because he didn't know who I was, didn't recognize me. Not after all those years, not after our mother told him I was dead. Everything would've *still* turned out all right if Jonathan hadn't killed himself, if Philip had waited for his money and then gone off to Mexico without hurting anyone.'

'So what went wrong?'

'Everything.' She began fooling with the cigarette pack, trying to decide whether to light another one, and then finally tossing the pack on the table in disgust. 'It was a horrible night, Philip screaming at Jonathan about what a bastard he was for abandoning his family, telling him how we lived – Philip and me and

Mom – living rotten lives while Jonathan was out here getting rich, announcing to Jonathan that his daughter, that *I*, was dead.

'I knew who Philip was even before he told Jonathan, because I recognized that sobbing laugh of his, he'd been doing that ever since he was a boy. He told you I wanted to fuck him when he was here last Sunday, but that's a lie. I was teasing him a little, to show I wasn't afraid of him. I did the same thing when he talked on the telephone three days later, trying to put him off balance, messing with his mind so he wouldn't hurt me.'

'But when he *was* about to hurt you tonight – when he was going to kill you, why didn't you tell him then?'

'I couldn't! You think I have no morals, that I'd do anything as long as I thought I could get away with it, and maybe you're right, but there was one absolute in my life – keeping that secret. And I would've let him kill me, kill you, maybe even kill Jonathan, and I *still* wouldn't have told anyone who I was. That's why I couldn't go to the police.'

'But Jonathan did find out, didn't he?'

She held her right hand tightly against her mouth, staring at the floor.

I checked my watch. 'Not much time left, Mary. Even if Melvin Kelvin doesn't find that girl, he's going to call Land.'

She nodded, still looking at the floor, 'Jonathan was . . . you can imagine how he felt, having the worst mistakes in his life thrown in his face like that, especially the way Philip did it, with so much hatred.

'Jonathan agreed to pay the money and Philip finally left. I tried to make Jonathan feel better, but he was a wreck. I'd never seen him like that, so weak, full of such self-loathing. I told him that feeling guilty over past mistakes wasn't accomplishing anything. I'm an expert at forgiving myself.

'But Jonathan was having none of it, he kept going on and on about his daughter, what a sweet little girl she had been, how much he loved her, how he could have saved her life if he'd tried harder to find her.

'He said, and this really broke my heart, Jonathan said he was convinced now that he would go to hell for letting his little girl die the way she did.

'He went on and on about how he didn't deserve to be happy with me when he'd caused so much unhappiness in others, that it was all his fault to start with, and if he had the guts he'd cut off his dick just like Philip suggested.'

'Philip suggested?'

'Oh, yes – Philip gave quite a performance that night.'

'And that's why Jonathan did it, because of everything Philip had told him?'

Mary nodded – but then abruptly stopped nodding to stare at me. 'I want to lie to you right now, Teddy, with all my heart I want to say, yes, Jonathan killed himself because of Philip – but that's not what happened, not exactly.

'When I couldn't stand it for one minute longer, all Jonathan's self-loathing, I finally put my hands on the sides of his face and I made him look at me and I said . . . I told Jonathan, "Your daughter is a happy woman, married to a wonderful man who loves her, now stop it!"'

'That's all I said, but it was enough. He understood immediately, Jonathan *knew*. My secret couldn't be told by anyone except me, and although I didn't come out and say I was Nancy, Jonathan knew. Maybe he suddenly recognized his little girl's face in mine or maybe something had been working on his subconscious all along, but Jonathan knew what I was telling him, and then the first thing he said, he started screaming about those goddamn silly pictures.'

'Pictures?'

She took four Polaroids from the pocket of her robe and handed them to me. I remembered then that Philip had been looking at Polaroids before I shot him. In my rush to make sure Alfred was OK, I'd forgotten about the pictures, and Mary had obviously retrieved them when I left her alone with Philip's body.

They weren't really pornographic, Mary in four mildly erotic and amateurish poses, dressed like a schoolgirl in a black jumper, white blouse, knee socks, black patent-leather shoes. Her hair was done up in two ponytails that stuck out at the sides of her head; she wore ribbons and held a teddy bear.

In one pose, the white blouse had been unbuttoned and Mary was looking down in mock surprise at her left breast, pinching the nipple. In another pose, she was holding up the jumper's skirt, showing off her white underpants. The other two photographs were variations on the theme, Mary looking either innocently surprised or sexily poutish, an overage and overacting Lolita.

'It was just a joke,' she told me as I stared at the Polaroids, 'a little game that Jonathan and I . . . He took them right after we got married, seven years ago. Look, compared to what some men are into, I mean, the fantasies that Jonathan and I played around with were fairly tame. I didn't even know that Jonathan had kept those pictures. Philip found them in Jonathan's desk and made a big deal of showing them off while Jonathan was tied to that chair, telling Jonathan he was nothing but a horny old fornicator – and that his cock had caused more trouble than it was worth, Jonathan should just cut it off, and so and so on.

'What I guess I didn't realize was how deep that fantasy ran for Jonathan, which I suppose is why he kept the pictures all those years, taking them out of his desk and looking at them when he was alone, and maybe in the back of his mind, on some level, he was pretending I was his daughter, imagining that at long last he *was* making his daughter happy, and that was *his* secret, a secret that was OK to have as long as it was all fantasy. But when he found out he was *living* his fantasy, that he really had married his daughter, then everything Philip had said about him, accused him of, in Jonathan's mind it all became suddenly and horribly true.'

I put the four Polaroids in the pocket of my jacket.

'I was so screwed up that night, one part of me absolutely terrified at having let my secret out, but then, I don't know, I

suppose at the time I really did want Jonathan to know, obviously I did, I told him. I was so much in love with him, feeling his pain, and maybe I was thinking – it's stupid, I know – but maybe I was thinking it would bring us even closer together, not just man and wife but father and daughter, too, because . . .'
She shook her head.

'After . . . after Jonathan realized who I really was, he became *quiet*. He stopped talking about those Polaroids and then I couldn't get a word out of him. It was eerie. I reacted to his silence by prattling on and on, how everything could still turn out OK, Philip hadn't guessed who I was, no one else in the world knew, and what had been my secret could now be *our* secret. All we had to do was pay off Philip and get him out of our lives and then we could go on just like always.'

'What'd he say?'

She didn't answer.

'Mary?'

Still nothing. Then she cleared her throat. 'Jonathan . . . he wanted me to deny it. He said it wasn't true, even though we both knew that it was. He said, "You're not my daughter, you're my wife. You can't be my daughter, because you're my wife." I tried to explain how it happened, and that's when Jonathan broke. "Lie to me." He said it over and over. Begging. "Lie to me." I couldn't understand the point in lying if we both knew the truth, but Jonathan kept begging me, again and again, "Lie to me, lie to me." '

Jonathan Gaetan killed himself because he couldn't return the truth to where it had been hidden – because Mary wouldn't lie to him.

A knock on the door and then Melvin Kelvin sticking his head in. 'I'm sorry, Teddy. I never did find the girl, but I couldn't wait any longer. I called Captain Land.'

I told him it was OK. 'You go on downstairs and wait for them, I'll be down directly.'

As soon as Melvin Kelvin left, Mary asked me what I was going to do. Her face was colorless, hands squeezed so tightly together that the knuckles were white, the fingertips blood red. 'Are you going to tell?'

I didn't have an answer ready.

'You are, aren't you? It's some kind of code or something with you, isn't it? Like a point of honor.'

I stood there looking at her.

'Yes,' Mary said, nodding her head and squeezing her hands even more tightly together. 'Yes, I understand.'

29

Harvey Land was the first to come upstairs. Leaving Mary in the other bedroom, I took Land in to see what I had done to Philip.

Too weary to flash his lizardly smile, Land asked me if I knew that old joke about your mother-in-law going over a cliff in your brand-new Cadillac. 'Well,' he said, 'I have mixed feelings about this shooting, too.'

'How so?'

'Nailing the Lipstick Murderer, that's great, Teddy, but when we get into the official reviews of how this case was handled, a lot of people are going to be asking rude questions. The big one will be why didn't we let the other jurisdictions know we were investigating a connection between Jonathan Gaetan's death and the Lipstick Murders? Of course, the reason *I* didn't inform anyone is that I didn't know – which makes me look like an absolute fool.'

'We *weren't* investigating that connection, Captain, not until tonight. Not until Melvin Kelvin and Alfred ran that computer check and found out about Jonathan's son. Then I talked to Jo-Jo Creek – against your orders, yes, sorry about that – and learned that Jonathan collected gold coins, which pointed us to the motel. All that came out *tonight*, Harv. And as soon as you were informed, you informed the other jurisdictions, right?'

'Yes.'

'Any investigating that went on previous to tonight was just speculation on my part. I was following up Jo-Jo's lead on those money arrangements that Jonathan made right before he killed himself, that's all.'

'Why didn't you tell me?'

'Let's just say that, in a way, I was following up on *your* instincts.'

'My instincts?'

'Yeah. You were suspicious of Mary right from the beginning, which is why you asked me to question her in your office. You let Jonathan's death be ruled a suicide, because it *was* a suicide. But when Jo-Jo came in with that information about the money, I thought to myself, *Now what would Captain Land want me to do?* And the answer was – investigate this and then let him know what I find out. So I *was* following your orders, your implied orders. Kind of.'

'Such bullshit.' Then the lizard grinned. 'But I think we can sell it. By the time we knew that Philip Jameson was staying at that motel, he was already gone and we immediately put out the APB. Right?'

Lie to me. 'Right as rain, Captain.'

He nodded solemnly. 'Your debriefing, it's going to have to take place tonight.'

'Yeah, I figured.'

'And all the brass are going to want to be there.'

'OK. You get any word on Alfred?'

'He's going to be fine. I talked to the hospital on the way here. Is Mary all right?'

'Yes. She's waiting in that bedroom across the hall.'

'I'll have someone come up and stay with her. Kelvin said the girl still hasn't been found.'

'You got people looking for her?'

Land nodded. 'You're going to be hit with a shitload of questions downstairs, questions I don't even know the answers to myself. Jonathan's secret first marriage, his son showing up here out of the blue, the payoff money – are you going to be able to explain everything?'

'Yes.'

'Why didn't Mary come to us in the first place? And what was the point of Jo-Jo Creek filing those complaints against you?'

'I'll tell everything I know downstairs, OK?'

'Sure, Teddy – sure.'

'It'll be OK, Captain. We'll all come out of this heroes.'

'Let's do it then.'

He took me downstairs, the hallway and living room full of men from our department, state troopers, brass from the surrounding jurisdictions, FBI agents. They all stopped talking when they saw me. Land escorted me through the crowd, to the fireplace. All very unofficial, he began, saying that I was going to give a synopsis of the case because everyone had worked so hard that they deserved . . .

Land was interrupted by a commotion in the hallway, the father of the little girl pushing his way through, demanding to know where his daughter was. Before anyone could answer him, he began shouting her name.

Two troopers grabbed his arms, but as they were moving him toward the door, Penny emerged from the storage space under the stairway and ran to her father, the man from Iowa sweeping her up and hugging her tightly to his neck.

Penny had grabbed both of his ears and pulled on them insistently. '*Daddy!*'

'What, honey?'

'I want to go home *right now!*'

It got a laugh.

After Penny and her father left, all those eyes that had been watching them turned in my direction. Waiting for me to tell what I knew. I looked up at the ceiling, up toward where Mary waited, too. Finding a smudge in that otherwise perfectly white ceiling – a fingerprint that painters had left or perhaps a stationary spider, *something* small and dark – I locked my gaze on that little smear and told the story the best way I could.

30

Just over two years have passed since that night, and I've been retired for eighteen months now. Even though short on points, I was granted full benefits. Such are the accommodations we make for our heroes.

And I was right in my prediction to Land that night, about all of us coming out of it golden. Lord Alfred, wounded hero, was promoted to lieutenant and is now a model detective, computer literate.

Captain Harvey Land, massaging my story until it appeared that I was working on the Gaetan case under his explicit orders and direct supervision, quit the force a few months after I left. His corporate security company has made him a rich man living in Bethesda, Maryland.

And I was given a new nickname. Seems that when I shot Philip, the bullet went through the very center of his heart – purely by chance, I assure you. The shooting took place too quickly and my aim is too unsure for me to hit anyone's heart on purpose. But, making much of my advanced age and of the fact that I had faced down the killer all by myself, et cetera, the *Washington Post* quoted some unnamed colleague who referred to me as Heart-Shot Camel. And that became my new nickname.

It's just as well, too, because my other nickname no longer applies. I *can* be lied to, a fact that was proven when Lieutenant Bodine and his partner, Sergeant Kelvin, asked me to come out of retirement this past spring and talk with a young man who was suspected of being a jogging-path rapist. The kid denied it and in spite of putting on the Old Detector act, I couldn't tell if he was lying or not. Nothing came through during the interrogation, absolutely nothing. (He was apprehended four months later attempting to rape his fourth victim.)

But I'd had evidence of no longer owning that talent – unable to be lied to – long before Lord Alfred and Melvin Kelvin sent for me.

I live in a cheap A-frame on four acres of the Northern Neck of Virginia, spending most of my time building a small log house. Why, at my age and with my lack of visitors, I would need to build a new house is a good question. Something to do while I'm here, something to leave behind when I'm gone. I have a few lines out about possible part-time jobs with local police departments, so maybe at some point I'll do that, too, and I've started dating a short-order cook who works in the local truck stop, having made up my mind to redirect my kink for women, away from those rich and classy ones who cause you no end of trouble and toward those more practical ones who, when all else fails, can at least make a decent fried-egg sandwich.

We'd been dating for a few months and when we finally arrived at the part where you go to bed together, she made this rather studied announcement, asking me to go slow with her and please be understanding because although she was forty-five years old and twice married, she still was relatively inexperienced in sexual matters and was, in fact, kind of shy and nervous-like when it came to 'making love.' Then she eased me flat on my back and clambered aboard, pausing only long enough to spit, that little ball of saliva traveling a good foot through the air (reclined and wide-eyed, I watched its impressive flight) before landing expertly on target. She handled all the post-lubrication procedures with a similarly deft hand, just the way she flipped pancakes during the breakfast rush at the truck stop.

Inexperienced?

Hell, I don't care. I don't ask her any questions and she doesn't tell me any lies. That's the way I'm playing it from now on.

She keeps apologizing for smelling of cooking grease, claiming that even long hot soaking baths full of oils and perfumes don't always rid her skin of the odor. I say she smells fine, and we both believe me. Sometimes, after an eight-hour shift, she'll come out to see how I'm doing on the log house and ask if she can fix me something to eat. I always tell her that preparing food has to be the last thing she wants to do after eight hours of it, and she always says fixing food for me isn't like work at all, it's a real pleasure, so I always say, 'In that case, a fried-egg sandwich sounds great.'

The press played up the Gaetan scandal with front-page news stories about us police heroes and *Washington Post* Style section features on Jonathan Gaetan's 'secret' first marriage, the instability of his first wife, the deal his lawyers struck with her, and the terrors caused by *and* suffered by Jonathan's son, the Lipstick Murderer. One article mentioned the continuing mystery of Jonathan's daughter, who dropped out of sight as a teenager and was never heard from again.

But then there's this: Every morning in Washington, DC, people receive at their door a brand-new newspaper full of stories that have never been printed before, fresh scandals, murders committed just the night before, secrets being told for the very first time. Soon enough, the Gaetan story became one of the old ones.

Mary was right. She was never prosecuted for providing false information about the circumstances of Jonathan's suicide, she'd been through enough, people said. After all, she was only trying to protect her husband's good name. By the time those follow-up features began appearing in the *Post's* Style section, Mary was in Europe.

She was the world's best liar, so good at it that she ruined me as a lie detector. Mary had lied to me about Jo-Jo Creek, to name one more example. I eventually did check with a few people who had worked with Jo-Jo and Jonathan back when the Gaetan

Company was nothing more than a construction trailer, and those people told me that Jo-Jo was straight. Just a young woman in love with her boss. Which means that Mary *did* seduce Jo-Jo the day of Jonathan's funeral, manipulating her until Jo-Jo was so confused about her feelings and loyalties that she would have done anything for Mary.

Jo-Jo sold her stock in the Gaetan company and moved back to Oklahoma, a moderately wealthy woman. I read an article about her in *People* magazine last winter. Seems that Jo-Jo married a graduate student at the University of Oklahoma, a young man fifteen years her junior, and *People* was writing about her not only because she'd been involved in the Gaetan scandal but also because she was one more example of a recent phenomenon, older women marrying younger men. The story said they were happy with each other; the photograph of Jo-Jo showed her absolutely beaming.

No one prosecuted Jo-Jo for filing false complaints against me. She was just trying to help Mary protect Jonathan's good name. She'd been through enough, people said.

Last summer I stuck a bunch of my clippings, about what a front-page hero I'd been, in an envelope and sent it to my grandson in care of my daughter's address. Ten days later a bigger envelope came back with my envelope inside, unopened.

This summer I'm digging a ditch, pickax and spade, to put in a water line, digging by myself a thirty-yard ditch thirty inches deep, well below the frost line, local people have assured me. Those same people also say that the smart thing to do would be for me to bring in a backhoe and get the ditch dug in about an hour. And it was true, that in the beginning this ditch of mine did indeed seem too ambitious an undertaking for a man of my retarded enthusiasms, but now it's turning out to be a job that, at the end of every day, you can measure your progress in feet forward and inches deep – which is something.

When I heard that Mary had moved back from Europe and

was living again in her house, I sent off three of those Polaroids, saying in a note I had lost the fourth one. What's one more lie between Mary and me? She never wrote back.

In fact, the only mail I get these days is from Lord Alfred and other friends of some standing. They always use my new nick-name, *Dear Heart-Shot*, in those increasingly infrequent letters, and although that new nickname doesn't offend me, I don't think my friends appreciate how accurate it is – exactly how heart-shot I ended up being.

I don't know how anyone can kill a person, especially at close range the way I killed Philip, and not be affected by it. I keep replaying the sequence in my mind, keep seeing how he looked with that ugly hole in his chest, keep going over and over how final and irretrievable killing him really was. He might have deserved it, but the fact that *I* was the one who killed him made it quite impossible for me ever to carry a gun again. And for that reason as much as any other, I was retired early. Armed or unarmed, I'm tired of hurting people.

The reason I never got around to telling Mary's secret had nothing to do with larceny (no bribes, sexual or monetary, ever came my way), but neither did it have much to do with chivalry. I was just too heart-shot to tell. I had finally figured out that of all the secrets I had pursued in my life – a boy running over his father, a young woman allowing her baby to drown, a daughter's pregnancy, a wife's affair – my *exposure* of those secrets never saved a life, never eased anyone's misery. Revealing those secrets just caused more heartache. And telling Mary's secret would not have stopped the nightmares that Penny and Billy still have in Iowa, would not have brought back to life any of the people Philip killed. I don't want to own any secrets myself and I don't want to hear yours, either.

I'm not sure that Mary was correct when she said it's not the secrets that hurt, it's when the secrets get told, but I am convinced that Jonathan's last request was dead-on: Lie to me, *please*.

Epilogue

She asks him if he is absolutely sure.

'Yes, ma'am,' the private detective replies. 'In those red trunks, on that green towel there, no doubt about it. He wasn't that hard to find.'

She nods, taking from her straw beachbag a stick of gum, unwrapping it and putting it into her mouth, chewing slowly and keeping her eyes on the boy in the red swimming trunks. Then, as if suddenly remembering that the private detective is still at her side, she dismisses him by saying that she has left instructions at his office for a bonus to be paid. He thanks her and moves off to the parking lot, standing by his car to watch.

With forefinger and thumb, she removes the gum from her mouth and drops it into a trash barrel before stepping on to the sand, walking to a spot a few yards below the boy, between him and the ocean, spreading there a large beach towel that she has taken from her straw bag. She has been wearing a terrycloth robe that comes just below her waist and now she removes it, which is what the private detective has been waiting by his car in the parking lot to see.

He mutters an admiring word, watching until the woman sits on her beach towel, and then the detective gets into his car and drives away, his thoughts alternating between contemplating the size of the bonus he's going to receive and reviewing the sight of her in that black bikini. Although it was not one of those tiny string affairs that look really good only on *girls*, the black bikini worn by the detective's client was too small to hide the truth, and the truth it revealed was everything the detective hoped it would be.

The boy in the red trunks has been watching her, too. He is at that age when the allure of an older woman is potent, especially an older woman as beautiful as this one, but the fantasies that run through his mind are largely theoretical, because he is not the type to walk down there and attempt a conversation. He is too shy and he thinks he is too skinny and, just look at her, she is too wonderful, that thick reddish-brown hair, those long and perfectly shaped legs, toenails painted red. When she turns over on her stomach, her head in his direction, and undoes her bikini top, propping herself up on her elbows to read a book, the bikini top falling away so that the top halves of her breasts are exposed to him – the boy becomes feverish.

But then the inevitable occurs, the woman approached by this tall and well-built blond guy in a pair of skimpy racing trunks of the type that the boy wouldn't wear on a bet. The boy has a word for guys like this; he calls them stud-gods. This particular stud-god bends on one knee to talk to the woman, who turns her head to listen but does not otherwise alter her position. After an exchange that the boy cannot hear, the stud-god moves off toward a blanket full of girls (all wearing string bikinis) who have been mapping his movements around the beach and now cover their mouths in giddy anticipation of his arrival in their sector.

After noting the stud-god's successful landing among those giggling girls, the boy turns back to the woman, appalled to see that she is looking right at him, smiling in a line straight across her mouth as if to comment on the stud-god: *What a jerk!* So the boy smiles back to tell her, *Yeah, I agree.*

But still, he does not consider approaching her, even less so now, not wanting to be put in the category of just another guy hitting on her.

Within twenty minutes, it happens twice more, good-looking young men approaching the woman and trying a line on her (I bet each of them opens with the same one, the boy sneeringly thinks – *Watcha readin'?*), all of them shoving off after a few seconds of conversation, the woman smiling ruefully at the boy after each encounter. And the higher she raises herself on her elbows, the more her breasts are exposed, until little more than the nipples remain covered. He is aflame.

Finally, after the next stud-god hits on her and departs, the boy swallows hard, embarrassment so tightly upon him that his face flushes with an instant sunburn, calling down to the woman, 'It's a shame you can't just come out here to sunbathe and read without being—' But the sentence is too long to be shouted across the distance that separates them, and the woman interrupts him by shaking her head and touching her ear.

Now what? he wonders. Then, breathtakingly, she sits up, holding on to her bikini top so that only at the last available moment does it *not* fall completely away from her chest and expose to him the full, bare, throat-catching glory of her breasts. Sitting there, facing him, one hand at her back doing up the bikini top, she smiles and motions him to come down to her.

And although this is too comically sweet to sound true, the boy actually looks around to make sure she means him and not some stud-god who's been sitting behind him, her smiles and invitation meant for *this other guy* all along. No one is behind the boy, however, so he stands, trying nonchalantly to straighten his boxer-style red swim trunks as he traverses the several yards that separate them, walking shoulders back and not looking at her, the woman's heart breaking a little to watch the wonderfully and painfully self-conscious approach of all this innocence.

He drops to his knees in the sand, well off her towel.

Her eyebrows go up. 'What were you saying?'

'Oh, I just, you know, all those guys hitting on you, I was just saying it's a shame a person, someone like you, a woman, you know, it's a shame a woman can't just come out to the beach alone and read and sunbathe, whatever, without being interrupted every five minutes by one of those stud-gods.'

'One of those what?'

'Oh.' He smiles. 'That's just what I call them, those beach hunks. I call them stud-gods.'

She laughs, and when she does, he falls in love with the lines around her eyes, the way they crinkle to give her face an animation and a measure of character that, to the boy, makes this woman ten thousand times more beautiful and interesting than any of the bouncy coeds he sees every day. She has said something to him, something he didn't catch because he was too deeply lost in and around those gray eyes.

'Pardon me?'

'I said it's a label they probably wouldn't argue with – stud-gods.'

'Yeah.' When he realizes he is nodding like an idiot, he stops. 'Hey, what're you reading?' Damn, he thinks, I can't believe I asked her that.

'A sad novel.' She shows him the dark blue cover. 'Have you read it?'

'No. I don't have much time for outside reading.'

She asks him if he is a student.

'It shows, huh?'

She laughs again, and the way she does it, so genuinely, looking at him with such merriment in those eyes, God, he feels as if he is a genius of wit, the Oscar Wilde of the beach set.

'I have to admit,' she says, 'I didn't think you were a stockbroker vacationing from New York – and thank God for that.'

'Yeah.' He is smiling and nodding.

'What year are you in?'

'Uh, junior,' he says, upping his status by a full year and wondering if he should've gone ahead and tried to pass himself off as a senior. 'Over at the, you know, the college here,' he says, turning around as if he is going to point toward it, as if you can see the campus from the beach. Dumb!

'If I had known there was a college nearby, I might not have chosen this particular beach. Too much competition from nineteen-year-old coeds.'

'Hey, you're the one who's too much competition for *them!*'

'Well,' she says, her eyes actually fluttering.

He shrugs, his emotionally induced sunburn reddening more deeply.

'What's your name?' she asks.

He tells her and then asks for *her* name. The woman says a name, lying to him.

He offers his hand, which makes her smile at him again, the radiance of that wide-open smile blinding his thought processes, the boy unable to think of what he should do or say next, pumping her hand as if they have just closed an insurance deal.

'Do you feel them?' she asks.

'Huh?'

'Don't look around now, but all the spectators are watching you, can't you feel their eyes on you?'

'Watching me?'

'Of course. Whenever a woman is by herself, on a beach like this or in a bar, everyone watches the guys trying to pick her up. It becomes a real spectator sport, seeing who gets shot down and trying to guess who'll win – and now all the spectators are watching you, waiting to see how *you* do.'

'Yeah.' Come on, he chastises himself, you got to come up with something better than *yeah*. 'Are you here on vacation?' That's certainly brilliant, he thinks, cringing.

But she doesn't answer his question, suggesting to him instead, 'Why don't we give the spectators a real eyeful?'

'Huh?'

'You go get your stuff, I'll pack up mine, and then we'll walk off together hand in hand, do you think that'll deflate the stud-gods?'

'Yeah! Yes.'

So they do, the touch of her hand in his more exciting than any touch he can remember, and the spectators *are* watching, he senses their eyes upon the two of them, the young man walking proudly, grinning.

She invites him out to dinner, her treat, she insists, to repay him for rescuing her from the attack of the stud-gods. He has never had a woman's attention on him the way she lavishes hers at dinner that evening, laughing at things he says and nodding intently when he talks of serious matters, the boy unable to stop staring at her eyes, watching with slack-jawed astonishment when she leaves the table to go to the ladies room and then returns, the woman wearing a spaghetti-strapped black dress that fits her closely, showing off the richness of her body, fully a woman, and the boy remains so bemused by his incredibly good fortune that he doesn't even try to figure out *why*.

After ninety minutes at dinner with her, he feels as if they've known each other for years, that they have a *history*, and he is amazingly comfortable with her, no longer acting gawky or clumsy. But he remains male enough to wish for opportunities to prove himself to her, crazed drug dealers rushing in, brandishing automatic weapons, the young man taking them on barehanded, getting shot before subduing them, held bleeding in her arms, a brave smile . . .

He offers his arm when they leave the restaurant (she must have taken care of the bill on her trip to the bathroom, because none is presented, the waiter thanking them profusely on their way out), their silences holding no awkwardness as they walk like that, arm in arm, through campus and then along the beach, a walk that takes a full hour before he has summoned the courage to kiss her.

He is feverish all over again, this encounter too richly *good* to brag about to his room-mates, no, he will keep everything to himself, this event, the time – still happening but already a memory! – he met a beautiful woman on the beach and went to dinner with her.

And spent the night.

He is treated carefully by her, time proceeding slowly and softly – they whisper together and smile a lot – and now it is cast, because for the rest of his life, all women and all that transpires between him and a woman will be measured by this woman, this night.

It is decided in the morning that, yes, his academic career can indeed tolerate a week of missed classes. They drive away in her cherry-red Corvette, the boy's heart singing so loudly that those small, mean parts of his mind whispering *why?* are not heard.

It is a leisurely drive, taking four days and three nights, the woman finally telling him that she wants him to do something for her. He hears her out and then says yes; yes, of course.

In the afternoon of the fourth day, she pulls into a country lane and stops. 'Remember what I told you. He can't ever find out I was the one who brought you here – or anything about what happened between us.'

'I know.'

'I'm sorry to be so mysterious, but—'

'Don't worry, I can keep a secret.'

She smiles, touching her hand to his face.

He wants to say *I love you* but he doesn't, does not even lean across the seat and kiss her, the young man simply getting out of the car and – this is when he thinks he earns a measure of romance in her eyes – walking away without looking back.

While listening to the Corvette's throaty departure, he proceeds to the A-frame cabin and knocks, getting no answer. He goes around the side yard, to the back of the cabin, seeing a man working in a ditch.

When the man finally looks up, his face flashes concern, the expression quickly softening, however, and then the man smiles, asking the boy how long he's been standing there.

'Just got here. I knocked on the door first.'

The man climbs out of the ditch, wiping his forehead with his sleeve. He is dirty, his sweat making muddy stains all over his shirt. 'What can I do for you, son?'

'I came up from Florida to see you. I thought it was about time we met.'

There is a pause. 'David?'

They take halting steps toward each other, the man hesitating as he looks down at his dirty clothes, leaving it to the boy to make the first move, to do what she asked him to do ('Go right up and put both arms around him, give him a good hug, OK?'). Embraced like this, the man wonders if it really is the truth standing there with strong arms around him – and if it's not, Teddy Camel thinks, then please, son, just keep on lying to me.

The man has returned the embrace, the two of them holding on to each other awkwardly but with a great effort at sincerity, Teddy saying that name once again. 'David.'

'Poppo,' the boy replies, exactly as she instructed him to.

Now, it is now that Teddy Camel's shot heart races, pounding faster and faster until, leaping, it is set free, made true.

Acknowledgements

Large thank yous to Robert Dattila for ten years of honorable representation and wise guidance, to David Rosenthal for being smart, and to Arabel Martin for a life-saving rescue she performed.